'You're only going to get burned.'
'By what?'
'Monsters,' she calls into the night.
'And girls who go looking for them.'

D1594316

ROSIE CRANIE-HIGGS

WHITE LAND

A NOVEL

bhc
press™

Livonia, Michigan

Editor: Rebecca Rue
Proofreader: Lana King

WHITELAND

Published by BHC Press

Library of Congress Control Number: 2018968483

ISBN: 978-1-948540-72-8 (Hardcover)
ISBN: 978-1-948540-73-5 (Softcover)
ISBN: 978-1-948540-74-2 (Ebook)

For information, write:
BHC Press
885 Penniman #5505
Plymouth, MI 48170

Visit the publisher:
www.bhcpress.com

'Whither away?' roared the North Wind.
'To Whiteland,' said the King;
and then he told him all that had befallen him.

'The Three Princesses of Whiteland,'
East of the Sun and West of the Moon,
Peter Christen Asbjørnsen and Jørgen Engebretsen Moe

WHITE LAND

1

The wild

Too small. Too warm. Sparks flicker behind her eyes, and sleepless, she stares at the ceiling. It's dark, as black as black can be, but the roof slopes down and the room closes in. Beams jut toward her. The air is thick and heavy. Her heart constricts. She has to go.

Romy sits up. There's no light but the diamond through the shutters, no sound but Kira's breathing in the neighbouring bed. Too close. Too small. The breathing crowds her ears. The cuckoo clock ticks in the corner, whirring closer to the hour. In the next room sounds a mirror bird, faintly out of time.

Romy's temples throb. The need to breathe is too strong to resist. Gritting her teeth, she sweeps away the bedclothes, a cocoon of blankets half a foot high. Kira sighs in sleep. The bed creaks as Romy rolls over. She slips from the room like a wraith.

The fire at the end of the corridor crackles, the logs smouldering to cinders and ash. Moving blind down the wooden hall, Romy creaks down the old, cold stairs to the restaurant. The bar is shut, the tables deserted; post-midnight moonlight shines through the curtains as she moves barefoot among the chairs. Each place is set. Romy shivers. It's eerier than she would have expected; in the sharpened, listening silence, she could be the only soul alive.

There should be dancers. The instant she thinks it, they're there: a 1920s American party, a masquerade ball in a madman's mind. Tables of women in shimmering dresses, surrounded by long-nosed masks. Leering eyes, bow ties, the scent of ravaged food and lust. The bar shines with spilt liquor. Two ladies twirl, around and around, one in red and one in black with glistening, candlelit curls. Their skirts brush a drunkard's stool. Their heels click to a gramophone. Maniacal laughter echoes in corners. The gramophone keens on.

Silhouettes dance where there are no bodies. Voices exclaim where there are no mouths. The lace curtains flutter in a moonlit breeze. Romy blinks.

The scene fades out. Laughter escapes through gaps in the shutters, ghosts melting into rough wooden walls. A curtain sighs by an open window. Blinking again, Romy rubs her eyes. She should go back to bed; insomnia is often better than scaring herself in the dark. Heavens above, tonight she might *sleep*.

And I'm the son of a serpent. Romy shoves her disquiet beneath a table. No imagined ghosts will make her suffocation leave. She needs to touch the open air, to breathe without walls, to stop her very self from pressing against her skin like bugs in her veins.

First, though, she needs to make a pit stop. The idea arrives in a flash, and skirting the coat stand, she slips behind the bar. Three short towers of closed-bottle crates, upended spirits, and a low fridge clinking with lesser evils. They blink at her sleepily, her partners in crime. But who will win the jackpot? Who will get the prize?

Her eyes land on the second tower. Green glass bottles of a burgundy liquid, sidling close in a game of Sardines. 'You, my pretties,' she murmurs. 'Huzzah.'

Careful not to clink too loudly, she manoeuvres one to the fore. Sumptuous, wicked perfection; it's full. Shifting it lightly from hand to hand, Romy heads through the dusty moonlight to the door.

Chimes on the handle. Romy winces; she'd forgotten. They jar the quiet like nails on glass, and she bumps her hasty way out. The door snicks shut behind her. No way is she getting caught now.

Into a jog up the sloping drive, through the open gates. Her toes stick to the ice. Her skin is already chapping, raw. Coming to a stop behind a hedge, Romy sighs in the wind of the winter's night. Now. Now she can breathe.

And now she's pretty damn cold. Snow falls softly on her head, and she shivers. No shoes, no coat; just a pair of short pyjamas. Idiot. Cretin. Buffoon.

Wanderess. She shakes the snow from her scalp and the chill from her mind, forcing herself to shrug. It's not the end of the world; in fact, it feels good. The numbing cold, her piercing focus…the claustrophobic room and the stuffy evening fire are softly falling away.

Better an ice queen than suffocated. Curling her toes against the cold, Romy walks.

Up the face of the mountain, where yesterday's snowstorm blankets the ground. Across the cogwheel train line, tiptoeing through the night on its way to the summit. Onto the treacherous, icy road. The forest? Romy chafes her numbing arms. Why the hell not? It's barely a one-cow village, let alone a one-horse town.

Romy shivers. The Jäger slops inside the bottle, and she takes a healthy swig. Another, even healthier. It hits her with its spicy warmth, and a laugh bubbles up, from her belly to her lips. Her body is catching fire.

And the snow no longer burns. 'More!' She throws up her arms. The echo travels. Liquid trickles down her wrist. Let the whole village hear; it doesn't matter. She's free. So what if she can't feel her nose? Her toes?

Her *toes*. She rolls her eyes down. Ten disconnected bulges, they're a ghastly shade of purple.

Romy snorts. She can't do much about the purple, but the road *beneath* the purple…it draws her in, so vivid, so sheer, reflecting the moonlight back to the mountains and lessening the dark of the pines. So clear. So still. Not warm. Not small. Not stealing her breath. It's welcome as it chills her, as it clears her fear and fills it with a drunken haze.

What if Kira wakes up? a little voice whispers. What if Mum and Dad do, and find her gone? Guilt twinges hot, but Romy kicks it away. They'll do what they always do: sigh, search, chastise, and forget. It'll be over and done with by lunchtime.

Romy wipes her thoughts clean with a drink. She's sick of their sad suggestions of help, of their let-down, drooping mouths. Sick of being a problem with a capital 'P,' of hearing something's *wrong*—can't she *see*, she's *wrong*. All she needs is solitude, atmosphere, life. All she needs is this.

The wild. The wind picks up with a moan, lifting her hair to brush her arms. Romy smiles. Long and blonde against her skin, it's perfect: she's an ice princess, a snow queen, an otherworldly elf. Slowly rotating, she watches it drift. Beautiful. Her.

She takes a swig and carries on. The warmth seeps through her skin to her bones. She gulps again, again, tilting her face to the sky. The falling snow thickens, spattering her skin. Alcohol flies as her arms stretch wide, spattering the ground. It's a waste, but who gives a shit? She feels. She can breathe.

She can *be*. Catching snowflakes on her tongue, she slowly turns around. Around and around, around and around. It's unbelievably dizzying. She swigs and staggers on.

Where she is matters less with every step. Her mind is calm now, as frozen as her limbs, and it's wonderful. The road widens into the empty car park, and that's wonderful, too. With stark, gleaming hills to one side, the stiff forest line to the other, and shrouded tyre tracks in the centre, it's deserted, inviting, and dark. So dark.

A track leads onto open fields. Romy ceases her stumble in a vague attempt to focus. That way lie ski trails, fox prints, and deer. Lanterns hang from two low cabins, staining the surrounding hills. Moonlight slides across the snow.

Not tonight. Peering through the bluish light, Romy slugs from the bottle. Tonight, it's tree time. Tall pines, sweet in scent, swaying toward her in welcome… She squints, but still, they sway. Calling, luring, seductive, tarry-hearted, and heady. The mountain, all elitist fields and hostile hills, light and bright and cold, doesn't stand a chance.

'We dance around the halls as ghosts…' Bypassing a snuffling fox, Romy mumbles into song. 'With dimes upon our eyes.' She stumbles across Motalles and up the snowy bank to the forest. A hitching giggle burbles out of her. 'You are just a nightmare creature, and an imbecile as—'

A woodpile looms on the edge of the trees. She lurches out of its way. 'Rude.' She blows a raspberry at it. She's a child again, playing outside in the first snow of winter. She could make snow angels; she could build a snowman.

Or she could find the Jäger. Romy flexes her fingers. In her lurching, she appears to have dropped it. She frowns at the blurry dark.

It's on her foot. The pain is a distant pulse. Squinting again, Romy scoops up the bottle before all the liquid can spill. Red on her skin, blood on the snow—a spray from a knife, a spray from a gun. Holding her bounty tighter than ever, she rocks away into the trees.

At least, she tries. The moon doesn't cut through the crowding branches, and after eons of wading, everything is black. Unsteady, unsure, Romy wobbles to a halt. The gap where she entered the forest is gone. She's forging her own damn path.

As ever. Romy rocks and sways. *All that we see or seem is but a dream within a dream.* She's a blur, afloat. Is any of this even real?

Just drink.

But everything is spinning, and her body is unwieldy. The snow reels each time she sinks into it. The faraway treetops dance the foxtrot, and even her trusted bottle, which she had *such* a tight hold on, has forsaken her again. Romy pulls a feverish face. Why is the spinning so *violent*?

Her dead toes clump something hard. Her head swoons, distant and hot, and a well-placed log grabs lecherously, sending her sprawling to the ground. Her chin thumps snow. Whiplash. The scrape of wood against skin is dull. Just as dully, Romy rolls over, drawing her throbbing legs to her chest. Maybe she should stay here; maybe she will. The soft powder cools her cheek, and she's slumping into a burrow. It's too dark to find the hotel, anyway.

A giggle burbles. No; it's not too dark. She's too *drunk*. Another giggle plops from her mouth, and she nestles into the powder. Conviction blooms with her lethargy. Why not stay here and sleep? She's so tired suddenly, so close to passing out. The wind on her skin is lulling. Why leave?

She's cold. A distant echo tells her this, a ricochet in her mind. She's far too cold. Not only this, but something, somewhere, is telling her she mustn't stay. She mustn't close her eyes. Something, somewhere, is wrong.

Get up. The thought is thick. Before it can be snatched away, she lifts her weighty, snow-patterned head. Get *up*.

Okay. Planting her invisible hands in the snow, Romy presses down. Her arms sink to her elbows. 'Rude,' she mumbles thickly. Trembling, she tries again. Snow fills her pyjamas. Frozen clumps roll down her belly, her thighs. It's not soft anymore. It's hard. It's *cold*.

She's a marionette, her head lost to the moon. It takes three, four tries, but propping herself against the tree, she blows out a sour breath. Everything dances a violent dance, but she'll do it. She'll stand; she'll leave the forest; she'll find the hotel. Something, somewhere, is *wrong*.

Blearily, she peers at the darkness. The forest is blacker than her own depression; she'll have to be a homing pigeon. Does that work with humans? Homing humans? She exhales, long and measured. Her stomach churns. Her tongue is acid. How in all heaven and hell will she ever—

Her chest and mind sharpen. Flickering through the trees, there's a light.

Romy squints. Some of the heat in her head burns off; a *light*. Coiling two balancing hands around a branch, she squints harder. It flits away as soon as she focuses…but it's there. A spark? Two sparks…three sparks…four? With an iron grip on the tree and an unexpected push, she clambers to her feet and staggers off.

Low to the ground and teasing, the lights dance in the dark. Her hair is full of frozen drips. Her trudging feet are blocks. The air in her throat is white hot, rasping. Shivers rattle her spine, but she follows, weaving through shadowy trunks. The bark scours her wavering palms. The lights are always ahead, frolicking, flickering, beckoning, until, after an eternity, she comes to the lip of a low-bottomed clearing and sees. They belong to a fire.

Abruptly, Romy sits. The flames are fierce, far fiercer than she'd thought, more a bonfire than a handful of sparks. She can feel their heat, taste their smoke, smell their sweetened burn from here. They roar. They are vibrant, tall, and furious, orange and blue and searing white. A sensual dance, hypnotic and light. Her mind starts to fall.

Oh, but the flames are not alone. Romy's attention swings aside. Passing in front of the blaze are wisps of air, threads of fog. Pale, frail, swooping smokescreens. She narrows her eyes through the flames. Unease unfurls in her chest, her heart lining up to race. She can't focus. She has to. What are—

One of the wisps flits away from the fire. It hovers briefly in midair, and Romy's lips part. There's a hand, a head, a whole body even, paler than the snow and opaque. A delicate dress brushes bony ankles, thin hair snaking around willowy limbs. Romy's head begins to ache. It's a woman, a gleaming beacon in the dark, and in a flutter, it returns to the fire.

But now there's another. Another, and another. Moving with the first, in and through and around the flames, they intertwine until they're inseparable. Another, and another. They're a rhythmic spiderweb, a silent ballet, a ritual. A rite.

Will you, won't you, will you, won't you, won't you join the dance? The words purr in her head. She's Alice in Wonderland, stunned and curious, watching unreality unfold. Rapt, entranced, adoring as the women, five, six, *more*, beautifully pale and eerily elegant, twirl in the leaping flames. They're on-screen ghosts in a silent movie, acting like she isn't—

The first woman turns around and looks her in the eye.

Romy sucks a frozen breath. Where before there were un-honed swirls, now there's a fully honed face; a human face of sorts, faint and far away, and as it passes behind the fire, she knows she has to run.

She's no longer tired. She's no longer confused. The something somewhere was right; with a barbed, swooning spike of fear sweeping hot through her body, she knows. If she stays here, she'll die.

Using the pine behind her for balance, Romy heaves herself to her feet. Where's the moon? She needs the moon. If the moon comes out, she'll believe in God. She'll convert to scientology, whatever. Her heart thumps, viscous. Her stomach thumps with it. Turning her back on the clearing, she pushes off into the dark.

No.

Her head snaps back to the fire. The twinge is vicious, and she lets out a shout.

Which one?

The woman with the face is drifting toward her. One hand raised, she's a breath on the snow, her black eyes fixed upon Romy's. *Which girl?*

Panic swells in Romy's chest like an overfilled balloon. She tries to shout again, to wrench herself away, but she's stuck. She's a dreamer. Her head is stone. Her feet grow roots, digging deep in the snow. She has no choice but to hold the gaze of the warping, black-eyed face.

Rosemarie. Drifting closer still, the woman smiles. It twists like gossamer and burns like oil. *You're better than your sister.*

The fire-lit figure drifts to a stop. Poised on the edge of the clearing, she drops her smile.

The bonfire dies. Romy blinks. The forest falls to darkness. The woman has gone; all the women have gone. Extinguished with the flames, only after-glow remains.

Her pulse is deafening. The balloon deflates, just enough not to panic. The afterglow won't fade. Romy takes a stuttering gulp of air, widening her eyes at the dark. The shadows of trees. No trace of the fire. Her heart is an iron fist. She presses a hand to her breastbone. Is it—can she leave?

The first woman rises from the clearing like a ghost.

Romy shrieks, veering back. The balloon swells and bursts. Slammed with a terror that screams past panic, she topples, crumples, thumps. Her wrists jar on the flat-packed snow. The blurring head tilts.

'Rosemarie,' it says in a rasp of leaves. Slowly, it rolls its black eyes toward her. 'Anneliese. Time to come home.'

Stretching her mouth to an inhuman gape, the woman starts to scream.

2

The wander

Anneliese.

The name echoes like a clap. In an instant, Kira's awake. *Anneliese. Romy.*

Her sister isn't here. She can tell before she opens her eyes. There's no angry sighing or rocking of the headboard as she thrashes; no tangled kicking of the blankets so they thump to the floor. No cursing of the cuckoo clock, on the hour, every hour. Kira reaches for her phone: 9:34 a.m.

Well, that's a first. She sets the phone down on the mattress. Romy, rising of her own accord, leagues from midday? No way.

'Knock knock.' The words precede a tap at the door. A second later, Anna looks in. 'Oh.' She blinks at the empty bed and pushes the door wide. 'Where's Romy?'

With a cavernous yawn, Kira sits up, propped by the scarlet cushions. 'I don't know.' Creakily stretching, she screws up her face. 'I was getting around to wondering. It's'—another yawn shakes her bones, and rubbing her sleep-grain eyes, she pushes her piles of blankets away—'early. Is she not downstairs?'

'Not that I'm aware. But then again, I wasn't looking. I assumed she was still asleep.' Anna rubs her forehead. 'Maybe she went for a walk. You know what she's like.' She casts Kira an entreating look. 'Would you do us a favour?'

Exasperation glimmers, but Kira nods. This isn't the first time and won't be the last.

Anna dips her chin in a nod. 'If she hasn't turned up when you're showered and dressed, see if you can find her. We really have to pack.' She appraises the room, strewn with underwear and vests. 'I'll do your packing, too, as a trade-off. You seem to need the help. All right?'

Kira's second nod is knowing. Anna leaves with a distant sigh. Always longing for a lost mountain, a difficult and hidden cabin, always wistful when they have to leave. Always packing late, as if hoping for an unavoidable mess that means they have to stay. Her mother never changes. None of them do.

Half an hour later, Kira wanders from the room. The hallway wall is lined with relics, with wooden skis and boots. Splintered and faded, their curling roses, bows, and laces—their impractical resistance—never ceases to amaze her. She passes with a shiver. The narrow hall is chilled with winter, barely countered by the iron-set fire, burning low at the end. Wide windows line one wall, and Kira buries her arms in her cardigan sleeves. The mountain may be pretty, but flakes of white fall thick and fast. The world has turned to snow.

Kira creaks down the stairs. The restaurant is full. Tables of elderly couples, tanned around the eyes from fanatical skiing or wrapped in jumpers, with a morning beer; dark-circled parents yawning, bouncing children pulling needles from the Christmas tree. A dog the size of a buffalo pants, its frizzy coat spattered with snow. A waitress lays down a water bowl, a tray of fragrant pastries precarious on her arm. All this—all this *food*—and no sign of black-loving, cake-devouring Romy, scowling her way through a feast.

Although she has found her father. Standing by the bar, his voice is loud, and Kira turns her smothered laugh away. He would appear to be practising his German on the waitress.

Spying an empty table, Kira leaves him to it. He should know by now, after several days, that the reason Talie switches to English is because she doesn't speak German.

He should, yet still he tries. Kira pulls out a chair. The misted window brushes her side, and clearing a hole to peer through, she presses her face to the glass. Snow-filled fog obscures the day. A flash of red through the pine trees heralds the tiny whistling train, whirring round the corner below the hotel. A dark bird circles the blanketed fields. A middle-aged couple reclines in the jacuzzi.

Quickly, Kira sits back. The thick, blind air and falling snow are no mask for nudity, wobbling arms, or their slow-burning embrace.

A snort sounds behind her. 'Are they ruining the view?' Her father kisses the top of her head. Turning, she catches his wink. 'It'll be me and your mum next. Quick dip before we leave.'

'Oh, God, Dad.' Kira covers her face with her hands.

'You're welcome, love. Any sign of Romy?' His cursory tone suggests he doesn't expect a "yes." 'Mum said she wasn't with you. I suppose she could have appeared while I was talking to Talie, but…*speak*ing of Talie.' Easing into a chair, he taps a nail on the table. 'My German must be getting better. She's not switching to English quite so fast.' He inclines his head at the raven-haired girl, passing with a tray of coffees. The strong black waft combines with croissants, with cheese and eggs and cold. 'That's a good sign, don't you think?'

He lifts his eyebrows at Kira, the embodiment of his last seven words. His face shows hope. It shines with pride. It shouts *hey, I'm doing well*, like a child learning to write.

'Um,' Kira stalls. The truth, or a tactful lie? 'The thing is, Dad, your German's great, but Talie's actually Turkish.'

She quickly turns her head. On the wall hangs an oil painting, of stretching ice and wolves; it's been her go-to through every awkward moment of every awkward meal. She's analysed every brushstroke, every subtle blend of grey. It reminds her of Turner, of Peder Balke. She'd only be brave enough to try such spectral beauty in watercolour, if she'd be brave enough to try for it at all.

'Talie's the owner's daughter,' she says, after several moments of staring. 'I'm sorry. We meant to tell you, but…' She drags her eyes back to him, screwing up her mouth. 'She doesn't speak German, Dad.'

As slowly as a penny, Mathew's face drops. It's a picture: a frown, a deeper frown, and then a parting of his lips. 'You mean…' The penny drops further. His eyes widen. 'Daughter!'

He bats at her.

'Hey!' Kira jerks away. He bats again, his large hands half-hearted. 'It's not my fault! And I don't know why you were *trying* to speak German. We're not in Germany. Dad!' She scrapes her chair back. A crumpled paper lands on her lap. 'Take it back.' She returns it. It settles daintily upon his chest. 'You can't blame us for you being daft. You should have taken the hint.'

Mathew brushes the paper back to the table. '*You*'—he wags a square finger—'should have told me there were hints to be taken. Did you and Mum both…'

Kira nods, slowly, again, again.

Mathew shakes his head. 'Cheers, daughter.' He huffs a laugh. 'You're a witchy, plotting pair. Anyway.' He holds up his watch with more ceremony than the gesture requires. 'Time's getting on. I take it you don't want breakfast?'

Kira smiles. 'I never want breakfast.'

Too late, she realises what's coming next. 'Then can you go out and scout for Romy?' Her father smiles and stands. 'Witches or not, I should help your mum pack.'

With a hand on her shoulder and a kiss on her head, Mathew McFadden departs. Kira toys with the crumpled paper. He must have been doodling: one side is mapped by sketches of a tree trunk, with four thin branches and a dash for the ground. She crumples it up again and shoves it in her jeans. It might make a nice tattoo.

What won't be nice is her upcoming quest. Pushing up from her chair, she moves to the coat stand with all the excitement of an ox. Romy. Romy, Romy, Romy. Why is she such a distraction? Why is she such a *chore*?

That's not fair. Kira's sense of justice swoops in, armed with matching, empathetic swords. She's not a chore. She's...

Difficult.

That's not fair, either. Guilt gnaws at her stomach as she heads for the door. Anna told her once that your first thought is instinct, and your second is who you are. More often than not when it comes to Romy, she winds up hoping it's true.

Within a minute of being outside, Kira's first thoughts slink back. The snow is growing heavier, and she can no longer see the hotel for the mist. She can barely see her feet, lurking on the end of her legs. Does she still have feet? Her boots looked so pretty in the shop back in England, but their insulation is a myth. If Romy's the distraction, she's the hold-your-hands-up, guilty-as-charged, perennially unprepared.

They're as bad as each other. It should help, but it doesn't. Kira shivers, burrows into her hood, and shuffles up to the road.

The powder is fresh and merciless. Her footprints vanish at once. Kira frowns. Looking for Romy will leave her like Sisyphus, forever pushing a rock up a hill. Snow masks everything. They don't even know for sure that she's out here; there may be an attic she could have slipped into, a bathroom they didn't check...

No. Romy doesn't hide in corners, or lurk in lonely rooms, or act the poltergeist in closets. If she's anywhere, she'll be outside. Free. Kira snorts. Her free, wild sister, off on a jaunt. *I'm going on an adventure!*

The humour wilts and withers and dies. Her sister, off on a jaunt, again, and Kira, bringing her back. Again.

It's just like the first time. Kira's face contorts. If anyone else was around, she'd probably resemble a dischuffed frog. The first time, she tramped through the ocean's mist, panicked as to what was happening; now, she knows what's happening, but she'd really rather not. This feeling normal is not okay.

She pulls another face, uglier than before. The first time, there'd been a fight; it hadn't seemed much in the moment, the dog-tired theme of doctors or no doctors, but it somehow became the last straw. Romy took a cocktail of pills from the bathroom, swiped a bottle of wine, and left.

She wasn't hard to find. She'd gone to the beach. Kira came across her by her favourite rock pool, the water bobbing with pills and rain. Romy herself was drunk and asleep.

Kira's relief hadn't lasted. Romy became bolder, cunning, taking every outing as a challenge. She slipped away to less obvious places, mixed drinks, upped her drugs. Recently, though, she's been better.

Or not.

"'She was a wanderess.'" Kira digs her tingling hands in her pockets. 'She *is* a wanderess. Bonjour.' She nods to a group marching fast toward the train hut. Their replies fly back in a muddle, and with a farmyard of clattering gear in their arms, they lug their skis over the tracks toward the chuntering train. It emits an indignant whistle. Kira huffs. The same family have done the same at least three times this week, running and nearly getting crushed. Their disorganized luck is a puzzle.

After several hundred metres of deserted, cloying mist, the puzzle has lost its appeal. Colder than bones and sick of her task, it's impossible not to brood. The fog makes it dark, and the winter makes it miserable. The chalets along the roadside are shadows under trees. Kira frowns at the toes of her boots. Oh, Romy. She doesn't even like the cold. She doesn't like the heat much, either, but summer's a myth back home in Devon.

Come to think of it, so is winter. If Romy's out in this, she won't be prepared. She'll have treated it like she would in England, where all there is for four straight months is rain and fog and moaning.

Shutting her eyes, just briefly, Kira plunges the lurking worry into a nice ice-water bath. Won't she be prepared? She hates the cold, so she might have wrapped up. Maybe she has just gone for a walk, but chose not to tell anyone. She's probably fine. If the buvette's open, she might have just stopped in there for a while.

Either way, though, she hates herself. She could be sat in the snow in Motalles, feeling it freeze her butt. She could be making snowballs, chucking them at tourists until her fingers numb. If the winter freezes her, she won't care. It'll be a savage win.

A low hum breaks the silence, this well of speculation. Kira looks up. Crawling toward her like a steampunk turtle, a snowplough's headlights shine like ghosts. Vaguely, Kira steps aside. Cutting two thin paths through the mist, the snowplough rumbles past. Was Romy's coat missing from the coat stand? Were her boots on the rack? She should have checked. Her parents must have, surely, or they wouldn't have sent her on a one-girl mission.

Kira sighs. She's a long way down the road already, alone in this damp co-coon that both steals and stifles her breath. She might as well carry on. If Romy *is* out here, she may well need her help.

Kira clings to this with frozen hands. The snowplough illuminated the village, but now the world folds in. The mist is growing denser, syrupy and tangible, tightening its dead-zone hold. She shivers. On sunny days, this road gleams, the sky an unreal blue. The chalets are rustic. The trees are a painting from a copy of *Heidi*, timeworn and grand. Mathew whistles "Winter Wonder-land," and it's repetitive, but true.

Kira shivers again. 'Just to the forest,' she murmurs. At least she's not deaf, which was largely the point…but she hadn't realised how silent—how dead-ened by the mist and snow—the mountain had become.

'I'm only going to the forest,' she whispers. This journey *will* end, and soon. They can't expect her to go any farther. Even if it wasn't creepy, she's not her sister's keeper.

Another shiver. Kira brings her hands to her mouth and blows. It warms her freezing lips, if not her fingertips. She's *not* her sister's keeper. As much as she wants Romy back—and safe—this time, it's just too much. Kira blows on her hands again, wiggling her fingers. The queen of preparation forgot to bring gloves, but at least she brought resolve. Going to the forest is far enough. She'll die of cold. She'll lose her mind.

As if she hasn't already. She scowls, her decisiveness dissolving into derision. She's giving herself a silent pep talk and squaring up to the weather. There doesn't appear to be much mind left to—

A magpie shoots from an overhanging tree.

'Jesus!' Kira scurries to the side. Her thoughts take flight, scattering like the snow-sprayed leaves it sends whipping across the road. 'God. Okay. It's fine.'

Cawing, the bird melts into the mist. It's a magpie; a magpie. It's *fine*.

Breathing through her jangled nerves, she leaves the tunnel of trees. Around a bend, and the mountains open into a spread of fields. Gentle. *Fine.* Inhaling the woodsmoke from rickety chimneys, she longs for the hotel fires. At least she'd be neither cold nor blind. The mist parts for a signpost warning of deer, two children sledging in the field by the car park, and not a great deal else. This tiny part of Switzerland is by far the most remote place she's ever been. How does the village survive whole winters here, on such a faraway, isolated mountain? Do they hibernate? Do they—

Looming out of nowhere, two shadows blunder from the mist and almost mow her down.

'Sorry.' A tangle of brown hair above a ski jacket, the young man lifts a hand. His breath is a wheeze, his arm around a shivering girl with buckled knees. 'Didn't see you. I need to get her inside somewhere. She's probably—'

Kira's insides freeze to blue, blue ice. 'Romy!'

She lunges forward. Clad in pyjamas and covered in snow, her sister sways in place. 'Romy? What happened? Oh my God.' She wrenches Romy toward her. The man flinches back. 'Romy? What's wrong?'

'I found her.' Palms up, the young man jumps in. 'I was in the forest. Collecting wood. You can see how much we need fires…'

Kira ignores him. Blowing on Romy's fingers, she switches, rubbing her mottled cheeks. Her fingertips are bruised, both bony hands a mix of purple, blue, white…Kira switches back to them. They're cold, but not frostbitten. Right? Isn't frostbite black?

'Um.' The man rubs the side of his head with a thick, padded glove. 'I—ah. She was under a tree. I didn't know if she was asleep, unconscious, whatever, but I woke her up and got her moving.' He spreads his hands. His voice is Scottish. 'I didn't hurt her.' His hands drop when she doesn't look up. 'I didn't. Is she your sister? You really need to get her inside. She's cold as hell, and she's not wearing shoes.'

'She's not wearing *shoes?*' Holding Romy up—*oh, God, oh, God*—Kira peers down at her feet. She isn't wearing shoes. Her feet are blue. Her legs are as mottled as her face. How is she still walking? How is she still *alive?*

'The hotel.' Wrestling to rest Romy against her, Kira grunts and tries to keep calm. Romy's head lolls. Her temple knocks Kira's jaw. A wash of hopelessness consumes her, but no. She has to handle this. 'Um.' Her hood falls back, spilling snow across her skin, and she shivers. 'We're staying at the…the…' Her throat constricts. Not calm. Not calm. She brushes hair from her sister's eyes, clotted and matted with snow. 'The hotel. We need to…' Her words disappear. She can hardly breathe. This is the most destructive Romy's ever been. 'Romy?' she manages hoarsely. 'What happened? Can you hear me?'

Almost imperceptibly, Romy nods.

Relief rushes in, quashed at once by panic. She's conscious. She's frozen. She's alive. She's in pyjamas. She's back, but she's not okay. Oh, God, Romy, *why?*

With a heaving breath, Romy rasps, and Kira's flying mind stalls. Purpled with cold, her lips painfully cracked, Romy opens her eyes. 'Anneliese.'

She collapses.

'Romy!' Kira stumbles under her weight. Her own knees buckle as she fights to keep her balance. Her feet skid on the snow-covered ice, legs staggering, tumbling—

'I've got you.' Lurching forward, the young man grunts, heaving them toward him. 'It's okay. Ow.' His shoulder clicks, loud and popping. With another grunt and a grimace, he yanks them upright. Kira's head reels. She staggers. 'She needs to get inside. Unconsciousness is the enemy. Come on.'

Bundling Romy under his arm, he gestures for Kira to walk. Arms out, she teeters. 'Did you hear me?' His urging voice pitches. 'Let's go.'

Shock clatters round her mind like a dodgem. Grounding herself on the ice, Kira kicks her body into action. 'Sorry.'

'I don't mean to be impatient.' The young man cuts her a glance. Kira loops an arm around Romy's waist, and in a three-legged race, they walk. 'You're staying at the hotel?'

Kira grits her teeth with effort. 'Mmhmm.'

'Then we need to hurry back there.' He appraises her. 'I'm Callum.'

Kira gives him a smile to dissuade him from speech. This is a horrible time for small talk. Romy…

Her shock ricochets into guilt, and her heart skips in time. To think she'd been bemoaning Romy. To think she'd been calling her a chore, a distraction. Her temples thud. Her stomach thumps. The road ahead is invisible, masked by sheets of snow. To think she was going to turn back.

'Hold her up.' Kira stops. Eyes closed, Romy murmurs, slumping into Callum. Unzipping her coat, Kira shrugs it off. Right now, it's the least she can do.

The cold hits her like a thousand stinging slaps. Callum stares. 'What in God's name are you doing?' He looks between her and the mist, her and the snow, her and the black-limbed trees, as if checking it's still winter. 'It's minus thirteen. You'll freeze.'

Kira drapes her coat over Romy's mottled shoulders. 'She needs it more than I do.' She brushes the falling snow from her skin. Shivers skitter through her, a hollow ache settling into her teeth. She replaces her arm around Romy's bony waist. 'I'm Kira. This is Romy. We've been staying at Les Sapins.'

Bracing her limbs, she picks up her pace. Her sister isn't heavy, but she's taller and supporting none of her weight. Coffee, woodsmoke, hotel fires. Kira pictures anything, everything, whatever. Mathew, merrily whistling Christmas songs off-key. Romy's current favourite song. *We dance around the halls as ghosts, and leave our spirits here.*

Not helping.

The look on Anna's face when they first drove up here, and she opened her arms to the air. With a grunt, Kira tightens her arms around Romy. Her muscles are starting to strain. Vin cuit, custard creams. Her own current favourite song. *You hunt like a wolf in the dark and the snow.*

Not helping.

If I'm a shadow, will you be happy?

Good *God.*

'Listen to me.' Callum matches her struggling march. 'Put your coat back on. Your parents will be up the creek even more if you both get hypothermic.'

He looks pointedly at the side of her head. Just as pointedly, she ignores him.

'Kira,' he insists. 'Kira, she's already frozen. She needs to be inside before she'll warm up. You're going to make yourself ill.'

'Shut up.' He may be right, he may not, but she can't take that chance. She won't. 'I'm not going to risk her getting worse, so leave it.' Readjusting her arm, she pulls Romy closer. 'It's not much farther. I'm fine.'

Not without a noise of disapproval, he quiets. The mist eddies. The road levels out. As the train line sifts into sight, Kira's heartbeat speeds with her feet. Hurrying, stumbling, shuffling, anything. Her head has started to pound.

Anneliese.

The word slinks coldly back into her mind. *Anneliese.* A place? A person? Something she misheard?

Later. The air clears briefly over the tracks. Kira fixes on the blue-sky gap, and gritting her teeth, she breathes. Everything jitters. She should have had breakfast.

'Let go.' Scooping Romy off her feet, Callum hoists her into his arms.

'Callum!' Kira staggers, throwing out her arms, tugged off-balance on the ice. He's toting her sister over the line like a lolling, raggedy doll. Romy's caked hair drags on the tracks. Her cracking lips are parted, her jerky limbs bare. Kira's throat burns. Her mouth is heavy. Her skin is numb. '*Callum!*'

At the hotel gate, he ignores her. With shivers rocking her body and her piercings whipped with cold, Kira stumbles across the train line. Oh, Romy. Oh God, oh, Romy. What have you done?

3

The dimes

The restaurant's heat hits Kira like the cold. Shocked from ice to inferno, she quickly begins to burn.

Olive-skinned and pixie-small, Hazal shrieks from the kitchen door. Three tables' worth of people stop talking. The silence is a clap.

'Kira?' Hazal's hands freeze in midair. Romy lies limp in Callum's arms. Callum breathes in gasps, and Kira feels like falling. 'Callum? What happens?' She flutters her fingers at the ramshackle couches. 'Is that—bring her to chairs. Fast. Fast! What she…?' She indicates a scarlet sofa, looking back to Romy. Shallow breathing, ashen skin. Hazal blanches. Kira's stomach twists. 'Put her there. I get your parents.'

Shoes slapping, Hazal scurries away.

'And clothes!' Callum shouts after her.

'Clothes.' Fingers fluttering, Hazal click-clacks up the stairs, her low heels far too loud. 'Yes. Oh, my…'

'Hold her cheeks.' Stamping his boots on the *Bienvenue* mat, Callum lowers Romy to the couch, taking a seat by her feet. Kira sinks down on Romy's other side, among the smothering throws. Manoeuvring her sister's legs to face him, he lifts her feet and rubs. 'Hold them,' he urges. In a wavering daze, Kira barely hears; it's so much worse than the first time. 'We need to warm her skin. Rub a little; not too hard.'

Kira's fingers are alien, unwieldy, but she chafes Romy's cheeks between them. Callum nods. 'Like that, yes. You don't want to make her face sore. This…' Wriggling his coat off, he tucks it over Romy's arms, slipping her stiff, white hands beneath her pyjama shirt. At the touch upon her stomach, she puffs a small gasp. 'That's good.' He smiles fleetingly. 'Very good. She's conscious.'

'Romy?' The stairs erupt. Ignoring the handful of staring diners, Anna shoves through the tables in a rush across the restaurant. Mathew and Hazal creak down behind her. 'Romy? Oh, my—' Anna scrapes a hand through her pale hair. She shoots a frantic look at Mathew. One hand rubs his chapped lips, staring at the sofa, a knot of clothes hanging limp in the other. 'Call an ambulance. Mathew. An ambulance. She needs to get to a hospital.'

'She needs to get changed.' Callum glances up. If this feels awkward to him, he doesn't show it. 'I need her clothes. Or you can do it. Hers are just…'

Clotted with snow. Part frozen, part soaked. Kira chills just thinking about it, how they'd feel against her skin.

'Dad.' She manages one word, just one, and holds out her hand for the clothes. 'Please.'

'What happened?' Anna looks between them all, as Callum shields Romy's modesty with his coat and Kira manoeuvres her limbs out of the sodden, crusted pyjamas. Her brain can't compute this, any of this. Her parents fade out. The hotel fades out. She numbs herself to getting Romy into a sweatshirt, banning the sense of violation that comes with having her sister exposed, if covered, mostly, by a coat. This is madness. This is *mad*ness.

'Hold this.' Callum nods at his coat and takes the tracksuit bottoms, changing Romy so fast he could be a doctor, or at least someone used to crisis. 'Thanks.' He takes the coat back and drapes it over his lap. Kira's mind remains dull. Oh, Romy. Oh, God. 'That'll help a lot. We…'

Callum's voice fades out. Kira rubs her eyes as Anna's fades back in.

'…Have to book new flights,' she says, gripping Mathew's arm. Forever seems to have passed, but it's not even a minute. The cuckoo clocks tick on. 'She can't travel like this, can she? Can we even travel *in* this?' Scooping up Romy's dropped socks from the floor, she bends to work them onto her daughter's feet. 'Mathew?' She glances up and straightens. 'Can we?'

Mathew's mouth opens and shuts. His cogs are struggling, the face of Kira's mind: one daughter frightened, one semiconscious, bundled beside this unfamiliar boy.

'Ahem.' The unfamiliar boy clears his throat. It sounds so much like a stage cough that Kira shuts her eyes. 'You can travel. Snow doesn't stop the Swiss.'

'Mm,' is all the response Callum gets. Knees crack. Jeans creak. Kira opens her eyes. 'It's all right,' Mathew says as if he hadn't spoken, crouching beside the couch. 'I think…' He runs his tongue over his teeth. 'I think she's just cold.'

An open silence falls. 'I'll…'—Callum fumbles in his pocket—'…um, get on to the ambula—'

'"It's all right?"' Anna's eyes become moons. Her voice scratches at hysteria. '"She's just cold?" How can you say that? *Look* at her, Mathew! Look at her!'

Dropping into a shaggy armchair, she reaches for Romy's leg. Her fingers judder.

Mathew sighs. 'I'm looking at her,' he says quietly, pulling a reindeer-patterned throw over Romy's torso. Kira watches him. This is how it always goes, and normally, it's a comfort. Anna panics. Mathew forces calm. He rationalises. Now, though, his face is a battle. An epidemic. A war.

It's so much worse than the first time.

'She's okay.' Taking a breath, Mathew strokes Romy's arm. 'She's warming up fast. The best thing to do is what they're doing.' He looks up at Kira, still faintly massaging Romy's cheeks. At Callum, doing the same to her legs and feet. His face sags, soft around the mouth, before he stitches it back into control. 'What happened, Kira?'

Kira glances at Callum. He's on the phone, speaking French, no help for her at all. 'I don't know.' She shakes her head. 'I really don't. It just…' She bites her lip, droops into the couch. She sounds and feels guilty. 'It all just *happened*. I was looking for her, and I…ran into Callum.'

Mathew stares through her. 'It always just *happens*,' he murmurs. Turning away, he leans forward, resting his forehead on Romy's. Kira fights, and fails, to keep her face as tight as his. If Romy was awake, she wouldn't allow this; affection is her personal vampire, risky to associate with and downright dangerous to invite inside. Now, though, she looks like a child, letting Dad kiss her goodnight.

Kira twists her fingers into her cardigan. 'Callum…' She swallows. Every word is a block in her throat. 'Callum was bringing her back from the forest. She was asleep under a tree or something. I don't…'

Her skin grows hot, and she stops.

'An ambulance is on its way.' Callum steps in before Kira burns up. It's too easy to feel guilty when you're not. 'Even with the snow. It'll be here soon.'

Silent, Anna nods. Mathew lifts his forehead from Romy's. 'Where did you find her?' he asks without looking up, brushing Romy's cheek. 'In the forest?'

Callum is doing a very good job of showing only minor discomfort. He shifts on the sofa, one hand flexing. Again, it's too easy to feel guilty when you're not. 'Aye.' He looks between them all. 'Near part of l'Ermite. The...the...' he flounders. 'Um.'

'The walking trail,' Kira murmurs. 'With the wooden hermit statue. We've done it.'

On Romy's face, something flickers. Starting slightly, Kira drops her eyes. Romy's snap open.

Kira goes cold.

'Romy?' Anna whispers. Sliding down to her knees, she removes her daughter's hands from her stomach and enfolds them in her own. 'Thank God. Are you all right? What happened?'

Slowly, Romy turns her head. Anna flinches. It's a tiny movement, but a flinch nonetheless. Romy's hands fall to the couch. 'Romy?' she repeats, uncertain. Kira's stomach twists in time with her fingers. 'Are you—are you all right?'

Romy shifts back to face the ceiling. Kira's breath catches in her cooling chest. Her sister's mouth lies slack. Her eyelids are heavy hoods, her eyes shades deeper than their normal, ice-light blue. They're as blank as if they've been carved from slate, as dark as if there's nobody there. Empty enough to be nothing but seashells, left by the tide on a barren shore.

'I got lost.' She sighs. Her lips barely move. Her eyes flutter shut. 'Sorry.'

Silence. Although her skin is hot, Kira grows colder. Her insides could be chunks of ice. Romy's face is pinched and waifish, hollow beneath her cheekbones. The ice splinters and spreads. It's as if she's not there.

Something's very, very wrong.

'Right.' Whether he's looking elsewhere, or choosing not to see, Mathew stands up. 'Suitcases.' He slaps his thighs. The noise is jarring, the motion more so, and even he flinches. 'Come on, Annie. We can find out details later; the important thing is that she's okay. Her colour's coming back already.' He smiles down at Romy. Kira catches his eye, and he looks away quickly. 'See?'

Callum raises his eyebrows but says nothing. It's a lie chock-full of bravado. He can see it, Mathew can see it, and Kira can see it, but she clings to it regardless. Her father forces calm. He rationalises. If he was to let that go, then...

'She can't have been out that long. Don't worry.' Gently pulling Anna to her feet, Mathew kisses her worry-pale cheeks. 'She'll be okay, and we need to catch our flight.'

'Swiss doctors not cheap.' In the kitchen doorway, Hazal dries up a mug. 'Not always good, too.'

Mathew turns his hand palm up. 'Even more reason to get going. If she's not completely better by tonight, we'll take her to the doctor. I promise.'

He puts a solid arm around Anna's shoulders. Staring straight ahead, Anna's eyes are fixed in the way that says she's either uncomprehending or unconvinced. It mirrors Kira's mind, the over-brightness of his voice, but hugging Anna to him, Mathew carries on. 'First thing tomorrow morning, I promise.' He breathes a whisper, a kiss into her temple. 'She's going to be okay.'

Casting a last look at Romy's disconcerting stillness, he leads Anna away. They return up the groaning stairs. Hazal returns to the kitchen, and the diners return to their business. Kira and Callum are left alone.

In the silence, Callum sighs. 'Your father.' He stops. Kira glances at him, away from the galloping reindeer blanket. He looks like he's faced with a furnace. 'He doesn't seem that concerned, I suppose.' He furrows his forehead. 'Should I have introduced myself? I'm not sure he looked at me more than once. It was all…'

He clicks his fingers pensively, one, two, three.

'I know what you mean.' Kira lets her head sink into the cushions. If she's the furnace he felt he was facing, he clearly doesn't know how to light it. 'Very "business as usual."' She tugs a light lock of hair, snow-damp. 'I guess it is.'

Callum just nods, releasing Romy's feet. Flushed red, they're a stark contrast to her face, tinged with grey and wan.

Kira traces her dry lips. The cold is as dehydrating as the sun. 'She wanders off a lot,' she continues, for lack of anything else. He deserves an explanation; he's the reason Romy's here.

He's the reason she's alive.

Kira kicks this away. She *is* alive, and that's what matters. Gently, to not make Romy flinch—and also, if she's honest, a little wary herself—she returns to rubbing her sister's cheeks.

'Dad's trying…' Her voice sounds wonky. Kira swallows and clears her throat. 'I…I guess Dad's trying to react the same as always. Keep calm. Keep Mum calm. Fix things that need fixing when it's all under control. It's too serious this time, but he won't admit it. He just wants everything to be okay.' She pauses. 'He wants us to be okay.'

And by *us*, primarily Romy. Kira's hands drift still. Romy, Romy, Romy: lost, found, lost, found. Wherever she goes, and however she gets back, the important thing is always that she's fine.

A man and his granddaughter, spotting her by the roadside and driving her home. She was lost and drunk to the moon and back. The memory clatters through Kira like her sister clattered through the door, slurring at the man to bugger off. She's *fine*, she was *walking*, she didn't need help. The well-meaning neighbour, who came across her in the park one night. Even a friend from school, who rang Kira when Romy flipped and slipped out of a sleepover. Endless people, endless wandering. Endless suggestions that Romy get help for the darkness that opens its maw, chews her up, and turns her to spit and acid.

Out of some sort of stubborn pride, she won't. She's *fine*.

Except this time, she isn't. Kira's frail calm teeters. 'Romy's okay, isn't she?' She looks up at Callum. Shivers of panic begin to fizz. 'She's going to be all right? You know what you're doing?' Her eyes fall on Romy's pink feet. The bony shins poking out beneath the blanket, her thin shoulders, warming through. 'Is Dad right? Can she, I don't know, travel? Can we go home and take it from there?'

She squeezes Romy's arm. Her sleeping sister is warmer than she is.

Sleeping?

Something's wrong.

Stop. Kira breathes in, clenching her stomach, and out, long and slow.

Callum doesn't answer straight away. 'She's all right,' he says, scanning Romy's body. Kira's chest spikes. It comes out as *all right?*, his expression unreadable…far too unreadable to be anything but false.

'What is it?' she asks sharply. His hands return to Romy's blooming skin, lightly tracing patterns of distraction. 'Callum? What's wrong with her?'

He looks up. Her thoughts leapfrog. Patterned with melting snowflakes, thick, wild hair falls below his ears, matched by brown eyes wide and perplexed. Twenty, maybe? Twenty-one? Old enough for serious stubble, for none of the acne on the boys at sixth form.

Shh. Callum looks away, up and down Romy's body. It's warmed up to normal, bar the stillness and her pale, pale face. Kira forces herself to focus. 'She's fine,' he says. 'Absolutely fine. It's just…' He gestures at nothing. His forehead creases. 'It's just that when I found her, she was ninety percent snow. She must have been there for hours, which probably meant she was there overnight. I only saw her because I tripped over her foot.' He raps his knuckles on his knee. 'It doesn't make *sense*.'

Kira looks between them. Her chest tightens, as taut as a drum. It's not just panic; it's certainty. Something's so very wrong.

'Meaning what?' She looks between them. What could be a smile brushes Romy's lips, the smile of a dreamer in a pleasant dream. If she's awake, or aware, she's ignoring the world.

Callum runs a hand across his head. It leaves his hair even wilder than before, and Kira blinks. 'Meaning she shouldn't be okay. Look.' Pinching the top of Romy's left sock, he pulls it off. 'Her feet are red, but her toes are still white. She's got frostnip.'

Kira watches as he puts Romy's sock back on. It really is like she's a child. 'It sounds like there's a "but,"' she says, dropping her eyes, fighting her worry, picking snow from Romy's hair.

'There is.' Callum's hand hovers over Romy's. Gesturing vaguely, he shakes his head and rubs his stubbled mouth. 'She's just…frostnip is normal, right?' He looks up, not waiting for her to say she doesn't know what frostnip is. 'Covered by that much snow, though, and being out overnight…' He shakes his head, again, again. 'She should have full-on frostbite. She shouldn't be warming up so fast. She shouldn't be, you know, pink.' He nods at Romy's face, still pale but heating. 'It's not—*oui, ça va.*' He nods at a couple in the doorway, hovering with questions for eyes. '*Elle va beaucoup mieux.*'

He returns his attention to Kira. A beat, two. Thinning his lips, he sighs. 'Sorry for the bluntness, but your sister should be dead. I thought she was, at first.' He gestures at empty air. 'I don't know. I guess it doesn't matter. She's okay, whether or not she should be. Maybe I'm wrong about the snow. Maybe it fell from a tree and hadn't been on top of her long. But still, to be outside in those…' He nods at Romy's pyjamas, crumpled on the floor. 'Ahhh.' He slumps into the sofa, scratching his head. 'I'll take your dad's lead. The main thing is that she's okay.'

They lapse into uncomfortable silence. Not uncomfortable because they're strangers, but with Romy between them like a corpse set for autopsy, they're still attracting whispers.

Kira turns her full attention on Romy and tries her best to ignore them. The small, sleeping smile has grown. She's breathing strong and slow. Kira lifts her eyes beneath their lashes to Callum. It may be wishful thinking, but watching the TV on the wall, playing silent *Charmed* reruns, his face has smoothed out of its concern.

The staircase grinds into its groaning symphony. Laden with cases, her parents struggle down. 'How's everyone doing?' Mathew deposits his cargo by the bar with a sky-scraping stretch. 'We need to get ready to go.' His eyes land on Callum, and he moves toward the sofas. 'I'm sorry I didn't say thank you before.' He holds out his hand. 'I'm Mathew.'

Gently lowering Romy's legs to the sofa, Callum stands. 'Callum.' He shakes the proffered hand. 'Don't worry about it. If my daughter had been rescued by a stranger, I'd be unsociable, too.'

Kira cringes. Mathew bows his head.

'Still.' Squeezing Callum's hand, he lets go. 'Thank you, for finding her and staying. This happened at the worst possible time.' He rubs his forehead. 'Our flight's at four. Is she definitely okay?'

Somewhere in the hotel, a cuckoo preemptively strikes eleven. 'She is.' Callum rocks back on his heels. 'I work at Les Pléiades most winters, so I've dealt with similar things in the past.'

Not from what you just said, you haven't. Kira narrows her eyes. You and Dad should be friends.

'People getting lost in the woods.' Callum is still talking, zipping up his hefty snowboard jacket. 'People skiing into snowdrifts and getting stuck. It was luck that I found her when I did.' He looks up toward the tables. Kira follows his gaze: in pride of place behind them, the second cuckoo chimes. It's large, elaborate, and minute in its detail. She took stacks of photos to paint from.

'I'm sorry, but I have to go.' Callum pulls up his hood. The third chimes in. 'Romy's recovering really, really well, and I've got a posse of four-year-olds waiting to learn to ski. A posse with designer parents, no less.' He dips his chin: *you know the type*. 'They'll beat me with their Desigual gloves if I start the lesson late.'

Mathew laughs and claps Callum on the shoulder. 'Not a problem.' Kira cringes again. 'Not at all. One question, though.'

Callum lifts an eyebrow.

Mathew smiles. 'Where in Scotland are you from?'

'Hub.' Quietly, Anna steps up beside Mathew. 'We really have to go.'

Thank God for that. If she could, Kira would crawl into bed and force this bonding to end.

Callum makes his way to the door. 'Shetland.' He indicates the outside, swirling with snow. 'I hope you get home okay. I'm not sure when this is meant to lift.' He smirks. 'It was nice to meet you.'

His eyes meet Kira's. She can't help a smile. 'No, it wasn't,' she mouths. He snorts.

'Come on, daughters.' Mathew taps Kira's shoulder. 'Callum's right; it'll be a long drive in this weather. Can you get to the car, Romy? I'll carry you if need—'

'I'm not going.'

Romy's voice is dead. Her eyes stay closed. Her face settles back to nothing as soon as the words are out. In the doorway, Callum pauses.

'Why not?' Flashing Mathew befuddled bemusement, Anna lays a hand on his back. He responds with a frown like bumps in the road. 'You always hated it here.'

Romy opens her eyes. Kira stiffens; their flatness is unnatural, dimmer than coins. *We dance around the halls as ghosts, with dimes upon our eyes.* She rubs one arm. That lyric means death.

'I'm not,' Romy repeats, shot cold with insolence, 'going.' She looks up at her father, impassive. 'I refuse.'

Mathew's frown deepens, becoming valleys, ridges, hills. 'No, you don't,' he says. His words are more surprised than anything else. 'I don't think you have a choice. Does she?'

'No.' Anna folds her arms. 'Come on, Romy.' She flicks her gaze to Kira, and it softens. 'Kira. Let's get—'

'I'm not going!' Romy screams. Kira flinches into the sofa as her sister jolts upright, her spine cracking violently. 'Don't you understand? Are you stupid? No!' She scrambles over Kira and out of the way, batting at Anna's arms. 'I'm not! You can't make me! I re*fuse*!'

'Rosemarie, that's enough.' Mathew snaps back into control. 'You're being ridiculous. Get up.' He stoops for Romy's shoulders. Kira backs away, her stomach a seesaw. All at once, she feels sick, unreal. 'We're going home.'

'No!' Romy yells. With a backwards scramble and a flailing of her legs, she kicks her father in the stomach.

'Romy!' Anna shouts. Digging her nails into the sofa, Kira watches in slow-motion horror. Mathew doubles over. Anna grabs his arm. Romy slams angrily back against the cushions. 'What are you doing?'

'Never mind that.' Mathew unbends his middle with a wince. 'Someone just help me get her in the car.'

He stoops again. She wriggles away.

'For God's *sake*, Romy!' His voice rises to a shout. 'Stop it! You're nearly seventeen.' He leans toward her. She lifts her foot, taunting, and he flinches back. 'Christ. Why are you embarrassing yourself? Why are you embarrassing *us*?'

Just like that, her fury dies. 'Because you're not listening,' she says. Calmly, she tilts her head to one side, smiling a humourless smile. 'This is perfect.'

It's a purr, soft and sly. 'None of you know what's going on. You'—she flicks lazy fingers at her father—'think this is the last straw. You look vapid, all stupid blue eyes.' Kira's eyes widen farther. Her lungs feel like they've risen and shrunk, cowering beneath her chin. 'And you.' Romy tuts at her mother. The sneer curves into a darkening smile. 'You really should have known better.'

'Romy—' Anna steps forward.

'Start listening.' Romy's smile drops. Taking her right hand's fingers in her left, she bends them back with a snap.

4

The damage

Anna shrieks. Kira's lungs shrivel. All the unturned necks in the restaurant twist. Romy tilts her head to Kira.

'Bitch,' she says calmly. 'It could have been you.'

Romy lashes out. Snatching a fistful of hair, she rakes her nails down Kira's cheek.

Heat and pain and whiplash.

'Hey!' Callum lunges between them. 'What the hell are you doing? Stop!' Tearing Kira from Romy's one-handed grip, he half-carries, half-drags her to the bar. 'Kira? Are you all right?'

'"Kira?"' Romy scoffs. '"Are you all right?"' She pushes herself from the sofa. Her fingers are bloody and knotted with hair. Kira's head rushes with vertigo. Her hair. Her blood. 'Why are you protecting her? She's a bitch. Oh, let's try our best for Kira, the sun shines out of her *arse*—'

'Stop!' Mathew blocks her path. She flings herself against him. 'Stop it, Romy!' He cracks his shin on a coffee table. 'For Christ's sake, stop!'

Romy doesn't stop. Leering at a quickly departing family, she shoulders past her father and makes for the bar. 'Get off me!' she spits. Catching her arms, he whips her back around. 'Let me go! I need to—'

'You need to calm down.' His knuckles are strained and pale, holding her in place. 'That's what you need to do.'

'*Get off me!*'

'Stop it!' Mathew shakes her, hard. 'Why did you attack your sister? What's going—ah!'

Romy's teeth snap at her father's arm, and Mathew jerks away. 'No, *no!*' He snatches her back before she darts out of reach.

Her blue-murder howl jolts Kira back to earth. She could be an animal, primal, a fiend. Kira stumbles back. Callum shoves her behind him with rough, iron fingers. Around his shoulder, the hotel is bedlam. By the sofas, Anna covers her mouth. A stream of guests make for the door. Hysterical and ashen, Romy fights their father, one hand bent and broken. The other whacks his chest.

'Oof.' Mathew closes his eyes, tightens his grip, and opens them. 'Right.' Catching Kira's stare, he sets his jaw, hauling Romy toward him. 'Let's go.'

Romy bellows like a bull. Hoisting her up and over his shoulder, Mathew staggers toward the stairs.

The bellowing echoes down even once they're out of sight. Kira drops her eyes to Callum's shoulder. Her cheek is hot and pulsing. Her torn scalp is raw. There could be a butterfly trapped in her skin, skittish and trying to escape. She rests her other cheek against the cool ski coat. The bellows crank up into screams.

With a thump and a cry comes silence.

'Oh, God.' Anna drops like an anchor to the couch. 'Oh, God.'

'Indeed, oh God.' Ghost-white, grim-faced, Hazal hurries from the kitchen to the door. 'Everyone!' She turns on tiptoe to the remaining diners, her dishcloth in her hands. 'Attention, *s'il vous plaît.* Everyone! I am so, so sorry, *je suis vraiment desolée, mais...*'

Like a shepherd after a storm, she herds her guests out into the snow. Apologies fly in the wake of promises. A tinny bell rings in Kira's ears. The thudding in her chest is painful.

Morphing from shield to man, Callum places a hand on the small of her back. She doesn't, can't protest. It's madness; it's a blur. Keeping her eyes on the floor, she lets him direct her to a door beside the bar and into a dark-wood bathroom. It's madness. It blurs.

Callum stops in front of the mirror. The cramped room is dimly lit, and Kira doesn't look up. With her eye swelling and her cheek stinging, vicious and sporadic, she doesn't need to see her face to know the damage is real.

The damage. The damage inflicted by Romy. The damage inflicted by Romy, her sister. Callum rifles through the cupboard beneath the sinks, and Kira stares through him. The damage inflicted by Romy, her sister, angry and sad and unreachable but never, ever violent.

'I'm going to clean the cuts.' Standing, Callum turns on the taps. Kira blinks back to herself. 'Lavender'—he points at a bottle by a stack of tissues—'and frankincense. Hazal's all for natural remedies. Turn your cheek.'

Forcing a smile, Kira does so. His first touch makes her flinch, water brushing blood. Closing her eyes, she clutches the sink, gritting and grinding her teeth. The oils smell nice, but they sting like hell.

Eventually, Callum steps back. 'Done.'

Done doesn't feel very positive. Her cheek throbs and burns, and her eye is an awkward puff. Kira grimaces. 'Thank you.'

With a tense smile and a deep, deep breath, she turns to brave her reflection. Her left eye is cut at the corner. A light swelling blooms at the tip, but without the blood, the marks are shallow and thin. It's the fear in her face that chills her chest, the wildness of her scleras and the tension in her bones. Having never encountered it, it scares her even more.

It's an afraid, victimised version of her. A weak version. She can't stand to look.

'Jesus.' Shaking her head, Kira turns away. 'I'm—is this real? Is any of it real? I mean, I know it is, but *Jesus*.' Blinking hard, she rests her tailbone against the sinks. 'My sister attacked me. She *attacked* me. She's never done anything like this. Normally, she just…' She combs her hands through snow-damp hair, looking up at Callum. His arms are folded, his mouth a line. 'There's something wrong with her.'

Callum arches an eyebrow. It's so polished, so expressive. She wouldn't be surprised if he practiced posing in front of a mirror. A dash of amusement, a pinch of *you think*?

'Obviously,' Kira adds. Despite his sarcasm, guilt nips: he shouldn't be here. Is he thinking the same? That he shouldn't have gone to the forest this morning? He'd never have witnessed a personal horror film and never have dealt with the aftermath. 'I mean, obviously. But something seriously wrong, as opposed to the wrong that we're used to. She's never violent. She gets really, seriously down, and she wanders.'

Chafing her uninjured cheek with her fingers, Kira sighs. 'I don't know. Romy drank, she did drugs, but this…' She turns to the mirror. The girl inside is a blank stare. 'I don't know. I really don't. And I know it's not your problem, and I'm sorry for going on, but it's like…'

A gust of wind rocks the hotel. The floor lamps gutter. 'Like what?' Callum asks, stepping up beside her. In the mirror, their faces flicker. Kira shivers. They could be ghosts, there in the shadows but gone in the light.

'I don't know.' The wind moans louder, the howling of wolves, sneaking through cracks and crannies. 'It's like we've turned a really grotesque corner. Ugh.' Squishing her mouth between finger and thumb, Kira shakes her pulsing head. 'Maybe I'm naïve.' The words come out mumbled. 'Naïve in believing that people don't do things like this of their own accord. Maybe all that's wrong here is she's worse than we thought. Maybe...'—the lights flicker again, and she grimaces—'...maybe this is her breaking point, and our parents will finally force her to go to a doctor. Maybe they'll realise that the fights *are* worth the hassle. Maybe she'll get better, and—oh, *God*, this is hopeless.'

She tips her head back. 'I don't believe a word I'm saying. You know you can leave any time, right?' She looks across at Callum. 'You don't have to put up with my overanalysing. You've already saved both me and my sister. Didn't you have a lesson to go to, or something? Designer ski gloves and anger?'

'I'm collecting Brownie points.' Callum hoists himself up onto a sink, resting his head against the wall. 'But you *are* overanalysing. It'll be—'

The lights die. Kira's pulse judders. Irony, or pathetic fallacy? She stiffens. The afterglow glimmers bright. This is not the time for vocab.

Callum snorts. It makes her jump. 'Well, this isn't creepy at all.' His jeans squeak against the sink. 'If I scare you, will you hit me?'

Kira shivers. 'Absolutely. And, if we're done, we should go.'

They should. Kira tries to summon up movement, but the sudden dark is too...big. Too empty, and yet too full. How is it so easy to feel threatened, and alone, even though she's neither? She fixes her eyes upon the crack beneath the door and the tiniest strip of light. It's better than—

A wisp of shadow passes through the glow.

Kira blinks. Disconnects. Reconnects. Through? She narrows her eyes at the light. It's whole, and she's finally adjusting to the dark. Why through, and not past?

Because it came in.

The lights sputter back to life. Kira's panic ducks back into its lair. There's nothing there; of course there isn't. She breathes. There never was.

'Good to know the measure of new friends,' Callum says. Only a hand-ful of seconds passed in the dark; how is that possible? Kira breathes, deep and slow. *There's nothing there.*

'Nice of you to join us.' Callum spreads his hands to the lamps. 'I love storms. As I was trying to say'—kicking up a leg, he leans back against the mir-ror—'it'll all be fine. *Romy*'ll be fine.'

He taps on his knee. Kira doesn't need to look at him to guess what he wants to ask. Everyone has the same problem: to hedge, or not to hedge? 'What…' he tries. Pulls in his eyebrows. 'What exactly is…'

'Wrong with Romy?' Kira offers a rescue, allowing a half-smile to say *I won't bite.* He pulls down the corners of his mouth: *pretty much.* 'Who knows. She refuses to let a doctor in, so we've never had a real diagnosis.' Banishing her paranoid imaginings, she shrugs. It would be a lie to say Romy's never im-pressed her; even while wishing she'd give in, her tenacity, her convictions, struck a chord. 'She won't go to premade appointments. She locks herself in her room, or disappears, or won't get in the car. It's not like anyone's going to drag her.'

Except today. This halts Kira for a second: yet another indication Romy's gone too far. Way, way too far.

'It's always seemed like a test,' she continues, more thoughtfully than be-fore. 'To see how far our parents will go. Not necessarily to help her.' She flicks two uneven fingernails together. 'More to…act like things are okay before they force something? They haven't passed yet, clearly. I really wish they would.'

Her voice catches. She clears her throat. 'Severe depression is what most people guess.' She presses her nails together harder. The thinner one bends. 'Ei-ther those who know her or those who find her. Someone suggested bipolar; someone else, really, *really* wisely, suggested antisocial personality disorder.' She huffs a humourless laugh. 'That one made Mum angry.'

'Yes, it did.' The door creaks open, and her mother steps in. Arms tight across her chest, she keeps a hold of her bones. 'Sorry.' She offers a trite smile. 'I didn't mean to eavesdrop, and I wasn't there for long. The walls are worse than paper.' She holds out her hands. 'Are you okay?'

Pushing off the sinks, Kira lets her mother enfold her. 'The shock is the worst part,' she mumbles. Anna is mint tea and hair oil, witchy perfume linger-ing on last night's crocheted top. 'My face is fine; Callum cleaned it up. Are we going home?'

Kissing her temple, Anna lets her go. 'We…' she begins. Her eyes flick to Callum.

He takes the hint at once. 'I've got to get to work.' He slides to the floor. 'Have a nice…um…' he flounders, shoving his hands in his pockets. Kira's mouth stays still, but her mind is a smile. 'Never mind. Bye, Kira. Kira's mum.'

He leaves with awkward haste, their thank-yous afloat in his wake. Twinging with melancholy, Kira watches him go. One beat, two beats, three. His boot-steps fade. Anna sighs.

'We can't take Romy anywhere,' she says beneath her breath. 'For all your father's gusto, we just can't. Not in that state. He came downstairs just before I found you, and apparently she's only quiet because…'

She closes her eyes. A puff of air hitches and pops in her throat. Kira's stomach dips with unease.

'Because'—Anna lowers her chin to continue—'when he carried her into the bedroom, she threw herself about. She knocked her head on the bed frame, and although it didn't knock her out, she's stunned.'

Kira winces. Her unease dips lower, deep toward her spine.

'Oh, love, I know.' Swallowing, Anna squeezes Kira's arm. 'It's horrible; absolutely horrible. All of it.' Motioning for them to head back to the restaurant, she tugs the bathroom door shut. 'I've called an ambulance, but how it'll get up here I don't know. Just *look*.' She gestures out of the window. Fogged, heavy snow covers the train line, the station hut a white, hulking boulder. There's no sign of the road. 'It's meant to lift in an hour or two, but I…'—she halts in the middle of the floor—'…I can't believe…'

A sob cuts her throat. She brings her hands to her face, and halfway up the stairs, Mathew swivels. His laughter lines tighten. 'Annie.' Hurrying back down, he wraps an arm around her and leads her to the sofa. 'Annie, Annie, hey.'

It's a trap in Kira's chest, snapping shut on her breath. This is serious. She knew that already, but her parents' distress makes it real. Heart-sinkingly, chillingly real.

The glare of the snow is too light, too white. Migraine-bright on the edges of her vision, the gloomy hotel lamps make it worse. Tugging her cardigan over her fingers, Kira makes her measured way toward the bar. She needs to sit. The calm she'd almost mastered has dissipated, blown away with her mother's. Gripping her sleeves, she slides onto a stool. The second wall TV is blaring. Resting her chin on her arms and her arms on the wood, she stares listlessly up at it. English football and a screaming commentator. Sobbing parents and the howling wind. Her eyes sink shut.

A glass thuds down by her ear. Startled, she sits up.

'It'll take off the edge,' Hazal says. Having soundlessly appeared behind the bar, she leans on the wood and nods at the liquid. 'Trust me.'

Kira considers. Pungent and clear, her stomach blanches at the thought.

Not for long. Lifting the drink before she can think, she tips half down her throat.

Kira's face twists into magical shapes. Even Hazal has to laugh. She coughs once, screws up her eyes, and coughs again. A strange fizzing shoots through her nose. Her forehead and eyeballs are tingling, fiery. The liquid burns its way to her stomach, and she squirms. 'I…thank you?' She swallows again, shuddering. And she thought vodka was strong. 'What *is* that?'

Hazal tops up the glass with a humble pride. 'Herb brandy.' She pours another for herself. 'It works. Trust me. Some for all of you, I think?' She peers around Kira to call to her parents. 'If your daughter's reaction does not put you off.'

Her reaction doesn't matter a jot. Mathew accepts at once. 'Please.' Hollow-eyed, Anna nods. 'For both of us. And before I go back to Romy, I wanted to ask you something.' Taking Anna's hand, he heaves them up from the sofa. 'If that's all right.'

Pouring two more perfect glasses, the hotel owner shrugs. 'Go on.' She eyes him dubiously. He leans his elbows on the bar. Again, Kira cringes. His feigned ease is painful. 'Ask what you wish.'

Hooking a finger around his glass, Mathew clears his throat. His reticence is possibly more painful still. 'Is there any way…' He rubs his three-day shadow. 'Um. That…uh…' He clears his throat again. Kira squeezes her eyes shut. Please, Dad. Get it over with. 'That we could stay here a bit longer?'

The discordant clink of metal from the kitchen. The ticking of asynchronous clocks. Kira drags her eyes open. If this was a western, there'd be tumbleweed.

'I know it's a lot to ask.' Mathew speeds up. Hazal's eyes taper to cat-like slits. 'And you have every right to throw us out. It's just that Romy has to go to the hospital, and we need—'

'How long?' Hazal lifts her brandy, knocks it back, and pours two shots of a vibrant green. 'For me'—she drains half of the first—'and you.' She sets the second down before Kira. Sticky, spicy liquid sloshes over the rim. 'How long?'

Mathew tries to defer to Anna, but sipping her drink, she's half the world away. 'Indefinitely?'

Hazal calcifies. Kira hones in on her green oddity: this is going to go terribly.

'Within reason, of course.' Mathew rushes damage control. 'But we have no idea how long we'll need, or when we'll find another flight—'

'Not Romy.'

Shot with a pang, Kira looks up. Is that better or worse than terrible?

'I like you.' Hazal's olive cheeks are taut. 'I do. But I can't have her here. You understand?' She looks from Anna to Mathew, Mathew to Anna. 'She stay in hospital, and you stay here. I have no trouble with the rest of you. And she, she need to recover.' She angles her glass in Kira's direction. 'I mind her not at all. She can make friends with my daughter; Talie needs it. But when Romy leave hospital, you all leave.' She closes her eyes. 'Today was horror film. Bad for guests, bad for business, bad for me.'

Running his tongue over his lip, Mathew nods. 'All right.' Resigned, he nods again. 'After what we've put you through, that's fair. Anna?' He glances at her. Sinking in her glass, she shrugs. 'Okay.' He knocks back the rest of his brandy. 'Okay. Hazal, I'm so, so—ah.'

Tyres screech outside. Mathew swivels. 'Perfect.'

Slapping down his glass, he heads for the door. Anna is halfway to following, tying back her tear-stained hair, when Kira suddenly remembers.

'Mum.' She hops from her stool. Her mother turns. 'Romy said something to me. Before she passed out, when we were bringing her here. Me and Callum.' She bites her cheek. That rasp of a voice, that single word. 'It was—weird.'

Tightening her ponytail, Anna brushes it back. 'What did she say?'

Shh. It's Romy, smiling as she lies upstairs, smiling unconscious on the couch. The words are prescient whispers in her mind. *Start listening.*

Kira shakes it off. Whatever Romy is right now, she isn't telepathic. 'It was a name, I think,' she says, as two paramedics clatter into the restaurant with a stretcher and a generous helping of snow. Anna looks over her shoulder. 'Anneliese.'

Her mother's shoulders tense. Mathew is leading the men upstairs, his French broken but enough. 'Mum?' Kira prompts. Anna looks back. 'Did you hear me?'

A pause. With a sigh, Anna wilts. 'Sorry.' She rubs her forehead. The ceiling creaks, and she glances up. 'What did you say? What did Romy say?'

Shh. Romy's voice in her mind, motionless as the men tramp into their room. Smiling, serene. *You really should have known better.*

Kira blinks in a butterfly flutter. Either the alcohol is kicking in, or the morning has made her need a three-year sleep. Probably both. 'Never mind.' Sliding back onto the stool, she rests her head on her hand. Her mother is raring to tend to Romy, and suddenly, she's lost the energy to keep her. 'It can wait.' Nodding to the staircase, she tries for a smile. 'Go. Make sure Romy's okay.'

Anna hesitates. 'Stay here.' Wrapping Kira up in a rush of a hug, she murmurs into her hair. 'We don't want Romy to…to fly at you when she wakes up. We don't know why it happened before, so we don't know what might trigger it again. Just…' She pulls back. The ceiling creaks, from the room to the hall. 'Just stay here. I'm sorry.'

Her fingers trail along Kira's arm as she hurries from the bar. 'At least one of us will be back soon,' she calls over her shoulder. 'I know this isn't fair on you, but…'

Kira stops listening. *Fly at you. This isn't fair.* The understatements curdle with the liquor in her stomach. She really does need a good sleep; apart from feeling hard-done-to, Anna's words have brought Romy's attack swaggering back to her mind. Lashing. Scraping. Scratching. Blood. The absent eyes behind the demon.

Fly at you.
Start listening.

She's hot and cold and sickened. Grasping her glass, Kira drains it dry.

5

The life so far from home

If only Romy saw the benefit of passcodes.

After an hour of reading her sister's phone, Kira could combust. Implode, explode, both at once, as long as it's destructive. Nothing she's seen is surprising, and there's certainly nothing to indicate that Romy was skidding off course; but the self-hatred, the cynicism, what she feels when she's alone…it's harrowing, it's tender, and combined with this morning, it's far, far too much.

Letting the phone bounce to the bed, Kira exhales in a whoosh. It sounds feeble in the stuffy room, and she does it again, louder. She needs a distraction. In this state, exam revision is useless. *Worse* than useless. There's nothing to do in the village but ski, and they returned their skis last night. She knows no one, and her parents won't be back for eons. "Soon" is always a hopeful lie.

Drooping onto her back, she shoves her hands behind her head. She can think. She can brood. She can do both and have a party.

The cuckoo clocks chime their irreverent half-hours. Time has been positively crawling. Moodily eyeing the ceiling beams, Kira's mind flits to Callum, or rather, to his words on the sofa; something isn't right. Romy should be dead. She was outside in short pyjamas, potentially overnight, and she should be dead. She should have been dead when Callum found her, snowbound under a tree. She shouldn't have recovered so quickly when they got her inside. Something isn't right.

Of course it isn't. She broke her own hand. Kira presses her palms into her eyes, blinking through the fizzing dark. What happened to Romy last night? Callum found her in a normal part of the forest, littered with snowshoe trails that they, as a family, have followed at least twice. Yes, Romy never actually joined the family outings, having refused to leave the hotel unless it involved food, and the village tells tales of abominable snow, but the woods themselves…

Kira shakes her head behind her hands. The woods never seemed strange. Not at all. Shelters made from branches and lilting slopes, short tracks winding in on themselves and rough tarmac roads. Illustrated signs tacked to trees about imps and gnomes and local birds. It's all so normal; it looked so safe. What could have happened to Romy?

Unless she was attacked. The word slinks in, sleazy and grimy and grey. She doesn't want to face it, doesn't even want to think it, but no other explanation jumps out. An attack could make her lash out, furious at herself and others. It could send her retreating inwards, losing the life behind her eyes.

But that wouldn't explain the too-quick recove—

Kira rejects the looming thought and sits up. It's too small in here, too warm, and brooding in place gains nothing. At least by venturing into the cold, she has a chance of clearing her mind. The sky attempts a pastel blue. The mist has mostly lifted. The fresh air beckons; there's no reason not to go.

Besides, the room is chewing her up. Romy's phone is an infectious mountain of misery. Romy herself, dazed and cold, left this place on a stretcher.

Now Kira needs to go.

One beer-drinker holds the restaurant's soul. He nods at her as she weaves through the tables, ginger hair amok about his wide, blurring eyes. He's probably stealing the Wi-Fi again. Averting her eyes from the rumpled sofa, she plucks her coat from its cushions and leaves. The horror doesn't get a look in. Not again.

The air outside is fresh and frosted. Soothing her mind, it stings her throat. Is this what Romy wanted when she left? To clear her head, to breathe? She always did feel trapped by walls. Meandering up the drive, Kira verges on a smile. Maybe they aren't so different.

She crosses the train line and sinks into memory. All of them laughing at the Montreux market, as Anna's drink wound up tasting like pee. The weekend she, Romy, and Anna convinced a scandalised Mathew they'd adopted a pug named Jim. Romy's last birthday, where she inverted the glitzy Sweet Sixteen and had a party in an underpass. It was gothic, black, macabre, full of metal and retro stereos, and Romy couldn't stop grinning. It was perfect.

'Kira!'

The distant shout echoes. Kira stops like it slapped her, and the world re-forms. The sledging hill, the car park, the hulking forest on the far side; she's followed the road without seeing a thing. It's been ten minutes or more.

Turning from the mountains, rolling in valleys to the silver-grey lake, she peers at the crowd of tourists. The call must have come from there, but there's a horde. An army. A flock. She strains her eyes. Is someone waving?

Yes. A man-shaped someone, standing at the foot of the sledging hill. Clutching a snowboard and surrounded by children, he's signalling to her with his helmet.

Callum. Probably. Kira considers. Why not? If it's him, it gives her something to do, and if it isn't, well, any conversation is better than brooding.

Skirting sledges, rucksacks, and sodden paper plates in an attempt to avoid the crowd, Kira watches Callum turn back to his posse. '*Mes amis!*' he cries. Dropping board and helmet into a snowdrift, he vigorously brushes snow from his hair. A belly-high boy sets off an imitation, and within seconds the troop becomes a giggling horde of hedgehogs.

Stopping at a safe distance, Kira huffs a laugh. Callum snorts. '*Je suis sûr que vos parents vont adorer vos nouvelles coiffures.*' He indicates their tousled mops. '*Êtes-vous prêts?*' A sly grin grows. Sniggering, the children nod. 'Righty-ho.' He spreads his hands, and they brace themselves. 'One…two…three…run!'

The children burst like cannons. Callum jumps neatly out of the way. Barging past with a cheer and a salute, boards and helmets tucked under their arms, the race to the parents is on.

'*À toute!*' he calls, watching their snowy scattergraph with something akin to pride. 'Ah.' Spying Kira, he retrieves his gear from the snowdrift and trudges toward her. 'How are you doing?' He motions to the car park, and they walk. 'How's Romy? I'm assuming the ambulance was coming for her.'

Kira eyes him. 'Tactful.' She pushes her hands in her pockets. This time, she remembered her gloves, but they're as ineffective as her boots. 'You assume correctly, though. Mum and Dad went with her to the hospital, and as I've heard nothing since they left, I'm assuming everything's fine.'

Holding up a finger, Callum jogs to a cabin serving beer and pancakes, collects a pair of skis and boots propped against the side, adds them to his awkward load, and returns with a nod that he's listening. 'Why do you need—' Kira cuts herself off. The answer is probably obvious to a seasoned mountain-dweller, and she doesn't much want to feel stupid.

'Have you finished work already?' she asks instead. Passing a coach of day-trippers, they step from the tarmac to the stretching fields.

'For now. I'm off until three.' The snowboard slips from his shoulder with a thud, and he growls. 'Dammit. Can you hold these?' He loops the helmet straps over his wrist, tucks the uncomfortable skis beneath his arm, and hands her the boots. Furry buckets with a hundred buckles. She dampens a snort of laughter.

'I wasn't meant to work earlier,' he continues, obliviously bending to retrieve the board. 'But the kid who was called in sick. Got drunk last night in a barn, I think, and woke up puking like a beast.' He turns his sly grin on her. 'Have you ever been on a chairlift?'

Kira raises an eyebrow. 'Have I what?'

Relieving her of the ski boots, Callum points across the field. At the base of a gap in the trees whirs a creaky, clanking, antiquated, listing metal contraption.

'I am not getting on that.' Her voice rings out, too loud. A passing villager looks up, one she's seen before with a cowboy hat and a husky. Kira contorts her heating face. 'I want to look in the forest,' she amends. It may be a hasty attempt to avoid the contraption, but now that she's thought of it, it's as good a plan as any. 'Around the tree where you found Romy. And besides'—she watches uneasily as a chair soars into the trees—'I don't want to fall off and die.'

Callum bursts out laughing, loud and full and suited to a far bigger man. 'You won't fall off.' He bites down on his grin. The passing cowboy meets his eye, also suppressing a chortle. 'Hi, Ian.'

'Hi, Callum.' Ruffling the bounding husky's head, the man nods across at the chairlift. 'He's right.' He turns his amusement on Kira. 'You won't fall off. At least, not more than once. If you're anything like my daughter, it's a mistake you won't make—'

'He's joking.' Callum shoots him a half wither, half grin. 'Thank you, Ian, very kind, very kind. Bye, Wolfi.' Nodding at the dog, he turns to Kira. 'And I took ten six-year-olds up there this morning. If they can do it, you'll manage. Come on.'

He veers off toward the chairlift. Scowling at his back, Kira follows. Seasoned mountain-dwellers seem to lack empathy.

'How many British men are up here?' she calls, glancing across at the cowboy. Whistling, he tramps away, pulled by the panting wolf. 'Are all of you so witty?'

'Yes.' Callum nods back at her, his skis an unwieldy staff in the battle of ice and snow. 'We're a plague of hilarity. We're everywhere. That last bit's actually true.'

He angles his head, as if trying to see her without appearing to check. Kira puffs through her nose. Yes, she's still here. Call her a sheep or a toy on a string.

'I need to drop my stuff off,' he continues. 'At the top of the mountain.' He indicates the chairlift with his dangling helmet. 'Hence that. They'll store it until my next shift, so I don't need to drag it around. And if you come with me'—he brandishes the helmet—'I'll show you where I found Romy.'

Men. 'You found Romy in the forest behind us.' Kira speeds up, the better to protest to his face. 'Why can't I wait for you to come back down? If you're dropping stuff off, it's not like you'll be long.'

'Because it spoils the fun.' Callum winks and, before she's fully fallen into step, breaks into a jog to evade her. 'Mind the children!' he calls back merrily. Dragging his burden across the ski run, he has just enough time to avoid getting crushed. 'Too late.'

The flurry flies past. Kira jolts to a stop. It's madness: crouched for maximum speed, the children whoop and holler, poles in the air and little skis askew. Disgruntled humiliation shifts behind her ribs. Callum's right; they can't be more than six. What an abominable day.

'Why can't I wait down here?' she repeats. Callum only offers an exaggerated wink. 'Callum!' She throws her hands out. Waving his helmet cheerily, Callum turns away. 'Callum!'

If she goes down, it won't be quiet. Ready to argue until all the cows are home, Kira checks that no more flurries approach and trudges across the run.

She's almost reached him when he starts to move. Wielding his staff with his board for balance, he propels himself into the chairlift queue.

'Oh, come on!' Incredulous, Kira pulls up short. 'Really? Why—you know what, fine.' She slumps with resignation. It's not worth it. 'But if I fall off and die, it's on your head.'

Wading through the last of the snow, she steps in beside him. He gives her a gloved thumbs-up. 'I told you, you won't die.' He nods at the man in the wooden hut, hands on controls and watching keenly as the kiddie queue moves forward. 'These things wouldn't be here if everyone fell off. And they're fun.' He gestures for them to approach the barriers. The last three children slide up and away. 'But just in case you do'—he tangles his bundle under one arm—'try not to land on your head.'

Kira gapes. The barriers open. '*What?*'

'All you have to do is sit down.' Callum chivvies them through. The chair surges and groans behind them. 'Sit. Now. *Now.*'

Her legs are knocked from under her. Head swooping, stomach leaping, Kira sits with a yelp.

'See?' Comfortable beside her, Callum lowers the bar. He pats her thigh encouragingly. 'Fun.'

Kira slaps his hand away. 'No, not fun. Anything but fun.' Her voice strangles as the chair soars, rising through the trees at a clip to churn her stomach. Seizing the bar like a drowning man, she peers unhappily around. 'This isn't natural, Callum. I feel like I'm on a plane with no roof and no floor. No.' She half-lifts a finger, preempting his plague of hilarity, his amazing British wit. 'I'm on a plane with no roof and no floor, where the air hostess laughs in your face and kicks you to the curb at the end. Oh, God.'

She can almost feel the whites of her eyes popping wide with panic. Pine trees. Wavering snow. The quickly receding ground. Her predicament isn't over; it's only just begun. 'The end. What do I do at the end?'

'You run.' Callum pats her leg again. She'd kick *that* to the curb, the patronising thing, if she wasn't so scared of falling. She should have stuck to her guns and defied him. 'Have fun. This is much safer than flying, I assure you. At least you're attached to something.'

Moving as little as possible, she manages to nudge him off. 'That's not reassuring in the least.'

Callum grins. 'I tried. Don't worry so much.' He casts a look over his shoulder. 'I take it back. You're entertaining the children, so feel free to carry on.' He indicates the chair behind them. 'They're having a whale of a time.'

'You won't be when I push you out.' Folding her arms, Kira tries not to stare at the world with white-noise fear. The air is cooler up here, and inhaling it breath by breath by breath, a hint of calm trickles in. It's too beautiful to be afraid. It is.

A faint crack sounds. Kira looks down. Startled by falling icicles, a deer skitters off through untouched snow. Below it, a solitary snowboarder braves the vertical slope. She rouses a murder of crows in cahoots, and their shadows lift up from the ground. Kira watches them land on an old stone roof. Skimming black on white, their caws echo round the mountain. *How dare she be here?* they say. *Outrageous. How very, very dare she?*

Yet there she is. Slipping through the house's abandoned shadow, she weaves through broken tiles and the shadow cast by its crooked, jaunty chimney. Animal tracks lead away from the door, and Kira cranes her neck. Wistful, they wind off into the trees. If she had her materials, she'd paint it all: ragged birds atop a lonely house, deer prints, fox prints, someone wending their way through a fairy tale forest—

Jolting over a kink in the wires, the chair judders and tilts. Kira's calm jolts with it and wilts. Peaceful thoughts and observations fade with the broken house. She grips the bar with renewed fervour. Breathe, and don't look down.

She inches her attention sideways to Callum's lazy slouch. He's angled his goggles on the side of his head, his arm curled around his ski boots like they're a child in need of a cuddle. Skis and board slant across his torso, his helmet rocking in his lap. Tapping a muffled rhythm on the metal of the chair, he's a jester, a joker, a clown. He's got comedy for days.

Or he would have. Again, she's far too scared.

'Do you ski?' he asks suddenly. His comical head angles toward her. 'Or snowboard? Or both?'

Kira tries not to look grateful for the well-timed distraction. It's his fault she's up here at all. 'No.' She pushes back her breeze-blown hair. 'Well, I've been *on* skis, but I wouldn't call it skiing. More…'

'Falling with style?'

Kira catches his eye and can't help a smile. 'Yes, that'll do. Mum was pretty good in the end, but me and Dad never made the drag lift.' She stiffens. 'What are you doing?'

Lifting the safety bar over their heads, Callum nods at the landscape ahead. 'Getting off.'

Kira's heart stumbles. The chair is slowing.

'Oh, no.' Her head flushes, hot and cold. Panic spears her chest. 'Oh, no, n—how do I get off?'

Cresting the mountain, the chair reveals their exit with a flourish. There's a wooden hut, a pylon…and the chairs in front looping round to tip straight back down the drop.

'It's not stopping.' Kira clutches Callum's arm, then regrets it. What kind of feminist strength is this? God, she hates being dependent. Especially after Peter. But... 'Callum? I don't know what to do.'

'I know.' Gathering his gear under his arm, Callum narrows his eyes and tenses. Poised. 'Are you ready?'

Alarmed, Kira stares. 'No?'

'Walk fast.' He pushes her gently. 'Now.'

Their feet scrape the ground. With his hand on her back, she stumbles forward and scurries away from the lift.

'There.' Callum drops his hand. 'Easy.'

She feels like a blur of a person. Kira blinks at her boots, her jeans, at the hem of her heavy coat. They—what? She drags her head up. They're several metres away; they made it. Swinging around its wires with a clatter, the chair trundles back down the mountain. Somehow, she survived.

'Sorry.' Callum shrugs his apology. 'I'm aware that pushing you around isn't gentlemanly, but it worked. You did it.'

Regarding her with something between knowing and contentment, he hitches up his burden, wades into a snowdrift, and trudges off toward the leaning wooden hut.

She did it. Kira tips her head back in relief. She did it, and she's safe. She did it. She's returned to solid ground, and she's safe.

Letting out a sigh, she stamps lightly on the snow. Oh, solid ground. How truly underrated. Layer by layer, her panic sloughs away. Two elderly walkers saunter from their chairs, engrossed in conversation. Another chair empties—and another, and another—and she shakes her head. Easy.

The stone

Skiing from the chairlift with Julia and Karl, Lena watches the girl by the control hut. She's the twin of her mother; she's seen them around the village enough to recognise them by now. But why is she—

Callum. The figures fall behind her. Lena cranes her neck around. Stashing his equipment, hair static and wild. If the girl's with Callum, trouble is coming…and it's closer to home than she thought.

Lena doesn't do shock or worry; it isn't in her nature. Instead, she does resolve.

Resolve that fires to stone. Trailing her children over the moguls, she already knows her role. Get the girl away from Callum.

Or trouble will find them all.

7

The senses

'Done,' Callum announces.

Kira nods, in a vague *yes-that's-nice-dear*. His speedy shoe change doesn't compare to this, and slowly, enraptured, she rotates. She's never been so high up; it's entrancing. The pine trees meet the sky so soon, sooner than lower down the mountain. All she can see, for miles above the lift and beyond, is the towering forest and an ocean of peaks.

They shine in the pale sun, fresh and bright with snow. Wooden crosses top the summits.

Callum grabs her arm and yanks. Slamming into his chest, Kira yelps like he's thrown ice water in her face.

'Sorry,' he says in a way that means he isn't. 'I didn't much want you to die.'

She opens her mouth, but doesn't need to ask. A troop of skiers are zipping past toward a sculpted ski jump. One by one they shriek, one by one they fly, and one by one they spread their legs and clumsily fold into snowdrifts.

Whump. Whump. Whump.

Callum laughs. 'That could have gone better.'

Blinking away the shards of her hypnosis, Kira rights herself. 'Just a tad.' She steps away. She'd almost toppled into this stranger's arms, like a silly woman out for love. 'Thanks.'

Callum draws up the collar of his bright red coat. 'No problem, damsel.' Checking around the hut, he nods. 'We can head on down again now.'

He gestures toward the chairlift. Ten retorts for *damsel* perish. 'What?' Kira's heart seems to wobble. 'Don't point at that. Why are you pointing at that?'

Callum holds up his hands. Arrest me, officer, guilty-as-charged. 'I know I should have mentioned it before.'

'Mentioned *what*?'

She knows, though. Her heart wobbles off its ledge. He looks like he's guilty of poking a bear, or at least a little ashamed.

'I promise you, it'll be fine.' He glances at the ski slope behind him. 'We can walk down the mountain if you want, but there's a high chance we'll get skied into. Or indefinitely stuck.'

Kira peers around his gear-swaddled body. The slope isn't steep, the snow's not deep, and they won't be up in the air. 'I accept.'

Callum gives her an I-teach-children look. 'That wasn't a real suggestion, Kira. It'll take ages and wear us out.'

'Maybe so, but you don't have a hope in hell of getting me back on that.' Kira flicks distasteful fingers at the chairlift. 'No more coercion. It'll be ten minutes of psychological torture.'

'Kira.'

'No.'

'Please listen to me.' Callum steps toward her. 'There's nothing to worry about.'

'Maybe not, but I said—what are you doing?'

Her voice stabs like a knife. He's still moving toward her, his face thoughtful, and abruptly, completely guilt-free. 'Callum.' Kira raises her hands. Do seasoned mountain-dwellers, as well as lacking empathy, enjoy tourist ignorance? She steps back. He steps forward. Was this his mischievous plan all along? 'Please don't. Now is not the time for simulated free fall—'

To the high-pitched amusement of arriving children, Callum lunges forward. Grabbing her in a rugby tackle, he hoists her onto his shoulder.

'Hey!' she shouts, slapping his back. Target acquired, baggage secured. He holds her tight and walks away. 'Callum, stop it! I've known you three hours!' She turns her slaps into fists, fighting to wriggle free. He only holds her tighter, closer to his head. She can feel his grin against her coat. 'What happened to being reassuring? I thought you felt guilty?' She kicks out, but her legs won't bend enough to make contact. 'Callum! Three hours is not enough for this!'

Striding toward the chairlift, he ignores her. The creak and clank of the chairs fills her ears, dread pooling through her chest like water. Her doom is almost nigh; she can hear it in the whoosh of dismounting skis, feel it in her jerking limbs as Callum breaks into a jog. It's even more horrifying to watch from behind.

'I'll kill you, Callum,' Kira warns, but it's weak. Dodging a chair already descending, Callum stops on the brink of the vertical drop and waits for the next to rise. Her body tenses. His shoulder digs into her stomach, pinching her pinhole breaths. 'I promise you that. Once we're on the ground—'

The rocking chair roars up.

Oh, no. Nausea swirls behind her ribs. Kira squeezes her eyes shut. Oh, God, oh, no. If he makes even one mistake…

'On we go.' Sliding Kira unceremoniously from his shoulder to his arms, Callum leans back. 'Hold on.'

The chair jolts beneath them, sweeping them away. Kira cries out. Callum's arm is tight about her middle, but the lift propels them down at a horrifying angle. No. Oh, God, oh, no.

'We're fine,' Callum says, but what help is that now? Screwing up her face, Kira clings to his shoulder. Dependence be damned; she's not letting go. Lynx couldn't drag her away.

The chair clanks and rocks. Grunting, Callum shifts them around, and after a small, heart-bending forever, all at once it's over.

Slowly, slowly, Kira opens her eyes. The bar has been secured over their knees, and Callum is carefully reclaiming his arm. They sit side by side as if the panic never happened.

Except her heart drums up a percussion. Brushing back her tumbled, tangled hair, Kira tries not to breathe like she's just run a race. Callum's expression is smug—is it ever not?—as he surveys his snowy domain. With a burst of indignation, she lets her hair fall, curtaining him off from her vision. Who does he think he is? Her handler? A trainer of an obstinate dog?

'There's one thing you should know about me.' Kira speaks through gritted teeth. 'I'm honest, and I'm righteous, and—'

'Those are two things.'

'Shut up. Oh, God.' The chair jolts over a kink in the wire. Kira grapples for the bar. 'I'm honest, and I'm righteous, so when I say I'm going to kill you, I mean it. You may have saved my sister, but I don't have to like you.' She winces at the ice of the metal through her gloves. 'Nothing about this is fair. If I could, I'd push you out.'

Callum raises his practiced eyebrows. 'Yes, ma'am.'

For some reason, that brings the whole thing home. She's floating down a mountain on a metal couch, having suffered a fireman's lift, having been laughed at by a winter cowboy, and having lived through a horror film. Laughter boils in her belly and surges up her throat. 'Ridiculous.' Shaking her head, she slumps back in the seat, swallowing down the shakes. 'Wow. This is utterly ridiculous. You're such a wazzock, Callum.'

Callum grins. 'Wazzock.' He tests the word. 'I can deal with that. Why not.'

He shades his eyes against the glow of the mountains. The clouds are coming down above the tunnel of trees, the sun disappearing as quickly as it came, and as the gloom presses down on the landscape, Kira's laughter calms. Whether it's amusement, fear, or frustrated mania is a crooked mystery; but despite Callum's infuriating, king-of-the-castle confidence, she's grateful. If only a little, they distract her from Romy; and after this morning, a little is enough.

She certainly needs it now. They're almost at the ground.

'Don't worry.' Callum sweeps his hand at the approaching land as if it's nobbut a molehill. Putting an arm around her shoulders, he hoists up the bar and rushes them, stumbling, away.

'So what's the verdict?' he asks, once they've forced their way through the lift-side snowdrifts and reached the neighbouring field. 'Not so bad?'

'Definitely so bad.' Kira winches herself from the ungroomed snow, raising her hands to the heavens in relief. Solid ground suddenly feels like her only goal in life. 'It would only have been worse if I'd fallen off and died. Seriously. It was hell.'

Walking backwards, Callum grins. 'Not so bad, then.' Bending at the edge of the car park, he beats the snow from his body. 'Seeing as you're alive.'

Kira pulls an imaginative face at the top of his messy head. 'Fine.' She assesses her own snowy body. Her tight jeans are too sodden to attempt to beat dry, and she shivers. 'Where did you find Romy?'

Brushing snow from the tops of his boots, Callum lifts a finger. 'Bear with.'

The lull that falls as she waits is full. The whistle of the wind, the crackling of power lines, cars somewhere else on the mountain. She shivers again, tucking her hands in her armpits. Something in it all is unsettling; although happy shouts and laughter drift out of the resort, as the rush of the chairlift shrivels, she can't shake her rising unease. Something somewhere doesn't feel right.

The shadow she thought she saw in the bathroom. Romy's purring voice in her head.

That's called paranoia. Kira stamps her feet against the cold. How long does it take to—

Hello.

Kira looks up from her toes. A voice?

Hello, it whispers again. Kira becomes clockwork, in desperate need of winding. It's speaking, but at the same time, it isn't; breathy, enticing, and gone, like a rustling of leaves.

Leaves inside her head.

'Right.' Callum straightens, slapping his hands to his knees. 'Let's go. Romy—'

'Did you say something?' Kira interrupts. Movement returning crank by crank, she looks around. Is she going mad? Hearing the wind become whispers? There's nobody here but them.

'Yes…' Callum cocks his head. 'I said, "right, let's go."'

Distracted, Kira waves her hand. 'Before that. You know what?' She turns the wave into a stop. It's clear he senses nothing; no chill in the air, no electric eeriness. No voice. 'Never mind. It's just the thought of going in there.' She nods at the forest. 'Seeing where you found Romy, after the day we've had.' She lifts her shoulders meekly. It could be true. 'I'm paranoid.'

'To be fair, the forest does that.' Callum offers her a smile. Surprised, she returns it. 'Mum hates it. Anyway.' He turns to the trees, rubbing his thick-gloved hands. 'Romy wasn't too far in. Just a few minutes, I think.' He narrows his eyes. 'It was in a clearing, although there've been so many joys since then…'

His voice trails off with his body. Negotiating cars, two sparring dogs, and a half-buried motorbike, he wends his way toward the snowy bank.

The words take a handful of seconds to settle. One, two, and disbelief. 'Are you serious?' Kira cries after him. 'You find a girl under a tree, and you don't remember where?'

All guns blazing for a verbal war, she hurries to catch him up. Callum shoots her a deadpan steadiness, probably intended to make her feel small. 'I'll recognise it.' He tilts his head back to contemplate the bank. 'Don't worry. I've lived here for years.'

Kira has just about readied a scathing retort when he steps back, propels himself toward the snow, leaps, scrabbles, trips over a trap of thinly masked twigs, and lands gracelessly on the ground. 'Shit.'

Kira bursts out laughing. 'Oh, that was priceless.'

'Ignore it.' Vexed, Callum staggers just as gracelessly up. 'You saw nothing. And I think if we walk straight on from here…' He throws a glance behind him at the forest. 'Yeah. If we go on straight, we'll hit the clearing. I remember thinking it was odd, but Romy was probably too drunk to change direction. We'll find it no problem.' He appraises her standing at the foot of the bank. 'Are you deigning to join me?'

Mischief toys with Kira's lips. 'Of course.' Straightening her ladylike posture, she extends an elegant hand. 'If you would be so kind, good sir.'

Callum's eyebrows hit his mop of hair. Her smile stretches into a grin. 'Yes, I change like the wind.' She bats her eyelashes. 'I'm as fluid as you are annoying, but mercifully, I'm self-aware. Now, sir?'

She beckons him over. With a short bow, Callum pulls her smoothly up beside him. 'Milady.' He raises her glove to his lips. Kira grins again.

'Quite right, too.' She curtseys, no mean feat in knee-deep snow. 'After what you've put me through, I deserve some chivalry. Which direction?'

Direction. Callum's previous words resolve, and she frowns. 'What you said before.' She looks past him into the snowy, sombre trees. 'About Romy not changing direction. Why did you say she was drunk?'

She looks back to him. He flounders. 'Um.' He's a goldfish in a bowl. 'There was an empty bottle near where I found her.' A search-me expression flits across his face. 'Jäger. It might not have been hers, but I assumed it was.'

Just like that, Kira's lightness dies. 'Jesus, Romy.' She moves past Callum into the dismal forest. 'I thought that was done.'

Everything white, everything buried. Nothing stirs but their steady trudge. Laden branches mask the sky, and even the gaps in the clouds where the sun peeps through seem strangely far away. Kira's dismay swells to a bruise. How could Romy find her way in the dark? The trees are a web in the daylight. At night, they must be a labyrinth, deadly and dark and worthy of Pan. And with however much Jäger inside her…

Kira's insides hurt. Oh, Romy. Could she see anything? What *happened*?

Ducking her chin into her chest, Kira folds her arms. Away from the jovial paths, the forest is different; brooding, heavy, pressed upon by clouds. It surrounds them with a wall of white, spiked by bushes and Grimm-esque trees. No birds call. No miaowing jays, or squawking magpies; no foxes, no badgers, no deer, no tracks, no rustles in the undergrowth. The more they walk, the more she shivers. There's nothing here at all.

'This one, I think.' Callum stops on the edge of a clearing. It's a white, immaculate bowl, dipped low and surrounded by a grand ring of pines. Footsteps crowd a pile of logs, carelessly abandoned. Callum's eyes light up. 'Yes!' He clicks his fingers. 'Those are mine. My sticks. And Romy was'—he scans the trees—'there.'

He heads with bracing certainty toward a particular pine. Kira says nothing. The base of the trunk is a decrepit hollow. 'Just there.' He nods at it. Lined with flattened, scattered leaves, it's been crushed and crumpled. A bed. 'Half in the tree and half on the roots. Your parents won't like it, but she probably got drunk, couldn't find her way back, and decided to sleep here. Stranger things have happened.' He scratches his head. 'I've got a friend who slept in a thorn bush after a night out. On a scale of one to stupid, I'd say that was worse.' He huffs a laugh. 'She couldn't take a shit for a week without screaming.'

This isn't encouraging. Kira examines the miserable tree, her concern growing sadder by the second. The bark is withered and peeling, the splintered branches drooping to the ground, and the hollow itself is home to several small, rotting bodies. She closes her eyes. The picture in her mind is painful, so visceral she's almost there: Romy, unconscious in the dark, surrounded by death and decay. Close to death herself, drifting into a snow-covered silence—

No. Kira digs her knuckles into her eyes. None of this makes sense; if anything, the more sense she tries to make, the more it veers away. Romy's attacks, her too-quick recovery, her depersonalisation…could she just have been hungover?

She was hungover. She was drunk. She was out of it. Out of it *because* she was drunk; Kira grapples for this flitting hope, aware it looks like a straw. Peter once told her that his brother woke up, bleary from a night of brandy, and didn't know his girlfriend's name. Maybe Romy—

Don't be stupid. Even if Callum's right, alcohol wouldn't cause Romy to act as she did. There must be something else.

Kira turns in a slow, observatory circle. Trees, snow, the crisp, white bowl. There's nothing vivacious leaping out and shrieking *pick me! I did it!* Nothing human, or animal, or even disturbed. Nothing to say what Romy might have seen.

What Romy might have gone through.

Although…Kira's breath snags minutely. Surely not. It's not possible.

Is it? She takes a cautious step. The dipped clearing was pure. It was.

Her lips part of their own accord. A tiny ring of indents has appeared in the centre, each print as identical as the trees around the edge. Kira blinks. Focuses her blurred, squinting eyes. The rest of the snow is untouched.

'Callum?' she calls, hitching and tentative. He turns, the abandoned wood stack in his arms. She points at the footprints. 'What are those?'

8

The road

Relinquishing the wood, Callum comes to stand beside her. 'I don't see...' he begins. 'Oh.' Treading lightly, he moves to teeter, precarious, on the edge of the bowl. 'They look like odd little feet made—agh!'

The snow gives way. Sinking to his thigh in untouched powder, Callum frowns. 'Well, this is me now.'

Shaking snow from his gloves, he continues his stare.

But with the fall, something has changed. Kira looks up. It's all but imperceptible, but present nonetheless; a change in the air, or a shift in her perceptions. She stills, listening, sensing. The tiny footsteps—now that they've thought it, she can't take it back—are the same. She blinks, refocusing. The snow is so bright. Is it getting whiter? Is the forest darkening? The clouds descending, strangling the sun? Maybe the trees are edging closer, a gastric band of pines.

Doubtful. What isn't doubtful, however, is that the paranoia is real. Kira crouches to help Callum. She shouldn't have let it in; it's her mind playing games, inventing stupid comparisons to scare away her reason. Nothing's changed. This isn't a silver screen supreme, where the girl is left helpless when the trees attack. It's a normal clearing, in a normal forest, where nothing abnormal can happen.

Except it can. By the time they've struggled, heaved, sunk, and Callum has scrambled out of the snow, the tiny footprints have gone.

Kira stares. Looks over at Callum. His mouth has turned down, and she looks back. She's not mistaken: the footprints have gone.

And the forest is getting colder.

Apprehension creeps and crawls. A gust of wind whips into the clearing, blustering snow from the trees. Kira shivers, tensing her limbs. The sky is disappearing under dimming clouds. Her temples throb dully from the change in pressure. The wind drops away, and the forest is silenced.

She wasn't being paranoid; something isn't right.

'Can we go?' Kira's voice is minute. Her apprehension melts into anxiety, stinging in waves like the bite of the wind. The pines are too tall. The rise across the clearing slopes up too far. The tree trunks are too dark, too straight, too thick; they stand like pillars in a war-torn wasteland, gliding with a roar across the clearing, reaching to take her in their withered arms—

And now her feet are sinking. Fright thrills through her. Sinking as if the clearing is quicksand, the white slips and slides and glistens in the sun that's no longer there, covering her knees, thighs, chest, mouth, her cheeks and nose and eyes—

Kira clenches her fists. The sharp nail on her little finger slaps her back. She blinks, hard, screwing up her face. Again, digging her nails in deep enough to dent, and the forest is normal.

At least, not trying to consume her. What is *happening*? Drawing a lung-straining breath, Kira scans the clearing. Her anxiety—no, her *fear*—is rising by the second. It's a phoenix, lifting in vivid bloom. If she doesn't act, she'll burn.

'Let's go.' Kira looks to Callum. His eyes have unfocused, staring into the distance. 'Callum.' She touches his arm. 'Let's go.'

He starts as if ghost-struck. His eyes lose their glassy gloss, and with a dead man's slump, he nods. 'O—yes.' He nods again, more definitively. 'Yes.'

Rubbing his eyes with clumsy hands, he's the image of how she feels. With the blood in her temples and her fingers trembling, out of sync and not hers to control, she's about as real as the quicksand snow. Maybe less so. Locking Callum's hand with hers, she hauls them both away.

'Wait.' Forehead creasing, Callum stops.

'What?' Kira asks. Anxious to leave, her impatience is a beast to keep at bay. Callum rotates, surveying the clearing. Kira folds her arms tight. '*What?*'

Resting his arms behind his head, Callum's words are a puzzled exhalation. 'Which way…' He rotates again. The crunch of his boots is painfully loud. 'Which way did we come?'

Kira points ahead of them. 'That way.' God, just let this day end. 'What's wrong with your memory? We walked in a straight line, like you said, and now we're following—oh.'

Through the trees ahead is a circular clearing, dipping to a bowl of untouched snow. Their clearing.

'I take it back.' Kira turns a quick one-eighty. They must be missing something.

They're not. She scans the forest, flick, flick, flick. They're stood where they were before, between the tricksy bowl and the sad, hollow tree. Callum's fall still tramples the snow. She glances over her shoulder: an identical clearing, replacing their line to the car park. The pulse in her temples throbs.

'That's not possible.' Callum shakes his head. 'It's an optical illusion.'

'Maybe.' Kira starts to walk. Cautious at first, carefully retracing their path toward the bowl, she speeds up until she's almost running. Bypassing Callum's bewilderment, the crash site, the fallen firewood, she stumbles around the edge of the clearing to the rise on the other side.

Half-bent bushes, scratching bark. She scrabbles up the slope with her heart in her windpipe and a budding idea of what she hopes not to see. She wasn't paranoid. She must be.

Is she?

At the top of the rise, Kira reels back. Where the trees thin out and the ground should level, the clearing appears again.

It's a perfect replica. Her lungs stutter. Her stumbling run marks the edge of the bowl, the firewood haphazard by the hollow tree. Just for a second, there's a shadow of Callum. Entwining her fingers, she tries not to scream.

A tiny, rustling movement, somewhere to her left. It sighs and stirs, and she wheels around. A laugh, a dance? The original clearing is empty bar Callum, trudging stiffly toward her. Did she imagine it?

No. Chittering behind her, it lifts her hair. *Hello.*

The breath on her neck is the coup de grâce. Kira shrieks, whips around, and careers back down the slope.

'Something's up there—something—' She crashes into Callum, wild and shaking. 'What the hell is this? What—hey!' She staggers as he shoulders past her, forging a path up the rise. His face turns to snow at the top, and with a bare second's look, he slides back down.

'This isn't real.' He rubs his face so hard it must chafe. 'It can't be. I was here this morning, and it wasn't like this. I'm *always* here. It's never like this.'

'Walk. We'll just walk.' Panic bursts like a blood blister. Grabbing Callum's arm, Kira wields her blocky feet. Back around the bowl, back toward the firewood, back the way she *knows* they came, even though it mutated. She marches to the hollow tree and beyond, ignoring the hissing in her head about mirrors, mirrors and magic, entrapment…it's ridiculous. Impossible. Unreal. If they walked here in a straight line, they can sure as hell walk back.

'Kira, we don't know where we're going.' Jerked along by her jogging insistence, Callum tries to jerk away. 'Maybe we should—'

'What?' Breathless, Kira cuts him off. Breathing hard, marching hard, watching hard. She can't stop now that she's started. Who knows what might appear if she does? 'Maybe we should wait for it to go away? That won't help. It might not go away. It might'—she gulps at the entrance to another clearing, one that surely cannot be—'change even more. We need to get out.' She swerves around the rim of the bowl, marked anew with Callum's fall. 'Which won't happen unless we try.'

They hit the slope at her final words. Releasing Callum's hand, she powers on up. Can't stop; mustn't stop. If she stops, she might be paralysed, overpowered by fear. Unreality would float her on the string of a red balloon, and she might never get going again.

'Maybe—' She slips, flinging out her arms. The steep slope is wet underfoot, dotted with holes from trees dripping snow, but she won't slow down. She can't. 'Maybe we're snow-blind.' She pushes on her knees for yet more speed. The low rise sang so sweetly of innocence, and now it never seems to end. She daren't look back, though. The way things are going, they could have climbed a mountain. 'We could be imagining it all. Stranger things have happened, right?'

'I'm not entirely sure.' Callum speeds up, too. He may be far less out of breath, but urgency creases his voice. 'And as much as I'd like it to be, this isn't snow-blindness. Snow-blindness—'

His sentence dies as they crest the rise and trip to two startled halts. On the other side is a road.

Callum lifts an arm and drops it. 'Well, that shouldn't be there.' He looks left, right, left. Hemmed in on either side by snowdrifts and pines, the thin, white road is straight and neverending. He runs a hand over his head. 'That should definitely not be there.'

Everything is on fire. 'What do you mean that shouldn't be there?' Gasping, Kira thumps her weight against a tree. She couldn't be less stable in her legs, her lungs, her sanity. 'Where else should it be?'

'Not what I meant.' Callum takes a halting step toward it. 'I mean, I've never seen it before. I thought I knew the forest inside out, but…ah, bollocks.' A second step sinks into the snow. Swaying, he removes his leg with distaste. 'I miss Spain. None of this rubbish in Spain. And I know what you're going to say.' He glances at Kira. 'You're going to say we should take it, even if we don't know where it goes. You're not a girl to dither.'

Kira raises an eyebrow. Why would *any*one dither on a day like today? Quite apart from the madness, it's freezing.

'We *should* take it.' She treads lightly up beside him. Her jeans are soaked as it is, and her feet don't bear thinking about. When she gets home, the queen of the unprepared is resigning. 'At least it's not another clearing.'

Callum shrugs. 'I suppose.'

Kira takes her careful steps off across the snow.

'Oh.' He snorts. 'You really don't dither, do you?'

'No.' She hops down to the road, stamps her feet, and looks around. As far as she can see in either direction march trees and this thin, white trickle. *The Thin White Line.* Her blistered, pounding panic slips. The less bloody version of Peter's favourite. That was not a fair trade for *Atonement*.

The deep snow crunches. 'Fine.' Callum sighs. She can hear the frown without turning around. 'But for the record, don't blame me if this gets us lost. I've already admitted that I don't know where we are. Left or right?'

Kira pulls up her hood. At this point, it probably doesn't matter. 'Right.' She burrows into the fleece, pushing her hands in her pockets. Solid and compact, the road is a gentle slant with no end. Although she can't see high enough to tell, the pines on both sides seem infinite, a lifeless mass of green-white quiet in an unfamiliar world.

An unfamiliar world that trades in tricks. They tramp, and trudge, and this wandering distracts her. If the self-crowned king of the forest doesn't recognise the road, who knows where they've ended up? They could be writing a fantasy novel, one wardrobe from Narnia. They could be where the wild things are. They could run into a giant named Grawp. Perhaps they'll find a diviner camp. Perhaps, through the trees, they'll see a clanking tin-man. They could have wandered beyond the wall, faced with the roaming dead.

Too far. Sweeping this away, Kira turns to walk backwards. 'I promise not to blame you if this gets us lost.' It's an unacceptably delayed response, but that doesn't matter, either. In this green-white infinity, they're the only two alive. 'Although I think we're already there.'

'Phones.' Callum stops. His face shifts in odd slow-motion. 'We have…'

'Phones!' Smacked with the galling realisation, Kira fumbles in her jeans. 'All this time, we had civilisation. How did we forget? We're the internet youth.'

Fiddling with his scratched device, Callum offers it full disapproval. 'Magic forests do that. Even to youths.' He shoves the phone in his inside pocket. 'It's not working, anyway.'

Kira frowns. It was fully charged this morning. 'We tried.' She flicks her dark-starred case. 'Have you really never seen this road? You seem like you've lived here forever.'

'You do realise'—Callum squints at the thick white sky—'that no matter how many times you ask, the answer will stay the same? Yes, I've lived here for years. Yes, I've explored these woods to death. Yes, I thought I knew every path, every clearing, and pretty much all of the trees. But clearly, I was wrong.' The teasing in his voice wilts. 'Asking "are we there yet?" won't suddenly make it right.'

Kira's cheekbones heat. 'That's not what I was doing.'

She turns away. 'Hey.' Callum grabs her arm. 'I'm not—agh.' He shakes his head. His expression is pained. 'I know you weren't saying that. I'm not trying to be patronising. It's just…'

He mouths for a moment. Kira waits. Despite what he's saying now, he's made her feel stupid. It's not party town for her, either.

'Whatever that was'—he sighs eventually—'it can't have happened.' He waves a bleak hand behind them. 'There's no way it can have happened, but it did. And I'm trying very hard not to think about it, or this'—another wave—'because none of it should be happening. Honestly, I'm happy to assume I was wrong about knowing every inch of this forest. If it explains it, I'm game. Magic clearings, magic footprints. All of it.'

Kira watches his eyes flick around them. He truly does look thrown. Lost.

'So what do we do?' She starts walking again. She'd rather stay peeved, but the look in his eyes…it settles in her stomach like sickness. Maybe she had been hoping that eventually, they'd be "there."

'We walk.' Callum sighs again. 'In theory, it shouldn't be long before we find somewhere with people. It looks like unpopulated heathen-land, but you can't go far around here without hitting some random hamlet. And then'—he spreads his hands, preaching ruefully to the masses—'we'll work out exactly where I went wrong. Whoa.' He stops. 'What's that?'

9

The restless

The trees taper into distance perception. Stuck in the road before that, a *something* has come into view. Callum's insides hiccup.

'A sign?' Kira's voice is ambivalent, as though the *something* is a joke, a blemish, and a threat. 'Here? Pointing to what?'

She rekindles their approach, more watchful than before. Uncomfortably, Callum follows. 'I don't know.' Although he'd rather not admit it, this development is not a comfort. It's *wrong*. He's never seen anything like it. Not in the forest.

Not anywhere.

Fifty metres, twenty, ten. They're far too close; his skin prickles, and not from fear, but an oddness in the air. It's electric, heady, like a storm.

He's never been a fan of storms.

'Oh.' Kira stops, high-pitched, surprised. Callum brakes to avoid collision. He'd been considering defeat, admitting his unease, his spider-senses, whatever, in order to try the direction that *doesn't* have a magic sign. 'It's a window.'

Callum's unease eases. She's right. A frame nailed to a splintered post, the small, wooden, air-filled window is comically vigilant and pointlessly alone.

Kira tilts her head to the side. 'It's adorable.'

She smiles, at it and him. It's subtle, inquisitive, different from the grin that makes her eyes crinkle to nothing. It's adorable in itself.

It doesn't prevent his snort. 'It's useless.' Jogging the last few metres, he pokes his head through the gap. Blinking once, twice, thrice at the empty air, he manoeuvres back out with a shrug. 'Yep.' He flicks a dismissive hand. Thank

Christ for easy solutions. His spider-senses were bollocks. 'Useless. Although it does have a nice motif.'

Hello.

Callum looks up from the etching. 'What?'

'I didn't say anything.' Bending until her head is level with the frame, Kira contemplates the view. The road is captured perfectly, so barren and picturesque it could be a winter postcard. The scene is all there is, though. No framing of something specific; no hidden message carved into the wood, unless you count the mocked motif. A tiny engraving of a sketchy tree trunk, it has four thin branches and a line for the ground. That's it. That's all there is.

Disappointment clunks inside her. As much as she'd love to prove Callum wrong, the wooden window is useless. She lifts her head. The real-life scene is still. Rotating her lips in twisty contortions, she peers back through the gap. Over the wood. Back through the gap. Everything is the same: the same sky, the same winter, the same impatient Scot signalling to get a move on…

Or not. Kira leans closer to the frame. Something *is* different; something she missed, or that hadn't been there. Tucking her hair behind her ears, she parts her focused lips.

'There's a fork.' The words are a breath of disbelief. 'Callum.' She glances up, grasps his attention, and quickly returns to the gap. 'The road forks. Look.'

Callum swings around beside her. 'No, there isn't.' He swings back. Kira narrows her eyes. Parting around an island of trees stretch two ramrod roads. 'Is this some oddball trick of yours, or is one of us actually blind?'

'You.' Standing, she shifts from the postcard-path to the real-life road. The fork remains. 'Definitely you. I'll prove it.'

Either she's gone mad, or he has. Callum scratches the back of his neck and watches Kira march away. After the length of a beginner ski slope, she throws out her arms. 'See?' she shouts, breathless but satisfied, clumsily swivelling to face him. 'You must be able to see it now. It's right behind me.'

He's in that experiment where no one sees the monkey. Callum shades his eyes, but it makes no difference; right behind her or not, there's only one road. He stoops to squint through the window. The same image greets him, and exhaling through his teeth, he shuts his eyes. If he's being made fun of, she'll be right back on that lift.

Callum straightens up. Blink, slow, deliberate: no fork. Again: still no fork. Again.

At the fifth, Kira jolts into focus. Callum wavers in surprise. He hadn't noticed she was blurred. 'I still don't see anything,' he calls. Irritation barbs his chest. 'Is this payback for the chairlift?'

Giddiness swoops in a swoon. 'Jesus.' Swaying, he slaps his hands to his knees. Nausea curdles like rancid milk. Unsteadily, he looks up.

The giddiness crashes straight back down. Shuddering, splitting, distorting around a narrow belt of trees, the way ahead reshapes itself. Behind Kira, just as she said, curve two white roads.

Rocking a hand to his spinning head, Callum wobbles up to his feet. A glance at the window, up at the fork. Deceitful, dizzying monstrosity. He resists the urge to kick it. Some monkey. What a little shit. What a wazzock.

With a final, cursing glare, he slogs after Kira.

It takes an age too long. Collapsing beside her, he emits a queasy groan. His woozy limbs are exhausted by the minuscule hike, as unhappily unwieldy as the arches of his feet. 'I need to sit down,' he mumbles after the fact. 'Don't mind me. Stupid monkey. Stupid goddamn monkey.'

Settling into the snow, he drops his head into his hands. Stupid monkey? Whatever. The restless words slip away. In the short time it took him to get here, Kira's mind metamorphosed, from an energetic, curious whirl to a vacant, staring mass. Cocking her head, she stares through Callum. She's blanker than the time she tried to write a book. Even her memories are fading.

What?

Whatever. The events of the day are drifting away, and like snowflakes, she lets them go. Romy, the clearing, the fork. The cuts on her face that pulse in the cold, the man she met this morning. They sink into tar, and she's nothing.

Nothing but a numbness in a swaying bag of bones. No concern. No wonder. No attempts to understand. It's her seventeenth birthday, two-point-oh. She almost giggles. Over-drinking to nirvana. Now, it's not as nauseating but just as rich, as harmonious; it leaves her with a dreamy floating, a faint flurry at the edges of her senses, and a vague sense that she's not herself.

With her thoughts a sluggish, oceanic rumble, Kira glances over her shoulder. The prongs of the fork are identical, straight and white and lined with the booming, marching trees. 'Which…' she mumbles. Her tongue is treacle. 'Which way?' The question takes eternity. 'Which way do you want to go?'

After an endless pause, Callum shrugs. It's as listless as if he, too, feels and wonders nothing. 'Right,' he murmurs in a weary breath. Heavily, Kira helps him up. 'You know. For consistency.'

Why are they carrying on? A voice beats at the base of his skull, but his senseless brain ignores it. Why are they pretending this is okay? None of it is. None of it can be. Why aren't they running for the hills?

They should be. They have to. He's a swimmer in a dream, or a somersaulting monkey, crashing cymbals and chattering, inane. Mindless, barely there. If he let himself, he could spread his arms, fall back, fall *in*, and—

A monkey?

With a tremendous, deadweight heave, Callum hauls himself back. He'd been thinking about monkeys, or one specific monkey, and he snatches it with papery hands. The monkey. A video of an experiment, one about attention that he studied at school. The teacher presented it with glee. *How many of you*, she'd started by asking, *think you'll spot it straight away?*

He had.

Callum grasps Kira's hand and tugs her into movement. Whatever's happening, to them and their minds, he can't let it win. She doesn't protest; she doesn't seem to hear. In fact, and the image washes him cold, she looks worryingly like Romy. Inanimate, grey-faced, and very far away. 'Come on. We need to get out.'

Neither of them see, as they slowly turn right, a smiling wisp of a woman. Neither of them see her restless tendrils pale into the air.

Hello.

10

The worlds she's never known

The numbing fog was creeping back. Kira's might never have begun to lift, but at a sly slip of wind down his neck, Callum is awake. They're trudging through a growing, weighty daze, and he stops.

'No.' Disentangling their hands, he jabs his nails into his skull. 'Stop. Jesus. Kira!' He grips her shoulders. 'Kira, wake up.'

He could shake her, but he doesn't. She hasn't spoken in far too long, hasn't done anything except be led. Is it too late? Has it gone too deep?

'Hmm?' Like fingers clearing a misted window, her eyes suddenly spark. 'What?' Kira looks up at him. His swell of relief is startling as she blinks, a dreamer out of touch. What would happen if she'd been lost? 'What's wrong? Has something happened?'

'No.' Callum lets her go. It feels like a wrench. 'We're fine. Everything's fine. It's just…' He gestures around them, at the flat sky, the trees, the road. None of it ever ends. 'This place. This atmosphere. I don't know; something. The forest is never like this. It's screwing with our brains.'

He rubs his hands down his face, rough and repeated. 'Making us sleep while we're awake,' he continues, muffled by his fingers. 'You know if you're watching a film, and you kind of know what's going on, but most of your brain is thinking about waffles? When you wake up, you expect to be able to pick up where you left off, but you can't because a bouncing snowman's joined the cast, someone's turned the city to ice, and you have no idea how it happened. That's what's going on here, and we have to make it stop.'

Kira stares through him. Her mind is sharpening fast now that he's shaken her fog, but not enough to fully function. 'Are you comparing this to watching *Frozen?*' She blinks at him, half-amused. A further level of fuzziness lifts. Somehow, she smiles. *It's screwing with our brains.* 'Does this mean you've *seen Frozen?*'

'Men do many things for women.' Callum turns his attention to the road ahead. Kira sees something register. 'Oh, come *on.*' He tips back his head as if to say *Lord help us.* 'Really?'

Where the road had been strong and unfailing, now it ends. Kira's shoulders slump in a way she thought reserved for cartoons. There's a break in the road, a break in the trees, a break where the land falls into the sky, a clean-cut precipice that troubles and exhausts her. She speaks in a sigh. 'Do you want to go back?'

'No.' Callum shakes his head, although he looks like he'd far rather nod. 'We've come this far. We might as well go to the edge.'

Kira tugs a hand through her tangled hair. If she was writing the book she didn't finish, she'd say she was flabbergasted, or flummoxed, or any other words that are intricate but contrived. She'd probably use all of them. At this point, no single option is enough.

'Kira?' Callum prompts.

Kira brings herself back. 'Sorry.' She gestures emptily. 'This is all just so…'

'Impossible.' Callum nods along. 'I know. I'm starting to hate that word.'

Twisting her gloved hands into knots, Kira follows him toward the drop. The air is sharp, stripped of weight. The pines are more like incense, perfumed. Or is it madness?

Madness. Everything is madness. This holiday has only lasted a week, but that's enough; enough for anyone to know that no part of the land just falls. There's nowhere where the sky takes over the land, where the mountains, the valleys, the lakes disappear. It's no longer a case of Callum losing his way, if she ever believed it was…and as they peer out on the edge of nothing, suddenly, she's afraid.

In the nothing lies a blanket of unbroken cloud. White seeps into pale blue, darkening to indigo, purple, violet; where it creeps along the horizon, it fuses into snow-cloud black. It's a melancholy sunset without the sun, and it pinches Kira's breath.

But the cloudscape is not what has Callum's attention. Following his cheerless gaze, she gasps; below them is a drop, a cascade of land and air. Carved into the mountain, their road falls fast, curving down steeply and tapering to nothing. Kira leans gingerly over the edge. No; not nothing. Treacherous and frozen, it's there when the slope opens up again, winding through the cluttered trees.

And beyond the trees…Kira wavers. Madness. Madness is all there is. Half of her wants to step closer. Half shouts to get the hell away. Beyond the trees rolls a turquoise ocean.

'Where are we?' she whispers. It's vast and transfixing. She can't not stare. Sky and water, a strip of land. There are no buildings, no mountains, no roads. No other side. Just the churning waves, a faint roar slapping the shore, and the burst of the sunless sunset. 'Callum?' She drags her eyes away. The colour-bright water is painful, but hypnotic. 'Surely this goes beyond—is that a *hummingbird*?'

A speck of blue flits through her afterglow. Hovering behind Callum's head, the tiny bird bobs serenely. Golden wings tremble, beaded eyes curious, and it watches before darting off with a hum.

Into the sunset, a beautiful buzz. 'Not like any I've ever seen.' Callum shakes his head as it vanishes, swallowed by the boundless sky. 'Not that I've ever seen a real one, but still.' He scratches his head. 'We really need to leave.'

He turns his back on the water. 'Wherever we are, we need to leave. There's no ocean here. For God's sake, the country's landlocked. I won't use that goddamn word again, but it's definitely time to go.'

'Agreed.' Kira spares the precipice one last look.

The fog sweeps in like wind. Her mind has cardboard walls, and they flutter off with the bird. Nirvana. Oblivion. She's teetering on the alcoholic brink, and all she can do is stare.

Shimmering water, burgeoning clouds. Unchanging, stalking trees, burning and scarring her brain. Her world was never anything else. She smiles. The colours of the clouds are mesmerising, merging with the sea. Waves upon waves and shore upon trees…she thought she'd hit nirvana before, and on her birthday before that? She'd had no idea what it meant. It's this, here, watching the tides, watching the wispy moon forge a threadbare home. It's the night creeping in and the day flying out.

'Kira.' Callum taps her arm. 'Let's go.'

Her eyes don't falter as she brushes him away. The sunset; the sea. The smiling of the moon. It's home. She frowns. 'No.'

If he notices her irritation, he ignores it. 'Come on, Kira.' He pulls a face at the ocean. 'There are more important things than staring at *that*. If you really want to eye up a large body of water, I'll take you to Lake Geneva. Hell, I'll take you to France, if you're feeling committed. Right now, I don't care. I just want to get away from here.'

Kira doesn't move. Her irritation is flowering, to anger, to rage. Maybe if she settles to stone, Callum will leave her alone.

'Kira.' Seizing her shoulder, Callum turns her toward him. 'This isn't right. Come *on*, let's—'

No.

'Get off!' Kira screams. Wheeling around in a surge of crimson, she slaps him so hard her arm socket cricks.

Time staggers. Kira boils inside, like she's turned to acid. Stunned, Callum stares at her, his cheek flushing scarlet. The sound of the impact echoes round the mountain. A gunshot in ricochet, it bounces back, once, twice…and as it fades, so does Kira's rage.

The curtain lifts. The crimson greys. The acid turns to water.

'Oh, my God.' Kira claps her hand to her chest. Her heart beats faster than a panic attack. 'I'm so sorry. I don't know what—'

Her voice cracks. Blankly, Callum probes his skin. Biting halfway through her lip, horror seethes in her belly. Black scratches at her vision, and she blinks. Blinks. Blinks. The ocean begs her to turn again, be burned again, enraged again. It's a furnace, an oven, a bonfire, licking at her back. She wraps her arms about her body. She won't give in. She won't be like Romy.

'Callum, I'm so, so sorry.' Her throat aches, hot. She can't bear to look at him, to see the handprint on his skin and his trepidation. 'I didn't mean it. I don't know what happened.' She swallows. It hurts. The furnace is heating up, and her resistance is frail. 'You were right.' She looks up desperately. 'This place is screwing with our brains. We should go. I feel like I'm going insa—'

Closing the gap between them, Callum cups her face, draws her close, and kisses her. 'It's okay.' Kissing her again, as soft as whispers, his tears start to fall. 'I love you, Kira. I know you didn't mean it. I know you don't want to hurt me.'

'Hey!' His touch could be electric. Kira jerks away. 'What the hell? What are you doing? What are you *saying*? Christ.' Slapping his tears from her cheeks, she stumbles back toward the edge. 'I met you this morning.'

Callum takes a step toward her. His glazed eyes well up again, close to angst, to pain. 'What's wrong?' he asks. His voice is thick.

She continues to retreat. The road to home is in her sights. Her slap still stains his skin. If she has to run, she just needs to dart into the trees, skirt round him, and then—

Kira stops. A slap. A kiss. Callum, touching two fingers to his lips, his face closing in like someone who expected more than this. Callum, slowly lifting his gaze.

Callum, meeting hers. 'Oh, God.' Abruptly, his expression clears to a focused, reddening horror. His eyes grow slow-mo-movie wide. 'Oh, my—oh, *God*.' Ducking his head, he swipes his cheeks. 'I—don't know. I actually have no clue.'

'You do,' Kira says quietly. A slap. A kiss. The fog. This place. 'We both do.'

Callum runs a rough hand across his scalp. His face is a wild disorder. 'It's a leech.' He sweeps a look around, at the trees, the ocean, the sky, the snow. 'A parasite.'

Kira shivers. 'Let's go.'

He nods, and together they run.

Away, away, away from the drop, pelting toward the parting roads. The fork is still a fork, and they skid to the left, past the deceitful wooden window. At least the original road hasn't changed. As unsettling as it was when they found it, right now, its lonesome consistency is the warmest thing in the world.

Although.

Digging in her heels, Kira trips to a halt, flinging out her arms for balance. No sooner has she thought it than she knows she was wrong; not everything is the same. There's something, a sound. A flutter in the air. As Callum blunders to a stop beside her, the racket of their running drops away, and it comes to fluting life.

Birdsong. Chucking. Tweeting. A crow caws, high above, in a flurry of beating wings. A raucous jay flaps from one side of the road to the other. Kira slumps in relief, a whoosh of a sigh. The songs and life jar after what felt like years of stillness, but it's even more warming, more welcome, than the road. She cranes her neck back. Even the sky is alive, returning to a pale blue-grey.

And as if they were there all along, Kira's ears are full of voices.

Children—laughter—a sputtering engine, igniting and driving away. The creak and sway of the chairlift, a dog's lopsided bark. They're back.

The wind has left their sails. Kira's strained limbs shake. Without a word, she and Callum traipse toward the commotion.

Except it isn't commotion; it's normal. In seconds, the road's end blurs into sight. Kira's face breaks into a smile, caught between confusion, an urge to cry, and a freedom that floats like a thermal. What to think, what to say, what to do? The car park swims into view, blocked by a frozen metal gate; beside it rests the bank they climbed so very long ago. Flashes of cars, the hut selling pancakes; she can even see people—*people*—clustered by a cross-country ski instructor. As quickly as things went wrong, they're right.

Nobody notices Callum push through the gate or Kira grind her aching legs into a jog to keep pace. He speeds up with every moment that reality remains, looking left to right as if to tell himself he's safe. She can't help but do the same.

Out of breath, lips parted, scrutinising everything. Throngs of families stand by cars, winter gear littering the deep, shining ice. Groups on peeling benches, with food and cans of beer. A line of motorbikes roaring past, the couples coat-and-helmet-less despite the pointed cold. Even Hugo, the hotel cat, pouting, scowling, and grooming kids for attention. Everything that says without a doubt that they're back.

At the bottom of the sledge-infested hill, Kira's pocket rings. She starts. Her childhood Pearl Jam favourite: fitting. Eddie Vedder sings that he's still alive. Bizarrely, so are they.

'Dad?' Kira listens for a moment. 'All right.' She nods. The word is calmly controlled. 'Yes. No, I'll see you soon. Bye.'

She stows the phone away before winter sends it to an early grave. 'Sorry.' She shrugs. Callum's patience seems to be dwindling. 'I have to get back.'

Nodding at her pocket, he doesn't seem to hear. 'Wasn't that dead?'

'What?' Kira skips from the path of a reversing car. 'Um.' She shakes her head. Mathew's words linger like sweat on her skin. 'Sorry. Dad's coming up to take me to the hospital. Romy wants to see me, apparently. To apologise, or something. Which is good, I guess, but it means I have to go. I wasn't meant to leave the hotel.'

Her attempted smile fades when Callum says nothing, eyeing her with something close to suspicion. 'What?' she repeats, uncertain.

He regards her a moment longer. 'Nothing.' He looks away to the sun. 'Probably nothing. Did you see the time? On your phone?' He hunches his shoulders. 'Regardless, I'll either have to go back to work or explain to Miguel where I've been. I'll come see you before you go home.'

Hopping up onto the snow of the hill, he stomps away toward the chairlift. He brushed her off as quickly as a leaf on his arm.

Kira stares. Incredulity doesn't cover it; is that it? After everything that's happened, that's all he has to say? A robust figure in the afternoon sun, he shows no signs of coming back. He didn't even acknowledge, now they're safe again, that what they just saw was extraordinary. None of it could have taken place. It could have been all in her head.

She sighs, a long, frustrated grumble. Despite the day, he *is* a virtual stranger. What else would there be to say?

That was strange, creepy, and embarrassing for us both. Or, perhaps, *let's dissect it, piece by piece, and analyse how we've gone mad.* Kira nudges a ball of ice with her foot. A kiss and a slap, anger and love. It'd take a hell of a lot to explain it, whatever it was. *Wherever* it was. Was it even real? The nudge becomes a kick, and the innocent ice skids away across the road. Is that why Callum stormed off? Did she make everything up, ranting and raving and riddled with delusions, so he couldn't wait to get away?

Kira snorts. If he had, he'd have a point; the more she thinks, the less she knows, and the less she knows, the more her mind wants to judder and stall. No, thank you, human, try again tomorrow. She had enough of that when she was learning to drive.

I'm trying very hard not to think about it, or this. Pushing her numb, twinging, blocky feet up the road, Kira sets off for the hotel. *Because none of it should be happening.*

It shouldn't. It's im—

The winter closes round her, and she shuts off her mind.

11

And so she burns

The restaurant is deserted. Kira couldn't be more glad. Apparently, her mind doesn't like being dampened, and cradling her frozen limbs, riddled with newfound shock, she scoots upstairs and crawls into bed.

Straight away, she crawls back out with a groan to shake the giants. These clothes will give her frostbite, or flu, or something, but damn, she just wants to lie down. Also, if Mathew arrives, and she's asleep, maybe he won't wake her up. Maybe she won't have to face the hospital.

And I'm the son of a serpent.

Wrangling her numb limbs into a baggy T-shirt, Kira stops. That's a Romy thing. She made it up when she was twelve, and was so very pleased that she spouted it for three years straight.

Okay. Slowly, goose bumping, Kira drags a cardigan with her onto the bed. Okay. Okay. *Okay.* She huddles back in her blanket swarm, foetal position, massaging her toes. She has to face the hospital. She has to wake up. There are so many Romy things, and so much Romy. Romy, her sister, who—

Nope. Clamping a fat pillow over her head, Kira blocks out the room and her mind. Hell, no.

One hour. Three days. Six weeks. Forever. One hour of singing Nickelback in silence, three days of mumbling Nickelback out loud, six weeks of reciting Edgar Allen Poe, and forever of firm denial. Huddled in her blanket swarm, she's warming through and dozing when her phone buzzes under her thigh.

'Mmm.' With another groan to wake the sleepiest of giants, Kira clumsily tugs it out. The white screen blinds her in her stuffy cocoon.

I'm outside, with little green cakes.

'Mmm*dad*.' He knows her. He knows how to get her to move. Kira's stomach growls with a wheedling whine, and scooping her outerwear off the floor, she creaks down the stairs. Toying with table placements, Hazal doesn't look up. That's fine. Kira slips past her, unobtrusive. She'd really rather not talk.

Which only worsens the problem of her parents. Kira pulls down the corners of her mouth. She can't tell them what happened, and she certainly can't tell Romy. Her family doesn't need another escapade of insanity. Not today. Not *ever*.

The rental car loiters in front of the gate. Kira's heart sinks through her stomach. Why is she the sibling that can't lie? Romy would have prepared three days' worth of stories before even considering leaving the hotel.

Except for last night.

Kira scolds her wayward thoughts and drags a smile onto her face. 'How's Romy?' she asks as a two-pack of cakes is placed neatly on her lap. Mathew squeezes her leg, kisses her cheek, but says nothing. The 4x4 is stifling. 'Dad?'

He remains silent long enough for her dragged smile to droop. 'Her hand's been put in a cast,' he says. He looks tired: his under-eye pouches, his bristling hair, as if he's been scraping through it with his square, ridged nails. 'She's under observation for hypothermia. Not that I could catch that, but Annie mostly told them the truth. Apart from what Callum said, about how long she'd probably been out.' His brow creases. 'And her hand. What she…' He sucks in his cheeks. They stay taut long after he lets out his breath. 'I'm not sure what she said about that. Kira, I don't *know*.'

He slaps the steering wheel. The car swerves right. Starting, Kira swirls, uneasy. She's rarely seen him angry at anything other than Romy.

Threads of worry stir. This *is* Romy. It's Romy, and so much more.

'I should never have suggested this place.' Mathew changes gear with a lurch. 'I've never felt so *useless*. I can't speak to these people—oh, get over it.' He glares at the Mini, blaring its horn and making a show of veering out of their way. 'Twats.'

His fists strain on the steering wheel. His skeleton is tense enough to split through its skin. Kira sits rigid, the cake box awkward on her legs. Which kids' film is it, with a panicked line about confrontation? *Toy Story*?

'Dad,' she says, pulling at the plastic. 'Do you want to go somewhere? A café, or—'

'I don't know, Kira.' Mathew's voice is terse but calmer. He hardly seems to know she's there. Kira fiddles with the paper label. Suddenly, she's not hungry. 'From what we've been told, Romy's going to be fine. Mum wants to put what happened aside, though, so it'd be wise not to mention it.'

Pausing mid-fiddle, Kira doesn't return it. 'What?'

Mathew shoots her a look, between pleading and we're-in-this-together. 'She wants to move on.' He sets his jaw. 'She thinks that what Romy did was just a…a'—he waves a hand, wincing—'a blip on the radar. An anomaly. Whatever. It sounds like outright denial to me, but I promised her we'd leave it until we get home. Whenever that ends up being.'

She can feel his hope vying for her attention. See his head angling, trying to catch her eye. Kira stares through the green, gooey, chocolate bomb cakes. *Carac, 2.90. Produit de—*

'It'll make everything easier, okay?' Mathew adds. Now he does sound pleading. Anger lifts its serpentine head. And so he damn well should. 'I don't know what else to do. There's no…guidebook for this, and Mum…' He flexes his fingers on the wheel. 'Please, Kira.' His cheeks move, in and out. 'I'm not saying we *will* forget it, just that we should go along with this for now. And "for now" is only until we get home…'

His words peter out. The serpentine head hisses. And so they damn well should.

'Are you serious?' He's a vocal Medusa, turning her to stone. Kira forces herself to look at him. 'You're going to act like nothing happened? You're going to ignore what she did to me? What she did to *herself?*' She holds up her fingers, mimes them breaking. 'How can you ever get her help if you "put aside" everything she does? Especially this. This is worse than anything she's ever done before.'

She thumps her head back against the seat. Her mouth twists. He's as mad as she is. 'It's five times worse. Ten times worse. How can you forget it happened, even for a few days? Won't that just make her think it's not that big of a deal? So Mum doesn't like it.' Her fingers clutch at the air, grasping for his logic. 'I don't mean to sound uncaring, but whatever. Romy needs help as soon as we can get it. Surely even Mum can see that. She needs to see a doctor, a psychiatrist, whatever, and we can't do that if we're playing happy family. I know you've never wanted to force her, but at this point'—she lifts her shoulders—'you pretty much have to.'

Mathew's fingers flex. 'I know.' He stares through the windscreen. The curving road, the mountains on the other side of Lake Geneva, Vevey's approaching lights. Kira watches him watch. If he gets any tenser, his skeleton might not have a choice. It'll break through and scream for freedom from his mind. 'And I'm trying. You have to understand, though, that this is a compromise.' Voice measured. The calm before the storm. A storm that, if she had any sense, she'd be trying to dispel. 'It has to be. I agree with you, but I also know what Annie's—oh, come *on*.'

The traffic lights blare red. Braking, Mathew stalls the car. 'Christ. Bloody hell.' He wrangles the gearstick. 'Kira, it's a horrible thing for us all to deal with, but it is what it is.' The car jerks. He growls it back into motion. 'We'll be home before long, so we can talk about it then. Romy's safe in the hospital, and even if she wasn't, I'm sure this was just a one-off—'

'Yeah.' Kira returns her attention to the cake packet. Paper label shredding, control almost dead. 'So you said. It's a blip on the radar, an anomaly. You're not even convincing yourself, Dad.'

The steering wheel rubber starts to squash. 'That's not going to help,' Mathew says curtly. 'I know this is hard, but you're eighteen, and this attitude—'

'Don't tell me I need to grow up.' Kira twists in her seat to face him. 'If I do, then you and Mum sure as hell do, too. Romy broke her own bones. On *purpose*. Is that not worth remembering? Not worth doing something about? Do you not care that she hurt both of us? *Shit*, Dad.'

Kira slams back against the seat. Her temper is hotter than it's been for years. Anna wished that away, too. 'You'll forget everything just because Mum doesn't want to deal with it? Because she doesn't want to understand that what's better for her isn't necessarily better for Romy?' She glowers at the cakes. Sliding off her knee, they lie skewed by her feet. 'This is bullshit.'

'Kira, *enough*.' Mathew yanks on the gearstick, his anger drowning in the engine's roar. The car smells of rubber. 'Do you really want to dwell on what she did to you both? Do you not think I'm considering that? All I see when I blink is her screaming. She attacked you, broke her hand, and didn't give a damn. I never said we wouldn't get her help. Christ.'

He sweeps around a bend, ice be damned. The car jolts and skids. 'I'll carry her to the doctor's if I have to. We've been irresponsible. Call it cowardly if you like. But as I've been trying to tell you, we can't do anything until we're home, and in the meantime'—another growling bend, too close to the mountain's edge—'Romy needs to feel that we support her. How can we do that if we're stuck on her violence?'

'If we're stuck on her—' Kira mouths for a moment. This isn't *real*. 'And there it is!' Peering around corners at things under shuttered lids. *I don't like confrontations.* She rests her head on the window with a clunk. They're all spineless cartoon dinosaurs. 'Peace of mind doesn't mean you write something off. Jesus, you—are we ostriches?' She waves her hands, widens her eyes. 'Dad, this is awful. If nothing else, think about the effect upon Romy of us ignoring what she did. Could we be any more upper-class British?'

'We're not.'

'That's not the *point*, Dad!' Gritting her teeth, Kira breathes through her nose. Calm. 'How was she when you left her?' she asks stiffly. One beat, two beats, then, 'Attacked anyone else?'

Not calm.

Mathew doesn't rise. 'She was fine,' he mutters. The car is becoming a theme park ride, complete with popping ears as the altitude drops. 'Compared to earlier, at least. She was the same as she was at first, when you and Callum brought her back. Now please'—he exhales briefly—'just leave it.'

Kira had been fully intending to leave it. Her last snap opened the floodgates to guilt, but this is something *else*.

As quick as it came, her resolve dissolves.

'The same as when we brought her back?' she exclaims. Images flash through her head: Romy grey, weak, ruined. 'You mean she looks inhuman? Half-dead? Actually, no—she didn't look half-dead. She *was* half-dead. She should have *been* dead. How does that make her fine? Although I suppose we shouldn't think about that, either, right?'

For a second, her mind slows her. Abruptly, she shuts up. Isn't that what she and Callum are doing? Denying what happened in the forest?

For a second, her mind allows doubt. Abruptly, she shuts it up.

'What happened to her last night?' Kira spreads her hands, palms up. 'By all measures of science and logic, she shouldn't be alive. We should get the police involved. We should at least alert the commune. Will we?'

One second, two seconds, three. Mathew doesn't speak. 'No.' Kira twists around and turns her back. 'No. I thought not.'

Her mind buzzes. Shock, rage, concern. She could shatter. Kira forces herself to focus on the road. Less snow-caked, it's turned to slush, winding through a lopsided, multicoloured village. Christmas lights above windows flash red and green and white; plastic model Santas climb ladders flung from balconies, jaunty sacks of gifts hanging down their backs. A lone donkey stands on the pavement. A boy in a gnome hat grips its reins. A faint-pink sunset daubs the edges of the sky.

Kira's rage ramps down and numbs. Something isn't right. Something more than what happened in the forest; something to do with Romy.

'Why does Romy want to apologise?' she asks. She's not calm enough to speak, but it'll have to do. The silence was thicker than blood. 'She doesn't say sorry. Well, she does'—Kira twists her mouth with her fingers—'but only with this sort of—'

Mathew doesn't look at her Romy-mimed sneer. Despite herself, or because of herself, Kira twinges with guilt.

'Kira.' He sighs, dips his chin, and sighs again. The sound is muddied with anger. 'Just appreciate the gesture, Kira. For your mother's sake'—his fingers flex—'we need you to be mature.'

Kira raises an eyebrow. 'I'm sure my *mother* can deal with it,' she says tartly. 'Just like I'm dealing with your stupid way of coping. Mum's not weak, and she's not some victim. She just doesn't want to face what's going on.'

Mathew shoots her a glare so fast his driving glasses bounce.

'It's true, though.' Her chest flutters. This is baiting. He's her *dad*. 'Mum's the one dealing with Romy while you're working, so I don't understand why you're acting like this. You're both being so *stupid* about—'

'Just shut up, Kira!' Mathew shouts. 'You're a bloody broken record!'

The car's front wheel bumps the roundabout. Kira's funny bone bumps the door, and she chills with panic and idiocy. 'Dad, I—'

'You can't begin to imagine how much this is killing us.' The car kangaroos through the exit. The indicator tick-tick-ticks too late. 'Do you know why that is? Because we're adults. We don't voice our every frustration, and believe me, we have them.'

Kira twinges again, but it's a battle, a war. Guilt is cold and anger is hot, and she fills with them both like steam. 'Maybe if you did, I'd understand.'

'Be quiet.' Mathew lifts a finger off the wheel. 'Just stop. Until you have children of your own, you can never understand what it's like to see your daughter the way we saw Romy today. She was brought back to us unconscious, frozen half to death and in her pyjamas, by a stranger. *Dammit.*'

He swerves the car violently. Kira slides into the door. Knocks the pavement, barely missing the red-and-white hospital sign. His savage distraction almost cost him the turn. 'Jesus, Dad.'

'"Jesus, Dad" me when you're acting your age.' Mathew growls down the twisting roads. A speed-checker board lights up in red. A sad face. Fifty-six. 'I'm not asking you for much. Don't say anything inflammatory, for all our sakes, until we can sort this out.' He glances at her. 'Which we will. Now can you please leave it alone?'

And he said she was a broken record. 'I was only pointing out that Mum isn't weak.' Kira keeps her voice as civil as she can. 'If you're under the impression that she is, then you clearly don't know her.'

Anna, handling school sanctions that Mathew knows nothing about. Anna, holding them both whenever Romy let them get close. Anna, combing the county in the car while Kira tried to track Romy down through Snapchat. She never broke down. She never gave up.

Something here isn't right.

Mathew doesn't reply. Ramming the 4x4 into park, he's out of the door and away.

Kira can't decide whether to roll her eyes or cry. She crossed more lines than she knew existed, but nothing she said was wrong. It all had to be voiced, and if not now, when?

Climbing from the car, she hesitates. The cake packet lies askew on the floor, icing smudging the box. Pushing down the lonely sight, Kira scoops them up. One of them *was* for her.

Keys. She pulls them out and locks the car. Amusement almost sparks at her father's stormy exit. His glasses lie crooked where he flung them on the dashboard. It'd be the cherry on top of a hell-to-pay day if someone stole the rental.

The hospital is blocks of white and glass, stacked like childhood Duplo. It's more imposing than protective, more money than charitable. Approaching with a plastic packet of cakes, Kira feels like a little girl. Her family's in there, though, and they need her.

Pushing through the glass doors, everything but her urge to cry spikes, quavers, and dies.

'Dad?' she asks. Her voice is tiny. He's thrown himself onto a shiny metal chair, his head on his arms on his knees. Ignoring the receptionist, white-coated and interested, Kira takes the neighbouring chair and puts a tentative hand on his shoulder. 'Dad, I'm sorry. I didn't—I don't know...'

With a hefty breath, Mathew sits up. It's the slog of a man with a hundred thousand monkeys on his back.

'I know.' He tips his head back against the wall. 'None of us know anything.' Shaking his head, he sighs again, staring at the air. 'It's okay, K.'

Kira pulls in her lips and squeezes them tight, as if crushing the life from the sudden ache. 'You haven't said that in years.'

Mathew rolls his head along the wall to face her. 'Because you told me not to.' He smiles, but it's flat. 'It's okay, Kira. Really. I just need a minute.' He nods at another glass door. 'You go on up. Romy's one floor up from here. The door at the top of the stairs, and the bed at the end by the window. You know how much she loves light.'

He smiles again, and this time, a glimmer of his normal bravado peeks out. Half-hearted, Kira laughs. 'She's a vampire.'

'Maybe light will do her good.' Mathew squeezes her knee. *We're adults. We don't voice our every frustration.* 'I'll be up in a minute. I promise. You go.'

Carefully placing a cake on his thigh, Kira goes. The thick block stairs are white. The glass doors are framed with white. Even the ceiling lights are white. Its brightness is blinding as she emerges onto the first floor, the only colour a pale lake painting, peaceful on the door in front of her.

The door at the top of the stairs. Apprehension fizzes through Kira's chest, sudden and heady. This is the ward.

She hadn't thought to feel so unprepared. It's only Romy; if the roles were reversed, she'd power on in, blustering and banishing illness from the room. Years ago, she did.

This isn't reversed, though, and it isn't only illness. Bronchitis; she'd coughed like a champion. Battening down a rush of anxiety, followed by guilt, followed by anxiety over her guilt, Kira puffs a preparatory breath and nudges through the open door.

The ward is brimming. Vibrant red flowers wobble on tables, televisions murmur on the walls. The air-con blows like the day is drenched in summer. Everything smells of lemon. Kira makes her self-conscious way to the other end of the room. Romy picked the perfect time to issue a summons; twice she's barged into, as doctors, nurses, or visitors pass, and twice she almost trips over a trolley leg, a table, a chair. She's clumsy at the best of times. As much as her mind hums, it's amazing she doesn't go flying.

Romy. There, in the very last bed beside a large, bright window: Romy and Anna, as silent as space.

'Mum.'

In a tired chair between Romy and the window, Anna looks up. 'Hey, love.' With a pale smile and a sigh, she gets to her feet. Her face is bleached by the hospital lights, her eyes flicking over Kira's shoulder. 'Is Dad not with you?'

Uncomfortably, Kira folds her arms. 'Downstairs.' She shifts her weight to one hip. Even averted, the sight of Romy scratches her eyes. It's nails on glass, a muffled scream. Wan and sleeping, stiff against the pillows, she's more than unnerving. She almost *died*. 'We argued in the car.'

Anna's eyes widen, enough to register faint surprise. 'What about?'

Oh, the guilt. Two pangs, three pangs, four. 'He told me I shouldn't bring up what happened because you want to forget it.' Kira scratches the side of her face, her chin. 'And I said you weren't weak. Basically, I think we're okay now, but he said he needed a minute.' She retrieves the remaining carac from her pocket. It's smushed and cracking. 'How's Romy?'

Glancing down the ward, Anna takes the proffered half. 'Unresponsive.' She sighs. Cagily eyeing the little green cake, she bites into it regardless. 'For a while, she was adamant that you had to be here, so maybe she'll start talking now that you're here. She hasn't moved in over an hour, though. Mmm.'

Mouth full, Anna indicates her recently vacated chair. 'Sit, have some coffee. See if she wakes up. Whatever you feel like, really. The best coffee is on the third floor.' She attempts a small smile. With her sugary, chocolatey delight already gone, Kira nods. 'While you decide, I'll go find Dad. He must have got the wrong idea when I said we shouldn't dwell on this. All I meant was that we should focus on the present.'

Anna tightens her ponytail. Kira notes it with a pang of sympathy. The tighter the ponytail, the deeper the worry. 'Primarily,' Anna continues, 'getting Romy well enough to go home and sorting out new flights so we *can* go home. Mathew's got himself into such a state, which is completely understandable, but to pin it on me...'

Her words drift off, and with a headshake and a tracing-paper smile, she moves away.

'Mum.' The word comes before Kira plans it.

Shielding her crumbling cake, Anna turns. 'Hmm?'

Kira hesitates. 'Is everything okay?'

The ward fluorescents are blinding. She's had too much madness on too little sleep. She's had too much madness, full stop. For a second, there's something in Anna, a sharpness that threatens to razor her edges, simmering, glittering gold. It's a touch she's felt before when she's thought one thing, looked up, and found her mother thinking the same. This time, it's wild.

Winter. Pine. Fires. Herbs.

Anna doesn't say everything's fine. Anna turns and walks away.

Kira watches her leave. Her upper body lifts and tightens, nothing but a tiny pocket of air. Something isn't—something—

'Kira.'

It's a whisper, almost inside her head. Nipped again by the hospital ward, Kira braces. Romy. Any second now, and she'll be ready to face her. Any second.

Ish. Squinting, grimacing, and dropping it all, Kira turns around.

Romy's eyes are open. Her head tilts quietly. Her expression is mildly curious, moderately cold, and highly unsettling. Kira turns to slush. Just like this morning.

'Why did you want to talk to me?' Taking Anna's bedside chair, Kira sits on her hands. Notes her mistake, removes her gloves, her scarf. Something to do, anything. She drapes her coat on the arm of the chair, careful and meticulous. Her gloves come next, folded in together. The blue scarf Anna crocheted, delicate on top. It feels mean, but Romy's stare is unbreakable.

Harsh on her bent head, eventually, it's too much. Fiddling with her cardigan, Kira looks up.

She could scream. Romy lies still, too still, staring and emptily absurd. 'Why are you staring?' Kira spreads her hands, keeping the biting cry from her voice. Exasperation and fear, worry and distaste. The eyes, the eyes, the *eyes*. 'What do you want? Please, Romy.' She crushes her eyes with the heels of her hands. If only Romy's scrutiny could just be ground away. It feels like disease. 'Stop *looking* at me.'

When she drops her hands, her wish has been granted. Romy's gaze has slid to the window, angled over Kira's head to the trickling snow. Kira digs her nails into her fingers to stop her shaking her head. Propped against a hillock of pillows, Romy's bandaged hand flops limp, pallid on the sickly blue sheet. A thin gown hangs from her thinner body, and her hair, incongruous beside the rest of her, lies combed and shining to her ribs. Kira swallows. Anna must have brushed it. Anything, everything, to coax her daughter back.

It makes the image so much worse. Gaunt. Creepy. Dead.

'Mmm.'

Kira starts. Humming, Romy rolls her head along the pillow. Despite its innocence, the movement is unnatural. Kira's breath sticks, somewhere cold between her throat and her chest. She can almost hear moaning, screaming, laughing, the sick creak of the bones of the dead. Romy's eyes are flat. Her smile is bruised.

When she speaks, all else is lost.

'I know where you've been,' she whispers. Her voice is sore, but firm. 'You and him. I know where you've *been*.' She sits up stiffly, jerky like a jump cut, backing into the headboard. 'Pinky promise.'

Kira raises an eyebrow. The flippancy quails inside her. Romy has never said that in her life. 'And where is that, exactly?'

Righting her head with an awkward spasm, Romy smiles. 'Whiteland.'

12

Incinerating

et me out, let me out, let me out, let me—

It's an infestation, a puppeteer. Romy screams and shouts, but nothing's there, no one hears. Kira wavers in front of her. Her long hair brushes her fingertips. Hers and Kira's. So often, they're the same. Same hair. Same skin. Same love of piercings. Same longing for tattoos.

So often, they're different. Kira's sense of justice. Kira's lack of hatred. Kira's safety.

'And where's that, exactly?'

Kira's words come through in a bubble. It's like she's drunk. Her sister's blue eyes, wide. Her sister's lips parted, the front teeth slightly bigger than the rest. The bony bed. The evening through the window. The foreign language jabber.

The soul incinerating her mind.

Kira, she's mad. Romy scrabbles to fight, but she needs a window, and she only has a crack. Lost footsteps, covered by snow. No sooner does she think than she's smothered. *She's playing a game, and she's laughing. They're all laughing. They went mad before we were born. I can't—*

Breathe. Romy darkens, suffocated. The puppeteer smiles and drowns her. 'Whiteland.'

13

Warning words

Although the name means nothing, Romy's confidence knocks her. She's making eye contact. It's disconcerting. Leaning forward so the chair squeaks, Kira struggles with nonchalance and draws out a sigh. 'Whiteland?'

Romy nods, once. Sure.

'That's not a place.' Kira sighs again, forced, weary. 'If it is, I haven't been there. We went to the forest. I wanted to see where Callum found you. I wanted to see if we could tell what happened.'

Mirrored clearings, the impossible ocean. Kira frowns and swipes it away. 'Oh, but he made me go on the chairlift. You know how we refused all week? Believe me, we were right to.'

Nothing. The silence stretches like space.

'How could you know where we've been, anyway?' Kira fiddles with her sleeves. The quiet with Dad was blood. This is yawning, torrid, layered, hiding the underworld. 'You were here the whole time. And it's only the forest. We saw it every time we used the car.'

Romy's laugh cuts the words from her mouth. A tinkling sound, high and pretty, it's at odds with the rest of her. 'Whiteland *is* the forest.' She spreads her hands, condescending and amused. 'Are you stupid? The forest, and the footprints, and the paths that change. The road from the cliff to the river. Although I bet you thought it was an ocean, didn't you?'

Kira's expression drops. Oh, God. Oh, my—

'Oh-ho, there we go!' Romy laughs again with a sick clap of her hands. 'I knew, I knew, I knew I was right. I knew that's what you saw! Are you scared?' She sits forward, away from the pillows, an odd smile parting her lips. 'You are.' The smile morphs into a gash of a grin. Kira's every atom tenses. Nodding, Romy leans closer. 'How *lovely*. But are you scared of me, or what you saw?'

Closer, closer still. Her cold breath flicks onto Kira's face. It smells of metal.

'If you're scared of what you saw, you're more pathetic than I thought.' Romy looms over her. 'You didn't go nearly far enough to see anything worthy of fear.'

Kira resists the urge to shrink in her chair. 'How do you know where I've been?' How can Romy be so larger than life? Cornering her like a giant in a fairy tale, a witch with a waiting oven? How can she know about any of this? 'It's impossible.' *I'm starting to hate that word.* Kira tightens her fingers on the stingy chair. 'The cold messed with your head, or you've got a fever, or something. None of what you said is true.'

It is, though.

And that's not Romy.

It's a thrill of realisation, a matching thrill of fear. Whoever, or whatever, this incarnation is, it's not Romy. It's barely human.

'It is true.' Romy breathes. Despite herself, despite the horror budding and stealing her breath, Kira hushes her mind to listen. 'You know full well it is. It's probably what you're thinking right now.'

Kira tenses, further, further still. Now her skeleton will be the one to split its skin. None of this should be—

'See.' Romy smiles, dead. 'There's no point denying it. You've been to Whiteland; you saw the wooden window, you felt your mind slide. And now that you've been there'—she drops her voice—'you can't go back. Stay out.'

She lets the words hang. Their gravity is discordant. 'What?' Thrown, Kira narrows her eyes. 'Why would I go back?' She leans forward on her arms. Jack fought the giant, Hansel and Gretel burned the witch; no protagonists win by getting tangled in their minds. She can't let Romy see the knots. 'I don't believe there's a separate land somewhere in the forest, but after what happened today, I do believe I never want to see another tree.' Disquiet wants her to frown. Instead, she cocks her head. 'Anyway, why does it matter to you?'

'Ørenna.' Scrambling to kneel on the edge of the bed, Romy's face contorts. 'You'll want to go back.' She twists the sheet in her hands. Kira can't help it; she flinches. 'I know it. You'll want to find out if what you saw was real. You'll want to see if there's something there that explains what's going on.'

Metal breath. Veined eyes. Their faces are inches apart. The rest of the ward is beyond the world, out of the atmosphere. Kira's breath feels moon-walk-thin.

'And what *is* going on?' she whispers. 'What happened to you in the forest?'

For a moment, she thinks Romy didn't hear. No change in her face, no change in her posture, hunched on the edge of the bed. She doesn't blink. If anything, she shrinks. A vein shudders in her neck.

But then she bows her head.

'Curiosity kills more than cats,' she says flatly.

When she looks up again, she's begun to change.

It's a subtle change at first, but one Kira can't ignore. Romy's eyes darken in her paper-pale face, and as they grow dark, they grow wide. Deepening to black, the blue leeches into the white, and in a matter of seconds each socket reflects the night that left her lost.

Kira's heartbeat shudders and skips. 'What was that?' Romy looks away, warped with a grimace, but it's too late. 'Are you okay? Do I need to get a doctor?'

'You can't go back.' The short words jerk. Her grimace grows in grooves, her eyes rogue and gaping. She hides her face in her hands. 'You can't go back to Whiteland.'

The seconds seem to throb. 'But what *is* Whiteland?' Kira asks. Against all her better judgement, she's still sat, still close, still alone with her sister in the atmosphere. What is *happening*?

'Romy?' she ventures when Romy just breathes. Shoulders heaving, a rasp in her throat. 'Are you sure you're okay?'

No response. Kira extends a cautious hand, retracts it. She's not brave enough for that; not now.

Brittle enough to break, she's half an inch from bolting. Romy's face. Did it change? Was it a trick of the light? Intense fluorescents can mess with your head. Or a reaction to medication? The beginnings of a seizure? Kira bites her lip, hard. She thought her sister barely human. She thought it wasn't her, but Romy looks so vulnerable, so forlorn, crouched on the bed in a hospital gown. Whatever hides behind her fingers, Kira can't help but hurt.

'Romy?' She extends a hand again. 'What's Whiteland, Romy? Why can't I go back?'

Romy's fingers drop like a shot. 'You can't,' she hisses. 'You. Just. Can't.'

Kira's doubts fly away. It wasn't the light; Romy's eyes are black, and growing, growing, growing.

'You can't,' she repeats. Her eye sockets stretch. Taut, pulsing veins, both bulging and caving. Kira's stomach plunges, like she's had three coffees too many and not enough to eat. 'Not ever. You mustn't.' Her eyes flash blue. 'Help me.'

Kira's mounting fear hitches. 'What?' With those two words, the distorting girl before her sounded like… 'Help you? How?'

Beyond the curtain, a nurse rattles in, her cheer ringing out of tune. The ward door opens and closes. Why has Anna not come back yet?

Romy takes a long, rattling breath. 'Help me.' A pause, then, *'Help me.'*

Her irises flicker blue again, a spark in the black. They latch onto Kira's like a fishhook and pull her into the night.

Romy, alone, naked in the dark. Shadows lick her skin, not two-dimensional but thick like tar, like an oil spill coating a bird. *Help me.* She scrambles to her blurring feet. *Kira, I can't get out. Kira. They're dead, they're the Kyo, but listen to her.* She plunges forward. *Listen, don't go back, Kira. The Whispers are planning to—*

The hospital glare is blinding. The oily black wanes. It sucks Romy's fleeting image with it, the naked form that starts to scream.

KIRA, NO, I CAN'T GET—

Kira's head swoons. Reality swoops. She's back like a frozen slap.

OUT.

The shriek inside her mind snaps off. Outside, the cataclysm is loosed.

'I believe you heard her.' Romy's distorted face wrenches back, ferocious, whitening to bluish ice. Paper for skin, stretched across her cheeks like a skull. Eyes protruding as her face recedes, turning to fire with the depths of the dark. They're black holes and caverns, 8-balls and obsidian. 'Listen to me, she said. She *said*. You can't help anyone.'

She cranes her neck forward and spits in Kira's face. 'And you. Can't. Go *back*.'

'Romy—'

Kira's cry perishes. Romy's mouth is stretching, her words becoming a gargle as it elongates to a rattling hole. As black as her eyes, but longer. Yawning. 'You…' She wheezes. Her neck cricks with her tilting head. Now, she *is* inhuman, dark corridors and haunted asylums and hunching figures in *The Blair Witch Project*. 'Can't…'

A noise rumbles from her throat. Washed with breathless, wildfire terror, Kira scrapes her chair back. The noise is a groaning, creaking moan, and it swells and grows and grows and swells until Romy flies forward and screams.

'You can't!' She snatches Kira's shoulders. Nails pierce skin, and Kira cries out. Romy drives her down into the chair. 'You...can't...go...back!'

Every word is a shake. The bawling becomes a wail, a screech, an animalistic howl. Kira's head snaps back and forth. The pain is hot and jarring. Back and forth, back and forth. She can barely see. Flying like a rag doll, she can barely breathe. Why is no one hearing this? Why does no one *help*?

Whatever's in Romy doesn't want them to.

'You can't!' Romy shrieks. 'Out, out, out! Get out! *Get the fuck out!*'

Kira's vision blurs. Dizzy, nauseous, assaulted by the smell of metal and Romy's peach shampoo, she flails for her sister's arms. Her head is burning. The jerk of her neck throbs through her skull. 'Get off me!' She gasps. 'Get off! Ah—'

Catching the hospital gown, she yanks. Romy tumbles to the floor with a keening cry. Unsteady, chest heaving, Kira scrambles to her feet, backing up against the wall. 'You're not Romy.'

Romy's distorted face wavers up. She landed on her head, but undeterred, she sways on her hands and knees. 'I am.' A hacking laugh rips from her throat. The pain of it rings off the walls, a wheeze like a fox's screech. 'I am, I am!' She grins. 'I am!'

Kira shakes her head violently. 'No.' She presses tight against the wall. Cold white nips at her spine. 'You're not. You're not—'

Human.

'Help!' Fear paralyses her, but also makes her scream. She tries to move her head but can't.

Can't?

'Somebody—' Her voice cracks. '*S'il vous plaît?* My sister—'

'No one will help you.' Romy continues to laugh, holding fast to the bed and scrabbling to her feet. 'They won't even hear you. Not anymore. Can't you feel it?' The air seems to throb. 'Little huldra, you're alone.'

Kira swallows a whimpering sob. 'No.' She shakes her head, again, again. She's stuck. Can't run. Can't see the room, can't hear a thing but laughter. 'Please, just stop.'

Regaining her balance, Romy reaches out, stumbling toward her. 'Why?'

'Romy, please.' Terror swells up in her throat. 'Just stop. Leave me al—ah!'

A pair of hands hauls her away from the wall. The ward blurs. She spins, her body flung a few feet toward the door, and the owner of the hands, a woman in a flowered dress and a Matrix coat, plants herself before the monstrosity of Romy.

'Stop,' the woman orders. Stepping toward Romy's rocking, keening body, she is commanding and resolute, a confident north-European drawl. 'What do you think you're doing? Leave them alone.' Another step, slow and watchful. 'You shouldn't be here.'

Her limbs tense, wiry and taut. She looks, Kira thinks distantly, like a predatory cat. 'You're an abomination.'

Romy's laughter pitches. 'That's what you're calling it?' She throws her arms wide. 'Lena, Lena, Lena, don't be so *polite*.'

With a great heave, she sends the laughter into a howl. Kira starts to shake. She needs water, she needs air, she needs the toilet. She needs to scream. 'That's not Romy,' she stutters. It strangles in her throat. 'That's not my sister.'

The woman looks round. 'Correct.'

She pushes Kira half-behind the curtain. With that one word, fresh horror swoons, swooping up to hysteria. That's not Romy. It's not even human. If it was, it isn't anymore.

Then what is it?

Kira stares through the paisley curtain. Breathe in. Breathe out. Romy's obscured, and someone's in control. The woman, whoever she is and wherever she appeared from, seems to know what's wrong; and even if she doesn't, she's better at crisis management than anyone else in the ward. Either that, or Romy's right and nobody could hear.

Not possible.

Is any of it?

Kira shuts her eyes and keeps them still. Breathe in. Breathe out. Iodine slithers up her nose, mixed with curdling hospital food, lavender perfume, the bright red flowers. The ward behind her is growing louder, more confused, shouts and questions and scurrying feet. Romy's sunk back to concave laughter, shrieking something unintelligible.

Breathe. Kira digs her nails into her palms. She'll be getting permanent grooves. It's impossible to tune out, even as the words become clear: *we're all dead here, we're all dead here—*

In a sudden dying sputter, Romy's mania subsides.

Kira's eyes flick open. Beyond the curtain, perfect silence descends. She twists the hem of her Aztec top around her fingers. Is this the lull before another storm?

Stepping back, the woman gives her a nod. Kira hesitates. Three seconds, five seconds, ten. The blood is loud in her ears, but biting hard at her cheek, she pushes back the curtain.

Slumped on the bed, Romy's eyes are closed, her skin warming from its uncanny, death-white grave. She could be asleep; apart from her skewed limbs, she could have been all along.

Fraught, drained, as if she ran a race that ended too soon, Kira turns to the woman. 'What did you do?' Her voice is limp, incredulous. She clears her throat, dodging the arriving cavalry. A bustling clamour of questions and fretting, the nurses, part annoyance and part concern, bundle her sister back into bed. 'Is she going to be—'

'She's fine.' The woman's black eyes burn into Romy, sparking with a tight-lipped, white-lipped rage. Faint sweat trickles from her spiked black hair, melting into her collar. Righting her Matrix coat, she turns to walk away. 'I didn't touch her. Just do what she says.'

Kira backs into the wall to let her pass. 'Do what she—what? In what—what respect? How?'

The woman skirts a worried doctor, raises her hands above her head, and mimes a snap. 'Don't go back to Whiteland.' Dropping her hands into her pockets, the woman ducks her head and picks up into a stride. Struck dumb, Kira stares. Nurses, visitors, patients, they part before her, Moses with the sea, and she's almost reached the door before Kira jolts back to her senses.

'How do you know about that?' The word ricochets around her mind. 'What's Whiteland? Wait!' She raises her voice, close to a shout. The woman sweeps through the open door. 'You can't just leave!'

At the top of the stairs, the woman shoots a short, sharp look back. The warning is obvious, even with the whole of the ward, a doorway, and a corridor between them. 'Just listen to the—your sister,' she calls. Kira's bewilderment swells. The woman is already turning away, her words a strain to hear. 'She's right. You'll be safer.'

Kira lets her hands fall back to her sides. 'Safe from what?'

Safer *than* what?

'Kira?' The door bangs open. Anna shoves through. 'Romy? Kira!' Her eyes land on Kira, and she forges an unforgiving path down the ward. 'Oh my God, Kira, what happened?'

The commotion surrounding Romy hits her mother like a train. Kira watches any last colour leave her skin, her body reeling in a double take. The nurses, the newly arrived doctor, her unconscious daughter…her eyes fly between them, stretching. 'Oh, God.' She lifts a hand to her mouth. 'Oh, *God*.'

Kira doesn't know what to say, what to feel. 'What happened?' Mathew barges up behind them, stony hands clapping Anna's shoulders as the chaos hits him, too. 'Christ on a bike.' He tears his attention from the doctor blusteringly questioning her cluster of nurses. 'Kira?'

'We were just…' Kira shakes her head, again, again. Just what?

'*Madame?*' An angular nurse taps Anna's arm. '*Est-ce que je peux parler avec vous?*'

'Kira?' Mathew prompts, as the nurse starts to jabber to her mother in feverish French. 'You were "just" doing what?'

Her mind is a mess of nebulae, cloudy, tainted, far. 'I…' She works her mouth. 'We, we were talking, I guess, and then she went crazy. Again.' She ducks her head. 'Shouting at me, and groaning, and laughing. I don't even know how to describe it. Her *face*.'

Black holes, caverns, 8-balls, obsidian. Kira swallows and hugs her ribs.

'Come here.' Mathew pulls her to him and wraps her up. She hugs him back hard. 'It's okay.'

It's not, but he's her dad, and that's what dads say.

'It's mad,' she mumbles into his coat. The puffy material squeaks. 'It *was* mad. It was scary. Her face didn't look real. Her eyes, and her mouth, and her skin…' She shuts her eyes, her whole body tensing. 'And then she threw herself at me, and I pushed her off, and, and'—she pulls away, gesticulating—'she was coming after me, making this *noise*, and then…'

Her eyes trail over to the bed. Better not to mention the peak of what she doesn't understand: the way Romy *stopped*. Moving from floor to bed in a second that no one saw, returning to normal on the orders of a stranger. 'She collapsed. Just fell down, like she fainted. I told you, Dad, she needs help.' Her voice climbs, either desperate or despairing. At this point, probably both. 'That's the second time today she's attacked me.'

It was meant to be accusing, but it goes unnoticed. Anna turns back from the nurse, offering them a weary, seesaw smile, and Mathew's attention is with her at once.

'She's moving Romy to a private room.' Anna inclines her head at the doctor, bending intently over Romy's bed. 'And she recommends that we take her home as soon as she's well enough. Physically speaking, because of the cold. Mostly. She—' Anna puts her fist to her mouth, her insides scooped and emptied. Her eyes close. Her chest shudders. 'She said that because Romy needs serious psychiatric care, we need to sort it out in England. One of the nurses overheard some of what she said to Kira and saw most of what happened. Romy flew at her unprovoked.'

She presses knuckles to teeth. Kira forces her face not to move. How much did the nurse hear? How much did she *see*?

'I'll deal with this.' Taking Mathew's hand, Anna sighs, the brittle smile peeking back out. Kira looks up at her father. Troubled, silent, strained. 'Because of the language. Not that there's much to deal with yet'—she gestures at the doctor, the nurses, the ward in general—'seeing as they don't understand what's gone on. The nurse I just spoke to said Romy's asleep. Not unconscious; asleep.'

Mathew's trouble deepens, to dusk, to night. 'So she threw a fit and fell asleep?' He blows out through his mouth, long and slow. 'This…okay. Okay.' He rests his hands on Kira's shoulders. Kira glances up. And he thinks he's confused. 'I'll go with Kira back to the hotel. Get us flights home. Two days' time? Three?'

Anna lifts a hand, lets it fall. 'Whichever works out best. Ideally, as soon as possible.' She hugs him quick, tight. 'Look after her.'

It's a whisper, a breath. It's probably not meant for her to hear. Kira averts her eyes, a little chilled. She always could read lips.

Look after her.

You'll be safer.

Anneliese.

'Mum,' Kira says suddenly, as Anna hugs her, too. 'Who's Anneliese?'

Anna's lips pause on her temple. She steps back again, smiling, tightening her ponytail. 'I've no idea. Why, love?'

14

Eradicating

'You should have told me.'

Halfway to his room, grapes, Berliner, and beer in hand, Callum stops. The voice is faint, but when it comes again, he carries on. His mother. From the other side of her door, what else did he expect?

Something creepy. He lowers elbow to door handle, lips moving in a way that could be a smile, if he let it. A portent, or the ghost of Christmas yet to come. The Grim? He rolls his eyes. Dear God. Today's "The Day That Was."

You have a perverse interpretation of catastrophe.

He stops again, rigid. The handle bounces up to knock his funny bone, but the oddity is distant, barely felt. He didn't think that.

He didn't hear it, either. It was…his forehead creases. Air, or words in leaves. A hiss through rain. Something he never thought he'd have to describe. Was it actually there?

You have a perverse interpretation of catastrophe is not a phrase he'd imagine hearing. *Come on*, he thinks; a real, solid thought. Whoever she's talking to, best to leave her to it. The beer will get warm; the grapes will go soft; the doughnut is dropping sugar on the rug, and after work, followed by the forest, followed by work, all he wants is to finish Parmenides and have a damn good sleep.

His mother is speaking again. Despite himself, he listens.

'It's not perverse when people were there.' Carol's voice is sour in its fury, and Callum does a double take. His *mother*? Really? 'Did you give any thought to that? Did you give any thought at all to what would happen? Hazal *does* have a catastrophe on her hands. Everyone ran out, and who can blame them?'

They will not know what they saw.

It's cold, a sigh and a rustle. It's almost there on his skin, snaking around the base of his neck.

No. He shakes his head sharply. He should move. Forget Parmenides; he should sleep. This is called being madly overtired, making a mountain out of the other end of a phone call. Paranoid, like he and Kira were—

'It doesn't matter if they know or not!' Carol snaps. A sighing, rippling pause, then, 'You should have told me what was going to happen.' She drags her voice down to a painful hush. 'I could have—'

The beer bottle slips from Callum's hand. He hadn't realised it was loose, but it thunks to the wood, and the words snap off. 'Dammit.' He crouches, fast enough to stop it rolling. This is the perfect time to leave. He can stop listening, devour his snacks, and forget about today tomorrow.

The door opens.

He heard. Not one voice, now, but two, three, a swelling sigh of wind. His mother's face is slate. 'What did you hear?' she whispers.

Behind her, the wind pulses. Callum straightens up. A hundred versions of *nothing, really* skitter through his mind, but is there any point denying it? He's treading on invisible eggshells. Everything inside him is cold, but he doesn't care for lies. 'What did you not want me to hear?'

Carol steps forward. The hem of her cardigan lifts, her hair fluttering up from her collarbone. She's scared.

This is definitely something creepy.

'Everything,' she says, and then he thinks nothing more.

15

Everything that hides

Kira throws a ball against the wall of her room, time and again and again. A museum souvenir from one of Romy's lighter moods, it's a St. Bernard and a bottle of rum, sat contented in a snowstorm. The dog's grin seems to grow every time the ball returns. As a result, she throws it even harder. Stupid rum-drunk happiness. It's neither the time nor the place.

Throw, catch. Throw, bounce, catch. Mathew taps on the adjoining wall, his third-time plea for her to stop. Frustrated, she pushes out her lips. The monotony's keeping her sane. Dulling her mind into doing nothing, just making sure it continues. To be fair, it's probably exceedingly annoying.

That doesn't mean she'll stop. She could do something else—go and talk to her dad, distract them both—but she did that after tea and only came out worse. It wasn't that Mathew hadn't tried; for once, he just hadn't managed to transmute his own worry into reassurance.

Or maybe, this time, she's seen too much for it to work. He put his arm around her, and they had a beer while he searched for flights and she talked about something, anything. Her January exams, the hospital, her current paintings, Romy, New Year's Eve plans, how they acted in the car. All of this, he said, has shocked him enough to short-circuit a house; he shouldn't have lost his temper, even if she was, and he smiled weakly, very much losing her own. When he added that he'd had a feeling since landing in Geneva, a feeling that had *pulsed* when they drove up the mountain, she was done.

It was too much. At the same time, it wasn't enough. Her insides were coiled, jittery, and after what she and Callum had seen in the forest, hearing her dad talk about pulsing atmospheres, strange feelings, and the creepy isolation of the village was winding her up to break. She finished her beer, hugged him hard, and said she was going to study. That she was feeling strung out, too, and might as well be productive.

It was true; but she was, and is, far too antsy to focus. She tried revising *The Handmaid's Tale*. She tried getting her head around metallic minerals, again. Taking geology is one thing she'll always blame Dad for. She tried thinking up rewards for if she passes, but so far, the boomerang ball has been the only thing to work. Now, even that's falling flat.

If only Mum would get back. Kira's pout morphs into an impatient, restless scowl. At least there'd be something new to mull over. They wouldn't be *waiting*.

Who's Anneliese?

I've no idea. Why, love?

The scowl smooths into a sigh. It loops in her mind, snags on a hook, and won't let go. Anna didn't wonder at her question. A denial of knowledge, an extra hug for her and Mathew, and off they went. She has a thousand things on her mind, but still. When the word was something Romy came out with…

Catching the ball, Kira rolls over. A hefty sigh whooshes. The hefty bed creaks. The tiny ticking cuckoo clock announces 9:00 p.m. She closes her eyes. It means nothing. Let go.

You can't go back.

Help me.

That's not Romy.

Correct.

Lying in a muted, face-mushed gloom, Kira's hearing sharpens. The chimes on the restaurant door. Glasses clinking from the bar. The crackling fire on the landing.

Footsteps.

She listens. They continue on, past her door, merging into muffled voices on the other side of the wall. Kira worms her arms beneath her chin. Think of the devil; at least, if nothing else, she's broken the silence.

When the tap comes on her door, Kira doesn't need to look. Winter and mint precede her mother into the wooden room.

'How are you doing?' she asks, soft. The bed depresses as she perches on the edge.

That's not Romy.

Correct.

Anneliese.

Kira says nothing. Staring at the headboard, at every gnarl of wood and groove of carving, she sighs; the question is an unavoidable roar, yet she'd rather study metallic minerals than ask it. Not knowing is bad enough, but knowing could be worse.

She'd also rather ask it than live in her thoughts. She sighs again. 'What's wrong with Romy?'

She regrets the phrasing at once. 'No.' The words hang heavy, an anchor not quite scraping the ocean floor. 'I mean. I mean, is she going to be okay?' Wriggling to sitting, Kira holds up her hands. 'Sorry. I really didn't mean it how it sounded. Do the doctors know anything yet? Why she collapsed, or why she's being so violent?'

It's Anna's turn for silence. Her narrow cheeks move in, and out, as though she's considering options. 'Not to my knowledge,' she murmurs. Then, as if this is the only answer Kira needed, 'What happened at the hospital?'

Kira fights to keep her eyes on her mother. Romy, screaming *you can't go back!* 'Did no one tell you?'

Looking up, Anna sits back, one blanket-reindeer farther down the bed. 'I heard some of it from the nurse, but I'd like to hear it from you.' She shifts again. Her eyes have manned the guard posts, and the drawbridge has been raised. 'She didn't understand all of what you and Romy said.'

Kira dips her head. Something else unavoidable, roaring. Anna's watching, another half-reindeer between them, but Kira's got nothing to give her. How can she even attempt to explain? How can she describe Romy becoming someone else—some*thing* else—who knew what happened in the forest? Who launched herself from her bed, warped and impossible, because they were talking about a place that can't exist? Who was then sent to sleep by a stranger who didn't touch her, or *says* she didn't touch her? Kira fights to keep her face innocent. What can she say? What *should* she say?

'I understand,' Anna says when the quiet starts to ring. Kira looks up. She'd bet her painting of Karliquai that her mum really doesn't. 'You don't want to talk about it yet, or you can't. I understand that. What Romy did today is awful, and it's obvious she hasn't been…'—she picks her words carefully, treading even more so—'herself.'

It's inadequate. Her eyes narrow. *Age of the understatement*, Kira thinks but doesn't say. No one needs Romy responses right now.

'Love.' Anna takes her hand. It's subdued, concerned: maybe Kira's face is speaking for her. 'Like Dad said, we'll sort this out. To be a cliché that you'll hate, today was the straw that broke the camel's back.' She squeezes Kira's fingers. 'Okay?'

Kira nods, slow, thinking. 'Will you take her to Dr. Beech?'

The psychiatrist Romy refuses to see, an efficient, smiling city man. If he can help, then this is not the disconcerting web it appears; and if that's the case, maybe the events in the forest can also be explained. Explained *away*. Mistakes caused by disorientation, the confusing similarities of the landscape, hallucinations beckoned by the morning's horror—maybe by snow-blindness, ignoring dictionary Callum. Maybe she was riddled with delusions, and he was dying to get away.

Either way, everything Romy said would be irrelevant. Brushing aside the uncanny knowledge about where she and Callum went, and the woman in the flowery dress, it's all coincidence. Ramblings that struck a chord but meant nothing in the end.

This is how she lies to herself; this is what must be true.

'...But we'll help her however we can,' Anna finishes. Whatever else she said, Kira missed it, and she drags herself from her fervent thoughts. Anna is watching the window, the glowing colours from the train line lamps, a fox scurrying into the snowy field, the stars above the mountains. Kira frowns. Gazing at the night, she's perfectly composed. It's not like her. She's tears and fear, as she was this morning; she's worry and fretting and edges. As much as it isn't true, Anna never seems strong.

'Has something changed?' Kira leans into her pillow mountain. 'You're...' She pulls a scarlet woollen blanket up around her shoulders. She's what? 'Calm, I guess. If me and Dad can stop worrying so much, that'd be great.'

Pinpricks in the gloom, Anna's eyes shift to her. 'I'm as worried as you both.' The tiniest hint of a huff. 'I'm always worried. But I've—'

She stops. Kira waits, but nothing else comes. 'You've what?' she prompts. Staring through the bedclothes, Anna's pinpricks are wide. 'Mum?' She sits up properly, head tilting. Anna's expression is shadowed. 'What have you done?'

'A lot of thinking.' Rubbing her forehead, Anna folds her hands atop her jeans. 'And I realised that I've been worrying so much because we've never done anything. We're making the decisions now, not Romy. To use another of your hated clichés'—she rises from her perch, brushes creases from the bed, and offers a smile—'it was a lead balloon, and I should have recognised it long ago.'

She moves to the door. 'Wait.' Kira scrambles across the bed. 'That's not what you were going to say.'

She slips to the floor. The golden bedside lamp doesn't reach over here, and in the shadows, she's sure: Anna knows something she doesn't want to say. Maybe it's the greyscale dark, giving hazy, shifting impressions of secrets, but they're close, almost eye to eye. Her mother is unsettled.

'What is it?' she asks. Anna's smile is holding, but wearing thin. 'What were you going to say?'

A pause. Grainy, aware, full of the ticking cuckoo clock, voices in the restaurant, the lingering smell of fondue. Anna nudges the door open, her hand on the wood. 'Kira,' she says lightly, in the parent-tone that says the subject is finished. Stepping into the hall, she starts toward her room. 'Give me a minute to freshen up, and we'll go down for a drink. I think we deserve it.'

Everything about this is strange.

'Why did you stop speaking?' Kira follows Anna into the fire-lit hall. With the smile refuelled, Anna turns.

'Everyone forgets what they're going to say.' She shrugs, thin and delicate. 'Everyone gets distracted.'

Kira winds her fingers into her sleeves. Questioning her mother is uncomfortable; she's rarely felt the need. 'You didn't forget,' she says. Call it instinct, or intuition, but there's *something* here that isn't right. There has been since she ran into Callum in the mist. 'People only use "everyone" when they're defending something they shouldn't.'

Kira half-expects her mum to laugh, to say she's being silly. But all she gets is a measured look. 'Leave this alone.'

Anna's smile is gone.

'No.'

Kira hurries down the hall. Blood *dum-dums* in her temples. *Leave this alone. You'll be safer. Look after her.* Three-word proclamations, and they rip her inner lies to shreds. '"This?" What's "this?" What aren't you telling me?'

Anna tips her head back. 'Nothing.' She fixes exasperated eyes on a beam. 'There's nothing. I'm just tired.' She glances at her closed room, pulling her hair from its band. That, at least, looks true. 'Can you please not give me the grilling you gave Dad? I'm not keeping anything from you, and honestly, your attitude toward us is getting a bit much.'

Anna moves to open the door.

'I have an attitude because this is madness.' Kira steps to block her path. 'There's something you're not telling me, and it's insulting that you won't admit it.' She spreads her hands. 'Do you think I'm too young to understand? Is there something about Romy, or, I don't know, our lives? Our family? Come on, Mum.' Her face screws up of its own accord. Disdain, discontent. 'Surely we should be together on this? Instead of keeping secrets?' She pauses. 'Have you even told Dad?'

The door opens. 'Told Dad what?'

Blinding light slices the hallway. Pulse leaping, Kira starts. Mathew is a silhouette.

'Do you—' She clears her throat and regains her composure. 'Do you know what's going on with Romy?' She shifts her weight to one hip. *Dum-dum.* Blood. 'What's really going on?'

'Leave it, Kira.' Anna's voice is clipped.

Mathew's eyebrows lift. 'What do you mean?' He fixes on Kira. His beer can groans in his hand, his eyebrows sinking low. 'Anna?' He looks to his wife. 'What's this about?'

'She knows something about what happened to Romy.' It comes out in a desperate blurt. Kira carries on regardless. 'She's acting like she doesn't, but she does. She slipped up when she was in my room—'

'*Shut up!*'

Anna cuts across her, hoarse and fractious. It echoes about the rafters, a ricochet of shock. 'Just stop! You asked what was wrong with Romy, but—what's so wrong with you that you can't—Mathew, she doesn't know what she's saying.' She shoots her husband an odd entreaty, buckled and ineffective through her anger. 'She's upset. It's been a horrible day for all of us, and she's searching for an explanation.'

'Don't patronise me.' Kira snaps the ends off her mother's words. 'I'm not clutching at straws, if that's what you're saying. Why are you *lying*?'

'Kira,' Mathew begins, a warning rumbled low.

'If you're so concerned with secrets, why don't you tell us what you and Romy were talking about?' Anna lifts her shoulders: *well, go on, then.* 'How about what you did today when you were meant to be in the hotel?'

Kira folds her arms. 'I went to the forest to see where Callum found Romy.' It's not the whole truth, but it's enough.

Deflating, Anna's shoulders drop. She didn't think she'd get an answer; it's in her posture, her widened eyes, the cogs working behind them. The silence is loud again: the crackle of flames, a door shutting in another branch of the hall. Tick, tick, tick. The asymmetrical clocks click on.

'Fine.' Face twisting, Kira turns her back on her parents. Anna lost for words, Mathew out at sea. The stairs creak and moan as she flings herself down them. It's not worth it. If Anna won't even tell Mathew the truth, she'll never tell *her*, and there are far better ways of wasting time than raging at a mother-shaped wall.

Tearing her coat and boots from the stand, Kira blusters a storm through the restaurant.

'Do you know where Callum lives?' She pulls up short in front of Hazal. Halfway through the kitchen door, the woman turns. 'You know each other, right?'

Hazal nods pointedly toward the tables. Restive, impatient, Kira follows her gaze. Heads have turned to stare, drinks paused in hands. It isn't silent, but quiet. Whether or not they understood it, they must have heard the whole familial exchange.

Normally, she would have been flushed and contrite. Now, she tosses them a sweeping glare. 'Please.' Lowering her voice, she steps closer to Hazal. 'I need to see him. It's important.'

Upstairs, a door slams. Hazal's gaze flits to the ceiling, and subtly, she steps back. 'Important to me you don't disturb everyone.'

Every bone is stern, her expression engraved. Kira winces. Her parents' muffled voices roll toward a fight. 'I know.' She fights not to jig her leg from impatience and a stirring embarrassment. The argument is heating fast. 'And I'm sorry. I really am. You have no idea how much I—we—appreciate what you're doing.' She pulls a face, pouring it full of rushed regret. She has to get away. The walls are pressing in. She wrestles her coat on, flushed with heat. 'I just—I'm trying to figure out what's going on with Romy, so we can all get out of here.'

Hazal turns away.

'Please?' Kira rushes into a plea, unintentionally childlike. 'I know it doesn't make much sense, but I need to find Cal—'

'Left of the train line, first house up.' Hazal pushes through the kitchen door. Soup and chocolate drift out, mingling with the fondue. 'Use the little steps.'

The kitchen door snaps shut. Kira is dismissed. Pulling up her hood, she ducks her head and hurries out into the night.

16

Go

I t's hard to decide what's more suffocating: the blanketing cold or impenetrable dark. All at once they're upon her, thick, smothering, crisp, and she's infinitely glad she doesn't have to go far. The only light for miles floats from gallant stars and train line lamps. The moon shirks its duties behind snow clouds. The hotel's heat falls rapidly away. *Left of the train line, first house up.* It's not far.

Up the drive, through the hotel gate. The left side of the tracks are unblemished, the snow dotted with an embedded path of stones. Kira stops at the bottom. Brushed with powder and a glint of ice, they wind up from the road like lilies on a pond. "Steps" is a loose term. One foot wrong and she'll break her neck.

Or at least a leg or two. Bleakly, she starts to climb.

It's a miniature winter wonderland, a spectral night of ice. A thick, frosted archway heralds the top of the stepping stones, rough-hewn from the hedges bordering the garden. Stray twigs brush her coat, snow evading her hood to nip her skin. Surveying the box-cut scene, Kira shivers. The garden is a long, sweeping square, rising sharply to meet a small wooden chalet; the windows shine with a dim, flickering glow, and Christmas lights line the balcony, twitching red, green, bright red, out. Footprints lead steeply to the door, distant in the dark.

Kira groans. 'Seriously?' She lets her head droop. 'Has today not been enough?'

Apparently not. The footprints are all she has to go on, and it's a close-to-vertical trudge. Gulping frozen air, she grips her knees and resigns herself. This is the last time she acts on impulse. At least at home, the worst thing she'll hit is the beach.

At the final snowdrift, the door opens. Light spills around a silhouette, so similar to her father's. If this ends in shouting, too, she'll sleep for a year. She'll—

'Are you the English girl?' a woman asks. Straight up, no preamble, as if she already knows the answer. She plants her shadow on the threshold like an uptight butler.

Heaving up to level ground, Kira bends over, exhausted. 'Yes.' She gasps. Hand on her chest, thudding up a storm. She really should exercise. 'I came to see Callum. I was told he lived—'

Stepping back into the house, the woman slams the door.

'Here.' Kira straightens up. 'What?'

Too late. The house is closed. The woman has gone. 'Rude,' Kira mutters. Hovering just in case, she frowns at the silent, motionless door. Nothing. No explanation; no apology. Just a wooden rectangle hung with a wreath.

After thirty seconds, she gives it the finger. Callum might not be in there; there could be nightlife lurking somewhere, or a girlfriend. What did he say about drunks in a barn?

Not enough, or she'd be joining them. The garden resembles a ski slope she'd never plunge down. Beyond it, there's nowhere to go. Hole up in the hotel bar? Weasel out of Hazal that green liqueur, until today is a ringing in her ears?

That's not her. That's—

The chalet echoes with a barrage of noise. Stairs thundering, exclamations, and the door behind her flies open.

It crashes off the wall. A hand seizes hers. Kira spins so fast her head wavers. 'Wh—'

'Sorry.' Callum lets her go. 'I didn't want you to have left already. Bloody women. All they do is gossip, and now she thinks you're Satan.' He shakes his head in bewilderment. 'Come in. It's freezing.' He rubs his bare arms, sidestepping to free up the doorway. 'I'll handle Mum.'

But Kira's mind is prickling as much as his skin, and although Callum offers her a welcome bow, she holds back. 'What do you mean, she thinks I'm Satan?' she asks, wary. Suddenly, the night and the cold seem inviting. 'People have been gossiping about me?'

Callum flashes his eyebrows. A quick motion, up and down, as if he knows something crucial that she doesn't. 'From what I've heard.' He rubs his arms again. In the pooling light, his goose bumps are brazen. 'Which is only snippets. But if you're coming in, I'm sure we're about to find out. Speaking of which.' He shivers, a full-body shudder. 'I didn't think my rescue mission through.'

One angry stranger, or two angry parents? Kira considers Callum. The steep, shining garden. The chalet, seeping warmth. The hotel roof, visible over the hedge. Callum again, edging meaningfully toward heat and light. It's a rock or a hard place, and bracing herself, she follows him inside.

They land in a cluttered lounge. Heavy, mismatched curtains shut out the night, bulging where they drape over piles of books and bedding. A chequered armchair nestles beside a log fire, a black cat basking in its heat. Three boys, controllers clutched so fiercely that their knucklebones strain, stare avidly at a flashing TV, a painting of a red elephant ruling the wall above their heads. A gargantuan, sleeping dog sprawls across the red cloth sofa.

Despite herself, Kira smiles. A mess of brown-black fur, its shaggy sides spill to the floor, and she's about to beg Callum if she can please, please, *please* hug as much of it as possible when his round-faced mother reappears.

'I said no, Callum.' Dangerous and Scottish, she emerges from a door between the elephant and the curtains. Picking her stony way toward them, she is shoulder-length brown hair and glasses, leggings and woollen slippers. Kira takes an awkward step back. Maybe she should have chosen her parents. Or the bar. 'I won't have her here, especially with the boys. Oh, *Nibbles.*'

Her displeasure is marred by a second cat, weaving through her legs. Callum steps neatly into the distraction.

'Give me ten seconds.' He watches his mother scoop Nibbles into her arms. 'Five, even. There's no reason Kira can't be here.'

Depositing the cat on the sofa-back, his mother sidesteps the oblivious, enraptured boys. 'That's not for you to decide.' She opens the chalet door. The cold marches in. 'I'm sorry if it sounds harsh, but for once, no means no. Everyone knows what she did, and I don't want her in my house. Quite frankly'—she regards Callum with something like disillusion—'after seeing it for yourself, I can't believe you let her in.'

Callum's eyebrows fly.

'Yes, I know you were at the hotel.' His mother waves a hand. 'Even if Hazal hadn't told me, it's all over the village.'

Enough.

'What's all over the village?' Kira's voice is biting enough, defensive enough, for one of the boys to look round. It's a surprise to her, too, but this day never *ends*. 'Do tell me. I appear to have forgotten.'

She plants one hand on her hip. The woman's mouth whitens to an affronted line, but Kira ignores her. What *is* any of this? Why is she being victimised, over and over? She's the only one with any sense. 'You can talk to me as well as about me,' she says pointedly. 'What exactly is "the village" saying?'

'That you're mad.' Bookended by two less interested parties, a mini-Callum has stopped playing to grin. 'You broke your own hand and attacked people. What?' His voice pitches with innocence, shrugging at his mother's startled *Jay*! 'That's what you and Estela were saying.'

He returns to *Rocket League*, unfazed by the fact she might be dangerous. With an inward slump, Kira's lightbulb moment hits.

'There are two of us.' She can't hold out on her exasperation. 'Two English girls. My sister—' She swallows. 'My sister *did* break her own hand, but she only attacked me. Well.' She frowns. The memory is a blur of movement. 'She might have pushed someone out of the way, but that was only to get to me. Again. Look.'

She holds back her hair. To her chagrin when she saw them earlier, the fading cuts are still stark. 'I'm not the one everyone's talking about.' She drops her hand. 'I guess they left me out.'

'And exhibit B.' Callum lifts her other hand. 'All fingers functional. Can we call off the inquisition?'

The dog grunts in its sleep. The boys crow as one, the television playing a victory jingle.

'Okay.' Slowly, the woman looks between them. Millimetre by atom, she shuts the door. 'I'm sorry. Apparently, I wasn't given the whole story.' She lifts her eyebrows, a mirror of Callum's earlier gesture. 'Cup of tea? Beer?'

She moves past them to a door at the foot of the rickety stairs. A little gruff, but reconciliatory. 'Either of you?'

Callum looks to Kira. 'Which one?'

Kira blinks. 'Um.'

Callum considers her. 'One for each hand, please.' Giving her a half-smile, he motions for her coat. 'Sorry about that.' Hanging it up, he shakes his head, the way her mum does when she says *men*. 'Have you ever lived in a village? The people are vultures. They really hate losing their scraps.'

It's a daze. Another world. Surreal. Kira smiles back, small but there. 'I know exactly what that's like.' She slips off her boots, adding them to the endless line running along the wall. 'Not quite a village, but I've lived in a small town all my life. Picture this.' She arranges her fingers into a frame. 'It's early on a Sunday. People are out, either because it's summer or because they're going to church. A stranger is seen leaving a woman's house, and by the afternoon, it's spread that she's cheating on her husband.'

Callum cocks his head.

'Some people'—Kira smiles properly, mischievously—'say she's sleeping with the gardener. Some think he's a high school sweetheart, and some whisper that he's a plumber, fixing more than her pipes.' She drops the frame. 'Turns out he's her brother, leaving for church. So as much as I wish I—Romy—wasn't the current piece of meat.' She scrapes her hair back from her face. With the front door shut, the fire is a furnace. 'I get it.'

Callum lets out a laughing snort. 'Good, I suppose.' He starts toward the roaring bubble of the kettle. Waking with a grunt, the dog shuffles after them, but as much as she previously wanted to hug it, Kira barely notices. If the lounge is a riot of colour, the kitchen is just a riot.

It's hard not to gawp. Pots and pans litter both floor and surfaces, one box of cutlery and many of food spilling beside a line of animal bowls. A menagerie of cleaning products, tins, and dog treats recline by the back door, unhappily bowed clothes horses ringing a table and chairs. On the wall lists a small, bony sketch of a tree, stripped of its branches in winter.

'The sink leaks, the dryer's broken, and we have an ant infestation.' Callum's mother sweeps her eyes over the dripping laundry, the open, empty cupboards. 'I didn't know it was possible to have an ant infestation in winter, but here we are. Everything comes in threes. Fours, actually. Callum, you do the beer.'

Callum moves to the fridge. It rattles and clanks. 'Do you want one?'

'No, thanks.' The woman's eyes stray to the countertop. 'But I will have a small whiskey.'

She helps herself to the bottle of Bell's, nestled among a liquor stash that would fill Hazal with pride. Awkward and lemon-like, Kira tries not to fiddle. With their familial normality, she feels like a thumb, or an embarrassing third wheel.

'Our beer stocks are low.' Knees popping, Callum straightens. 'Corona, or…'—he squints at the green label, patterned with herbs—'whatever the hell this is. Our stocks really *are* low.'

'That's because you keep drinking them.'

Kira huffs. Callum's mother meets her eyes, crystal whiskey glass at her lips. Behind it, there's almost a smile, and faintly, Kira matches it. The guard's still up, but at least the woman appears to have downgraded her from the devil. What's slightly less than devil? Siren? Succubus?

She'd rather be Satan.

'I'll have the whatever-the-hell-this-is.' Kira nods at the greenish beer. 'Fits with the day we've had. Also, you look like you'd rather burn it than drink it.'

Callum snorts. 'Only if it tastes how it looks.' Twisting off the caps, he hands her the bottle. 'Cheers.'

They clink. His mother lifts her glinting glass. 'Cheers. Do you take sugar?'

Kira blinks. 'No?'

The woman finishes the tea. 'Then they're ready. Boys! Bedtime!'

Clapping her hands, she leaves the kitchen. Callum sets the tea on the table. 'See?' He looks between them and the beer. 'One for each hand. Best way to be.'

'Thank you.' Kira cradles the mug gratefully, warming her hands. 'I think. What's the fourth thing?'

Callum arches an eyebrow over his mug. A happy reproduction of Eeyore, it conceals most of his face. 'Your mum said things come in fours.' Kira perches on the edge of a chair, cautious of the occupying pasta tower. 'Is there a fourth thing?'

Callum glances back through the kitchen door. The three musketeers are piling upstairs, the beaded curtain at the top of the steps clacking in alarm. 'Them, I think.' He takes a swig of beer. 'They've been here the past few days, but I keep forgetting to ask why. Only one of them's ours.'

'They're Valerie's.' His mother sweeps back in, collects her drinks, and departs.

Callum watches her follow the boys upstairs. 'Well, that answers that. I don't know a Valerie.' He nods at her greenish beer. Everything the Swiss seem to serve is green. 'What's that like?'

Kira sips it. It's the weaker, lighter version of Hazal's burning shot. 'It tastes like'—she sips again—'freshly mown grass. And herbal tea. And a little bit like that.'

She points to the Corona. Callum screws up his face. 'It sounds horrid. Do you want to move?' He nods at the vacated living room. 'I feel like you're becoming one with the pasta, and it doesn't look very fun.'

Kira steps after him over the dog, a sleeping mound in the doorway. 'Has something happened?' Callum asks, sinking into the sofa with a contented exhalation. His tea is so close to slopping that Kira's mind flinches. 'To bring you here.' He sets the beer on the floor with a smirk. 'To find out where I live.'

Kira sets her drinks on a side table, sinking down beside him. Awkwardness wriggles through her, warming in her chest. What to say? Where to start? Her phone buzzes, and she pulls it out, hoping for a springboard. She doesn't have a specific reason for being here, other than *everything*, and coupled with the pathetic "my parents were fighting," it's not a lot to go on.

As all good employees do, her phone delivers at once. She stills. 'What?' Callum asks. 'Is everything okay?'

Kira types a quick reply. It wasn't the distraction she wanted, but it gives her something to say. 'Dad wants to know if Mum's with me.' Looking up blankly, she puts the phone away. 'That's all it says. She was at the hotel when I left, but they were arguing, so maybe she stormed off.' She sips her oddbod beer. 'I don't know. It's not like them at all, but they can sort themselves out.' She reaches up to scratch the reclining Nibbles. 'I don't really want to help her right now.'

Callum lowers Eeyore to his lap. 'Why not?'

He cricks his neck back to see the staircase. It's empty, the clacking curtain silent. 'Actually, before you say anything, I want to apologise. For how we left things earlier. I just...'

He waves at the air. Kira shakes her head.

'It's okay.' She smiles across at him. Nibbles grumbles at the movement, nosing the back of her head. 'I didn't deal with what happened any better. I went back to the hotel, curled up in a ball, and recited Edgar Allen Poe until my Dad arrived. Over and over and over, just so I'd stop thinking.'

Callum's eyes drift off to the side. '"All we see and all we seem is but a dream within a dream."' He settles into the corner of the couch, cocking his head. 'Did I get it right?'

Kira wiggles her hand. 'Ish. A-star for trying. Is this weird?' Seeing him lounging, the thought strikes her in a rush. An awkward, wriggling, hot-cheeked rush. His house, his life, his family. They only met this morning. 'Me, I mean. Finding out where you live, as you said, and showing up here like a stalker.' She grimaces. 'I've kind of wreaked havoc for you, so I can...'

She trails off. Callum has fixed her with a derision that clearly says, *don't be stupid.* 'Why don't you want to help your mother?' He taps the arm of the settee. 'All I did after the forest was work and nap.' One finger, two fingers, three, all four. 'I take it your day was stellar.'

It doesn't take long to tell him everything.

'Do you think it's insane?' She tugs an owl-patterned cushion to her chest. Callum stares through the fire, gnawing the inside of his lip. The silence is full. Her toes curl. She poured out a waterfall, offloaded an avalanche. Maybe she should have kept some to herself. 'All of it? Any of it?'

The fire spits. Overhead, there's a thump and a giggle. Kira swallows the last of her beer. 'Alternatively, I can leave.'

'No.' Callum taps his knee, shakes his head, blows out, heavy and long. 'You don't have to do that. I think it's insane'—he looks up at her frankly—'but I don't think *you're* insane. I don't know what I think.'

Reaching over the arm of the sofa, he produces a log from a wicker basket and tosses it onto the fire. The sparks jump, flying with the flames. They spit out at the black cat, lying spread-eagled and dead to the world. 'I will say, though,' he continues, scratching his mop of hair, 'that I don't think your mother's lying. What good would it do her? What good would it do anyone? Sometimes, people just sound shifty.' He moves his tapping to her elbow. 'Do you ever feel guilty when you're not?'

All the time. 'I guess.' Kira buries her chin in the owl. 'But if that was the case, why would she and Dad be arguing? That's why they were fighting when I left.' She pouts, pensive. 'Unless they're both lying, and were arguing about telling me.'

Callum smirks. 'So now it's a conspiracy?'

'No, but...'

'But what?' He prods the fire with a poker. 'Do you believe what Romy said about the forest?'

Kira executes a several-second fish impression. 'Whiteland?' she says, forcing it to stop. Callum nods. 'Um. I don't know. I believe what we saw, because we saw the same things, but it's hard to even consider there being a different land.'

Something nudges her toes, and she glances down. A puffed-up tabby cat has wandered over, its wet mouth dribbling onto her sock. She recalls her legs to the sofa in distaste. 'It goes against science, against logic, and everything we've grown up knowing. If we believe it, where would we—' Holding up a hand, she brings herself to a stop. 'You know what? I don't want to think about it. Any of it. It's like a dream that's bending my brain.'

She rubs her eyes. Through her knuckles, Callum nods. 'An impossible dream, no less.'

Kira huffs. 'Right. An impossible dream, when all I want is to go home, focus on my exams, and forget it ever happened.'

Callum sticks the poker back in the cinders. 'You can, can't you?' He shrugs, matter-of-fact. 'Once Romy's well enough to travel, you'll leave. What she said, and what we saw, might follow you home, but nothing else will.'

'Won't it?' Kira stifles a yawn. Nibbles wriggles out from under her head, and she burrows deep into the cushions. 'What happened to us earlier, Callum?' She locks her arms around her curled-up legs. The heat of the fire, the stress of the day. They settle on her like quilts. 'Where did we go?'

'I thought you didn't want to talk about it.' Callum's voice is drier than the logs on the fire.

Kira pushes out her lips. 'I don't. But if we're using dream metaphors'— she rolls her head along the couch toward him—'it's recurring.'

Callum smiles then. Not a smirk, not teasing, not smug. A smile. It does something strange to her sleepy chest, and all she can do is return it.

'In answer to your question then, I don't know.' He shifts his gaze to the dribbling cat, gunning for his feet. 'I don't know where we went. I don't know how it happened, when I know this mountain back to front.' He meets her eyes. The smile falters. 'But unless you leave for home tonight, I reckon we're going to find out.'

17

The note

ight-forty-seven brings curtain-filtered sunlight, hammering knuckles on the wooden door, and her phone buzzing in her pocket. Two cats erupt in hissing shock, but Kira is slower to wake. Groggy. The noise is a haze of confusion.

I don't have cats is her first thought. *Then I am where?* is the second.

Lifting her head, she squints through the daylight. Callum's arm lies loose across her feet. Her legs are curled over his knees, his body slack with sleep. They haven't moved all night.

Oh, dear. Sitting up, she fumbles for her phone. How did they fall asleep propped this awkwardly? She rubs her face awake, grateful for the thousandth time that makeup is a strain. Why is her phone so hard to reach? It vibrates something dreadful, painful on her hipbone. Nearly…nearly…

There. Prepped for the apocalypse, she screws up her face and answers to her father. 'Dad?'

'Kira!'

'I'm coming!' Callum's mother hurries down the stairs, securing her dressing gown at the waist. Spotting the occupied sofa, she slows. Her throat works. Her cheeks pull taut. Stiffly, she opens the door.

Guilt twists cold and curdling. A twinge for her, and a twinge for Mathew, speaking fast in her ear.

'Have you heard?' A flowered dress, heavy overcoat, and snow boots stride into the chalet, propelled by a gust of wind. Plonking herself on a squashed red armchair, the woman crosses her legs. 'Hazal's had more trouble.'

Kira's attention flits. Mathew. Women. Too much information for her early morning brain.

Dad. '...Don't know what to do, where are...'

Woman. '...Fighting last night, and she ran off. Said she was going to take a shower, but when she didn't come back...'

Dad. '...Come back, so we can figure this...'

Woman. '...Found the water running, but nobody there.'

Kira snaps herself into focus. 'Okay.' She rubs her eyes and tries to breathe. 'Dad, I'm coming now.'

The woman's eyes flick to the sofa. Ending the call, Kira tracks her gaze. Callum stretches like a yawning cat, looking in sleepy bewilderment between the women. 'Mum.' He furrows his bleary brow. 'Lena.'

'She still hasn't come back.' Glancing at his mother, the woman cuts him off. 'I've just been round there. The husband's going crazy, asking every guest that comes in if they've seen his wife and his...'

Her gaze flicks to Kira.

'Daughter. Yeah.' Manoeuvring her mannequin limbs off the couch, she lets her sarcasm spill. 'And I'd love to stay and fuel your gossip, but unfortunately, I can't. I have to go create more gossip. Have a wonderful day.'

'Wait.' Callum heaves himself up as she retrieves her boots, scanning the room for her coat. 'If you want, I'll come with you.'

'It's fine.' Coat over her arms, Kira yanks the door open. 'I really have to go. Now. Sorry,' she directs toward Callum's mother. Arms crossed, she has a face like a garrison. 'I am. Really. Your fire was warm, and we fell asleep. Don't kill Callum over it. Thank you for the beer, and the tea.'

It's inadequate. Again. Guilt does more than twinge, but she's out of the door with the words afloat, carelessly wading down the garden and through the frosted arch. She can't think about guilt. Can't think it, can't feel it, because Mum... She chews on her cheek, worrying it raw, stumbling, shivering, blinded. The morning is bright.

And her mother is gone.

Gone, with no note, no warning. A lie after last night's argument, slamming away for a shower. Kira missed some of what her father said, but she caught this: Anna's phone lies abandoned, and her winter-wear is missing. The car hasn't moved. No one's seen her. She's gone.

Gone.

At the hotel gate, Kira stops short. The flowery woman. The heavy-coated woman. She'd hardly looked at her, but dammit, she should have. Everything about her suddenly knits.

Her dress. Her accent. Her spiked, black hair, no longer wet with sweat. She's the woman from the hospital.

Later. Frustration spikes, but Kira keeps moving. The woman is around, known to Callum, known to Hazal, but Anna has gone. She needs to get back to her father.

Mathew is waiting on the reindeer-blanket couch. 'I'm sorry,' Kira says, the moment the door chimes announce her arrival.

'Kira.' He stands like a guard on watch. His face sags. His eyes widen, everything taut and relieved.

She links her arms around his stomach. 'I'm so, so sorry. You have no idea how sorry I am. I fell asleep. I was with Callum, and we were sat on his sofa, and we just…' She pulls free, gesturing emptily. With everything that's happened, it sounds selfish. Unthinking, inadequate. Again. 'We fell asleep where we sat. I'm so sorry.'

Tugging her close again, Mathew rests his chin on her head. 'I'm glad you're okay.' He reels her in tighter. 'At least I could assume you hadn't moved since you messaged. I'd have liked an update, or for you to actually come back, but at least I had an *idea*.'

His chest empties, refilling, full and deliberate. 'Like I said, I'm glad you're okay.' He rubs her back, up, down, dropping the words into her hair. 'Right now, it's enough that you haven't gone crazy or disappeared completely. We can have the staying-over-with-strange-boys talk later, alongside the one where you don't send your dad mad with worry.'

Those words are definitely going to haunt her, hunt her, and skulk through her mind for a long time to come. Pulling free again, Kira casts her eyes around the restaurant, as if Anna might be hiding beneath a table, in the jacuzzi, behind the Christmas tree in the corner. More guilt right now will cripple her. 'You really don't know where Mum is?'

Mathew shakes his head. It seems to weigh too much for his body. The bravado has gone without a trace; never, even at the hospital, has she seen him so undone. So close to crying, or maybe collapse.

'I tried, Kira.' He scratches his cheek. Bloodshot eyes, unshaved chin, a hint of sweat. He never smells of sweat. 'I searched the village, I spoke to the neighbours, I spoke to the hotel guests. I even went to the hospital after she'd been gone most of the night and drove around town when they told me I couldn't just wander in and look around. Now she's still not back, and I don't know what to do. I can't help feeling I'm to blame.'

Kira wilts. 'Dad.' She blinks, hard. 'It wasn't just you that was arguing, Dad.'

'Not just this.' He pinches the bridge of his nose, fighting down a yawn. 'Everything. I don't know. Could you check your room, see if there's anything that says where she might have gone? I've turned ours upside down, and had a quick look in yours, but if you could…?'

Wretched and hopeful, rumpled and crumpled in yesterday's clothes. Kira has to blink again. Again. Swallow down the painful air that rushes up inside her. He's barely a parent, more of a friend, desperate and in need of her help.

'I'll check again.' She struggles for a limp smile.

He smiles limply back. 'Thank you.' He nudges her in the direction of the stairs. 'If you could do it now?'

Halfway up, Kira looks back. Blowing out his cheeks, he sinks heavily into the sofa, reaching for a half-empty brandy glass. Tired and parched with the sun barely up, like an old alcoholic or a weathered cowboy in the shade of his porch. It's only a day since things went wrong. It's only a night since Anna's been gone.

The painful air rushes up again. Pushing into her bedroom, Kira carelessly sheds coat and boots and tips face-first toward her blankets. Drinking early, drinking alone, and not changing his clothes. She horse-kicks the door shut, crawls farther onto the bed, and smothers her face with the pillows. She'll check her room in a while; right now, she needs ten minutes to mope.

After considerably longer than ten minutes, plus a shower, plus a search that throws up nothing and leads to a long ten minutes more, a knock comes on the door. Kira grunts but doesn't move. The door creaks open, the bed depresses, and she doesn't move. Having built a pillow fort and layered herself in blankets, she's forced a serenity that any shift might rock. There hasn't been this peace in a long time, even prior to yesterday; she's warm, ignoring the world, and content to bob on the thoughts of her uninteresting—*deliciously* uninteresting—home.

The sea. The gulls. The bright little houses crammed on the hillside. The wind, the rain driving down three days out of five, the parties by the colourful beach huts; even the uneventful days where she and Romy would go to college, return from college, eat fish and chips, and lead uneventful, separate, yet companionable evenings. The days she'd previously counted off with vigour, in anticipation of leaving. The days she never thought she'd—

'Are you all right?'

Kira jerks upright. Her body heats from the stomach up. She hadn't, in a month—no, a *year*—of Sundays, expected him to be the one to come in, catching her curled in an unflattering position, butt-first, with an ocean of pillows for protection. Sweeping her hair from her face, she clears her throat and tries for normalcy.

'Sorry.' Callum's smirk doesn't look sorry at all. 'I didn't mean to scare you. I like your fort.' He nods at the rudimentary structure. Kira's flush seeps into her jeans, down to her thighs and calves and toes. 'Genuinely. Best episode of *Community* was when it all happened in a pillow fort. Or a blanket fort.' He shrugs. 'Whatever.'

Averting her face, hot from shame and pillows and contemplating the shame and pillows, Kira hastily dismantles her stronghold. 'That episode was embarrassing.'

'No, no.' He wags a finger at her. 'That's an irreconcilable difference right there.' Gathering her rejected pillows, he tugs them toward him. 'Anyway, I think showing up in your bedroom trumps showing up at my house, so that's one thing you don't have to feel weird about. I meant to come with you earlier.' One on top of the other, he starts to build a tower. 'I'd got my shoes, coat, everything, but before I could actually leave, the kraken was released. I had to listen to a speech about how bad it looks that a girl I don't know, and especially one with a feral sister, slept with me on the couch.'

The tower falls down. Eyeing it disapprovingly, he misses Kira's grimace, the spark of fire at the word *feral*. 'Mum was livid, and Lena spent the whole time with her angry, beady eyes boring into my skull. I don't think she's ever not angry. Even her gossip is angry. Anyway.' He taps on the biggest pillow, woven with a chalet and a boy on skis. 'The upshot was that it's a bad influence for the boys, and I may be an adult, but it's still her house. Oh.'

His face creases, his nonchalance sliding into shame. 'Sorry. Ah.' He scratches the back of his head. 'Sorry. I shouldn't have said feral. Romy's not feral, but that's the word they both kept using.' He closes his eyes, his chin knocking his chest. 'Goddammit. That makes it worse. I should probably stop talking.'

'Don't.' Putting the fort-tower back in its place, Kira tosses the remains onto Romy's bed. 'It's all right.' She props herself up against the headboard. Callum lifts both eyebrows. Its truth is as much of a surprise to her; the spark of fire has sputtered out. 'I know.' She smiles fleetingly, almost sheepish. 'You'd expect me to get righteous and offended, all puffed up in the chest.'

A pause. 'Like a cartoon character,' she adds. 'Before you take that the wrong way.'

Callum nods, a tad too deliberately. The burning body heat threatens to return. He's a man; of course he'll take it the wrong way.

But all he says, despite his eyes lingering on hers, is, 'And you're not going to?'

'It's not like it'll stop people saying it.' Dropping his gaze, Kira crosses her legs, neatly tucking in her ankles. The gnarled headboard hits every knob of her spine, and she's still too close to a flush. 'And she was actually quite feral.'

She huffs a wry laugh, twisting her checked shirt between her fingers. Callum deflects his gaze to the window. A smile tugs at his lips, and watching him, one tugs at her own. He's trying to batten down its hatches.

'You're allowed to agree,' she says dryly. 'I happen to not be feral. And I'm sorry that your mother's upset.' She pulls her mouth to one side. 'I get it. I shouldn't have stayed. After persuading her I'm not the devil, I became a different devil. I can apologise to her properly, if you think it would help.'

Slipping off his coat, Callum drops it beside Kira's. 'I don't know that it would.' He moves more comfortably onto the bed. 'It's no more your fault than mine. But if you really want to, let her calm down first. Maybe for a few hours, by which time she and Lena will have taken so many turns shouting about it, along with everything else today that they perceive to be wrong, that she'll be worn out and almost pleasant.'

He sticks his hands behind his head, reclining against the newly arranged pillows.

Kira's smile tugs again. 'Make yourself at home.'

Callum grins. 'Cheers.' Tugging off his sweatshirt, he drops it on top of his coat. 'And it's fine.' He replaces his hands behind his head. 'You really don't have to apologise. I told Mum you were upset, and being the advantage-taking fellow that I am, I persuaded you to stay the night so I could "comfort" you.'

He quotes with his fingers, rolls with his eyes. 'Now she just thinks I'm a dick. Ow.' He frowns. Wriggles his back. '*Ow.*'

'Ow?' Kira shifts aside. He wriggles again. 'Ow, what?'

Callum rolls over, colliding with her legs. 'Ow, there's something sharp in the bed.' He lifts up the blankets, angling his neck in a three-point-turn to peek inside.

'What are you, the princess and the pea?' Kira tilts her head. Callum is rooting around, grey T-shirt riding up and away from his jeans. 'I think I'd know if there was something in my bed.'

'Not all of us are princess material.' He pulls back the sheet to reveal the mattress. 'Aha!' Producing a creased slip of paper, he holds it out with a satisfied grin. 'Looks like you've got mail.'

'What?' Kira snatches it. The half-light is hard to see through, but her mother's writing is clear.

I know you know. Going there is the best I can do.

'What is it?' Callum sits up to read over her shoulder. The hotel clocks cuckoo, ticking out of time. Downstairs, laughter bursts. The paper smells like her mother. 'What does it mean?'

Kira holds the flimsy note up to the light. It reveals nothing: not another hidden sheet, not a lemon juice postscript. Aunty Nat taught her that as a child. 'It's Mum's writing.' She swallows. The words came out hoarse. 'But I don't know what it means. Something to do with Romy?' Her heart starts up a flutter in her chest. An idea is forming, but if she looks at it head-on… 'She knows I know she was hiding something?'

Slowly, Callum nods. 'But where's she had to go?'

Kira looks at him, and a look is enough. It's in the uncertainty of her eyes, the growing, reluctant line of her mouth.

'You think she's in the forest.' It's smooth and not a question. He forces his voice even. 'You know it's just trees, right? Not some phantom fairyland your sister made up?'

Kira looks away. 'The forest is linked to what happened to Romy,' she murmurs and falls silent. Patient on the outside, Callum looks out of the window. A bleak buzzard weaving through damp, low cloud, yellow sunlight weak through the wisps. 'And it's all I can think of.'

Kira keeps her gaze down. Long hair falls in front of her face, damp and tangled and mussed from her fort. His ex, Ivet, the girl Jay not-so-affectionately nicknamed "The Poodle," would have started preening the second he arrived, shooing him out until she was perfect.

Perfection is subjective.

'Mum knew something about all of this.' Kira rubs her eyes. Callum drags his mind down. 'And from her note, it sounds like she's left as a result. She didn't take the car, and the trains had already stopped when she left, so where else does that leave?'

'Walking.'

'Callum.' Kira levels him a blank, tired look. 'One of her daughters nearly died because of walking, at night, in the snow. Do you really think she'd risk the same?'

'She's risking the same if she's gone to the forest.'

Kira scrapes a hand through her hair. It catches in the tangles. 'That's not what I meant.'

'I know what you meant.' Callum slumps back into the pillows. 'But it's just a forest, and not even a big one. Other than more trees and more mountains, the most your mum would find is the next ski resort.'

He pauses. Is he overstepping a line?

Probably.

'Kira...' He lifts the edge of the note. It seems almost alive, a frail thing with a fluttering chest. 'Kira, Romy got maybe three hundred metres into the forest. She curled up and went to sleep in that clearing; you saw the tree for yourself. Why would your mum fight with your dad, leave you a note, and disappear if she was going to poke around the edge of the trees? And how do you know'—he shifts his head to look at her, fiddling with the hem of her shirt— 'that Romy *wasn't* making up what she said? You're basing the entirety of your thinking on the words of a mad girl, who claims we went adventuring in fairyland. Believing her means you believe in this land, and that your mum also—'

'Romy isn't mad.' Kira's eyes snap to his through her hair. For the barest of seconds, she's as fierce as her sister. 'She's not all right, but it's not madness. It's something else.' She drops her eyes again, her face hard. 'I just don't know what yet.'

'Okay.' Callum levers himself back up. 'Okay. I'm sorry. But the fact remains that Romy could be saner than a saint, and it wouldn't mean this place exists.'

He tugs at a loose thread on his T-shirt, an idle façade of indifference. That's a bridge in his mind he'd rather not cross. Kira said it last night: *it goes against science, against logic, and everything we've grown up knowing.*

'Yes, strange things happened in the forest.' He pulls the thread to its death. 'Really strange things, as a matter of fact. But it doesn't mean we wandered into Narnia.'

'You weren't saying that last night,' she says tersely. And he's the one calling out madness. 'You weren't saying it while it was happening, either. You were just as confused as I was, and just as worried when we thought we were losing our minds. You can back out all you want, claim that we saw things, felt things, that weren't there, but you're not convincing me.' Kira looks at him sideways. 'I don't even think you're convincing yourself.'

She can only assume he's listening. As bad as she is at keeping still, he's found another thread to tug at. 'You said that what we saw was impossible,' she continues, less accusatory than before. Her own coping strategies are hardly perfect. 'Whatever Whiteland is, whether it's a real place or a name Romy chose, she still knew we'd been there. She knew what we saw, and she'—she flicks her fingers, fishing for words—'it was like she had a list. Checking things off in her head. The river that we thought was an ocean. She knew that, too. That we thought it was an ocean. And the wooden window.'

She thumps back against the headboard. 'How could she know that, Callum? How could she know any of that, unless it belongs to a place? A place she'd actually been, where something strange happened? You found her in the clearing where everything started.'

Watching her warily, Callum nods.

'Right.' Sitting forward again, Kira crosses her legs. 'And something strange had happened to her when you found her. Strange is going to go the same way as impossible, but it's the only one that fits.'

The shirt hem finds its way back to her fingers. Outside, the train whistles, a car honks its horn. 'There's a pattern,' she continues with a little less gusto. 'All three of us experienced something in that part of the forest. And going back to my original point'—she determinedly meets Callum's eye—'Mum knows what happened to Romy. What happened to Romy is linked to the forest. Even if this wasn't such a messed-up knot of *stuff*—she flicks her fingers again, pausing them in place for emphasis—'where else would Mum go to find answers? If she's trying to bring back her daughter's mind, and she has to go somewhere to do it, where would she start but the place that took it away?'

Callum huffs. 'I thought Romy wasn't mad?'

Kira opens her mouth. Closes it. 'I…' She pulls a face. 'She's not. Not in herself.' Her mouth winces. 'But I didn't tell you everything that happened at the hospital. I don't think she's mad, if we're even allowed to say things like that, but I think something mad is inside her.'

Romy, alone, naked in the dark. *Help me.* The image that took her, and shook her, and sucked, and then flung her back to life.

KIRA, NO, I CAN'T GET—

In a hush, she relays this. Only a hushed part of her mind can stand to remember.

Callum doesn't laugh. He doesn't brush it off. He doesn't say anything.

He doesn't speak for so long that it's the worst reaction of all.

'Romy asked for my help.' Swivelling, Kira slides from the bed. She can't sit in silence. She has to do something. The room seems to swirl with absurdity, as thick and pungent as smoke. She can't look at Callum. 'So I'm going to help her.'

She retrieves her outerwear from the floor. Only when she's put it all on does Callum speak. 'Going where?'

Kira shoots him a look that says clearly, *are you stupid?* He tips his head back on his neck. 'The forest. I'm not religious, but I'm praying for your soul.'

He'd be praying for his, too. The dread that ballooned up his throat as she spoke, as she described the shitshow, the horror show, the horror…it's impossible to vocalise, but it shut his vocal chords, clamped them with a pressure he didn't know existed. All that comes out is a burning desire for none of this to be real.

'I take it you're not coming, then,' Kira says shortly. Buttoning her fur-ry-hooded coat to the neck, she stamps into a pair of pixie boots and grabs her phone from the bed. 'Good. I don't want to feel any more like a fool. I know this is messed up, Callum, but it doesn't make it any less real.'

She's cutting so close to the truth he can almost feel the knife. 'Oh, I'm coming.' Scooping up his coat and sweatshirt, he follows her into the hall. 'Just wait.' He grabs her sleeve. 'Wait a second.'

With a sigh, Kira turns. 'What?'

He falters. Three seconds. Four. Five. 'Don't feel like a fool.'

She narrows her eyes, searching his. Three seconds, four, five, then, 'All right.'

Callum relaxes. 'Then let's go.' He makes himself smile, makes himself tease. 'I might think your knowledge of life is based too strongly on seventies horror, but I'm coming. It's the most scandal this village has ever seen.'

Kira casts him a motherly exasperation. 'If you mean *The Evil Dead*, that wasn't the seventies.'

They clatter down the stairs. He grins. 'You know your horror films.'

'I know a lot of films. And I don't believe Romy's been possessed by the trees.' Kira pulls on her gloves, pulls up her hood. 'If you're going to try to be clever, you should really do it right.'

'Wait.' Halfway across the restaurant, she turns. Her hip butts a chair. 'Ow.' She rubs her leg, heading back to the bar. 'Hazal?' she calls into the kitch-en. Wincing at how demanding it sounds, she adds, 'Sorry.' She rests her awk-ward arms on the bar. 'I just—are you there?'

Slowly, the kitchen door swings open. 'I'll meet you at my steps.' Callum touches her arm. 'Supply pit stop. Better safe than hungry.'

Kira nods, and he leaves. With an expression that looks deliberately blank, Hazal emerges from the kitchen, an embroidered tea towel tight in her hands. 'Yes?' she says, looking Kira up and down. 'Is all okay?'

It's like the typical British thing of asking *how are you?* and expecting only *fine* in return. Kira nods, although clearly, nothing is okay. 'Do you know where my dad is?' she asks. 'I guess he could be in his room, but I didn't hear anything.

Last time I saw him, he was down here, and—' She cuts herself off. Not the time to waffle. 'Sorry. Um, have you seen him?'

Hazal's face doesn't change. 'No.'

That's it. No elaboration. Kira's face starts to heat. Her leg starts to jig. 'Okay.' Looking away, more awkward than ever, she digs around in her jeans. 'I have—' She pulls out the note. 'This.' Folding it small, she places it on the bar. 'If you see him, could you give it to him? I'll message him, too, but he needs to see this. I found it in my room.'

Hazal's hands tighten on the towel. Her eyes trail down to the paper. Sitting between them, it feels like a gauntlet, far, far bigger than its palm-sized square. Kira fights the urge to snatch it back.

Weirdly slowly, carefully slowly, Hazal picks it up. 'Okay,' she says. Without looking, she slides it into her apron pocket with what is definitely fake apathy. 'I give to him.'

She turns away. Kira forces a smile into her voice. 'Thank you,' she calls, as Hazal returns to the kitchen. The door swings shut. Kira flinches. Dismissed.

In the pantry, Hazal waits for the chimes on the hotel door to sing. 'Good thing,' she says, 'she is polite.' She nods at Mathew asleep between the shelves. 'If she came in to look for me, you have to do that to her as well. These people.'

Straightening judiciously, surrounded by leaning stacks of goods, Lena regards the rumpled man. Mouth half-open, ragged, unwashed, he looks like a tramp in the dark, cramped space. 'One nosy English person is enough.' She nudges him with her boot. 'We need to get him back to his room before your staff come back.'

Hazal lines a packet of cinnamon sticks up with the rest. 'And he won't remember?' she asks. The Whispers. Mathew going where he shouldn't, as if Anneliese is hiding in corners. Lena, thinking fast.

Lena sighs. For a moment, she looks so tired. 'No,' she says. 'He won't.'

18

The night

Past a troupe of tiny children, dragging snowboards and helmets; past the cars that never move, the pines, the chalets throwing out sweetened wood-smoke; down the same road, but this time with a quiet trepidation reserved for presentations or the two attempts it took to pass her driving test. Kira watches Callum from the corner of her eye. If he shares her cold worry, a sheet of ice in her chest, then he's a far better actor. Hands in his pockets, humming "Johnny, I Hardly Knew Ya" shamelessly off-key, he could be going to the shops, or the pub.

Skirting the ice beside the sledging hill, the forest snakes into sight.

No; it doesn't snake. Kira drops her eyes. It marches. It taunts. Callum can think her gullible, superstitious, whatever, but anything could wait inside. Things worse than whispers in her ear, oceans, and pretty little birds.

Listen, don't go back, Kira. The Whispers are planning to—

KIRA, NO, I CAN'T GET—

'Why go when you're so nervous?' Abruptly, Callum stops walking. 'No one's making you.'

The very real voice slices off the memory. Forced from her thoughts, Kira starts. 'What?'

Callum lifts three fingers. 'You stopped talking the second after I showed you my pockets of treats.' He drops one. 'You've been walking slower than a kid sent to see the head.' He drops a second. 'And'—he gestures across the car park—'you're acting like the trees might eat you if you're fool enough to look them in the eye. If you want to go back, go back. I'm sure your dad would prefer not to have someone else wander off.'

Callum sways his upper body behind them. It demands more effort, but manages to look lazier than turning his head. 'You could go back to the hotel, be his drinking companion. You could go back to the hotel and be my drinking companion. It's been enough of a day already that I'm ready for a beer. Or'—he sways back to the forest—'you can swallow your fear, follow your mother, and help your sister. I don't mind.'

A smile ghosts toward Kira's lips but stops behind her teeth. 'I thought'— she rubs her uneasy mouth—'you were praying for my soul.'

On the sledging hill, two craft collide. Voices squeal, laughter erupts, a voice warns Kevin to stop.

'I am.' Callum pivots at the English. Kira doesn't need to: over the last several days, in several places, she's heard the same unruly Kevin chided for several unruly things. 'But I can do that whether I'm drinking beer or traipsing into fairyland. The choice is yours, madame.'

Kevin hits a bump with a squeal of glee. On the spur of her amusement, Kira chooses. 'You tell yourself that,' she says, moving into the car park before she can think better. 'Tell yourself you're humouring me, that you're here for the ride. That it's just the most scandal this village has ever seen.' She tips her head, bats her eyelashes. 'I'll believe that when you do.'

Callum pushes her head upright with one finger. '"I'll believe that when you do,"' he mimics, a young-girl imitation. 'Come on, if you're coming.'

Ignoring the frozen ground, iced to a perfect cake, he picks up speed toward the barrage of trees. 'You're a child, Callum,' Kira calls. 'You're a child in denial.'

'Oh, I'm not in denial.' Refusing to stop at the edge of the tarmac, he hauls himself boldly up the bank, leaps onto a precarious woodpile, and looks expectantly down his nose. 'I'm very self-aware.'

Kira snorts. Yesterday, she said effectively the same.

From the smugness of his smile, he remembers. 'I thought you were curious?' Extending a hand, he waggles his fingers. 'Treat it like you're in *The Hobbit*. "I'm going on an adventure!"'

Kira shifts her weight to one hip. 'Because standing on sticks is an adventure.'

She forges a cautious path up to Callum's castle. The king is not amused. 'They are not sticks.' He spreads his hands: *see?* 'They are logs. I'm still not a child. And I don't see you up here, daring to conquer.'

He's right about that. The scent of the logs is refreshing, newly cut pine in the biting cold, but calling them precarious is kind. Kira turns toward the trees. Stark stalwarts against the off-white clouds, they're the true kings, bushes and saplings tangling around them like subjects before a throne.

'I'm doing what you said.' She shoots him a wide-eyed innocence. Disgruntled and clumsy, Callum jumps to the ground. 'You told me to treat it like a joke.'

'I did not.' Stoically, he ignores her, clapping snow from his gloves. 'I said treat it like we're in *The Hobbit*. There's a difference.'

Offering him a sweet smile, Kira says nothing. His ego could probably use a break.

On the edge of the clearing, they stop. 'What happens now?' Callum asks. The bowl stretches away from them, its glittering snow unmarked.

'I don't know.' Kira rubs her hands for warmth, flecked with disquiet. 'I didn't think that far ahead. I just wanted to feel like I was helping. Or trying to, at least.'

Callum nudges a strip of wood with his boot. There are several around. Kira almost feels sad. He never did get his kindling. 'Well…' His boot pauses. He frowns. 'I was going to say we can look for some sign that your mum's been here, but it's all just snow.'

It's all just snow.

'Whatever we do'—Callum nods at the bowl—'I'd rather not stay here. I can't explain yesterday, and I don't fancy having another go.'

It's all just snow. Kira slumps inside. His words strike a chord of futility: what is she trying to achieve? Did she think she'd find Anna, trotting through the forest like a faun? A note, pinned to a tree, explaining what happened to Romy? A trail of breadcrumbs?

It's all just snow. What if it is just a forest?

'Kira?' Callum is watching her, hankering for a decision. 'That offer of beer is still—'

Sliding from her face, his eyes narrow over her shoulder.

The back of Kira's neck prickles. He's craning to see better, lips parting as he peers through the trees. 'What is it?' she asks uneasily.

Callum's voice is as bewildered as his gaze. 'Mist.'

Mist, and a lot of it. The path back to the car park is entirely, immaculately white, inching toward them in a desert-style dust storm. Kira falters, double takes. Not inching; it's moving, creeping, *sweeping*, encroaching upon the trees until they fade to white themselves. She steps back.

'That…' She retreats until her hand meets Callum's arm and her ankle brushes the tree. 'That wasn't there before. Was it?'

'No.' Callum's face is oddly blank. Colder than the shade within the trees, colder than the sporadic gusts of wind, the mist crosses the last patch of ground and enfolds them. 'It wasn't. And I think we should leave.' He looks over his shoulder at the growing haziness of the clearing, to the clarity of the forest beyond. 'Now.'

A shriek cuts through the mist.

Kira freezes. 'What was that?'

Another cry slices behind them. It sounds like a bird taking chase.

Callum jerks for her hand. His grip isn't warm, like he's offering comfort; it's cold and crushing, as though he needs hers. 'I don't know,' he whispers in the dead, muffled silence. 'But we really need to leave. It doesn't feel right.' He urges her away from the tree, farther into the clearing. 'It's not right. Mist doesn't come from nowhere.'

Another step. Another. Kira can't help but remember the voice, the tickling snicker: *hello*. Her hand crushes under Callum's fingers. Another step, soft and crunching. The air is clammy, breathy. Another.

They've almost reached the fringes of the mist when a low growl curls through the trees.

Kira whips around. 'What was—' she stutters, but a large, dark shape, looming from the white to their left, stops her words in their tracks. Callum's hand goes slack around hers. Her heart bounces down to her belly and back. 'Oh, shit. Callum?'

His voice is garbled. 'Yes?'

The truth is here. With a snort, the shape ducks its head to charge. Kira grips Callum's fingers tighter. 'You need to start believing.'

Yanking Callum with her, she spins around. His weight is unbalancing—*run*, goddammit—but she pelts across the clearing, stumbling, tripping, thumping through untouched snow to the rise.

The bird keens as they scrabble up the slope. Flail over the top, continue to run. The shriek echoes again, joined by a thudding, low like the thundering of hooves. Kira's legs almost cave. It's following them.

Into a different clearing, pretty and dotted with benches. Crash out the other side, blunder through a weaving, winding, snowy tunnel, every bush and every root itching to interfere. Callum flings his arm out as Kira trips, cries out, grabbing her wrist to tug her faster, faster, past small, frozen pools and snow-laden shelters, burnt-out campfires, and dip, rise, dip. The forest is never-ending.

And the mist is catching up. Kira dares a look back. Another cry strangles in her throat; she thought they'd been fleeing, flying ahead of its damp, white curtain, but now, it's almost here. Her heart bashes its head bloody. Her breaths come fast and barbed. How do you escape what doesn't get tired?

Hurtling through the trees, bark scrapes her palms. Thorns snag her jeans. Her tiny boots are coming to pieces. A branch catches her hair and she shouts, again as it tears from her scalp. Pain blooms hot, her hair in her eyes. No sign of Callum anymore, she's a whirlwind. Her senses tunnel. The forest is thickening, spiking into barriers, interweaving and churning with ice and leaves and rot—

Until, with a snorting roar behind and a beating of wings above, it drops away and she falls.

Kira crashes to the ground with a yell. Slippery snow propels her downwards, through buried woodchips and hidden thickets, a vertical descent too chaotic to stop. Her foot catches on a root and she screams, snow burning her face and twigs tearing her coat as it jerks her brutishly around. *This is it*, she thinks wildly; this is how she goes. She'll slam into a tree, or a rock, and that'll be the end, smashed to pieces at the bottom of the slope. At least it's more of a bang than a whimper.

Unless the monsters get there first. A feral snarl ricochets behind her, the hoofbeats drumming on the forest floor. The air throbs in dizzy waves as something sinks down, down, down, the mist creeping closer and colder and colder and closer to bead wet upon her skin. How much farther can she possibly fall? Twisting, bumping, thrashing down a sheer, endless hill, blinded by spraying powder as she tries to dig in her heels. What happened to Callum?

Throwing her arms in front of her face, Kira wards off a thicket's prongs. What happens if she reaches the bottom intact but still, there's no escape?

Just as she thinks this, the forest spits her out. Swooning at a second of free fall, she tumbles over a short ridge and slams into a road.

The wind flies out of her. For another second, or two, or three, the mist is forgotten; she's a crumpled, aching heap, a rag doll flung to the snow-covered ground.

Along the same ridge, a larger doll rolls, hitting the ground with a whump. Head whirling, Kira squints at it. Callum?

'Callum!' she cries, a rasp, a gasp, struggling up to her bruised elbows, her twinging, shaking knees. Heavily, Callum lifts his head. His temple is bloody. 'Are you—'

Up on the ridge, the hoofbeats die. Kira's words die with them. Oh, no.

The mist is slipping down the slope toward the road. Within it, poised in the air and paused on the ground, are two dark, colossal shapes.

Everything turns to static. The shadow on the ground tips back its head, and Kira scrambles to her feet. Can she slip away? Melt into the mist as it enfolds her, run when she's far enough—

A howl cuts the air. A drawn-out battle cry, a call to arms, pierced and full and haunting. It thrums with inhumanity. Kira's stomach falls away. She throws her eyes around the road, close to frozen, filled with fear. Callum, on his knees and breathing hard. The desert-storm trees, greyed and useless. Paw prints around her, the marks of raquettes. There must be something. Are they going to have to run?

No. 'Callum!' Hope balloons as she spots the little building. Lurking in the haze down a snowy stub of road, it's better than nothing. He hauls himself to his feet, and she runs.

Across the road and down the slope, to the sound of a volucrine cry. Arms up for impact, she collides with the stone and scrabbles around the walls, slapping, searching for a window, a door. Callum is beside her in seconds, pushing past like he knows where he's going, and as hooves scrape the ground and wings beat the air, he falls on the door and hauls it open.

Light spills in. Callum groans. 'Oh, Christ.'

Kira's hope plummets with her stomach, with her lungs. There's no space, no room; axes and shovels and broken furniture scrabble for space on the floor, and there's no way, no way they can fit—

As the howl comes again and the hooves shake the ground, the air a rush from the flapping of wings, Kira barges her way inside. She's not being eaten by phantom creatures; not today. Scraping along the wall beside the door, she wrenches Callum in against her, slams the door shut, and kicks at the stacks of precarious tools. *Not today.*

Darkness crashes down. A landslide of shovels clatters to the floor, toppling what sound like rakes. The noise outside hits a crescendo.

The noise outside dies.

Kira waits. Her heart thuds a tattoo, but nothing happens. Nothing pounds on the door; nothing scrapes, or scratches, or smashes its way through. She listens harder, pushing out every sense. The smell of must, as dank as an attic or a boarded-up basement. A sharpness in her throat from effort or screaming or both. Callum's hands on her thighs, vices through his gloves, his boots crushing hers.

Kira closes her eyes against the dark. Have the creatures gone? Are they lurking in silence, hoping for a false sense of security? Is it socially acceptable to spend your life in a disused storage hut?

Time is immortal when it can't be measured. After long enough that Kira has considerably calmed, Callum exhales, long and shaken, and uncramps his fingers. 'Add that'—he lowers his head to hers—'to the list of things we're never, in a million fucking years, doing again.'

Kira opens her eyes. All she can see is his neck, damp with sweat and mottled with snow and pine needles and grit. Heaving a shuddering sigh, she wraps her arms around his waist. Whether or not he's had enough of close quarters, she sure as hell needs the comfort.

'I don't know what you're talking about,' she murmurs into his coat. 'I love your normal forest. It's great.'

Callum snorts. 'Yeah, I forgot to mention the flying, roaring horse.' He squeezes her once before she pulls back. 'It runs rampant this time of year. Blame Appenzeller. There's nowt so queer as Appenzeller. Do we reckon we're safe?'

Kira twists her mouth. 'We won't know until we're alive or dead. And I thought Appenzeller was a beer.'

'It is.' Callum tugs at rakes and shovels gloomily blocking the door. 'It's also a canton, and a bloody weird one.' He kicks a reclining axe, shoves an anonymous pile of implements, and rests his fingers on the handle. 'Now?' He gives her a questioning look. Pulse hiccupping, she nods. 'All right.'

One creaking iota at a time, Callum cracks the door ajar. Kira watches as he peers through, heart hiccupping again, and again, and again. It feels like there should be violin music, or the theme from *Requiem for a Dream*. If she was a Victorian heroine, she'd have fainted long ago.

'All good.' He opens the door. Kira blinks at the night. After the muffled hut, it's sharp, cut with ice or glass. The mist has dissipated. The dark is quiet and clear. 'Let's go before the snow becomes quicksand, or we get beamed to Jamaica.'

Tiptoeing over the remaining tools, Kira huffs. 'I wish I could see that as one hundred percent joking.' She breathes the fresh, unimpeded air. 'Considering the fact we've seen a magical ocean, three mirrored clearings, and some Roald Dahl and Stephen King beast amalgamations, anything could happen. Wait.'

She stops. The realisation is a shift in air pressure, a rush of blood to the head. 'It's dark.'

Callum stares at her. 'Well done.'

He's halfway into *are you stupid?* when his face rearranges. 'Oh, delightful.' His mouth curls, open partway. 'It's not quite Jamaica, but it gets points for trying.'

'It shouldn't.' Kira lifts her arms, letting them clap to her sides. When they entered the hut, it was morning, but the night is as full as if it's fallen for hours. Stars prick the fringes with the clarity of winter. The moon hangs high, glinting off the trees, casting bluish shadows on the snow. 'It'll get too big for its boots.'

Whatever "it" is. Kira regards Callum bleakly, more resigned than any other adjective she probably should feel. 'What do we even—'

She swallows the rest of her sentence. In the shadow of the building, something moves.

'You're stupid,' a harsh voice snaps before she has a chance to be afraid. 'The pair of you. You're lucky they haven't knocked this place down yet, or you'd be dead.'

A woman strides into the moonlight. Kira's heart jolts; the flowered dress, the coat, the snow boots.

'You were at the hospital.' Her voice is more reverent than accusatory. She cringes inside. 'I thought I recognised you this morning.' She tugs on her coat sleeves and makes herself stop. Callum's face is growing long with surprise. 'What did you do to Romy? What do you know about…'

She gestures wide. With a bony hand, the woman waves it away.

'Psh.' It's an oddly feline hiss. 'That's not important. What *is* important is the fact you ignored me.' She sweeps both hands around, a mocking mirror of Kira. 'All of *this* is what I was warning you about. Staying away from Whiteland.'

Whiteland. It looses a deep wave of cold, spreading through Kira in a waterfall, a torrent. Hearing it from Romy was one thing, but hearing it again, from someone she doesn't know…they haven't been chasing the wind. There's a place in this forest that shouldn't exist.

'We're not in Whiteland.' Callum's voice borders on exasperated. 'You know we're not. This is the old commune building; you came to the last fête. Your daughter fell in the trough.' He points to a gnarled wooden basin, ice filling its belly and hanging from the spout. 'What's going on, Lena?'

Lena, Lena, Lena, don't be so polite.

Romy knew her.

No. Kira watches Lena watch them, her fierce, birdlike face unreadable. The thing *inside* Romy knew her.

With a shake of her head, Lena turns away. 'Go home, Callum.' The words are short and dismissive. 'You're only going to get burned.'

Callum spreads his hands, palms up. 'By what?'

Lena doesn't look back. 'Monsters,' she calls. The word rings off the stone and into the night. 'And girls who go looking for them.'

Kira steps forward. She doesn't feel real. 'What does that mean?'

Halfway up the road, Lena melts into shadow. 'This isn't your fight, Kira. Neither of yours.' The fading, echoing footsteps pause. 'Your mother knows what she's doing.'

The words are barely there, as insubstantial as the whisper in the trees. Kira chills, again, and again. *Hello.* 'My mo—what?'

'Wherever she is,' Lena continues as if she hadn't spoken, 'she'll be taking care of what happened to Romy. Don't'—the footsteps crunch away again—'go looking for her. Don't go looking for anything.'

The crunch fades to nothing. 'What are you talking about?' Kira's voice cracks. Her mind is roaring. 'Do you know where she is?' A futile step forward. 'Lena! Where is she?'

Where is she? She? She?

The echo flies to the peaks around them, high in the night like legends of stars. 'Let's go.' Callum's voice is a worn thread, pulled too tight and fraying.

'We could follow her, but God knows where she's going. That way'—he nods at Lena's footprints—'just leads to the forest. More of the forest. Christ, she's maddening.'

He tips his head heavenwards. 'It's like she's playing a game: "How to be a plot device in one easy step." Or two, I guess, if she's the woman you saw at the hospital. Dropping hints so our story progresses.'

He makes a sprinkling motion with his fingers. Kira doesn't smile, and he drops his hand. 'Whatever.' He rocks himself into a trudge up the opposite road to Lena's. 'We'll question her tomorrow. She can be as mysterious as she likes in the dark, but not today, Lena. Well, not tomorrow…'

Kira lets his words blur and drift into humming. All she hears are Lena's, warning, discouraging. Telling Callum to stay away.

That, and starkly, irrevocably confirming Romy's threat. The knowledge pierces like a poisoned arrow, seeping from her core to her bloodstream. Not only does Whiteland, or whatever lies in the forest, exist, but it's a part of something they're not meant to discover. It's there, taking Romy. It's there, taking Anna.

It's there, and they're pissing it off.

19

The fallout

Exhaustion hits as the road levels out and sweeps off into the car park. As though they're one bone-weary body, Callum slows, trains his attention on a nondescript building beside the empty beer hut, and veers off. Flush with crude graffiti, it's better than nothing.

'First-aid hut.' Callum retrieves a key from somewhere in his coat. Kira wouldn't have questioned his choice of pit stop, but nods all the same. 'I don't know what that fall did to me, but you look appalling.'

Kira lifts her eyebrows. 'Thanks,' she says as the door grunts open. A pale strip light flicks on. She shields her eyes from the glare. 'So we're staying here until everything heals?'

Callum motions to the full-length mirror. 'Just until you don't look like that.'

Kira snorts. 'Charming.' Her eyes drift to her reflection. 'Oh.'

Her cheeks blush red from the cold. A swelling, bloodstained bruise joins yesterday's marks, and her jaw is scraped, snow and twigs and leaves and ice matted in her hair. Her clothes are stained and torn. Her boots are scratches with leather tacked on.

'See?' Callum nods at them both. The gash on his temple is dried and lumpy, a gathering of tiny bruises ugly on his cheekbone. Woodchips skulk in his hair, and brushing them off with a vigorous hand, he slides his coat and gloves to the floor and delves into the cupboards.

Kira does the same and stares. Yesterday has nothing on this; she's never been so battered in her life.

'Don't worry.' Callum reemerges with several small boxes, catching the end of her unhappiness. 'It's fixable. And what's not fixable will make a good lie.' He looks her up and down, depositing the boxes on the sink beside the mirror. Long names, little bandages. 'Yeah, you can lie. Slipping on ice. Tripping over your own feet on the train line. You're clumsy, so you'll get away with it. Here.'

He turns Kira to face him. A burning overrides her indignation, and she squeaks. 'Sorry.' He lets go. 'I didn't realise.'

Kira flexes her fingers. In, pain. Out, relief. 'Neither did I.' He motions for her to look up, hold still. 'And I'm getting the feeling I should learn first aid.' A little dry, a little rueful as he tends to her cheeks. 'This is the second time in two days you've had to fix my face.'

Callum gives her half a smile, concentrated, close. 'I can fix your arm, too, if you want,' he murmurs. 'Shake it up a bit.' He steps back. 'Would you mind sitting on the sink? You're a bit…'

Kira eyes him pointedly. 'Average.' She hoists herself up. Her arm complains, brash and bright and slicing. 'You're just tall. And was that a polite way to ask if I'll take off my shirt?'

'If you want your arm seen to, then yes.' Callum returns to her face, cotton swab in hand. Gentle, the medicinal smell mingling with winter and cologne. Kira's skin shivers. 'There's quite a lot of blood.'

The shiver ends. 'What?' She flicks her eyes down. Her shirt's red checks are darker than they should be, a deep, damp scarlet seeping through her right sleeve. 'Oh.' She blinks at it blandly. 'Oh.'

'Pretty much.' Callum flashes his eyebrows. A plaster for her chin, one for her temple, and he steps back. 'Do you want me to look?'

Kira chews the inside of her cheek. 'I guess so.' She drops her eyes from Callum and her fingers to her buttons. 'I can't blame that on ice, too. I must have been caught by a branch or something.' She pulls the shirt off quickly. '*Ah.*'

The wind leaves her lungs, ripped like the material from her cuts. Closing her eyes, Kira clenches her jaw. 'I could have done that better.'

'Perhaps.' Callum rummages through his long-named boxes. Grimacing, Kira keeps her eyes closed. How bad is it? 'But it's actually all right. Just one big cut. How does it feel?'

'If I can't see it, it's not there.'

Callum snorts. 'And if it's not there, you can't feel it?'

'Yep.'

But it is there, and she feels it even before Callum sets to work. The pain has nothing on periods, or the time when a football hit her in the head, but it's enough. Enough to make her fret about seeing her dad. How, even with Callum's treatment, can any of it be explained? Her arm, her clothes, her boots? If it was just her face, she could say she tripped, but she looks like she's survived a gale, only to hit a tornado.

And how can she explain where she's been? *Sorry I didn't message, Dad, but time passed in the blink of an eye. Literally. And then I sat in my bra with a stranger, after we ran for our lives.*

Kira shivers. Her shirtless-ness suddenly feels so naked, so vulnerable, exposed. She can't tell her father. Not about this, not about the mist, not about searching for Anna. Certainly not about Whiteland.

'Done.' Callum taps her forehead. With a jump, her eyes flick open. 'I need to take care of my own war wounds, but feel free to leave. It is'—he checks his watch—'nearly ten. Your dad will have gone beyond kittens.'

'He'll have hit foals, at least.' Kira hops from the sink. 'Let me check my phone, and I'll be with you.'

Carefully, she manoeuvres her crumpled shirt over her bandaged arm. Callum shrugs, his eyes averted. 'Up to you. You don't have to.'

'I know.' Kira fastens her buttons, quicker than necessary. Her chest squirms as she pulls out her phone, squinting at the screen, dreading the—

Nothing. Relief flutters and settles. Nothing bar a reply to the message she sent as she left the hotel—a message, somehow, from *hours* ago—saying she was going for a walk. Nothing bar that and one further message: *Off to the hospital. See you later, K.*

'I guess he's not having foals.'

Kira looks up. She'd almost forgotten Callum was there. Her luck is incredible. 'No.' She types a quick reply. *Sorry, my phone died. Went to Callum's again. How's Romy?* 'He went to the hospital. I guess he's still there.' She shoves the phone away. 'Now instruct me.'

Callum consults his watch again. In the strip light, the glass glints with scratches. 'You really don't have to.'

Determinedly, Kira stifles a yawn. 'True. But two things.' She holds up a finger. 'One, you've spent two days helping me, so the least I can do is help you. Or try to, with step-by-step guidance.' She lifts a second finger. 'And two, I don't want to walk back, alone, in the dark. I'm starting to believe literally anything could happen.'

Callum laughs through his nose. 'You're just lucky. It's not normally like this, trust me. The most exciting thing that happened before yesterday was...' He screws up his forehead. 'Actually, never mind. Nothing exciting has ever happened. It's all bickering neighbours and figuring out why there are so few people, yet so many cats. And it'd be nice if you'd stay.' He pauses, scanning his medical supplies. 'Despite your sarcasm, your lack of common sense, and everything that's happened since I met your family, I'm actually starting to like you.'

Kira's eyebrows fly sky-high. 'Is that meant to be a compliment? If it is, it needs work.' She cocks her head. 'In fact, most of your comments need work. When we first came in, I looked appalling, and now I'm sarcastic, stupid, and part of the Addams family? Thank you, Callum.' She brings a hand to her chest. 'I don't know what I ever did without you. You're a one-man ego boost.'

'It's how I win all my women.' Callum passes her a wetted cotton pad. 'Knock-em-down-to-build-em-back-up. Is it working?'

'Well, you did get me in my underwear. What am I doing with this?' Kira waves the cotton pad. The cold water smarts. There are cuts galore on her fingers, too. 'You're lucky I still want to help you. "Knock-em-down-to-build-em-back-up."' She fights her face stern. 'You're horrid.'

Callum flashes her a grin. 'I try.' Positioning himself in front of her, he considers the mirror. 'I'd start with that beauty.'

He directs her pad to the gash on his temple, gritty and already crusting. His knuckles are a swollen violet-blue.

Kira pangs with dismay. 'Callum!'

'They're fine.' Catching her gaze, Callum brushes it off. 'I bashed my hand on a tree stump, but I don't think I'm warm enough to feel it. That'll be tomorrow's joy.'

Kira's mouth pulls down at the corners. 'You shouldn't have come with me.' Softly, she fixes her gaze on the gash. Blossoming, bruising guilt makes it hard to meet his eye. 'You shouldn't have got hurt, and you certainly shouldn't have cleaned up my face.' She glances at his hand. The tower of contrition builds up, up, up. 'Not with bruises that bad. If you'd told me what to do I could have done it myself.'

She dabs at the last of the blood. Callum hisses through his teeth. 'Honestly, it's okay. At this point my hand just feels...cumbersome. Ow.' He winces at another cut, small but gravel-clotted on the underside of his chin. 'Didn't know that was there.'

'Sorry.' Kira removes her pad. 'I'm done. What next?'

She turns to the scattered tubes of cream. His undamaged hand grabs her arm. 'Wait.'

The word is filled with such intent, unnatural and new, that she does. The jokes have dissipated like smoke. His brown eyes are cutting, and Kira's chest hitches, stuttering over a breath. Her head swoons, rushing, hot. She's spinning, spiralling. Callum's face is paling. Through it flit wisps around a fire, ghostlike and intricate, pale in the dark. A waif by the wooden window, staring straight—

The strip light fails. Kira jolts, sharp and clear again, jumping beyond her skin. Callum's hand drops from her arm.

'Automatic when nobody's moving,' he says. The light blinks back to show him rotating, scratched arms outstretched. 'Nothing strange. And the cream with the purple writing.' He indicates a tube. 'That's next. After that, I think we can go.'

Kira nods. The previous moments blur. 'I'll be quick.'

20

The flight

At four o'clock, the birds are asleep. The sun isn't trying to overcome the snow. And the ward is cold and silent.

Stealing out of bed, she recovers her clothes, dresses, pulls on a pair of spiky-flowered boots, and pads to the window. She could arrange a distraction; she could make her bed look as if she's still in it, huddled up and asleep. But what would be the point? They'll soon realise she's missing, and she only needs time to leave the car park. After that, they'll never find her.

Masked by gauzy curtains, the window hardly squeaks. Leaning out, she nods: a stack of bin bags, piled in a skip, more or less below her. It looks feasible, but even if it didn't, she'd do it regardless. This has to happen *now*.

Winching herself onto the windowsill, she wriggles to face the drop. The early morning is black, frosted. Ice stings the air, a breath of snow on the breeze, but it has no hold. She's used to the cold. As she slides from the window, it's a breath-stealing rush.

In her mind, Romy screams. Landing with a *whump* on the bin bags, the woman climbs from the frozen skip and runs.

21

How carefully they tread

Kira wakes up cold, uncomfortable, and curled in last night's towel, damp beneath her on the bed. Rolling arthritically out of it, she peers through sleep-fogged eyes at the window. Daylight edges through the cracks in the shutters. Everything is closed. The room is freezing.

Goose bumped, Kira props herself up. A draught snakes in from somewhere, creeping around like frostbitten breath. As she shuffles on the bed, it wafts into her face. Her shuddering, wide-open door.

Well, that was stupid. Kira rolls off the bed, forces clean clothes over unwieldy limbs, and drowns herself in blankets. Why did she leave the door open? Why did someone else leave a *window* open? Her room might as well be outside.

Kira pauses by the ramshackle wardrobe. She didn't leave her door open; she tripped down the hall from the bathroom, chilly in nothing but a towel, and slammed it behind her. She then collapsed on top of her bed…and stayed there until now.

Kira casts her eyes around the room. It may have been Mathew, but suspicion blooms in bloodstains. The two beds nudge each other for space. The beams dip low. The cases teeter by the table. Still, though, there's *something*.

It's paranoia.

It's not.

It is.

Blankets trailing like a wise man's robes, Kira moves warily to the door. The wind lows. The door hinges judder. Investigating seems like the worst of ideas, but she'll have to leave the room at some point.

Threads of unease rap up her ribs. She steps out onto the landing.

From staircase to fire, all four windows are wide. Kira drops her guard and the blankets. It's madness. Quickly, quietly, she closes the glass. Madness; one window is often cracked, but four? The corridor is frozen. Powdered snow drifts across the floor. The fire, smouldering day and night, is nothing but ash. They must have been open for hours.

Combing the knots in her hair, Kira retreats from the glass. Windows; is that all? After the last two days, it's not surprising she's on edge; it might be weirder if she wasn't. Still, th—

Kira and her thoughts stop dead. Her parents' door is open.

Crudely hacked into the wood is a thin, bare-limbed tree.

Unease seeps into dread. Four lines for branches, one for the ground, and in one corner…

'No,' Kira whispers. The ground feels set to fall. Stabbed on the edge of the symbol is a curling metal flower. 'Please.'

Kira takes a faltering step. Silver and delicate, the flower is familiar. Solid. Cold. Its long stem splinters the door. The wood cracks as she yanks it out, turning it over in her hand. If she only *had* been paranoid; she could go back to bed, close her eyes, and dream about the ocean.

She can't. She has a calling card and the symbol from the wooden window. Whiteland.

Images flash through her head. Romy kicking one leg over the other at the gate in Gatwick, the flower on her boot hanging by a few threads. Romy, buying the very same boots, smiling in a way she never does. Romy, insisting these flimsy boots will see her through a Swiss Christmas.

God, how alike she and Romy can be.

'Dad?' Clenching the pointed flower in her fingers, Kira banishes every single thought except the here and now. 'Hello?' She nudges the bedroom door. 'Dad? Are you there?'

The room beyond is empty. Rumpled bed, strewn sheets. Kira's vision shimmers and settles. On the crocheted carpet, aligned beside Mathew's wallet and phone, is the other silver flower.

No.

'Dad!' Kira wheels around. Flinging herself down the landing, the stairs, she tumbles into the restaurant. 'Dad?' She throws her eyes around the tables. Into corners, behind the bar.

He's not here. Not lounging by the TV, or practising his German. No one's here, bar the ginger man stealing the Wi-Fi and a woman with a coffee in the corner. Her dad's not here, but Romy has been. Her flowers. Her boots.

Kira doesn't think. Grabbing her outerwear, toppling the coat stand, ignoring the crash, she runs.

The train whistles, screeches, and whines as Kira crosses the line. Ignoring black ice, the trees spraying powder, holidaymakers' cars blaring horns and swerving round her, she slips and slides and runs. Normally, she'd feel bad, but they're irrelevant. Trifling. They can't see the horrors running races in her mind, her fear for Mathew, Romy, Anna. What Lena said. What lies in the forest. The silver digs grooves in her palm, and she runs.

'Kira.'

Snow. Chalets. Cars. Trees.

'Kira.'

Fields. Sledges. Waffles. Wine.

'Kira!'

A hand grabs her arm. Jolted back, recoiled like a rope, Kira spins around.

Callum. His face contorts at his bandaged hand, but she barely sees. Can't think. Can't acknowledge. Can't stop. He's a bubble. A blur.

'I need to go.' Gulping air, she jerks away. 'Let me go.'

'No, no. No. Wait.' He plants himself in front of her, wincing and grasping her arms. 'What's happened?'

Everything. Nothing. Kira glances at the forest, wicked, wild, waiting. It waits for her to come to her sister, dad, mum. She doesn't have time for this.

'Callum.' It's almost a whine. Normally, she'd feel bad, but it's irrelevant. Trifling. She doesn't have *time*. 'Just let me go.' She tries to sidestep out of his grip. 'Please? I can't explain right—hey!'

She stumbles as he pushes her backwards across a small patch of snow. 'What do you think you're doing? You can't—' Her back hits a wall. 'Hey!'

Callum slaps the wood on either side of her head. 'What's going on?' Blocking her in, he glares. 'I'm not in the mood for you to lie or to tell me it's nothing. I've just come from a royal bollocking for being unable to work today. I probably won't be able to work for the rest of the holiday, thanks to my hand, so I don't have the time or the patience. What'—his voice drops decibels—'is going on?'

Wither for wither, Kira matches his glare. 'Back off.' She nods at his face, almost butting his chin. Does it look like *she* has the patience? The time? The desire to be stared at by tourists? 'Now.'

With a grunt, he leans back.

'Very kind of you.' Kira brandishes the flower. 'Romy's been to the hotel.'

On either side, Callum's arms stiffen. 'What?'

'Exactly.' Kira flicks the silver. It tings. 'This is from one of her boots, the ones she wore to the hospital. It was stuck in the door of my parents' room. She'd used it to—can you back *off?*' She jerks her forehead forward. Callum leans back farther. 'It's obtrusive. Romy messed up the room, and carved that Whiteland tree into the door, and…' She pauses. Her breath flutters, her mind with it, skitty as a panic attack. 'My dad's gone. Romy took him.'

This doesn't have the desired effect. 'She took him?' Callum lifts a sardonic eyebrow. 'Took him where? The forest? Is that—' He ducks his head. 'That's where you're going. Really?'

Kira lifts her chin. 'Yes.'

Deadpan, Callum looks back up at her. 'You think your sister has escaped from the hospital, kidnapped your father, and taken him to the forest. Our favouritest, favouritest forest.'

'You wanted me to tell you what happened, Callum.' Kira resists the urge to stamp on his feet. 'That's what I'm doing. If yesterday still doesn't make you listen, let me go. I have to find my family.'

They're in there, and they need her.

'No.' Callum shakes his head. 'No, you don't. Not in the forest. Think about it logically.'

'I am.'

'You're not.' He leans in again. They're attracting attention, but Kira couldn't care less. Curious or concerned, passersby can go to hell. 'You're really not.' Callum grates his hands down the wood, the heels pinning her shoulders. 'Can you stop with the William Wallace for a second? Riding into an unequal battle didn't go well for him, and it won't go better for you.'

Kira wrenches at his fingers. He's bigger, though, with a better angle, winters-cutting-firewood strong. 'This isn't *Braveheart*, Callum.'

'I know.' Callum's hands don't waver. 'It's Whiteland. You at least need, I don't know, food. Water. Things pivotal for survival. Plasters, maybe. That's— dammit, Kira!'

Pain flashes through his foot. Stomping on his toes, she ducks beneath his arms and makes a break for the car park. 'Kira, stop! This is ridiculous!' He tosses out his arms. Skirting cars and skidding on ice, she ignores him. 'Ridiculous.' He scrapes his uninjured hand through his hair. 'Fucking ridiculous. Kira!'

Hitting the snowy bank, Kira clambers into the trees. 'Oh, for Christ's—' Callum spins, as if expecting the world to back him up. The boy on the tele-bob stares. Three girls with sledges watch and murmur, hushed like they think they're being subtle. A middle-aged couple, bundled garishly up to the ears, exchange a look. 'Christ.'

He has about a minute before she disappears. Cursing every single god and more, he jogs toward the buvette, yanking out his wallet. Water. Chocolate. Peanuts. Crisps. With his pockets stuffed, he runs toward the trees. Thirty seconds. He should get a prize.

Struggling up to the forest is a riot. 'I hope you realise you could be chasing nothing,' Callum calls. With a stinging foot, a throbbing hand, and the bulkiest, most unwieldy pockets ever known to man, his mood has soured even further. Ahead, not snow-wise enough to have vanished, Kira pushes on. 'You could be putting yourself in danger for no reason. I bet your family are back at the hotel, having tea and crumpets.'

'Nobody said you had to come.' Clambering over a fallen tree, Kira shoots him a withering look. 'You don't owe me anything. Go home if you think it's stupid.'

'I'd love to.' He vaults the tree and spreads his hands. 'I'd sincerely love to go home, have my own tea and crumpets, and complain about the weather. A perfectly dull, perfectly British day, seeing as I may have lost my holiday job. But no!' He waves his hands dramatically. Rolling her eyes, Kira tramps off. 'No, instead I have to follow a crazy blonde girl into magic fairyland because that's where she thinks her family is. What are they doing here, Kira? Building snowmen? Searching for wardrobes?'

Kira gestures over her shoulder, hand tricks that may or may not exist. 'I'll kick you if you carry on.' She trudges into the clearing, past the immaculate bowl and across to the other side. 'Then you'll be useless as a father as well as a ski instructor.'

Laughter barks from Callum's throat. 'Nice.'

'Don't mock me, then. Not after yesterday.'

Callum speeds up. 'All I'm saying'—he falls into step beside her, tugging up his collar against the cold of the trees—'is I don't think this is a good idea. I thought it was a bad plan yesterday, and I think it's an even worse plan now, specifically *because* of yesterday. We nearly got eaten.'

'We did not nearly get eaten.' Coming to an abrupt halt, Kira wheels to face him. 'We got chased. We don't know what they wanted; we don't even know what they were. And I'll say it again.' She forms a frame with her fingers. 'You don't have to come.'

Each word is pointed, enunciated. Eyes wide, hair wild, she could be a forest sprite or a creature born from the mountains. He read a book like that once, with a fox and a forest and a girl made from snow.

'I never even asked you to,' Kira says. Callum blinks himself back. 'I was going to come by myself. I would have, if you hadn't been all "I don't have time for this, tell me what the matter is."' She quotes him with her fingers and a drawn-out eye roll. 'You ignored the warning of girls who look for monsters, so you have no right to complain.'

The sprite image flits away. A shivering breeze settles to silence, as if the world is on mute. 'I'm Scottish,' Callum says. 'I complain for fun. And actually, I do have to come.'

Kira cocks her head. 'Do tell.'

He hesitates. 'After the last two days, you can't be in here alone. No one can. Who knows what might happen.' He shrugs. Casual, even though it's not. If he tried to explain his protective urge, she'd shout her independence and kick him to the curb. He wouldn't blame her, either; it's just as strange for him. 'It's not safe,' he adds, when she regards him critically. 'And no one else can go with you. Knowing what I do, I'd feel guilty if I left.'

Kira huffs. 'Knowing what you do?' Her criticism turns shrewd. 'So you accept things when it suits you, and deny them when it doesn't?' She nods, imitating his earlier tone. 'Nice.'

It's probably deserved; he did pin her against a wall. 'It's not the easiest situation to get my head around.'

'That's an excuse.' Kira shivers, wrapping her arms around her paltry coat.

'Kira.' With a rush of sympathy, Callum sighs. 'I can't say I understand, but I can tell this is hard. This whole situation is hard, and screwed, and largely insane. But hear me out.'

Her frown deepens to grooves.

'Why…' he tries before she can protest. None of this will go down well, but you have to start somewhere. 'Why would Romy want to kidnap your dad? And why would she bring him here? To the forest—the forest within the forest—' He rubs his eyes. 'Whatever. You know. How on earth would she have managed it?'

'It's not—'

'Wait.' Callum holds up his hands. Kira pauses, angling away. 'Physically. That's what I'm getting at. I'm six foot, your dad's taller, and Romy's just…not. She's taller than you, but she's skinny as anything. How can she possibly have taken your dad, in the early morning, without—'

'I don't know.' Kira's voice judders with cold and irritation, defence, desperation, doubt. 'I don't know, okay? But she did. All the windows were open, and…' She rubs her face, up and down. Her skin is raw and numb. Her hands fizz, mottled. *Unprepared.* 'And, I don't know, Callum. You saw what she did to me in the hotel, and what she did to herself. Dad could barely control her then, when she was half dead and he was awake. If she caught him when he was asleep, and she's fully recovered?' She ducks her head. 'I don't know. I really don't know. I just know she's strong and that none of this is right.'

Kira stares through the snow until it glints an afterglow. Callum just stares through the snow. 'I know that normally,' she continues softly, 'Romy can't overpower Dad. She can't take him anywhere, no way. But none of this is normal.' She looks up at Callum, open, raw. 'I keep saying that, as if it makes it okay. That none of this is normal, so anything is possible.' She shakes her head. 'I don't know. But I think…'

The thoughts are incense. They smoke, they smoulder, they form shadows from nothing. Kira breathes. It takes an age to exit her lungs. 'I think I know why she's taken Dad.'

Callum nods. For once, he's watching, eyebrows down, mouth lined. In a planetary ski coat, he's a beacon in the clearing. 'Why?'

'Dad wasn't there when I got back.' Kira tugs on her split ends. The thoughts are still unrolling. 'Still. When he did get back, he said he'd spent a long time telling Romy everything—and I mean everything—even though she was asleep. He wanted to get it straight in his head, to figure out what's going on. He said talking to her was as good a way as any.'

Callum nods again. 'And you think…?'

'That Romy wasn't actually asleep.' Kira holds up her hands. 'Maybe. I don't know. Maybe, while he was talking, she realised where Mum is and left the hospital to follow her.' She lets her hands flop, loose by her sides. 'To stop whatever she's doing.'

Callum frowns. 'Which we haven't figured out.'

'No.' Kira taps on her jeans, one, two, three. The air is growing colder, a sharp, tangy curtain anchoring around them. Knocking on her pulse, her nerves. 'But Romy was insistent that we don't go back to…'

'Whiteland.'

'If you really want to call it that.'

'I'm calling a spade a spade.'

Kira narrows her eyes at him. 'You choose to do that now?'

Callum shrugs. 'Yeah.'

Folding his arms, he says nothing more. The word twists through her chest, dragging blood behind it. Blood, or a vaccine, or anything else that pierces your veins and floods your body with cold. 'Okay.' She rubs her arms through her bobbled sleeves. 'Um. I don't know if it's better or worse that you're with me.'

Looking up, Callum meets her gaze. 'Madness loves company, right?'

A smile plucks Kira's lips. 'That's misery.'

'Same difference.' Callum shrugs. His eyes catch hers, wary and snagging. He works his hesitant mouth. 'Why…ah.' He shakes his head and looks up. 'I'm sorry. I'm only really good at being blunt. Why did Romy take your dad?'

Kira shivers. It's easy to forget where they are, in the middle of a forest that taunts them. 'To try and blackmail Mum into stopping?' she suggests. The trees sigh. She shivers again. The atmosphere is dead, airless. 'For company? I wouldn't put anything past—oh.'

Her head jerks up like a puppet on a string. Something's changed. The air was pressured, but now it lifts, a glittered sharpening of the trees, the snow, the clouds. Kira sweeps her gaze across the clearing. The hollow tree, the way they came. She lifts her chin. 'It's happening.'

The snow is close to a painful brightness. The trees grow focused, angular.

'Is that a good thing?' Callum asks. Lifting his bandaged hand, he lowers it again. 'I can't tell.'

The breeze sighs. Kira can almost see it, skittering over the powder. 'You feel it,' she murmurs. 'It's sharp and kind of strange. Like when you've had too much coffee and the world seems detached. Also…' She turns in a slow, slow circle. 'Ah. As much as I hate to say it, it looks like a video game.'

Peter, for thirteen hours straight, hooked on *Red Dead Redemption*. Herself, for a meagre seven hours, capering on a CGI horse.

'A really good game, though,' she adds, 'that's close to being real. The recent kinds that are still too bright and jerky but are great otherw—'

'Cliff.' Abrupt and alarmed, Callum grabs her arm. 'In this game, there's a cliff.'

'Wh—'

'Don't move.' Hauling her toward him, Callum stumbles back farther into the clearing. The forest whirls. His gloves grip her in place. His heart beats against her chest. Kira's fizzes. He's so— 'Over your shoulder. Look.'

Gingerly turning her head, Kira looks. 'Oh, wow.'

'Exactly.' Carefully, Callum slackens his grip, and carefully, Kira turns. Where there should have been trees, a sheer cliff face falls, bare rock and drifts of snow tumbling into a gully. On the far, far side, the forest continues, rising in shrouds of cloud.

Dusted shadows in a sandstorm. Telegraph poles as the sand takes over. Kira moves back, back, back, bumping Callum through the snow. Her eyes stretch wide. Her mind is cold, dropping by degrees, leaving her losing her breath. Are they safe? If the forest can do that at will, what's to stop it from creating a chasm, and…

'…There, and then it was,' Callum says. Kira snaps her spell of chaos. It could be another burning ocean, reeling her in to its maw. 'I didn't see it happen, but we were standing on the edge.' He eyes the cliff face uneasily. 'I guess we're in, boys.'

The drop is clean, vertical, down to a river no wider than rope. If Callum hadn't grabbed her… 'And I guess we're not getting out.'

Doubts rise up to burst their banks. Get out now, or ever? If the forest *does* change at will, how will they find their way? How will they search for Anna and Romy? How will they *survive*, unless the forest wants them to?

It's too late for that. They'll have to plan as they go. Whiteland is beckoning, and they can only obey.

22

The doors

On a bench at the tip of the mountain, Lena stills, looks up, and knows. As surely as she knows her own name, she knows. Whiteland has opened its doors.

Idiots. Standing, she scans the play park for her children. Even after her warnings; even after the Whispers sent the mist. What absolute, godforsaken idiots. 'Karl!' she barks, spying her brood. 'Julia! Time to go.'

Throwing snowballs at an older boy sheltered atop the slide, the brood reluctantly migrates. 'Come on.' She claps her hands, and they scuttle behind her. Performing a smart one-eighty, she slides down the snowy hill toward the train line. 'Oh, my days, come *on*.'

The train, a tiresome locomotive if ever there was one, chugs into motion. 'Come on, come on, come on. I don't have—yes.' Grabbing the twins' hands, she hauls them over the tracks, ploughing through snowdrifts to the footpath and skidding down to the village.

The ten-minute descent takes five. Karl and Julia gasp for breath, whining to slow down, but Lena can't. Won't. There's no *time*. Mounting the snow-sprayed steps in a heartbeat, she ducks the frosted arch and struggles up the slope to slam her fist against the door.

Carol answers at once. Lena ushers her grumpy children in and they topple onto the sofa, loudly lamenting their awful ordeal to the boys in front of the screen. Carol turns to watch them go. 'Come in, by all means.'

'You have to take them.' Lena cuts her off. It isn't a plea but a statement, intent beneath her breath. 'I don't know how long for, but I can't ask anyone else.'

Carol's eyebrows only rise. She pulls down her cardigan sleeves. The winter is blowing in cold through the door, but there's no time to go inside. 'Take who?'

Lena splays her hand on the doorframe. Tense, taut, fingers tapping. 'The children.' She nods at the sofa. 'Karl and Julia. I have to go somewhere, and they can't come with me.'

Carol glances over Lena's shoulder warily, suspiciously, as if the somewhere lurks behind her. 'Where?'

Lena merely looks at her.

'No.' Carol's shoulders slump, deflating like the wind has been whistled from her wings. 'No, no, no, Lena, *why*?' Her voice pitches, high but hushed. 'Why would you go there?'

Lena shoots a glance at the children. Engrossed in a garish, glaring cartoon, they aren't even half-listening. 'I have to.' Urgent, her fingers tap-tap-tap. 'Carol, that's where she's gone. You think she'd know better, or at least be subtle, but no. That stupid bloody woman.'

Carol's expression hardens. 'So?' Windows shut, shutters down, she battles for control. 'The whole point of watching is to watch, not to follow. I can't believe you'd risk your*self*—'

'I'm not. Not for her.' Lena's face twists into a bony grimace. 'I'm following Kira. That goddamn *family*. I tried to warn her off, but she's gone looking for her mother, and now I have to go and get her back.'

Behind them, the TV hops. Advert, news, a snippet of music. 'Why?' Carol raises her shoulders, her palms. 'We don't know her. Why does it matter if she's followed her mum? I assume it was her choice.'

She's going to have to spell it out. 'Carol.' Lena shoots another look at the children. Jay, giggling, shoving the TV remote up his T-shirt. Julia, trying to grab it. A gastric band tightens her chest. 'Carol, Callum went with her.'

The shutters drop. Carol's face is disbelief, horror, ash. 'What?' she whispers. Her crow's feet crease at the corners. 'Why? I knew I shouldn't—I shouldn't have let her in here, but...' She shakes her head. Her mouth opens, shuts. 'I thought he had more sense. I thought he'd be able to fight it. How is he already so—'

Her voice catches and snaps at the end. Lena looks away. Her twins are inside, sprawled beside the dog, and Callum is lost. Out there, unprepared, doing the very thing she told him not to: following Kira McFadden into hell.

'Does he know?' Carol pushes out, each word a flutter. 'Does he know what he's got himself into?'

Lena doesn't answer right away. It might be easier for her to believe he doesn't.

It might, but it's a lie.

'He knows.' She sighs. Lying is unsavoury. 'From what I can tell, he knows as much as she does, which apparently isn't enough. If it was, they wouldn't have—Carol.' She takes her friend's hands and grips them. Pale and pained, close to distraught, Carol has started to shake. 'I'll find him. You couldn't have stopped this from happening, so don't you dare think you could. You know that Callum was the one who found Rosemarie, which was godawful timing, and you know what they're both the daughters of. He didn't stand a chance.'

Carol's face caves in. Lena grimaces again; it was meant to be a comfort but came out like a slap. 'All I meant is that it's not your fault.' She squeezes Carol's hands, hard. 'Look after my children. I'll get Callum out.'

Releasing Carol's hands, she steps back. Whiteland is beckoning, and she can only obey.

23

The dark

Dusk falls so fast it takes Kira by surprise. One second it's daylight, in three more it's night; and in a world that's not her own, she's not herself.

They passed the wooden window almost straight away. The symbol had quietly vanished, and they peered through the frame for the fork; but there was nothing. No change to the tree-lined road ahead; no change to anything at all. After that, they could only walk.

It was so monochrome that Kira ceased to think. Ceased to see anything but the road, slowly sloping, ceased to hear anything but flat, dull steps.

Until the night flicks on like a light.

She sways. 'How long has it been dark?' She spins on the spot. The road tapers off into darkness, their footprints hardly there. As monotonous as if they've been walking in place, hour after hour after hour. Disquiet unfurls behind her ribs. They're anywhere and nowhere. 'How did we not see it happen? At least, how did *I* not—'

'It's the same as yesterday,' Callum muses.

Kira bristles. Rude. 'I was speaking, Callum.'

'Mm.' He stares off into the darkness. She shoots a glare at his cheek. 'I know.'

Rude. Disrespectful. Uncouth. Kira clenches her fist. She could almost hit him. If she did, he wouldn't interrupt again. He'd have neither the breath nor desire, bruised in the throat, in the teeth—

Oh, God. Kira grabs her fist. It was reeling up and back, and she chills from her skin to her roiling insides; he's right. It's exactly the same as yesterday. Turning her back on Callum, she stretches out her fingers, one by cramping, clamping one. The redness, the fury, is fading fast, but she can't take any chances. Yesterday, she let it win. Yesterday, she hit him.

'Are you all right?' Callum touches her back.

Kira jerks away. 'Don't touch me.'

The fury simmers. She closes her eyes. Unclenching her fists, she breathes. 'I'm sorry.'

'No, I'm sorry.' Callum's voice is full of love notes and tacky romantic films. 'I really am. What did I do?'

Cautiously, Kira turns to face him. Her anger spikes and dies. 'Nothing.' She lets out a breath of relief. His eyes, his anguish; none of this is real. *None of this is real.* 'It's this place. It's messing with us already. It's making me a psychopath, and you'—she points—'a lovesick fool. Again.' She circles his face with her finger. 'You're looking at me like Frodo looks at Sam.'

Vacuous, Callum blinks. 'What?' He lifts a hand, lowers it. At the fourth blink, his face clears. 'Oh, fuck me.' He rubs his eyes with his knuckles. 'Why has that become a thing?'

Kira grips her arms and shivers. 'Because we let it in.'

Her own words chill her. Now that she's awake, there are other things, too; the icy air, the lifelessness, the night's uncanny quiet. How did she not see it, feel it, hear it, smell it, even? Were they so far away inside themselves that the outside ceased to exist? There should be owls. There should be foxes. There should be rustling, the smell of pine, the wild scent of snow.

There should have been a sunset.

'I don't remember seeing anything since we passed the window.' Kira casts a baleful eye around them. This is all feeling like a huge, giant, supernova mistake. 'Do you?'

Callum opens his mouth. 'We gave up looking for the fork.' She nods. 'And then…'

His face goes blank.

'I.' He mouths for two seconds, three. In her mind, his thoughts go tick, tick, tock. 'Well, that's a bit of a bugger.'

Kira flashes her eyebrows. 'That's one way of putting it. We really need to…' *Be careful* is an appalling understatement. Stay awake? Stay sane? Stay *them*? 'We need to have our thoughts on guard, or something. I know it sounds stupid, but whatever "it" is, it's getting to us way too easily. We should stay distracted. We should, you know.'

Her voice trails off with her thoughts, eclipsed by a sudden, sweeping sense of *what the hell are we doing?* This, all of this, this risk, this madness…they have no idea—*no idea*—what they're getting themselves into. If they let it, this place will chew them up and spit them out for fun.

'You know, we can still turn around,' Callum says, as casually as if it's an option. His voice cuts through the deadened night, and at once she knows: they can't do that. *She* can't do that. Yes, this is crazy, and she's basically bringing an apple to a battle, but she can't go back. It's cowardice. This may not be bravery, but it's certainly bravado.

'No.' Folding her arms, Kira hugs her elbows. The word feels more real, more hefty, more anchored than anything else so far. It's a commitment. She needs to find her family. She *will* find her family. 'I mean, *you* can.'

'Don't be daft.'

'But I—' She stops and blinks at him. 'I'm not being daft. You could go back. You have every right to leave.'

'True.' Callum crooks a finger at her, the trees, and the sky. 'But I'm not going to. What kind of shitty man would I be if I left right now?'

Kira digs her nails into her arms. 'Yes, but—'

'No "yes, but."' Callum shakes his head. 'No, no. No, no.'

Kira turns away from him. 'But I really don't want you to—oh.' Her voice pitches. Reality bends. 'That's new.'

Callum barks a 'ha!' of surprise. Kira flinches. The sound travels on, and on, and on. 'Amazing,' he remarks. 'Some more moving trees. Did you see it coming?' Shaking his head, he sticks an elbow on her shoulder. 'I didn't. I definitely didn't see it coming.'

His sarcasm lightens what could have been dread. Instead of its endless forever, the road cuts off abruptly, a dark, dense, dead-end line of foliage in its place. With a fairly delirious disbelief, Kira surveys it. A thin, wood-chipped path winds in, and slicing the snow in front of her, its message is clear.

Fine. *Fine.*

'You know.' Leaning into Callum's elbow, she sighs heavily. 'I'm not sure, but I think'—she points—'and correct me if I'm wrong, but I think the forest wants us to go this way.'

Callum snorts. 'The forest is annoying.' He calls up to the treetops. 'Do you hear that, guys? You're annoying.'

'Shh.' Kira elbows him.

He grins. 'What? It is annoying. Ordering us around like this; who does it think it is?'

Kira pulls out her phone. 'Probably master of puppets.' She presses buttons, taps the screen: no response. By now, she wasn't expecting one. 'Do you have a torch in your hamster cheeks?'

She gestures at his pockets. Shooting her a look that says *shush*, Callum digs in his jeans. A keyring emerges jangling, flush with keys, a fluorescent lighter, a beaming maple leaf—*Canada!*—and a teeny, tiny torch. 'I do.'

Kira tilts her head. 'It looks like you meant to shrink your kids but pulled a faulty lever.'

Callum detaches it. 'Don't knock Trevor. We'll show up for animals, and that's the main thing.'

'What?' Kira's mockery pops and fizzles. 'Animals? What do you mean?'

Callum frowns. 'I mean animals?' He waves the torch around them. 'Kira, we're in the Alps. We're up a mountain in the Alps. There's wildlife.'

Ruefully, Kira hugs herself. 'I know, but...'

'You were hoping for something cute?' Callum smirks. 'Wild horses?'

'It's not the New Forest.'

'Good. I'm glad we've cleared that up.' Callum drops the teasing. 'I'm just going to say it. There are lynx around here, but they shouldn't approach us, especially if we're visible.'

For a moment, Kira gapes. 'This is the worst idea I've ever had.' Rotating, she rakes a hand through her hair. 'I should paint a fresco.' She frames it with her fingers. '"The Mistakes of Kira McFadden." Or, better yet, sculpt a frieze and fill it with reasons why we're doomed.'

'Hey.' Callum taps her arm. 'Listen. I've only ever seen a lynx once in the wild, and it wasn't in magic forest land. It wasn't in a forest at all. And.' He taps again. She angles herself away. Being tapped is so irksome. 'They might not even exist here. The only creature we've seen so far was that hummingbird. And the rampant mist beasts, but we were in the real world when that happened, so they don't count.'

He tenses, then shakes his head. 'Wow.' He laughs. 'That sounded insane. Do you realise what you've done to me? I'm talking like this is believable.'

Kira *hmm*s. 'Not logical, though.' She twists her mouth. 'If anything, the rampant mist beasts count times a hundred, because Whiteland's where they came from. And we must have been at least on the border then.'

Callum clicks the tiny torch on. Its equally tiny beam illumines the dense, hulking trees, hip to hip and front to back and swallowing the night. 'I was trying,' he says, 'to make you feel better.' He swings the torch around. 'I resign.'

Kira hugs her ribcage and doesn't even *hmm*. The wood-chipped path is no longer funny, the demise of the road more menacing than cliché. Anything could be hiding in the dark. 'What was it doing?' she asks. 'When you saw it?'

Callum turns. The less-than-blinding beam turns, too. 'Um. What was what doing when?'

Kira lifts a hand to block the light. 'The lynx you saw,' she clarifies. 'What did you see it doing?'

'More or less running straight at me. No, wait!' Callum holds up his hands as Kira's head whips round, aghast, astounded, sick. 'I'm sorry. That was an exception. It thought we were deer.'

'How on *earth* did it think you were deer?' Kira cries.

'We were standing in the dark and not making any noise.' Slowly, Callum lowers his hands. The torch rights itself. 'My ex was taking photos of the lights along the lake, and I was trying not to distract her. If we keep moving, keep the torch on, and make noise, we'll be fine.' He swings the narrow beam toward the narrow path ahead. It wanders in a crooked line, as dogged as the trees, as far as Kira's straining eyes can see. 'Trust me.'

And this is her travelling companion. Such fun. 'If you want me to trust you, work on your reveals.' Kira lays a hand on her juddering heart. 'Dropping bombs like "there are lynx in here" and "the first and last time I saw one it attacked me" is not the way to go.' She steels herself. 'Okay.'

Blowing out her lips, she walks into the torchlit trees.

And this is his travelling companion. Callum stares. 'I thought you were afraid.'

'I am.' Kira glances back, a silhouette flickering in the painted yellow glow. 'But I'd rather get it over with. Overthinking is an art form, and I'm better at it than I am at oils.'

'How good are you at oils?'

'Very.'

Callum flashes his eyebrows. 'Fair enough.'

'And besides.' Kira lifts her voice. It wavers. 'Based on the way the trees became a cliff, we can't just head on home.'

She has a point. Begrudgingly, Callum steps onto the woodchips. Their crunch is muted. He'd rather it was loud. For all his joking, he's afraid, too.

'We're going on a bear hunt!' he mutters, as the road fades and the forest enfolds them. The silence is an eiderdown. No rustling leaves, no creaking branches, no shifting of a breeze. No cheeping birds, of the kind who wake you at dawn in the spring. He pulls a series of faces, each more gaudy than the last. It's far too bloody quiet.

'Oh, a *forest*!' he continues, soft beneath his breath. The eiderdown stifles his mind, smothering his lungs. 'A really tall forest! We can't go over it, can't go under it. I guess we're going through it.' He sweeps the torch beam behind them. Snow, skeletal branches, dark. 'We're going on a bear hunt.'

'There'd better not be bears in here.' Kira shoots him a look. 'If there are, you *really* need to work on your reveals. Riddles are also not okay.'

In two long strides, Callum is beside her. 'There are no bears,' he says, shining the torch into the trees. 'It's a kids' book.' He arcs the beam back to the path. 'It seemed to fit. You said we need distractions, to ward off the psycho and the lovesick fool.'

Kira nods. 'Now *there's* a book.' She thinks for a moment. 'What about *The Psycho, the Fool, and the Aimless Wander?*'

Callum waggles the torch side to side. 'Mm. Sounds like literary criticism, or something equally fun.'

Kira pushes out her lips. 'True. *The Psycho and the Lovesick Fool* could be the first book, followed by *Those Without a Plan*, topped off with the great *No End Game.*'

Callum laughs, actually laughs, with a kind of pleased surprise. 'Maybe you should be a writer. Those are actually cool. Although those without a plan really should make a plan if they don't want to wander forever in the dark.'

Kira nods and nods again. They lapse into silence. A plan. First port of call: somewhere to spend the night. Second port of call: come up with a third.

Her thoughts stall, sucked by a bog. She's dreaming. Drunk.

Oh, God.

'Beaches,' she says. It can't grab hold already. It won't. 'I counter your bears with beaches.'

Powder drifts from a body-sized branch, dancing in the yellow light. It could be gauze, a net curtain, summer rain. 'Beaches,' Callum repeats. 'You want to talk about beaches?'

Kira raises her hands, palms up. 'I live by the beach. Romy always moans, and it always rains, but that's where I am right now. There's nothing remotely scary about it.'

Callum thinks. 'Jellyfish?'

Kira sidesteps this. 'Ice cream,' she says wistfully. She doesn't care for ice cream, but it's bright, and she's hungry. 'Ice cream, and parties in beach huts, and cursing the sand and the wind. The thought of relaxing on the beach is always better than reality.'

Callum eyes her scornfully. 'No, it's not.'

'I assure you, it is in Devon.'

Callum draws a circle with the torch. 'All right.' His words twitch with humour. 'Sharks, then. You can't just snub me and think about food. Failing jellyfish, there must be sharks.'

Kira taps his arm. 'There are, but you lose. Since 1847'—one tap per syllable, see how he likes it—'there have only been two unprovoked attacks off the British coast. If you're trying to ruin my haven, do better.' She shoots him a torchlit smugness. 'Ha.'

Quietly, Callum laughs. 'You know sharks?'

'Dad studied marine biology.' Kira stops the hand with the torch tracing an infinity line, a star. Apart from being inattentive, it's dizzying. 'He never got a relevant job, so he sprinkles it over us at home. When we were kids, it was a new fact every few days, and he'd test us in the car.' Sat in the passenger seat, Romy in the back. *How far can ocean trenches reach? The reward is Maltesers.* 'Most of them don't stick around, but that one's nicely reassuring.'

Callum nods. 'What does he do, then? Whoa.'

The woodchips swerve steeply, golden-brown in the beam. 'He owns a used motorbike company,' Kira says, swaying to stay on the path. 'But he only really enjoys marine—what was that?'

She stops. A rustle flits through the trees ahead, faint but undeniable. 'Leaves?' Callum suggests. 'Or—'

The torch burns to black.

24

The spectres

The rustling dies with the death of the light. Kira stares at the spot where the beam should have been, uncomprehending, dumbfounded. The darkness bursts with afterglow. She hardly dares to breathe.

A rough slap and grunt cuts the quiet in two. 'Work, goddammit,' Callum mutters, hitting the torch against his palm. Prickled with jittery, nervous heat, Kira tries to summon a smile. In the middle of a forest, in the middle of the night, it's still the way to fix electrics: slap and hope for the best. It's familiar, comforting…and at least they aren't being attacked.

Yet.

The smile slips to the forest floor. What happened to the rustling? She stares around at the useless dark. The only sounds are Callum slapping and her heartbeat thrumming in her ears. Her vision isn't adjusting. The disorientation is giddy, the heady dark complete. She can't see so much as her breath.

They can't go forward. They can't go back. *We can't go over it, can't go under it. I guess we're going through it.*

Great. He also said they need to keep moving, keep a light on, and make noise.

Great. Worry expands in her chest like air. The Mistakes of Kira McFadden, part two: all the reasons this was poorly thought through.

A pinprick of brightness flickers into view. Kira blinks. Far in the distance, it doesn't seem real. It's her eyes playing tricks, scuppered still by afterglow and her ache for the torch to live. Shutting her eyes, she looks again. The pinprick, the beacon, the fire winks on. And if she's not mistaken, it's brighter.

'Callum.' She reaches blindly for his arm. Her voice is uncomfortably loud, and she drops it. 'Callum, there's a light.'

Callum looks up; or rather, he believes he looks up. The night is too thick, too heavy to tell. His sense of grounding is Kira's hand. 'Where?' he whispers, balance wavering. Looking around will knock him flat. 'I can't…'

The light splits in two, and suddenly, he can. '…See.' He finishes on a downward breath. The lights pulse. God almighty, strike him down. Shrinking and flaring like a lighthouse in the fog, they split into four.

The rustle wakes up.

'They're coming toward us,' Kira whispers. In his peripheral vision, she's a shadow, where before she was words in the black. Transfixed, Callum nods. 'What do we do?'

Pushing the torch back into his pocket, Callum sets his mouth. 'We don't have much choice.' He tears his eyes away. Kira's face is brightening, spotlit. 'We either stay here, where we'll see what's coming at us, or we bugger off into the dark, where we could meet something worse that we'd never know is there.'

'Loving the optimism, Callum.' Kira flexes her fingers, warm in thick wool, scrunching her numbing toes. Every muscle sits coiled and afraid. 'Lights can't kill us, though, right?'

'You'd hope not.' Callum meets her eye, and she quails. There's more than apprehension; he's just as afraid as she is. 'Maybe if we don't stare at them too— Jesus!'

Kira snaps her head around. Sixteen lights now glide toward them, throwing the trees into stark silhouette. The rustle rushes louder, whirring feathers and breeze-blown leaves, lifting her hair, and the lights…Kira's breath slips back into her lungs. The lights are growing, morphing, weaving past each other in a weaving dance. No longer a blazing white, they blur into blue, emerald, gold… and as they swoop closer, dipping through the trees, Kira sees.

'They're birds,' she whispers. Her hand drifts to Callum's arm. 'The wings. That's what we can hear.' She shakes her head, faint with wonder. 'Callum, they're *birds.*'

They are. Setting the dark alive with colour, they're birds, and they're mesmerising. Feathers flash as they approach—the outline of talons, the arch of a head—but the lights, glowing bright on their wingtips, are what lull Kira, entranced.

'I hope this is a good thing,' Callum murmurs. Open-mouthed, Kira can only stare: alighting on branches and treetops, the birds settle a crescent moon around the wood-chipped path. Absent in voice, their wings crescendo. Fourteen, fifteen, sixteen, they land, until, draining of colour and sound, the trees become darkly still.

Kira holds her breath. For a moment, nothing happens. The trees are as statuesque, speechless, and black as if the birds were apparitions. Callum draws her toward him, and she lets him. Her pulse is a thunderstorm, his body on edge. The birds can't have disappeared. They must be there, perched in the dark, waiting for something to happen.

A soft white bursts into tiny, bright life, miniscule and hypnotic. Lifting from a branch directly above them, two sparks soar into the sky. Kira cranes her neck back. Higher and higher they rise through the black, beating a steady pulse. She smiles. Her head comes to rest against Callum's shoulder. The lights dance where the stars should be, cresting the shadowy trees. It's beautiful, dreamlike, otherworldly magic; and suddenly, it stops.

Raven-dark, fifty feet high. Larger than an eagle, refined as a stork, the silhouetted bird hovers, beating its wings. It feels like it's watching. Its eyes are a pressure. It craves comprehension, and slowly, it arrives.

The sound of leaves leaps back to life. The treetops rush like wind. Pockets of air flow through the forest, drifting over in drafts. The branches creak at takeoff, and the birds begin to fly.

But not away. With their curious colours growing, the lights glide behind Callum, buffeting the air in the direction of his back. Bewildered, he glances down. He can feel every inch of Kira's head, still resting on his shoulder. Her body heat warms his front. She's fused, fusing through him, staring up. For a moment, he's riveted, caught. Illuminated and far away, she's ethereal: an Icelandic kind of pale, her eyes a frosted blue. A fairy. A pixie. A ghost.

The words roll through his mind, and he's struck by how she fits. As much a spirit of the forest as the birds, dyed by the lights as they grow and glow.

Resisting the urge to put his arms around her, Callum shakes his fascination. They're close to strangers, and they could be in danger. The birds are behind them; they need to think, speak, move.

Kira lifts her head and walks off. Again.

'Hey!' Callum flings out his arms. 'What are you—'

A sweep of air pushes him in her wake. He shoots his disapproval back at the birds, part indignant, largely concerned. They did that on purpose. Was he being too slow?

Shadowy wings make the air throb, buffeting him on with the breeze. The pulsing lights move with them. 'Of course.' Callum turns to face the front. The bird above the forest casts a glow through the trees. 'They're taking us somewhere. Lovely.'

The air swerves, and he stumbles. Up ahead, Kira steps off the path.

'Kira!' Callum follows unwillingly behind her. She didn't question it; she didn't look twice. 'Hey! Why are you following them?' He jogs to catch her up. 'How did you know that's what they wanted? We were warned this place was dangerous. They could be taking us to our deaths.'

The breeze nudges right. His forehead furrows. Smooth and effortless, it sweeps them along, like the rapids at a swimming pool. It isn't unpleasant, but it's *strange*.

'They could be the mist fowl,' he continues. Kira's stillness is disquieting, her silence even more so. Has the forest got to her? Have the birds? 'Or'—he puts a hand on her shoulder, ready to pull her out—'they could be taking us nowhere. They're birds. Weird birds, granted, but birds. What happens if they get us lost?'

Kira pulls her mouth down at the corners. Relief sinks through Callum like an innocent witch, plunging to the river's depths.

'We were already lost,' she says. Her face is a ghost of wing-tip colour. 'I know it's strange, but they're helping us. I felt the shepherd bird watching me, and when I looked up, I knew.' Bemusement glimmers over her face. 'It goes beyond strange, in fact.'

Callum's eyebrows lift, lift, lift. 'You don't say.'

Bemusement blends with discomfort. 'It's better than standing in the dark.' Ducking her head, she mumbles into the folds of her coat. 'They wanted us to walk, so I did. I knew that, just like I know we'll be safe.' She lifts her shoulders, meek and bleak. 'Call it mad, but at least I'm not trying to hit you.'

Callum sighs. Sighs again, more for bluster and show. 'True,' he concedes. Her dejection is chastening. 'And at least I'm not the lovesick fool.'

Kira smiles, small but there. 'It'll be a proposal next.'

Callum narrows his eyes at her. 'Funny.'

He looks back to their iridescent, spotlit path. It's a trail of breadcrumbs. It's a trap.

It's a mind game *and* a trap.

He sighs, neither for bluster nor show. It's all they have. God*damn*.

Out of Kira's line of sight, he shoves his hands in his pockets and surrenders himself to the birds.

25

The spark

When the white from the shepherd bird veers to the left, the jerk in the air is a shock. Callum staggers. Kira grabs him, fighting to stay on her feet. Her heart swoops with her stomach, her head. The billowing air realigns behind them, and the birds light their path anew.

Despite the eerie, dancing colour, the forest seems to have darkened. Darker, deeper, denser, nefarious. The trees knot closer together; the undergrowth crackles obtrusively, wily and sly where it juts from the snow. Kira shivers. Spine-like bushes creep up to her shoulders, forming arches and hurdles and warrens and webs. Before, she felt safe, but with the eras, eons, ages they've walked, both trust and knowing have dimmed.

'Can I say I told you so yet?' Callum whispers. 'They're trying to get us lost.'

Kira twines her fingers together. 'They're not.'

Maybe, though. Maybe they are. Maybe whatever she felt was a trick. Maybe it's a wicked-witch trap.

Kira shivers again. It's too late for that; the forest is finally changing. It's brooding, watching. Breathing, waiting. As though they've left its extremities and are encroaching on the heart.

The stirrings of panic bloom cool in her chest. What if the forest *has* come alive and sent something after them? Masked by their human noise, shades or beasts or worse? An illustration swims to the front of her mind: thunderous fire pouring through a forest, a snorting fiend giving chase. The flames keep it hidden, but you hear its rumble, violence whooshing on the air.

The Minpins; that was it. It chilled her as a child, and it chills her now. What if the creatures from the mist are slinking—

A squat shape looms in the light from the birds. Kira's thoughts shatter. Her panic plummets cold. They're here, not behind but in front, arriving with a whimper instead of a bang—

Callum snorts. 'A cabin? No chance. Not a *chance*.' Doggedly, he shakes his head. Kira's panic falters. 'We all know how that ends.' He extends an arm to guide them away, but the buffeting air beats back. 'I don't think,' he insists, more urgently, 'we should let them lead us there.'

'Too late.'

Sheltered by trees, the cabin lies ahead, and while gentle, the wings push them on. Kira swallows her panic back into its pit. It scrabbles, but she locks the cage. It won't help. The birds slow, their lights dim. In seconds, they've arrived.

Callum exhales, long and displeased. Branches creak as the birds settle, nestling into the trees. 'I'm guessing this is us now.'

Kira ignores him. Made ominous by loneliness, the cabin in fact is calming. It's log-built, small, and crooked, with reindeer carved into the shutters, snowflakes drifting down the door, and, perched like the hat of a drunkard, a precarious chimney is warped on the roof. Her scrabbling panic stops beating at the bars. It has no path, no porch, no garden. Both windows are dark, but it's comfortable, cheering. It looks like a rustic home.

A rustic home with a homely aunt, hoping to bustle them in. Fire lit, tea brewing, black forest gateau on the table. After trekking through the day, and the dark, and the cold, it's so tempting to just let go.

With the sound of wind through leaves, the birds whisper back to life. Their wings flare, beating at the air. A gentle breath escapes Kira's lips. She shades her eyes, squinting. 'I...'

Her voice sighs back down her throat. In a scattered, graceful group, the birds lift into the sky. Slender shadows, they circle and soar, their wingtips violet, scarlet, rose. They are silent bar the air they move. They are phantoms in the trees. They blend to a single spark of white, and soon enough, to black.

The wind becomes a draft. The draft becomes the rustle. The rustle flutters into stillness.

'I...' Kira shakes her head. 'I can't believe they existed.' Swallowing, she turns to Callum, sizing up the cabin. The dark resolves around them. 'They were beautiful. Weren't they?'

Arms folded dubiously, Callum's voice is a frown. 'Indeed,' he says, a charcoal outline, a sketch. 'But I don't like their judgment. They've left us outside a deserted cabin, in the middle of a forest, in the dark.' His hand bashes her wrist. In her mind's eye, he's open-armed, informing the world that it's made of nit-wits. 'When has that ever been a good thing?'

Kira's beauty-fuelled awe dissolves. 'We're not in a horror film, Callum.' She sighs. 'Shut-up houses don't have to mean death. And this one's too cute. Or'—she waves to where it lurks in the night—'it was.'

'From the outside,' Callum retorts, full of Homer Simpson meaning. 'Anything could be *in*side. Have you heard of Hansel and Gretel? A house made of sweets, behind which hid a—oh, no, no.' He reaches for her as, mis-judging his location, she catches his side on her way to the house. 'No, you don't. Hey!'

Sidestepping deftly, Kira stretches out her arms, carrying on through the black. Her breath mists faintly, ghostly and pale. Snow crunches under her boots, a crisp, hard crust. If she listens to him, his words will start to itch, and then they'll be back where they started: sightless, lost, and vulnerable, inside and out.

'That's nice, dear,' she says under her breath as his teeth-gritted warnings chunter on. The cabin had been to her left, so if she moves in that direction, at some point she should…

…Hit it. Her hands knock wood, and she jumps. Fingertips brushing the logs, she moves right until they dip.

The door. Relief twists a scoubidou with nerves, apprehension.

Beneath her hands, the wood shifts. Her pulse skitters. Her head shoots hot. The door cracks open on its own.

Light blooms. Kira blinks. That was far too easy; without a *screee*, with-out a groan, with only the sense of a tired fellow lumbering from his slumber, the cabin invites them in. The itch has become a scratch. *Could* this be a wick-ed-witch trap?

Callum still hasn't shut up. Segueing from Hansel and Gretel, he's wound up somewhere in Russia, telling tales of Baba Yaga and endless impossible trials.

'Callum.' Kira pivots on the threshold. Callum looks like a baby presented with a maths book. 'Two things: one, Baba Yaga's hut sat on chicken legs, not frog's legs, and two'—she pivots back—'shut up.'

He might be right. He might not. It might be a trap. It might be an ark. Either way, her breath is pluming, the night is weighty, and she's tired. Kira steps through the door.

The light flares, sputters, and shrinks into a candle, proud on a stool in a corner. Unthreatened by witches, ovens, or trials, Kira considers it.

Reluctance steams off Callum as he enters. 'And that came from where?' Kira sighs and rubs her eyes. 'Shut the door.'

He lets out a noise between a grunt and a groan. It sounds like a frog in his throat. 'Kira.' He tips his head back. 'Kira, this is mad.'

'It is what it is.' Shutting the door decisively, Kira blocks out the night. 'Sentient birds led us here. It's all mad.'

A hearth to the left of the candle sparks. Kira starts. Crimson flickers in the kindling, and the high pile bursts into life.

Sweet resin, woodsmoke, a dry waft of heat. The rest of the cabin sidles from the dark. A wooden chair and table cosy in a corner, opposite the candle on its three-legged stool. A single bed sleeps in another, heaped with hefty woollen throws. The fire scorches against the far wall, befriended by a plump rocking chair and a scratchy, scarlet rug. It smells of warmth, of pine, of Callum's chalet. Unless there's a secret satanic basement, it's everything they need.

'There's no kitchen.' Callum looks around, again, again, as if it might hide in a wall. His surprise is amazing, his dismay is better, and his discontent is the best. Beginning to uncoil, Kira can't help but laugh.

'Your priorities astonish me.' She drags out the chair. It doesn't make a sound. Stalling, she slowly sits. Bizarre. 'Maybe it isn't a home.' She peels off her outerwear. Sweat spots damp beneath her arms, and she wriggles. 'It could be a refuge, like they have in the mountains. They don't always have kitchens, right?'

Callum drops into the rocking chair. The cushions puff and huff. 'No.'

'There you go.' Kira strokes the table thoughtfully. Scratched on the edge is the sketchy tree. 'Or maybe Whiteland doesn't do kitchens.'

Callum shoots her his full disapproval. 'What kind of place'—he extends it into every nook and cranny—'doesn't do kitchens? What's the point?'

Kira twists her hair around her fingers. She should have thought to bring a comb. 'If I were you, I wouldn't question it. This is the only shelter we've seen. I imagine whatever lit the fire and the candle can kick us out if we're rude.'

Her bladder twinges. Kira zeroes in. Suddenly, she can feel it straining against her jeans. Oh, dear. Never mind a comb; she didn't bring anything. Callum told her to, but she didn't listen. Impulsivity, as strong in her as it is in

Romy. Yet again, she's the hold-your-hands-up, guilty-as-charged, perennially unprepared. If Callum hadn't run into the buvette, they'd have nothing. No loo roll, no food, no deodorant. No soap. Heavily, oh so heavily, she sighs. At least her period isn't due.

'So there's a ghost in here?' Callum slumps and reclines. Hands on the arms of the rocking chair, he's a villain without a cat. 'Thank you, Kira. This gets better all the time.' He rocks to face the door. 'Do you have any more fun theories to—Jesus!'

The chair pitches as he flinches back, rocking violently toward the fire.

'What?' Kira whips around. 'Oh, God.' She scrapes the chair back, catches the leg, and crashes to the floor with the wood. 'Oh, *God.*'

In the doorway stands a shadow. Kira's head rushes hot. Punched with panic, a fist to her gut, she boots the toppled chair aside and scrabbles away. It's not a shadow; it's a figure, still and silent, cloaked and hooded with something like night. Hands press against Kira's lungs.

Softly, the figure looks up. 'Child.' Its wizened, hollow gaze finds her, and unreality swoons. Weathered and waifish, it's a woman.

Kira scrabbles back, back, back. Her bruising tailbone hits the wall. '*Nnn.*' She grits her teeth. The cabin blurs in yellow and pain. Oh, *God.*

'Child,' the woman repeats. 'Ørenna.'

Bowing her greying head, she's gone.

Yellow. Pain. They calm and settle. The room's too small, too warm, too closed. The fire pops. The candle wicks. Kira's blood thumps in her stomach and her head. Her eyes feel ready to burst.

'What in the bloodiest of hells was that?' Callum's knuckles strain white on the rocking chair. Slowly, he drags his head from the door, his eyes trailing behind. 'She knew you.'

Wordless, Kira shakes her head.

'She did,' Callum insists. 'She didn't look at me once. She was speaking to you.'

Kira exhales, long and shuddering. It feels as if her lungs are a fort and someone's pulled up the drawbridge. 'She can't know me,' she whispers. 'I've never been here before.'

'Maybe not,' Callum says, 'but she recognised you.' He rocks the chair to face her. 'Why else would she speak like that?'

A log collapses in the fire and roars. He watches Kira, waiting, but when the silent seconds reach a silent minute, Callum rocks to face the door. It never opened, and it never shut; they would have heard, if not seen it. Which means that not everything here needs doors.

And they're no better off inside than out.

'Are you tired?' Kira asks from her corner. Her voice makes him jump, but he rocks back around. If he thinks like that, somewhere like this, he'll probably lose his mind. Again. 'I'm tired,' she continues.

He smirks. 'You're subtle. But yes, we should probably sleep.' He scans the room. The fire, the rug, the tightly shuttered windows. The candle on the stool, the blank oak walls, the tiny, heavy-duty, slightly crooked bed.

'I'll be happy with the—'

'Take it.' Callum waves at the bed. 'If you give me a blanket and a pillow, I'll be fine. I feel like this chair's become mine.' He smiles. Hopefully it looks more relaxed than it is. He wouldn't bank on nodding off yet, anyway; the horror-movie darkness and the horror-movie trees press in on the cabin with a blood-pressure squeeze. 'Really. Take the bed.'

Kira gnaws her top lip. Spreading like an ink sketch, a map upon her face, the offer rallies against her goodwill. 'Are you sure?'

Callum's smile grows a little more genuine. 'Yes.' The word is firm and he settles back, sinking into the pine-green cushions. To be fair, it's heaven in a chair. 'I can keep watch better from here. And I'll make you a deal.' He shifts to look extra comfortable. 'Next time glowing birds lead us to a hut, or satyrs to a cave, I'll take whatever is serving for a bed.'

Sliding stiffly up the wall, Kira smiles. 'Deal.' She hands him a blanket, prickly and thick. 'Thank you. Although if satyrs ever do lead us to a cave, promise not to leave me alone.'

Callum laughs. Meeting her mischievous eyes is warm. 'If you're sure.' He jams a pillow behind his head. 'The same with sirens.' He grins. 'Or maybe not.'

As the fire dies down and the snow begins to fall and they ration out peanuts and crisps, the cloaked woman stands in front of the door. Quietly, mindfully watching the forest.

She's our child.

The cabin pales to smoke, to air. The spirits rustle round her. *We know.*

26

The leader and the led

She's lost in the world of Karliquai, the painting she took from a dream. An arcing field of moonlit snow, an indigo midnight bright with stars. A dark wooden chalet sits snug on a rise. Three dark figures look up outside it, watching a star leave the sky.

Kira was one of them. Romy was another, but the third she couldn't get a hold on. He was young, good-looking in a scruffy, shaggy way, and she felt like she'd known him for—

Kira wakes to an empty, growling stomach, a sharp-scented winter draft curling through the door, and the sense that someone's been following.

Sleepily, she sits up. Callum is crouched outside, ankle deep in snow with his hoodie sleeves rolled. Pulling the itching blankets to her neck, she peers at him blearily. 'What are you doing?'

She yawns, stretching her mouth at the corners. Her tongue is fuzzy and fairly gross. Her mouth is dry. Her skin feels fairly gross, as well. Here's to adventuring.

'Ah.' Scooping something into his arms, Callum stands and brings it inside. 'You're up.'

Kira eyes the cloth-wrapped bundle doubtfully. 'That had better not be alive.'

'It's not.' Callum kicks the door shut in a flurry of powder, bringing the baby-sized bundle to the bed. Butting her legs for space, he sits. 'I woke up, went out to make my own facilities, and found this by the door.' He prods it. A waft of cooking puffs out, like Christmas or Sunday lunch. He rubs his hands together. 'I'm praying the forest gods have given us breakfast, so we can save the Doritos for tea.'

The folds of the cloth fall back.

'Oh, God.' Recoiling, Kira bangs into the wall. Her funny bone yowls, and she grabs it. 'No.' She screws up her face. 'Oh, no, no, no. They're way too close to alive.'

Callum regards the skinned, roasted creatures with something like tenderness. 'Quite the drama queen, aren't you?' He smirks. 'They're no more alive than the cloth they came in. The forest gods are helping us.' He tilts his head thoughtfully. 'Or someone is, at least. They've been cooked, see?' He prods one golden flank. 'Don't tell me you're veggie.'

'I should be.' Rubbing her elbow, Kira leans forward. Revulsion battles empathy, and the pair of them battle need. 'They've still got all of their limbs.'

'Well spotted.' Callum lifts a creature by a tiny back leg. It sways like a crispy, grease-dripping pendulum, and he swings it toward his mouth. 'Mmm.' Frowning, he nods in appreciation. 'It's fine. More than fine. Probably a mouse, or a squirrel.' He indicates the second body. 'Try it.'

Kira twists her purple sleeves around her fingers. Her hunger may be a hurricane, and the aroma may be barbecues, summer fêtes, chicken, but eating a mouse? A squirrel?

'You were convinced last night this was some kind of trap,' she says as Callum dines with gusto. 'You didn't even think we should come in here, and now you're eating things left at the door.'

'Hunger.' Callum mumbles, gulps, and swallows. 'I'm starving. As are you.' He nods at her stomach. Kira clutches it, chagrined. 'Also'—he tears away the last of the meat, talking unattractively around it—'horror films are more believable at night.'

A growl starts deep in Kira's stomach. Gurgling around, it builds to the sound of a big-bellied burp. Disgusted—hungry—embarrassed—*hungry*—Kira averts her eyes. The meat could be undercooked; it could be bewitched; it could be deadly, designed to get them out of the way.

'If we die, I'm blaming you.' She reaches into the rough-spun cloth. It may be an age before they eat again, and refusing food is rude. 'Forever.'

Avoiding locking eyes with her breakfast, Kira cautiously starts to eat. 'Fine by me.' Callum wipes his greasy hands on the snow. 'We'll either be happy in paradise, so you won't mind being dead, or we'll end up endlessly rotting in hell.'

Kira wrinkles her nose. 'I'll definitely mind being dead in hell.'

Callum sits beside her again. 'No, you won't. If demons are shredding our fibres, you'll be too distracted to allocate blame.'

Kira rolls her eyes at his grin. 'Delightful.' She swallows and sets down the bones. He doesn't need to know it was delicious. 'You make such reassuring company.'

'I know.' Callum shakes his wet fingers. 'Want some snow?'

'No.' The reply is automatic. Kira lifts her hands in a preemptive defence. Surely it's too early for a fairyland snowball fight. 'No, Callum, but thanks for the look.'

He eyes her so patiently it ends up patronising. 'For your fingers.' He nods at her hands. 'The grease.'

Like a phone camera focusing, Kira's eyes hone in on her fingertips. 'Ah.' She wiggles the glossy things, tries not to feel too daft, and nods. 'Then yes. Thank you kindly.'

He tosses her a chunk. Again, trying not to feel too daft, she gingerly cleans her hands. The ice wants to stick to her hands.

'Okay.' Lobbing the melting chunk back outside, Callum glances at his watch. 'Shall we go?' Slapping his knees, he pushes to his feet. 'Whether or not it really is half nine, it's light enough to walk. Wherever it is that we're—agh—*ah!*'

He flinches. From the pocket of his jeans, a duck is quacking. Kira's face grows wide as he pulls it out to breathe. 'It works?' Last night, both phones had been dead, more dead than their sad little breakfasts. 'Who is it?'

Callum blinks his bewilderment. 'Lena, I think.' He scratches his head. 'You know. Don't-go-into-Whiteland Lena. You'll-die-if-you-do Lena. But look.'

Screen first, he holds out the phone. On it is an image of two small children, suntanned and eating chips. It's a standard holiday photo.

Kira frowns. 'There's no way to answer it.'

'Precisely.' The quacking continues, looped and abrasive. Callum taps the full-screen photo.

It dies.

The silence is as suddenly abrasive as the noise. 'We're probably supposed to take something from that.' Kira clambers from the bed. The feeling of being followed is back. It may not relate to Lena, but they can't know either way. 'You were right.' She drags her fingers through her knotted hair. Her long-abused scalp complains. 'We should leave. Whatever that meant, it can't be good.'

She straightens the bed, grabs the cloth, and gathers her things from the rug. 'Come on.' She motions for Callum to move. He looks about three light years behind her. 'You said it yourself. Let's go.'

27

And so they roam

istinctly lacking direction is heinous. The woodchip path was *going* some-where, but wandering, for thirty minutes, sixty, more, feels like going no-where at all. Last night's second port of call didn't happen. It's as if discussing what they're going to do will make it ever more evident that they really, really don't know, and so they just…don't. They walk. She, at least, shies from that conversation, even though she identified the need. They just walk. They wander. They're lost.

The same looming trees, the same empty snow. The same heavy, impene-trable silence. Even in daylight, the nothing is unnerving, and any conversation peters out.

Thoughts. Fears. Doubts. Where are they going, what are they doing, why did she think they'd succeed? All and sundry nips at her mind, from Romy to exams to her mother to her bonsai, alone on her windowsill. The unfinished watercolour festering on the floor. From his silence, she'd guess Callum feels the same.

Callum. Scotland. The holiday to Edinburgh back when she was ten. They tramped up Holyrood Hill in the rain while she and Romy sang like alley cats. *Why are we walking? Why-y are we wa-a-lking?* The year after that, they went to Whitby, to a warm, converted barn. It always smelled like fresh bread, and no one could figure out why.

In an instant, Kira sweeps back there. It was October and spooky, with witchy tales and bakery goodies and fairly unsuitable films. Her family. Her family, who have disappeared. It hurts in a sudden, tight balloon, filling up her chest. What happens if she can't find them?

Stop. Thinking like that doesn't help. It hinders. Holidays. Go back to holidays.

Cornwall. The year after Whitby, they went to Cornwall and gorged on huge beef pasties.

Pasties. Food. That's better. Right now, she'd die for a curry. She'd die for a lot of things, actually: clean underwear, toothpaste, a phone that works, water that isn't snow squished into their bottles and rubbed between their hands. Isn't snow meant to dehydrate you? One time, Peter got heat exhaustion, and no one at the hotel spoke—

WAKE UP.

The shriek slaps Kira back to herself. It cuts her cheek with ice as it slices her mind, keening past her and away. She stops, blinking. What—

She hears the wind before the words. The shriek rushes back through the trees. A white-hot wire piercing her brain, frost on the opposite cheek.

WAKE UP.

Kira spins on her heels. 'I'm awake!' she cries. Her mind is a muddle, a fog, a dream. 'Can't you see that? I'm a*wake*!'

There's no one there. Kira judders, double takes. The last of the dream-fog clears. She let her guard down. They didn't keep talking. Whiteland plucked her like a harp, pulling out memories, tangling her into a ball of wool.

Whisking Callum away.

He's gone. Kira's stomach bottoms out. While she got tangled, Callum disappeared.

'Callum?' she cries. Forcing herself to go slowly, she turns. Trees, snow, pine needles. No sound but her boots. She can't smell him anymore, his lingering cologne, washing powder different to hers. She hadn't realised it was there until it wasn't. '*Callum!*'

She rakes both hands through her hair. Her nails dig ten little grooves in her skull. How can he have gone so *completely*?

'Kira?'

A Callum-shaped blur appears up ahead. It's as if he stepped out of a tree. 'Kira?' he yells, but distant, muffled. Kira can almost hear someone laughing, a tickle inside her mind. They will not find each other. They will be forced apart. 'Kira!'

The word becomes cement, setting in her joints. She can't move. She can't reply. His head whips round in a frenzy to find her, but all she can do is blink. A numbness seizes her thoughts. Kira? Why so frantic? She's here. *Hello.*

'Kira!' Callum calls, high and scratched with relief. He breaks into a jog, crossing the space between them, but all she can do is stare. *Hello, hello,* the voice whispers. *You're more than a child.* 'What happened?'

Grabbing her shoulders, he searches her face. Kira says nothing, does nothing, thinks nothing. Everything is slow, sluggish, slothful. Sentient to un-reachable, second by dizzying second. 'Where...' She works her mouth. It feels as foreign as her very self. Focusing on his expectant face, she tries to think. 'Where did you go?'

Expectation morphs into confusion. 'What do you mean?' He releases her. 'Where did *you* go?'

Kira's mind shuffles clear. They will not find each other. They will be forced apart. Whiteland isn't just playing with her; it's playing with them both.

'Okay.' Kira shivers, pulling up her collar. 'So they tricked us, again. Who-ever they are, they—what are you doing?'

Slowly rotating, Callum doesn't answer. His concentration is analytic, as if every identical tree, every laden-down branch, every patch of powdered ground can help. An exasperated mother, Kira sighs. 'Callum, this is not the time to keep quiet.'

He holds up a finger. 'Bear with.'

Stopping his circle, he peers at the snow. A moment passes. Two. Three. Toeing the snow, Kira twists her lips. 'Callum, the forest will get in again.' He strides off. She throws up her hands. 'Callum!'

'Look.' Crouching, he gestures to the ground. 'Right here. Look.'

Three seconds is enough. Kira catches him up and looks away. The foot-prints are dizzying, heat and cold colliding like the Hadron inside her. She clenches her fists, enough to strain hot. The games are too much.

'Kira.' Callum comes to stand in front of her, concern trying to smooth itself certain. 'It's okay. At the end of the day, it'll only make us more careful.'

Kira wraps her arms around her torso. 'Will it?' She bows her head. 'We say that, but we still get caught. When you were shouting, I couldn't *move.*' She looks up at him, open, raw. 'I couldn't speak. I saw you and didn't care.'

'Kira.' Callum lifts a hand and hesitates. 'Okay.' He lowers it. 'Agh. Ah, I just…we're okay. It had us for a minute, but we're all right, and that's what I want to believe.' He scrubs a hand over his head, ferociously rubbing his face. 'I—we're—' He drops his hand. 'We're okay. Let's go with that. I guess we just have a lot to learn.'

Kira flashes her eyebrows. 'Clearly.' Uneasily, she glances back. A metre or two behind her, their footprints diverge. One path left, and one to the right. 'I was so sure I was alert.' She looks away again. 'I wasn't numb; I was thinking the whole time. It's this place.' She waves a hand. 'It's not stopping at switching us off. It's thinking for us, moving for us. We split up without even realising, and I thought I heard…'

She resists looking round. Why is she such a glutton for punishment? 'How do you walk, when you're walking *with* someone, in an entirely different direction? How do you not realise, unless you're so drunk you don't know your own name? At no point have we considered splitting up, but we did.' She shivers. Her body stays tensed. Muscles that shouldn't be taut are so tight they almost cramp. 'We really need a plan.'

'Agreed.' Callum retrieves the water, takes a drink, and passes it to Kira. 'Pretend this is liquid courage.'

She does.

'So, this plan of ours.' Callum squats, scraping snow from the ground. 'Beyond finding people, I have no idea.'

He squishes the snow into the bottle. Crouching, Kira gathers a handful. Glove-fluffy water. Yum.

'For now, I think that's all we can do.' She squishes the snow and rubs the bottle. Fairly inefficient, but it's all they've got. 'Look for signs of life. There must be people here.'

Callum packs the bottle back in his pocket. 'That woman last night was people-y.'

She'd rather not think about that. 'Very true.' She pushes it firmly from her mind and locks the cabin door. 'So, there must be people. I guess we look for footprints, fires. Remnants of camps?' She huffs with a wry ridicule of herself, of this, of all of this. 'I'm going for a snowy, old Wild West, in case you hadn't guessed.'

Callum turns down the corners of his mouth. 'Sounds right. So we cowboy along, hope to find people, and what? Explain ourselves?'

Kira turns down the corners of her mouth. 'Sounds right.' She meets his eyes. For a moment, it's nice. 'And then?'

'Beg for food. Trade for food. Sell our souls for food.' Callum sighs gustily. The little moment snaps. 'Give them outside junk in return for roasted squirrel.'

Kira's stomach squirms. 'Lovely. Apart from that, and explaining ourselves, we should ask about that symbol. You know.' She traces the sketchy tree in the air. 'It may mean something, it may mean nothing, but at least asking makes us seem a little less passive.'

Callum nods. 'Less, "Hello, strange world, we're entitled to your help."'

'Or accept your hindrance.'

'Precisely.'

'Okay.' Kira mirrors his gusty sigh. 'So, we have a plan. Ish. It feels marginally less...' A flutter of white drifts down to her glove. '...Oh.'

For a moment, they stare. Star-shaped, hand-sized, and gracefully intricate, the snowflake settles on the wool.

Callum tilts his head at it. 'Do snowflakes here not melt?'

Kira smiles. It's the antithesis of everything since the birds. The plan-ish makes things marginally better, and maybe this is hope.

Tipping her head back, she squints at the sky. A wisping mist trickles over the treetops, too thin to be masking snow. 'Hey, Callum?' Kira lets her eyes fall back to him. 'Can snow come from mist, or—oh, my God.'

She stiffens. Callum wheels around. 'What?'

A man stands a few trees ahead, still and looking their way.

Kira's stomach drops. Her heart quails. Slipping past her ribs to hide above her hips, it rejects one beat, and skitters through another. Against the snow, the man is stark, conspicuous by his humanity. Dark, woollen clothes hang bulky from his body. A thick-stitched hat fits tight on his head. His hair is grey, his beard a bristle, tangling around his face. His gloved hands rest on two thin poles, and his feet, encased in hulking boots, are strapped to long, wooden skis.

Kira's heart tiptoes from hiding. He doesn't look a threat: a bag of rough-hewn hide by his side, two wooden snowshoes strapped to his back. Still, though, he watches; and still he doesn't move.

'Who are you?' she calls. Her voice, at least, sounds brave. She resists the urge to slip her hand in the crook of Callum's arm. Will the man understand? They might speak Elvish here, or Dothraki.

But the voices spoke English. The woman in the cabin did, too.

'Doesn't matter.' Abruptly, the man tilts his head back. 'We need to go.' He jabs a pole at the sky. His voice is a grumble, verging on a growl. 'Now. The mist is coming.'

The mist is coming. Sharply, Kira looks up. She'd seen it through the branches, but she'd thought it normal. Now it's thicker. Now it's crawling. Now it's almost upon them.

'We?' Callum sounds like he can't believe what he's hearing. 'You want us to come with you?'

Kira grabs his arm. 'Callum,' she hisses. The mist's approach is clammy.

Stamping his skis, the skier turns himself around. 'If you want to live,' he says gruffly. 'Good luck avoiding the mist on your own.'

Ramming his ski poles into the ground, he heaves himself away.

Cold ghosts across Kira's cheek. Her heart crashes. She jerks her head around. Everything behind is white. Everything above is invisible. A single damp tendril creeps ahead to brush her skin, and her crashing heart becomes an orchestra, a band. The clashing of cymbals, the whine of violins. The mist is coming, and fast.

'Let's go.' Kira tugs on Callum's arm. He sticks in the ground, and she whirls around. 'What are you doing? Let's *go*!'

'Kira.' Glancing over his shoulder, Callum lowers his voice. 'Wait. Just wait. We have no idea who he is. We have no idea where he's going. He could lead us somewhere worse, somewhere with a whole lot more to worry about.'

'Than what?' Kira throws out her arms. 'The mist?' She can hardly hear herself for the cymbals, the violins, the drums. 'Callum, he said if we want to live—'

A shrill shriek echoes in the distance. Callum's eyes stretch and snap to hers. 'Okay. We need to go.'

The skier merely grunts when they catch him up. He's skiing away as fast as he can, flying toward a rearing slope, but with the snowshoes on his back and the bag at his side, the strain on his face is plain. At a second shriek, he skids to a halt. Unbuckling his smooth-worn skis, he slings them over his shoulder and runs.

A howl rips the trees as they hit the hefty slope. Kira flings a look back: the mist is keeping pace, snaking up around their heels, and with an urgent crash of guttural fear, she pushes faster, faster. Callum on her right, the skier on her left. They run and gasp with all they have.

And still the mist creeps on.

Not again. She can think nothing else, incredulous, frantic. It came so fast, too fast for reason. It rids the air of oxygen. It freezes her skin and scrapes her throat, and as they slip on pine needles, sinking in the snow, her peripheral vision turns white. Up, up—

'There!' the skier barks.

At the top of the slope, there's hope. It drops to a bowl-bottomed village, uneven openings huddled round the edges and a bonfire blazing in the centre. Kira's mind hiccups, gallops: *hope.* 'We need to get inside,' the skier shouts. 'Head for—'

A raucous howl drowns out the rest. The skier doesn't hesitate, careering down the slope. With a quick glance at Callum, Kira skids after him, hurtling into a sprint. Between two caves and onto the flat, past the fire and on. The village looked small on high, but no. Workshops abandoned, lesser fires quenched. Liquid spilled, the smell of hearty cooking, animal droppings, *life.*

'Inside.' The skier herds them through two heavy curtains, chopped and reeking of the wild. Kira's legs shake. She staggers after Callum. The curtains swing shut, catching her rear. Her legs tweak and fold. She sinks to the floor. Crumbly, earthen, the *whump* of Callum's knees. Wrapped by the dark, there's nothing.

Not nothing. A candle wicks on in a corner. A shadow beside it lifts a finger to its lips. A shape in its other hand drops to the floor, softly snuffed by the rock. Breathing in gulps, Callum shuddering beside her, Kira grips her throbbing legs and tries to quiet her lungs.

The air inside the cave grows cold. Their curling breaths puff up in the dark. No one moves. Callum's arm is warm against hers, the scrape of their coats too loud. Outside, the shrieks and howls give way to a thump.

Colder. Colder. Heavy footsteps cross the clearing, a deadweight body slamming into the ground. The shadow by the candle quickly blows it out.

Colder. The thump shakes the ground, entwined with coarse, scraping breaths. Kira digs her gloved fingers into her thighs. This time, they're actually done for. The rasp is too close, a wet gurgle of breath. She can picture the spit at its lips. Monsters, and girls who go looking for them; they should have listened to Lena. The mist before was a warning. Dammit, they should have listened.

But then she'd be sat on the hotel sofa, talking to police with her limited French, trying to leave out the parts of this that make her sound insane. She'd know her family were here. She'd know she could have followed. Maybe she's not the best of help, but at least she's doing something.

Mum. Dad. Romy.

Thump.

Mum. Dad. Romy.

Thump.

Kira hugs her legs. The cold ground shudders. If she'd stayed out of danger, that choice would have ended up feeling just as cursed.

The thumping stops.

Kira's mind hiccups. Oh, no. Oh, no, oh, no. The coarse breath inhales, a long, throaty rattle. They really are done for. It's right outside. The mist will drift in, damp on her face, and the beast, whatever it is, will make them Minpins until they—

With a last, rumbling thud, a sweeping over snow, the shadow, phantom, monster thumps away.

A second. A minute. An hour. Forever. Kira doesn't breathe until she absolutely has to. Soon, the beast's breaths merge with the blood in her ears. Soon, as the air starts to thaw, it's gone.

The candle *fluuts* alive in the corner. The skier releases a long, steady breath. 'Parasites,' he mutters above her, running his fingers along a ledge.

Callum offers her an unstable hand. 'Thanks.' Offering him a dim smile, Kira gets cautiously to her feet. In a swinging, swaddled holder, another flame flits to life, and with the taper flickering between his fingers, the skier holds it to four, five wicks until a ragged room takes shape.

Subtle staring isn't easy, but she tries. In the flame-lit gloom, the room looks bare, and rather like a hobbit-hole. A rug, two thick piles of furs, and an earth-and-rock-hewn fireplace occupy the centre, candle-littered ledges skirting the edges. A narrow passage winds farther underground. Intrusion hits Kira like a heated sheet, cringing in her mind. In the corner with the candle sits a table, a female version of the skier, and two young, clinging girls.

All three are silent. All three stare. All three are spectrally, undoubtedly human.

Their undivided eyes are uncomfortable. Kira looks away. She wants to goggle; she wants to talk to Callum, in private; she wants to *think*. Humans—ordinary, real-world humans—live here? Among the light-winged birds, the mist, the changing land? The idea of such a place, hidden in the forest, seemed so unnatural—so supernatural—that it hadn't occurred to her to imagine humanity. It seemed too hostile, too impossible. It's altogether too alive.

Igniting the fire, the skier straightens with a creak and an *oomph*.

'They would have died,' he says gruffly. It takes Kira a beat to realise it's aimed at the woman. She shifts her bone-cold stare to him, but says nothing. He sighs. 'They were lost.' He waves his glove at Kira and Callum, setting it down in a cubby hole. 'Did you expect me to leave them there?'

The woman's coldness deepens. 'What are they doing here?' Keeping her daughters close to her sides, she moves to the furs by the fireplace. 'Did they bring the mist?'

The skier regards her evenly. 'Both good questions.' He motions for Kira and Callum to sit. 'You're clearly not from the forest, and I don't think it's unreasonable to say that the mist wanted you.' His eyes flash a storm-cloud blue at them. 'Why?'

Creakily, he lowers himself to the furs beside his wife. 'Please.' He indicates the second pile, empty and waiting. 'At least until we establish whether I made a mistake, both in alerting you and bringing you here.' He laces his fingers. 'I would rather not have to make you leave.'

Hesitating, Kira sits. In silence, Callum joins her. How much to say? *What* to say? Explaining will either soften their welcome or throw it on the fire.

The silence ticks. Her face heats, blooming like a bruise from her cheeks. Should she make up a story, make up a name? Only relay parts that sound the least insane? Will *any* of it sound insane, considering where they are?

Tick, tick, tick. Callum clears his throat. 'Well, I'm Callum.' He sounds supremely awkward. Gesturing toward her, he clears his throat again. 'Ah. And this is Kira. Anything beyond that...' He taps his jigging knee. 'I don't really know how—'

'Outside?' a small voice whispers. Moon-eyed and intrigued, the skier's younger daughter ducks under her mother's arms. 'Have you come from outside?'

Kira and Callum exchange a blankness. 'Outside?' Callum frowns.

Thumb in mouth, the little girl nods.

'She means not from here.' Lifting his daughter onto his knee, the skier smooths her hair. The words are begrudging, a grumble. 'Whiteland.'

28

As common as crows

After all that's happened, it's the name that makes it real. Callum runs a hand across his head and nods. Slow-motion, reluctant, unsure: is it a mistake disclosing where they've come from? Or would it be more of a mistake if they didn't?

Either way, he nods again.

'Yes.' A glance at Kira, tense and looking lost. 'We don't know how we got here. Well, we do, but we don't. Not really.' He rubs his eyes. The skier is waiting, but this is so *screwed*. 'Ah. We're looking for someone.' He rubs his eyes, his forehead, his mouth. 'Actually, several someones. At least one of them is in some kind of trouble, and we think we followed them in here.' He flicks another hopeful glance at Kira. 'It's going on the basis of a note.'

'Huldra.'

The skier's wife spits it, vicious and loathing. Callum's flustered head snaps round. 'She's a huldra.'

The skier frowns. 'What?' Jaw taut, his politeness sounds stilted. 'What do you mean, she's a huldra?'

The woman's eyes fix on Kira. Her hands twist. Her eyelids tremble, as though Kira will mutate if she blinks. 'Huldra.' Her hands twist tighter, the knuckles glowing white. 'The girl is half Huldra. She shouldn't be here.'

Beside him, Kira stiffens. Her voice is a thread pulled tight. 'What's a huldra?'

Sweat beading on her forehead, the woman begins to shudder. Warily, Callum extends an arm, shifting in front of Kira. Paling, erratic, the woman sounds like Kira's description of Romy at the hospital…right before she attacked. 'What's wrong with her?' His eyes dart to the skier. 'Do we need to leave? Like, now?'

Resting a hand on his wife's leg, the skier murmurs something to his daughters. It's too low to catch, but they scurry away. 'I should hope not,' he says. Then, once the girls have clattered down the passage, 'With this amount of ignorance, I wonder that you're alive.' He regards Callum and Kira critically. 'You've had help.'

It isn't a question. 'Birds,' Kira murmurs.

The skier inclines his head. 'Hyrcinians.' He didn't need to think. Callum's eyebrows lift. Maybe in Whiteland they're as common as crows. 'Travellers' guides. There will have been others that you haven't been aware of, otherwise, you would be dead.' He considers them individually. 'The Huldra by far are not the worst of the forest.'

Callum turns his hands palms up. 'Then what are they?'

The woman starts to rock. 'Monsters.' Her voice is guttural, almost a groan. Her short dark hair slips in front of her face, stuck to her sweating skin. 'They're angry.' She picks at the skin of her fingers. 'So angry.'

Hell, this is unnerving. It can't be odd, or the skier would do more, but if this is Whiteland family life...Callum shifts closer to Kira. It's a shitshow. It's insane. Dammit, they should have stayed home.

'Iris.' The skier sighs. He places a hand on the woman's knee, more restraining than kind. 'The Huldra are known for their tempers,' he says. 'They're creatures trapped among the trees. In essence, they're beautiful women, bar the tail beneath their clothes.'

Callum wrangles his face straight. A *tail*? Well, Kira doesn't have that. He's safe.

'They spend their lives enrapturing men.' The skier zeroes in on Callum. Callum looks away. The sputtering fire, the basket of wood far more trickily crafted than his. Kira, carved from slate. 'If a man lets a huldra get close enough—close enough to talk to him, or hold his eyes—he's lost.'

Iris groans. Her shoulders rock, back and forth, her dogged stare unbroken. Her grey eyes bulge. 'Lost?' Kira twists her fingers together. 'How?'

Callum keeps his arm in front of her. It aches, and this is crazy...but crazy has a bite.

The skier fixes on Kira. 'Lost,' he says, 'in that no matter how hard the man tries, he can't escape. At the very least, he'll be seduced. More often than not, he'll die. He'll die,' he adds, his voice tightening, 'and although he'll be aware, he won't be able to save himself.'

Murderous succubae with tails. Callum wants to suppress a snort, but there isn't one to suppress. Although it sounds crazy, it also sounds real. Far too bloody, screwed up real.

$$\rightsquigarrow$$

'Eventually, it gains the huldra freedom.' The skier's rumbling eyes are hard on Callum. He tightens his grip on Iris's knee. The groan has become a low hum, and still, the woman rocks. Kira grips her twisted fingers tight. Still the woman stares at her, as if she's bathed in blood. This isn't okay. They should leave.

But they don't.

'The huldra,' the skier continues, 'can use its freedom to leave. Leave the forest, and Whiteland, if it chooses. It can live a human life. The tail disappears, and it's as any other woman…unless, of course, they're severely displeased.' He almost laughs, dark and dour. 'Then, they're said to be a beast. They regain the body of the monster. Iris?'

He turns to his wife, leaning in, murmuring under his breath. Kira narrows her eyes. He's lying; he must be. It's too absurd to be truth. He's making it up, spinning them a fairy story, laughing behind his stern, bearded mask. Either that, or it's not real: they've fallen prey to another trick of the forest, a fictional future played into their minds. Maybe they're out there, drifting through the trees, falling ever farther apart—

A stinging slap makes her gasp and knocks her into Callum. Kira's hand flies to her cheek. Too fast for anyone to stop her, Iris lunged.

'Huldra.' Manic and looming, she winches back her arm. 'Don't you ever—'

'What's the matter with you?' The skier flings his arms around her, heaving her bodily away. 'Look at the girl. There's nothing wrong with her!'

'Holy shit.' Standing in a scuffle, Callum heaves Kira up, dragging them both from the furs. 'Are you okay?'

'She's half Huldra!' Iris screeches. Kira's legs feel disconnected. The hobbit-hole is suddenly too small, too warm. It warps, it blurs, it turns her to a dreamer. The woman slapped her scratches, and now her cheek burns. 'How can you not see? That boy can't take his eyes off her. He can't stop protecting her. Just look!' She jerks her head in Callum's direction. 'I'm surprised you're not fawning over her, Erik. Get off!'

She bares her teeth, but Erik locks his arms. Backs flat like spies, the girls peer around the passage. Kira starts to back away. 'We need to get her out!' Iris bawls. 'Why won't you *listen*?'

'Because,' Erik growls, 'she's not a huldra.' Tendons strain in his neck. Iris continues to wrench at his arms. 'Do you really think she killed a man? She's from the outside, and she's tailless.' He staggers back, away from them. 'She's far too young to have set herself free.'

He looks to Kira, almost at the curtain. 'Ignore her.' The words are as strained as his neck. Iris emits a full, wronged cry. 'Years ago, she identified a witch. She thinks she can do the same for anything inhuman, but thankfully, she's not often right.'

Thankfully. Slowly, Kira retreats. If they should be thankful for this, she's been living her whole life wrong.

'So there are witches.' Callum plants himself like a bodyguard, firm and broad and glaring. 'Excellent. Murderous succubae with tails and witches. I can see why we'd be dead without help.' He takes a step back toward Kira and the curtains. 'Why does she think Kira's Huldra?'

The woman spits in his face. He flinches. 'Anneliese!' she shouts, her voice splitting. 'She's Anneliese's daughter!'

Anneliese.

Time stops, or slows, and Kira slows with it, caught in a Perspex bubble. The name Romy whispered before she passed out. The name her mother denied all knowledge of.

Her mother. Anneliese.

'Out!'

Time crashes back in a chorus of noise.

'She'll kill us if we don't get her out!' Iris screeches. 'Out. Get her *out*!'

It's the crack that shatters the glass. Kira's back brushes the curtained door. Wheeling around, she shoves through.

Away.

The cold is another stinging slap, piercing through her skin. Tendrils of mist traverse the clearing. The star-crossed snowflakes eddy into a blizzard. Kira whips her head around, left, right. Her mind isn't working. She was attacked.

Attacked in a foreign place, a foreign land, a foreign *world*. People mill about—tending the bonfire, talking in handfuls, chopping wood on the far, far side—but she ignores them. Her eyes land on the nearest snow bank. Her throat closes up. Kira runs.

She's halfway out of the clearing when a shriek spins her around.

'Anneliese!' Iris bawls. She's broken from her husband, forced her way past Callum, and now, raucous in the trampled snow, kicks at Kira's footsteps. 'She's Anneliese's daughter! She's Huldra!'

A rasping, gasping, maddened pause. Iris's eyes travel up the snow bank. '*Somebody catch her!*'

The world rushes in like a panic attack. The men beside the fire, the men chopping wood, people doing anything at all. They turn. 'Oh, God.' Kira staggers back. Other shouts join Iris's, and her words morph into a whimper. If she thought she was afraid before, she was wrong. This is fear. This is terror. 'Oh, *God*.'

Their first steps toward her are more than enough. Kira whirls. She scrambles. At the top of the bank, she blunders into a sprint. Shouts echo from the village, but she doesn't turn. There's nowhere to go, probably nowhere to hide, but running is better than waiting to die.

Running is better than waiting to die.

Light flashes in the corner of her eye. Dodging a grasping, hunchbacked tree, Kira veers away. Her fingers scrape resinous bark. Fire. Men and women giving chase. Thudding feet on snow. They have fire.

A sob gurgles up in her throat. She's been attacked, she's being chased, and the trees got what they wanted. Knees jarring, Kira pushes faster. Her feet are ablaze. They were throbbing already from running from the mist, but she can't stop. Her pursuers holler, drawing closer, Iris screeching in the distance. She can't stop. The trees got what they wanted.

They will not find each other. They will be forced apart.

Huldra.

Kira hits the next rise running. Snow in her boots, her jeans, her sleeves, and she breathes in heaving, short-term gulps. Her soles slip. She clutches at ice. Hot with sweat and frosted cold, she scrambles to the top...and sees the village from the opposite side.

Games. Kira's throbbing heart shudders. The last of her pursuers vanish over the snow bank after her. Ten people, twenty. This place is playing games.

Callum flies from the skier's cave. Shaking his wrist, he looks around wildly, notices her, and runs. Beside the fire, a boy sees, too. Pointing up, he starts to scream.

Another sob blubbers up. Kira turns back on herself, forcing a faltering run and hoping to God the troupe hasn't found her. Woodsmoke. Shouting. Endless crusts of crunching snow, sodden on her toes. Running, running, always running. Another rise rears between the trees.

No.

Tripping to the top, Kira lets out a moan. The clearing swims back to life. She screws up her hands in her hair. How can she escape? How can she try?

'Callum?' she yells. Her voice cracks in despair, but he's nowhere in sight; there's nothing but snow, nothing but trees and black butterflies that batter at her eyes.

She could let herself fall. She could curl up in a ball and hope it's a dream, the fiction she drew up in the cave. She could surrender to the swollen panic, the thunder in her head, to the butterfly forest closing in.

The fires flare into view, innocently bobbing. Orange through the bushes. Scarlet through the willow. She can't collapse. She won't.

Running is better than waiting to die.

Blinking against the butterflies, Kira stumbles left. The smoky smell is strong. A man shouts. A woman crows. The snow thuds with the wrath of thirty feet. They just need pitchforks, Kira thinks, and they'd be a medieval—

A ghost of a woman appears in the snow. Waif-like, wraith-like, smiling: *hello*.

The forest floor crumples. With a scream, Kira falls.

29

Hostile homes

The only sign of life is one wool-clad woman. Hunched over. Shaking. Forlorn. Masked by a straggling, frosted bush, Lena crouches low.

'You have to find the girl.' The weaselly woman is pleading, shuffling between the silent caves. 'Please go back after her. She's a *huldra*. She's *dangerous*.'

She steeples her fingers, the prayer so tight that her bones echo and crack. 'Please.' With a heavy, world-weary sigh, she shuffles to the next hostile home. 'Please. You have to find the girl.'

Lena crouches lower. A man has emerged from a cave across the clearing. Striding past the rowdy fire, crackling in the centre, he takes the woman's arm, leads her away, and leaves the snowy village deserted.

Foreboding blossoms, dark and viscous. Lena extricates herself from the bush. This could mean anything: Were they searching for Kira? Romy? Is it linked to Anna, or completely unrelated? The Whispers could help, if it suited them. She's tried to get through, two or three times, but other than ensuring she doesn't go astray, the Whispers are as quiet as their long-dead forms.

Of course they are. Lena casts the village a last grim look, retreating into the trees. Hitching up her satchel, she closes her eyes, letting the tug lead her on. They have far better games to play.

30

Where nobody goes

aint light, far above. It looks like sun through a part-closed skylight. That was their compromise, she and Romy, in their homely hotel room. Kira shuts her eyes. She's drifting. If she's back at the hotel…

Something tells her that she's not. Each knob of her spine is uncomfortable, as though she's beached on a rock. Her hips are twisted. Her pelvis throbs. Her boots squelch, soaking her toes. Kira's mind swirls out of sleep.

And the memories swoop back. The ghost in the snow. The chasing fire. The crazed, accusing woman. Crooked in the dark, a chill seeps through her. It's guilt and shame and fear. It's nausea. It's dread.

It's a film reel flicking into focus. Like a drill to her mind, she's awake.

Anneliese is her first thought. *Huldra* is her second. Kira opens her eyes. The faint light dances, blurry in her bleariness. *Huldra. Anneliese.* Who is she, what is she, why would being her daughter be such a scarlet letter? Why was she called her daughter at all? Kira presses her knuckles into her eyes. It's ludicrous; she's not a monster with a tail, and if she is, the tail is a damn fine master of disguise.

And yet…a thought that struck her in the cave snakes back. Anna. Anneliese.

Kira kicks this away. They visited Lavey-les-Bains four, five days ago, and neither her mother nor Romy had a tail. Anna certainly doesn't; she was the only one to brave the Turkish baths, and hell did not break loose. Erik said that freedom hides the tail, but still.

Maybe it's Mathew. He had a dalliance with a huldra and lived to tell the tale. Tell the tale, free the tail.

Stop it. Kira knuckles her eyes, but for each thought she blocks, more auld wives bustle in. The woman in the cabin, who seemed to know her. The sense that the forest *does* know her. The village in the clearing, living among such frightening, hostile instability, speaking the same language as she and—

Callum. Her racing thoughts become backseat drivers. Oh, no. What happened to Callum?

Kira heaves herself up to sitting too fast. 'Oh, my—' She screws up her face, riding out the pain. Her back is a wrenching protest, the bones in her wrist clicking and locked. Yesterday's injuries sting, pulse, blending into the whole. '*Ow.*'

Slowly, she breathes. Slowly, she straightens. Her shoulder knocks something vertical, a rock, a wall, whatever. Bracing her hands on the stony ground, she squeezes her deadweight eyelids shut, grits her teeth, and eases back.

It takes her weight. Okay. She breathes, untensing her muscles against it. It's okay; she's okay. Her knee twinges. Her tailbone moans. Her jaw thumps hot. It's probably cut. It feels like she's been thrown off a cliff but found mercy on the rocks.

Ish.

A wobbly memory paddles to the surface: falling through the snow like the snow was water. The ghost appeared, and then she was here, waking up in the dark. A dark that still surrounds her. Massaging her aching neck, Kira frowns up at the light. It's a pale, hazy glow and doesn't help the dark. Is that where she came in?

Another light flares from off to the side. Kira starts and inhales. It's close.

Another.

Another, in front of her.

Another, white and pointed, on her right. Uneasy, Kira's stomach dips. The nausea. The dread. 'Hello?'

Two more lights flare, brighter than the others. Kira shields her eyes. 'Who—ah!'

Her arms clap roughly back to her sides. Alarmed, she looks down: her gloved hands are pinned by invisible weights. She curls her fingers. Nothing.

Dread pools into fear. 'Hello?' She squints around, her voice pitching. The lights could mean anything; they're too bright to see past, and the dark all around is nothing but afterglow. She tugs on her arms: nothing. She wiggles her fingers: nothing. Inane, desperate questions balloon in her throat, but she clamps her mouth shut. They never help the captive.

She drags her knees slowly up to her chest. *Captive.* Is she a captive?

In a perfect circle of white, the lights flare and drop away. Kira shields her eyes too late. The afterglow is dizzying, hot, bright, red. The dark swarms around it. Slowly, her eyes adjust.

Quickly, she quails.

Dozens of women, still and straight, pale and blank and silent. The pool of fear freezes. It's a sword, a mace, a battle-axe sucking her breath as she stares. Their outlines waver in the settling gloom, cupping the stubs of candles. The smouldering glow doesn't reach their faces, but she'd bet her life, her *after*life, that the women are staring back.

Her mind backs into a corner, but her body knows what to do. Running is better than waiting to die.

Her hips crack. Her thighs groan. Her arms refuse to move. Pressing into the rocky wall, Kira scrapes herself up.

Until, after four whole seconds, the air slams her shoulders down. Unprepared, her knees give. The ground becomes a bullet in the buttocks. 'Agh!'

'No,' a voice says softly. Kira screws up her face in pain. 'No.'

The word rings and stretches. Kira's legs turn as numb as her arms. Her neck is stilling, and strain as she might, she can't slow it, can't make it stop. Hysteria mounts in her chest, up her throat. Her head is rotated to face the front. Her shoulders jerk flat against the wall, and there, in a matter of seconds, she's trapped.

On the whole. 'What the hell?' Kira cries, yanking at her limbs. Invisibly manoeuvred, invisibly bound, they're dead and dull and limp. 'Let go!'

She strains until her face hurts, until her breath flutters shallow and fast. The rows of women emerge from the dark. She doesn't want to look, doesn't want to see. Not their thin faces, their trailing hair, the dresses clinging to their brittle legs and swirling about their feet. Dying candles, bottomless eyes. *Hello.*

'Let go!' Kira yells. Manic tears scour her throat. The curving cavern mocks her. The rock-hewn walls echo her words, the skylight, its pale light dwindling. A hopeful star winks out. Swallowing hard, Kira shakes her head. 'Let go,' she croaks. 'Please.'

'No.' One of the women steps forward. It's the voice that said hello, the woman from the snow, a blurry glow ghosting her body. 'This,' she says softly, 'is the Kyo.' Her eyes are blank and black as she smiles. 'Here, we all are dead.'

The words echo in a murmur of voices. Kira bites at her cheek. Her breath is light. Her head swoons black. *Here, we all are dead.* Is she dead? She fell through the snow, and then?

The black coalesces. It's twilight, midnight, lurking on the edge of her senses. Dead?

'Am I dead?' she asks thickly, to keep herself awake. The speaker is watching her closely, her dress a flutter in a draught. 'When I fell, did I—'

A draught. Struggling through the night, Kira blinks. Again. An exit?

'Stand.'

The bond upon her arms is released. Her legs propel her up. 'You're alive.' The woman smiles. Kira cries out. Fighting for balance, her arms become windmills. In addition to having fallen off a cliff, she's now run a marathon. 'Just. You wouldn't be, had we not brought you here. We thought you far too interesting to die at the hands of fools.' She turns like a leaf. 'Come.'

A tug jolts behind Kira's ribs. Her feet stumble to follow. 'What?' She tries to hold back, but it's useless. 'Stop it. How are you making me move?'

The woman says nothing. Gaunt and haunted, the other women part, spanning a spectral path. Kira shivers. The cavern has murmured back to silence, candles smouldering in ghostly hands. The flurrying cold grows colder.

There must be another way out. Step by step her head clears, and step by step she chills. An opening that isn't a hole in the roof. There must at least be communication for the voice to be able to reach her. She wraps uneasy arms around her sick, unsteady torso. Both here and on the outside.

There is. An arch in the rock swims out of the gloom, and as the speaker drifts through it, Kira stops. Be careful what you wish for, she thinks morosely; the gap is dim and barely a fissure. It doesn't look wide enough for Romy, even, let alone her own non-willowy frame. What if she squeezes in and can't get back out?

The tug in her chest sharpens to pain. 'Hey!' Kira yelps, but it jerks her forward, hesitation be damned. Before it can ram her against the stone, she turns to the side, sucks in her stomach, and slides through into the dark.

On the other side, the tug slips away. Softly, almost caressingly released, Kira stops. The space around her is as black as ice, the draught flitting cold about her feet. Somewhere, the woman claps her hands.

The room imbues with light. With a gentle *puh*, Kira's lips part: candle flames upon candle flames, gentle and wicking and filling the air with the scent of a sputtering match. Cradled by stone bowls brimming with water, lining the ribs and the feet of the walls. Lighting a path to a pool at the end, to the breeze floating off it and the woman on the edge.

The blank-faced woman beckons. 'Closer.'

This time, Kira doesn't hesitate. She'd rather not risk losing her body again; not now she's back in control. Like a dreamer, she walks. This room is smaller than the first, and wilder; the walls rougher, the ceiling low, moisture glinting on the stone. Rocky stalactites jut down. It gives the cave an air of a jumbled, toothy mouth. Gems in amber dance with the flames. Amethyst sparkles in corners. She'd be thinking up a painting if she wasn't so afraid.

Alice falling through the dark, into a world of tricks. Reaching the edge of the pool, Kira twists her hands in her sleeves. If only the tricks could stop.

'They're not tricks.' The woman motions for Kira to sit. Grimacing at her aching bones, at the stone-cold floor, Kira sits. *These women read minds now*, Callum would say. His sarcasm makes her breathe. 'They are life. But you've never known life like it.'

Her dark eyes flick up to Kira's. Kira fights to keep her face straight. If her eyes widen, she betrays her fear. If she grits her teeth, she betrays her fear.

She betrayed her fear in the other room. The colts have already bolted.

'We can't blame you,' the woman says. Kira struggles to fix on her words. 'Whiteland is more than outsiders can think of, let alone think can exist. Creatures and men, more creatures than men.' She looks wistfully down at the pool. Three feet wide, it glitters with the ceiling, the breathing of the wind so tender on its skin. 'We watch it all from here.' She traces the water softly. 'And what we don't watch, we hear. I watched you on the outside, and I watched you in the forest, but I only heard you speak when you fell. Wondering about language, Anneliese.' She retracts the finger. 'Your friend.'

Kira looks up sharply. 'Callum? Do you know where he is?' Her nails dig into the pool's narrow ledge. 'Do you know if he's all right?'

The woman smiles. 'He was last on the list. Language, Anneliese, your friend.' She closes her eyes, and Kira's fingers spring loose. Startled, she folds them into her coat. 'It will all be dealt with. I am Enny.'

Nice to meet you isn't right. *I'm Kira* is pointless. Kira fiddles with the fluff inside her gloves and says nothing. Taking a breath, Enny straightens her spine. Her eyes smudge and darken. Kira flickers with disquiet. She's seen that change before.

'Languages are all the same.' Enny waves a long hand musically, with grace. 'Or, they are nothing. It's sometimes hard to say. They could be so different that they circle around and finally become the same. Loathing is close to love, is it not?' A shudder ripples through her. She blinks. Her eyelids are translucent. 'Is it not? I'm speaking to you now, and you shouldn't understand. You think that you're speaking your language, but you're not. Nobody here will speak your language, and you will not speak theirs; yet you speak. Yet *we* speak.'

She curls her hand, a royal motion, as if proving a philosophical point. Cautiously, Kira nods. What else can she do? Her heart has lodged itself in her sternum, but there's no way out. *There's no way out.*

And this ghostly, ghastly woman is mad.

'It must be, then,' Enny continues, mildly pleased, 'that there is no language. Not here. How can it exist if we communicate with fluency, yet never give it a thought? I am not conscious of speaking any language. I may have been when I was alive, but I no longer remember. Are you conscious of your language?'

She blinks her black eyes at Kira but doesn't give her time to speak. 'Maybe,' she muses. 'Or maybe not. Maybe the outside is different; maybe not. In the Kyo, in Whiteland, and in Urnäsch, I believe, language is irrelevant. There's just communication.' She tilts her head. 'Do you understand?'

No. No, she doesn't. Kira's insides crawl, full of spiders. Does she nod again? Make up a response? Is silence better than the *wrong* response and losing her body—or worse, her mind?

Enny trails her finger through the water. Kira's breath stutters. Any speech slips away. The water isn't moving.

We all are dead.

'Now'—Enny watches the water—'Anneliese.' Her voice lilts toward the absent-minded, light and sighing. 'She—no.' Stopping her tracing, she frowns. 'You're right. Your friend must come sooner. He will.' She snaps her chin in a fitful nod. 'I've seen him; I've seen them all. Your sister, your parents, the woman who follows.' She regards Kira inquisitively. 'This is quite the expedition.'

Kira's pulse thuds in her ears. Her body tenses, straining, stiff. On balance, she might have fared better with the mob; providing they didn't burn her first, she could have explained her way to release. Here, though... 'You've seen my family?' She balls her fists on her thighs. Here, she's a star on the edge of dark matter. 'And Callum? Are they okay?'

Dipping her whole hand into the pool, Enny merely sighs. The water ripples, colours sparking, washing up on the surface. As bright and irritated as a suncream reaction, Kira's eyeballs start to sting.

She blinks. Nothing happens. Butterflyquick, she blinks again. The pool shifts in swirls. She rubs her eyes, but the sting keeps building. Kira grits her teeth. Tiny, dotted pinpricks, her eyeballs burn, and as they draw a throttled gasp from her throat, the water-bound image comes clear.

Kira stills. It's a woman. A woman in a boat of reeds, sailing an endless blue. A woman, pink-faced with heat, wearing the white, black-treed vest she originally bought for Romy. Her mother.

Tears swell up, but Kira rams them down. Anna's here. On the ocean that isn't an ocean, her mother is alive.

Pain wires through her eyes. At her blink, the image reforms: Romy, struggling through the forest, her arm around Mathew to drag him along. Kira inhales, and it sticks. She can't breathe out. Mathew's face is semiconscious, haggard, a dark-shadowed white. It's so far away from the father she knows: the father of playful dream contests, poking fun at reality shows, trying to be a tower of strength. It's not the father from her eighteenth birthday, surprising her with a grove of art supplies while he and Anna beamed. It's not the father who hugged, who teased, who looked sad when Romy started shying away. It's a shadow. A tragedy. A ghost.

It's not the Romy she knows, either. Emotion threatens to swell and break. Where Mathew's face is gaunt, hers is almost withered, as if the thing that took her mind is too much for her bones. Kira bites at her lip, hard enough to feel her bottom teeth through the flesh. Oh, Romy. Writhing in the hospital, lying on the couch, lolling in Callum's arms. What's *happened*?

The Romy in the water glances up. A gash of a smile stretches her mouth as if she sees, as if she knows. Kira flinches back, rushing hot. Her sister's eyes are hematite, mischievous on her own. They should be blue. She always envied them, more frosted and glittering than her midwinter shade. They should be many things. *Romy* should be many things. Kira wants to choke. Her sister should be *alive*.

Before the horror can consume her, the image flits away. This time the pain is searing, a stab spreading out to her temples. Kira grinds her teeth against it. It's flicked to a woman against a tree, angular and slumped. She's fringed by snow, hidden in the centre of a thorny thicket, ringed by bullying, towering pines. Kira stops breathing again. Lena.

The image flicks before she has time to think. Her mind leaps, her vision spasms. Ignoring her throbbing head, she narrows her burning eyes: Callum. Callum, Callum, Callum, faint and silhouetted, crouched in a hole dug from snow. A chill prickles her chest. How long has she been gone? A web of branches weaves a door, and he crouches, peering through the cracks. Is he watching for her? Waiting?

If she can't get back, will Whiteland release him? He shifts his weight from right leg to left, leaning as close as he can to the web. Kira bites her lip through to blood. *Callum.*

Seeping together, the images melt. Kira's eyes are left wet and pulsing, staring at the pool as it ripples and stills. Everyone's alive. As much as they can be, they're okay.

For now.

Enny's dress rustles against the floor. Kira startles. She'd forgotten the woman was here, probably watching for how she reacts, waiting for the slideshow's end. Kira brushes the lingering water from her eyes. The woman is watching, but something has changed.

All her fear stampedes back. The change is visceral, calculated, chiming with the air: clearer, more metallic, like the taste of blood isn't just from her lip. An aura…and the eyes.

Kira's breath stutters. In the time of her distraction, Enny's eyes have grown, rounder and darker and lacking in life. 'You see?' she asks. A smile thins her lips, cut by a boning knife. She's all too sharply similar to the water-bound Romy. 'All will be dealt with, as I said. You have no reason to worry.'

Maybe not about anyone else. Kira forces her aching teeth to stop grinding, dragging her eyes to the woman's. 'Why am I here?' she asks. Her voice wavers. Dammit, no. She can't collapse if she wants to leave, and there's no way in hell she'll stay. 'You said I was interesting.' She shifts her legs, enough to spring up and run in a beat. Enny doesn't seem to notice. 'What does that mean?'

Looking up in a jerk, Enny laughs. 'I said that?' Amusement bubbles like boiling water. Merrily, it echoes, a clockwork toy on a haunted night. 'I don't know what it means.' She pulls her eyebrows together. 'We're not interested in you. We're interested in your mother and your sister. You?' She tilts her head. 'You're merely entertaining.'

Threads of anger start to hiss. Enny is trailing her fingers through the pool, regarding her like she's a pet. Kira clutches the anger with two clenched fists. Pointed at, laughed at, put on display; she will not be a circus animal.

She'll show this goddamn world her worth.

'Why?' she asks. Sparks flicker through her eyes. She bites back an exclamation. 'Why am I entertaining?'

With a pointed deliberation, Enny lifts her fingers. The pain in her eyes retreats, leaving them stripped, watery, raw, but Kira doesn't relax.

'Why are you entertaining?' The woman cocks an innocent eyebrow. 'First'—she dips a fingertip, causing a piercing flicker—'you don't know who you are. Second, you're so easily scared.'

She meets Kira's eyes for a blink. A flutter of images flit between them: Kira, afraid, in the car park; Kira, afraid in the mirrored clearing; Kira, afraid in the present, bruised and hollow-eyed. Kira shakes her head sharply, jarred and chilled. She's an older shadow of Romy.

Enny smiles, that glass-thin Chelsea grin. 'Third,' she says after a pause she seems to savour, tasting the dread upon the air, 'you're unaware of your danger. Fourth, although you don't know where you are, you still try to play the hero. And fifth...'

Shyly, she peeps from under her lashes. 'You don't know what we've done to your sister.'

The room seems to tunnel. The lights are too bright. *You don't know what we've done to your sister.*

Kira can't breathe. 'I have to leave.' She scrambles to her groaning feet. Her faded words come from someone else. The room sways. 'How do I leave?'

Another laugh tinkles. Enny's words are light. 'Oh, you can't leave. There is no leaving.' Gliding upright, she smiles beyond Kira. 'Not from the Kyo, my love.'

Oh, God. The other women are drifting toward them, folding into each other as they sigh through the arch. The candles wick to life in their palms.

Horror spools from Kira's chest, so potent she can smell it. The air is growing colder. 'What do you mean, there's no leaving?' She backs away from the pool. Every muscle tenses to run. 'Who are you?'

Enny's smile unrolls. 'I told you.'

'No, you didn't.' Kira swallows. 'You said you were dead.' She whips a look around. The women are encroaching, silent and soft. She backs away, away, away. 'Who are you?'

The woman cocks her head. 'We're the women of the Kyo. The raped, the murdered, the defiled. The denied.' The smile drops. 'The forever.'

A whisper of assent rises up from the shadows. 'No.' Kira shakes her head. The women surround her, but she has to get away. 'You're mad. You're all mad.'

'We are not.' Pressing her hands in a prayer, Enny sighs. Kira dips her gaze. Her tilted head and cratered eyes suggest the opposite. 'We are trapped, and we want to leave. Your sister and your mother and the Whispers, oh, they gave us what we need. One of us.'

A murmur rustles around the room, an almost melodic hum. 'I can't help you leave.' Kira's voice quavers high. Now she can't stop it; not anymore. If she thought she felt fear in the forest, she was wrong. The scale of her terror never ends.

'Unfortunately'—Enny sighs—'you can't.' It's the disappointment of kings and queens. If she wasn't so inhuman, her sadness would be pain and tormented, unbearable grief. 'So why should we help you? Your sister was useful.' She drifts across the stone. 'But you, my love, are nothing.'

Her head tips to the side, too far. Kira's mind fills with terror, her head with a roar. A click. Another. A third. Enny's neck jolts to ninety degrees.

It cracks. Kira's stomach curdles, souring, ill. She doubles over. The splintering echoes off the rock, and as Enny's face changes, as her mouth begins to scream, terror and adrenaline collide. Kira runs.

The screaming swells. The women blur. Their faces leap out as she passes, but now they're all the same: screaming, dead, contorting, *dead*, each adding to the holy chorus until it's a ricocheting, cataclysmic screech. Slapping her hands to her ears, Kira scrapes through the arch and away.

Icy darkness. Ringing ears. Her breath plumes in front of her. Unsteady in the black, she blunders, tripping on uneven ground. Her arms fly out. There's no escape. There's—

Her hands slam into rock and jar. Thrown off balance, Kira gasps, rebounding onto the floor. Her hip screams as she lands on the bone. A gasping sob rips from her throat. There's no escape. There's *nothing*. Nothing but stone…

…And the growing glow of candles.

Kira scrabbles round as it glimmers up the walls. The chorus swells, discordant. The screaming women drift through the arch, spirits, banshees, ghouls. Kira tries to stand, but her legs won't work. Another sob rasps. She can't feel her knees. Her thighs tingle and numb to nothing. She wrenches at them with anchor-heavy hands, and as the nothing spreads up her torso, her arms, she's shunted across the stone.

'Stop!' Colliding with the bone-cold wall, she gasps. Her spine roughly lodges in place, her shoulder blades sharp against the rock. 'Stop it!'

The women drift closer. The screams scream on. A manic laugh strikes up. 'Let go.' Kira shakes her head. Her skull scrapes stone. Pain blooms hot, and she sobs. 'Just *stop*.'

Hysterically, the laughter heaves. One by one, the screams cut off. The hellish women wait.

'I told you,' Enny calls as the shrieking echoes ring. 'There's no leaving.' Her broken neck has righted itself. She steps toward Kira, smiling. 'And now you're going to see.'

She waves a pleasant, gracious hand.

The flames extinguish. The women fly forward. 'No!' Kira yells as their long arms reach, trying to writhe, to escape. The laughter returns to ring in her ears. Her head is locked, her lips heavy. Her throat is a straw pinched shut. She can't blink. The stretching, leering faces scream. Their scratching fingers burn cold, searing through her skin.

Kira's terror takes her over. It's black and roaring, rushing in.

Here, we all are dead.

31

The monster carries on

Kira opens her eyes to green. Her heart is sharp and pounding, her mind a black, coalescing panic—what happened to the cave? The women? The paralysis? Is she okay? Is she dead?

Blinking away her speckled sleep, she squints at the canopy of green. Presumably, she's not dead. If heaven, hell, or any afterlife exists, it's unlikely to resemble a forest.

Especially not *this* forest. It hits her with a certain, dreaded relief: the women have dropped her in the forest. After all of that, she's back where she started, cold and lying in the snow. The sickly scent of pine has never been so sweet. Fingers freezing, palms slipping, Kira clambers to her feet. Brushes snow from her arms, her hair, her legs. Beats it from her back and breathes. Pine. Light. Clarity. Better.

Even better is the fact she can *move.* Kira stretches, relishing the clicks of her back, the pops of her arms and knees. Freedom: something she's never considered in a close, physical sense. Paralysis: something she never wants to again. Although its fear dwindles with the faintness of a dream, her body's not ready to forget. None of her is.

Which means she has to stay on her guard. Kira turns a complete three-sixty. This part of the forest is hardly different to where she and Callum met Erik. Blankets of snow, crisp and unbroken. Pillars of trees, marching in lines. Maybe, with a stroke of luck, it *is* the same part. She's well overdue for a coincidence and might actually come across Callum.

Or the village. The village with the torches. The village with the torches that chased her en masse. The memory arrives to scorch her eyes, as striking as the fire they bore. Kira's shudder almost makes her bend double. Maybe it wouldn't be luck after all. Who knows how long she was trapped in the Kyo? The village could still be searching, baying for her blood.

A crunch sounds behind her. Shot cold, Kira spins. It's the gravelly crispness of a boot on snow, and inhaling through her nose, she stills. Fifty metres off stands a man.

He's alone. His thick woollen poncho is much like Erik's, hefty boots ankle-deep in snow. His motionless back is to her. Tensed and wary, Kira observes him. Russet-haired and braced and tall, broad and stiff and staring.

The slow crunch sounds again, the boot over snow. Kira holds her breath. The man hasn't moved.

Which means there's someone else.

In a blink, she's on the sidelines watching the hushed, waiting scene. Hidden by a scraggly bush and a leaning, whiny tree, she starts. How is—what—

In a blink, it doesn't matter. Shock hits her, hot and dizzy: walking toward the man is her mother.

'Mum!' Kira shouts before she can think. Anna does nothing as she stumbles from hiding, doesn't show a glimmer of surprise. So what? After all the worry, she's *here*. She's alive. 'Mum—'

Kira staggers. She's back beside the tree. Disoriented, she grabs the trunk. Anna continues her slow, sly walk, her focus never leaving the man. Kira's head spins. A voice slinks in: *watch, my love. You'll learn.*

The words caress her temples, breathy and amused. It's as if she's back in the Kyo.

Terror plunges its hands through her chest, withdrawing them dripping and bloody. Kira slumps against the whiny tree. She should have known: this isn't real. Anna and the man aren't here. The women didn't drop her back in the forest. They're toying with her. It's a game.

She should have worked it out before her hopes ran high. Anna's face is younger than it should be. A thin, blonde braid loops over one shoulder, and not only is she wearing a dress, but it's long, and heavy and rustic and full. Kira bites her cheek. The lining is blistered. She saw in the Kyo that Anna hasn't changed from Romy's T-shirt and leggings. This is either a cruel illusion, or…

And now you're going to see.

Smoothly, her mother reaches the man, and now—only now—Kira knows. It's not Anna taking her victim by the hand, leading him away like a puppet. It's not Anna who, with a smug, curving smile, swishes off into the trees. It's not Anna's tail poking out from her skirts.

It's her mother from before. It's Anneliese.

I don't want to see this. Kira thinks it with such ferocity, such a gulping, bubbling horror, that Anneliese almost seems to hear. For a second, she pauses, as if she might turn. Fists clenched, face hot, Kira stiffens.

With a minute headshake, the monster carries on.

It isn't a blink that does it this time, but a tentative releasing of breath. Her head swoons, and it's night. Kira staggers back. A wall looms before her. She thought the Hyrcinian birds were impatient, but this is a whole new scale. Manipulation by teleportation.

If only Callum were here; that's the kind of thing he'd say. But he's in the real world, while she's tossed around a dream.

A dream that likes to toss her into things. Kira retreats until the wall stops looming, thrilling with uncertainty. It's not just a wall; it's a cabin. Smoke trickles from the roof. Around the corner, golden light spills onto the snow.

Kira's stomach tugs like a gentle fishhook. Briefly, she shuts her eyes. Okay. She's meant to see something, and she's meant to see it now. Resigned, she folds her arms tight and trudges after the light. If she doesn't, she'll get tossed there, too, and with every tug, every whirlwind movement, she's growing sick of being controlled.

The front of the cabin is a friendly face. Two windows wink on both sides of the door, and where a wreath or a welcome sign could hang, the sketch of a tree, portentous and skinny, digs its grooves in the wood. Kira shivers. Everything is light, cosy, and bright. With the ashy forest knotted around it, it should be the perfect woodland haven.

Without her mind's permission, Kira's feet start to move. *Hey* wars with *oh, my God*, and they both drown in cold. She'd have liked a few more seconds, a few more minutes, a few more years to prepare for what lies beyond the windows. The man, her mother? The man and her mother? Or something else entirely, the threat to beat them all?

Kira's feet line up in front of the glass. Staring through her toes, she steels herself. The cabin is silent; maybe it's empty? She can hear her breath and the wind through the trees, so the dream-truth hasn't left her deaf. The sharp tang of pine smoke curls from the chimney, and—

Her eyes flick up to the window's glow. The treetops whisper. *Watch, my love.*

On the cabin floor, the man lies sprawled, naked and staring at the ceiling. Kira's innards bunch and tangle and knot: he doesn't think, doesn't know, doesn't move. Straddling his thighs with her dress hitched high, Anneliese lifts a knife. He doesn't think, doesn't know, doesn't move, and she plunges it into his stomach.

He screams.

Kira opens her eyes to moonlight. Her heart is sharp and pounding, the echo of a yell raw in her throat—what happened to her mother? The cabin? The man? The crude knife that gutted him?

It's gone. It wasn't real. Kira shuts her eyes again. When the black swept in, and she crumpled to the snow, the cabin shimmered to nothing. The Kyo made her see it, and the Kyo pulled her out.

And now, they've dropped her…where? She drags her eyes open and forces them to stay. How can she tell if this is real?

It doesn't matter. In a blurring of her eyes, her mind reshuffles. The women, the cave, the paralysis; thank God she's out of there. Freedom: something she's never considered in a close, physical sense. She shudders. Paralysis: something she never, ever, ever wants to again.

A grim determination settles, and she pulls herself from the snow. One: find out where she is. Two: get back to Callum.

One: she's still in the forest. It hits her with a certain, dreaded relief. The moonlight is striped with thinning branches as spindly as Hallowe'en. It's bluish and cold, bright and bold. Something jars in her mind. The moon?

Kira's heart slips down, down, down, plunking like a stone in water. The moon hasn't risen since she entered Whiteland. For that matter, neither has the sun. Kira presses the heels of her hands to her eyes. What a beautiful, plausible game of the Kyo's, to drop her on the outside, back at the start. She can hear the manic laughter, the drilling banshee screams. *Let's drop the girl on the edge of the woods! She'll never get back in! Huzzah!*

They'd never say 'huzzah.' Kira almost laughs at the ridiculousness, the hopelessness, the impossibility fogging her brain. This is madness.

'This is madness.' She breathes, to ensure she exists. The puff of air through her lips grounds her. Swallowed by the trees, her quiet voice grounds her. Her sodden clothes ground her, clinging to her skin. 'Impossible.'

This grounds her most of all. Callum, and their scoffing at the word. Everything that's happened, and everything it means. Kira brushes back her snow-clung hair. She has to get back in.

Okay. She's here; she's grounded. To her left, right, and rear lurks thick, gloomy forest; in front lies a healthy swathe of moonlight, speckled with diluted trees. Let's go.

In a minute or so, she hits the edge of the forest. In a minute and a half, she knows. The Kyo have thrown her out of Whiteland.

To add torture to toil, she knows where she's been put. Her body sags like a puppet relinquished. A road cuts through the last of the trees, glinting white and straight. If she cranes her neck left, there's the metal barrier. If she cranes her neck farther, there's the car park. Yes, Whiteland is awful, with its raging, perilous social Darwinism, but she was there with a purpose—she was there for her family. If she doesn't get back, she has nothing.

Nothing, though. Poised in a moment of disconnect, she hovers above the road, above the forest, above her body, caught by the thought of letting this go. Right now, she could. Holding her frozen breath, she could. It's tantalising, almost a need, to let go of it all. She could take this road until the pavement ends, blinker herself like a horse, and live. Call the police. Work with them. Be human.

Is she not?

Not the point. Kira rubs her eyes, not to clear them but in the futile hope it'll help her think. The night is deadened, muffled the way only snow can manage. The world zeroes in when all you have is white, and a sharp sense of holding your breath.

'Shh.'

The sound is out before she can comprehend why. Once it is, though, it's visceral. Her lips purse, fairly awkward, and hold. She's telling herself to shut up?

Yes. Touching a finger to her mouth, she forces her hands to her sides, balling into flexing fists. Thinking is hopeless. Thinking outside of Whiteland is hopeless. Maybe the Kyo have thrown her out, but she needs to get back. Her chest twinges, cold and liquid. Mum. Dad. Romy. Callum. They're all in there. All that matters is getting them—

A tawny owl hoots. Kira chills, her twinging chest leeching cool through her limbs. That clarity, that sharpness of breath? She hugs herself, shifting her feet, kicking out thoughts of running away with the force of a mushroom cloud. No. *No.* Sure, she could flee, fetch food, water, chargers, but what would have happened by the time she gets back? Would she even be allowed back in?

The same owl hoots, sweeping in a shadowed swoop above the midnight road. Scanning the road, Kira curses it balefully. She'd trade a hundred owls, and a hundred normal worlds, for—

The curse gutters. Her breath sticks. Twenty metres up the road, a woman steps out of the forest.

Kira quashes the cartoon urge to rub her eyes and look again. Tall and curving and brazen, the silent woman is nude. It prickles Kira's skin just to look at her, but breathing deep with contentment, she spreads her arms and runs.

Kira slips behind a tree as the spectre flies toward her. No shoes, no clothes, yet she floats down the road. Her skin glitters, pale and opaque. Her hair sails out behind her head. It's as if she doesn't have a care in the world. Kira's arms goose bump. It's as if she isn't human.

Without a sound, the woman flies past like a ghost, or a flickering film reel. Counting to five, ten, fifteen, Kira cautiously reemerges.

Seven metres up the road, a fully clothed man steps out. Kira's chest jolts. Unreality rushes, distant, hollow, bright. She knows the blue shirt he was given for his birthday; she thought, at the time, they should vary what they wear, instead of both living in checks. She knows the battered brown boots that, try as she might, Anna's failed to introduce to the bin. What's more, she knows the reverse profile, the right ear that sticks out more than the left and the brightly silvering hair. Her dad.

He follows the woman, hands in pockets. A strangling dread takes Kira by the throat.

Kira opens her eyes to the sound of seagulls. Her tired heart pounds. Her mind is a blazing, tumultuous confusion, but the dream is already slipping away. The forest. The moonlight. The owl. The bizarre image of her father and the woman. It felt so solid, so material. What's real, if that wasn't?

Maybe she's losing the ability to tell.

It doesn't matter. In a blurring of her eyes, her mind reshuffles. She was adrift, as she often is, in the purgatory between asleep and awake. She lucid-dreamed again.

Thank God.

Propping herself on her elbows, Kira blinks her bleary eyes. Sea. Sand. Sky. She's sweating in a swimsuit, sunning on a towel, and surrounding her is the beach.

The beach opposite Lundy Island. The beach flush with surfers, seduced by the savage waves. The beach that, in winter, becomes her greyscale, melancholy, windswept love.

Home. Kira flops back onto her towel with a grin. Ahead of her shimmers the ocean, its salty breeze cooling her skin. Behind her trundles the high street. Securing her sarong, she sleepily stands, carried by her waking relief. Even the tourists are a relief: throngs, bands, *colonies* of them, cooing at the quaintness and clamouring for suncream, the bucket, spade, and ice cream shops thriving in the heat. Normality. All the rest was a dream.

If she's honest, it was a nightmare. A lucid nightmare, provoked by whatever she watched last night, whatever Romy wrangled her into. Heat causes nightmares, and movies make them worse.

Maybe she'll turn it into a painting, if the details don't slip away. Scooping up her bag and towel, Kira fans her face. It's far too hot. The sea breeze was short-lived, and with the beach at the mercy of the blazing sun, the world has tipped back to burning. It's definitely time to go home. Everywhere, everything, everyone is too hot. The lazing, reddened parents and their tired, reddened children. The dog lolloping through the water, panting up a storm. The young couple fanning each other, slumped beside a half-finished heart made of pebbles. Was it this hot when she fell asleep?

If it was, if nothing else, she didn't burn. She's got a tan to be proud of, and no pink in sight. Kira huffs. It's the least her body can do; her mind created Callum, then cruelly woke her up. He should be real. Even if he was insufferable, and persuaded her to eat a dead rat, or whatever. He was attractive, he was Scottish, or Irish, or Welsh, and, well…he wasn't Peter.

Kira flashes her eyebrows. What a creation. The creepy parts she'll save for telling Romy, the fantastical parts she'll save for telling Dad, but Callum she'll save for herself. How did the heat mould so much splendour? She must have been asleep for aeons.

And it's far, far, *far* too hot. Wafting air at her face, she sets off along the shore. Time to go home and hug her fan, tongue lolling like the sea-basking mastiff. She'll come back out when it's cooler and fetch her family a fish-and-chip tea.

Even the sea is too hot. Licking and spraying her feet as she walks, it's a friend of the sticky, damp air. Kira wriggles, kicking at the sludgy sand. Her gym bag has stuck to her side, and she pries the material free. Plastic on sweat, dotted with sand. The sooner she's home, the better.

Oh, shush. Kira angles away from the sea, trudging toward the town. Hot sand sifts across her sandals. It's just heat, and she'll be home soon. Besides, dusk is tumbling.

By the time she joins the mesh of streets, it's down. The air whispers over her skin, drying the plastered hair at her neck. The sun dips beyond the sea. The salty breeze whips up again, chivvying a shiver of cold. Kira rubs her arms. Paradise. Gently it eddies around the street, curling over the narrow cobbles, the chimney pots and broken tiles. Kira closes her eyes. It's beautiful.

When she looks again, *everything* is beautiful. The sky above the rooftops deepens to violet, the non-tourist side of town winding into shadow. It's a postcard from one of the beachfront shops, or the end of a whimsical film: the soft, settling quiet; the sunset chalking the ground in pink; the brightly coloured houses and their bursting window boxes, geraniums bobbing in the breezy, golden glow. The scattering of stars that pop overhead.

She's basically a tourist brochure. With a delectable shiver, Kira walks on up the street to the shortcut.

A tabby cat leaps to the moon and back as she turns off its alley. Kira starts. It clatters straight into a cluster of bins, bounding off more frightened than before. The echo clangs, reverberating. Kira winces. What did it think she was going to do? Give it an ASBO for loitering?

The cat scrabbles over a garden wall. Kira sinks back into her thoughts. A shower, a dewy Corona, and the last few chapters of *The Night Circus*; it sounds like a perfect—

A few feet from the end of the alley, a man steps into her path.

'Whoa.' Kira's hands fly up. Her heart skitters. She hadn't even seen his shadow. 'Sorry.'

Skirting around him, she pulls up short. He remains planted in place. 'Excuse me?' she tries. The man's face is hidden in gloom. 'I need to—'

Without a word, he grasps her arms. 'Hey!' she yelps, but spinning her around, he shoves her back against the wall. The air slams from her lungs. The stone scrapes, coarse on her skin. 'What are you—'

Her bag slips to the ground. She knows him.

It's anything but a relief. Something arcs in her chest, but it's nervy, jarring; she knows him, but she doesn't, but she *does*. Brown hair tumbles over his forehead, his brown eyes crinkled with distress. Five-day stubble scratches his chin. Wintry and snow-spattered, in a thick ski jacket, she knows him, but she doesn't, but she *does*.

'Kira.' The man docks his hands on the wall on either side of her head. In a cartoonish way, Kira gulps. Her chest feels shallow. He's pressing against her, trapping her.

What's more, he knows her name.

'Kira, listen to me.' The man cuts through her panic. His Scottish lilt is as familiar as his face. 'I'm not going to hurt you, but you have to listen.' He closes his arms so his hands touch her temples. It forces her to look at him. Her panic falters. His face is sincere. 'This isn't real.'

The words are a shiver. 'What?' she asks, bewildered. It feels like déjà vu. 'What's not real?'

'All of this.' He nods around them. Urgent, intense, his hands remain firm. 'Your town. Your home. Your family.' He nods at their crushing bodies. 'You and me. It's not real, and you need to wake up.'

Kira narrows her eyes. On her towel on the sand: then, she was asleep. Now, she's awake, alert, and on edge. 'You're talking rubbish,' she says. This is her life. Summertime laziness, bemoaning the tourists, haddock and chips and book upon book. She bats at her unease. 'I'm awake.'

'You're not.'

Kira shakes her head between his hands, but her unease refuses to quail. 'I am.' Raising defiant eyes to his, she juts out her chin. Doubt slithers in in the form of oddities, not saying anything but quavering, prescient. Reality is all there is, and yet… 'This is my life, in my town. I assure you, it's all very real.'

The man's forehead buckles. 'Kira.'

Determined, she stares him down. 'I'm real.' Desert heat. Rapid night. Her swimsuit would never be beige. 'Unfortunately'—she makes herself breathe—'you're also just as real. I've spent a normal day at the beach, and now I'm on my way home, hoping to God I didn't burn while I slept. So whoever you are'—she lifts her leg—'leave me the hell alone.'

She stamps down. The man kicks her foot straight back. 'I can't do that.' Setting his jaw, he shakes his head, pressing her back into the wall. Kira's panic flips and flies. She can't move a muscle. 'You need to listen to me.'

'Like hell.' Higher than she'd like, Kira raises her voice. There must be someone around to hear her. 'Get away from me. This is basically assault.'

Tensing her body, she tries to wriggle free. 'I said, get away—'

'I know what you said.' His voice is a snap. He leans in closer. He's all she can see, all she can feel, the smell of his skin so different to hers. His breath smells of nothing at all. 'And I'm sure this does seem real to you.'

'That's because it *is*.'

'It's not.' He lifts his voice over hers. 'Just listen to me, Kira. Sure, everything looks the same. You use the same towel you always use. You take the same shortcut you always take. You admire the same geraniums. But however much it seems the same, it's not. You need'—he flips his hands on their sides, gripping her head—'to wake up.'

Kira grits her teeth. Geraniums. The doubt sharpens its fangs. 'No,' she says in a voice too small. 'I don't know why you're doing this, but it's not going to work. Just let me go, and I'll carry on home, and the police will never need to know.'

'*Kira.*' The man tightens his grip on her head. Kira swallows a gasp. 'Because you're being an idiot, let me ask you this. What did you do yesterday?'

Easy. Kira lifts her chin. She can strike him down, replace fear with scorn. Yesterday, she...

Her breath sputters, retracts. Yesterday's not there.

That's ridiculous, she thinks, but at the same time, it isn't. Her mind is a coloured, blurry wash: not a flicker of a meal, not a hint of conversation, not the horror film she thought she might have watched. Not the clothes she wore, or the painting she worked on, or if she worked a shift at the shop. Beyond the beach and the murky, violet-green dream, there's nothing.

Kira sets her face to slate and glowers. 'Why does it matter?'

'Why do you think?' The man sighs in a whoosh. 'What month is it, Kira? What year? You must know that, right?' He pushes out his lower jaw, sarcastic and despairing. 'Jesus. Why are you being so *stupid*?'

'I'm not.' Kira twists her face to contempt. It's the only nonverbal ammunition she has. 'And you'—she musters all her conviction—'are insane. Either that, or you're playing some kind of game. A game in extremely bad taste, by the way.' She drops her voice to a hard, cutting hiss. 'Or do you actually believe what you're saying?'

He does. It's obvious even as she tosses insolence, even as she daubs him as delusional. He believes what he's saying, and her anger is failing.

She trips uneasily over his questions. What year *is* it? Is it July? August? An Indian summer in September? How old is she? Fourteen? Twenty?

'You're mad.' Her throat constricts; it's anaphylactic. She doesn't know who she is. 'You have to be. What's all of this if...' She closes her eyes, shaking her head, again, again, again. Her mind is misting, splitting at the seams. How quickly her clarity muddles. 'What's all this if you're not?'

You're mad. You're all mad.

We are not mad. We are trapped.

The words arrive unbidden. Kira twists her fingers. The joints crack but the pain doesn't come.

'Exactly that.' The man drops his hands to her shoulders. 'It's a dream like the others, except it's here to convince you you're awake. They want to keep you sleeping until you die.' He shakes her shoulders, short and sharp. 'Kira, *you need to wake up.*'

And now you're going to see.

'No.' Kira shakes her head vehemently. Murky, violet darkness. Trees, snow, screaming, ghosts. 'Stop it. Stop. Please.'

'Why don't you remember yesterday, Kira?' The man persists, squeezing her. 'Think. How is it so hot? You can't remember the month, but you know it's never this hot. It's not possible for England to *get* this hot. And you know you never tan.' Another shake, and she chokes out a sob. He's right, but he can't be. She swoons, sways. He can't, yet the darkness swims into colour. Burning torches, breaking hands, a woman breathing *child*. 'Why do you not know the year? Are you fourteen? Twenty? Why don't you *know*?'

He steps back suddenly, spreading his hands. 'How do I know exactly what you're thinking? How do I know your *name*? How did it get dark so quickly? It's four o'clock, Kira. Think.'

Tears glaze her eyes. 'I can't,' she whispers. Streetlamps and starlight. Leather-black night. An owl's call in the distance. Nails scraping skin, she rakes her hands through her hair.

Monsters, and girls who go looking for them.

Another voice, another woman. Kira digs her fingers into her scalp. Her legs are watery, her mind too full, her head too heavy, too light. The man wavers. She's drunk. He's drugged her.

Blurry at the edges, the night starts to fray. Grainy, paper-like, it merges with the sky. The alley tilts on its axis.

What's happening? She cries, but doesn't make a sound. Her hands on her skull are weightless. She rocks. A thinning poster tacked over a painting, the world is coming apart.

She falls. Her legs cave, and she floats to the ground. No pain. No anything. *Kira*, the man calls, like wind through a tunnel. Her vision crunches and crumbles to black. *Kira. Kira, wake up. Wake up. Kira, wake up. Wake up.*

Her head is immaterial. She tries to curl up, but her legs won't work. The ground is a breath of stale air. Spun by dizziness, she's a nauseous rush. She's terror. Nothing. She's nothing.

The man calls. *Kira.* Her mind fades. *Kira.*

The darkness sucks her scream away. *Kira, wake up.*

Wake up.

Kira, wake up.

32

Snow

'Wake up!'

The voice still hollers through a tunnel but closer, accompanied by a shaking, a shuddering that she wishes with all her fatigue would *stop*. Leave her in peace, leave her to lie. To lie, to die. It doesn't matter. Leave her alone. She's had enough.

'Wake up, Kira!' the voice shouts. Rough and creaking, it's right in her ear.

She opens her eyes with a start. A flutter of black sighs away into the trees like a curtain lifted by a breeze. Kira watches it go, unthinking. The voice had been so sure, so present, the shuddering more like shaking hands than the shivering of her bones, but there's no one here. She lets her eyes drift closed again. Caught between here and there, she wavers, clinging to an alley that seemed so real.

Go back. Sleep, sink. The colours were beautiful, the warmth was divine… but the harder Kira grapples, the more the dark town recedes. In its place lurches a burning, lacerating, unbearable cold, and as the last of her dream residue fades, the pain hits her like an avalanche.

A gasp sucks her breath away. Ice. Fire. She's freezing, surrounded by the heady scent of pine. She's Romy, curled up under a tree. Kira sharpens with her senses. If she doesn't move, she'll die.

Everything's so *heavy*, though. She could stay here a while and see what she sees; from her sheltered vantage point, clustered among roots, the world looks reasonably safe.

No. Kira drags her mind up, up, up. This isn't safe; this is Whiteland. Move.

Lethargically, she forces her weary mind to act. She can't let it linger half-asleep, susceptible and weak, or the *something* that creeps in to play with her thoughts will find a crack in a flash.

She's just so exhausted. Her arms feel disconnected, as though she's slept with them under her head. Her legs are feeble, flaky rods. 'Whoa,' she mutters, standing dimly, slumping into the tree. She's back in the forest; of course she is. It's only coming clear now that she's properly awake: she was a fool for believing in the dream. Reality has an otherness the mind can't recreate.

Later. Right now, it's snowing, and it's dark. Move.

Battling her balance, Kira pushes off the tree. Snowflakes patter her skin in a swirl before her eyes. Kira blinks. They land on her lashes. One foot in front of the other: repeat. Her legs have morphed into unwieldy pylons, walking a tightrope that sways in the wind. Everything, everything, everything hurts. One foot in front of the other. Be strong.

She trips on a hidden root and flails, freewheeling before she re-centres. One foot *carefully* in front of the other. The forest is thick here. Saplings and brambles and trunks dig each other in the ribs, but rather than bearing despair, it brings hope. Somewhere, there has to be a shelter of sorts. A hollow in a tree, or a tent of branches, low and heavy with snow. She casts her eyes through the undergrowth. Focus. The night is dense and claustrophobic, heavy with the clouds. God, if she could see. The snow is the brightest thing around, and it's muffled by falling flakes. *Focus.* With shelter, she'll survive the night. After that, she'll go after Callum, and after *that*, they'll find her family. Mum. Dad. Romy. They will.

Her mind flickers. Callum. Didn't she see him somewhere? In a dream, in the Kyo—Callum crouched by something? A snow hole?

Maybe. Kira's vision speckles. It's hard to remember. Dizziness washes in, and she sways, slapping her palm to a cool, dry trunk. Colours dance behind her eyes, churning with her stomach. She got moving too soon. She was worn out, cold, and weak. She didn't allow herself time to recover. A short rest, and she'll be fine. Come on.

But the dizziness won't abate. She's forgetting to breathe, and it's sticking, rasping. Her thoughts thicken to peat. She has to plough on, but her body—just—

She hits the snow with a thud.

'...Goddammit. If you die on me now, Kira, I swear...'

'...Sisters so fond of fainting under trees...'

'...Fat lot of good that first aid training is for supernatural bullshit...'

'...Song if it'll make you wake the hell up. Mary, mother of—at least you're breathing. What do you want? I know lots of Biffy Clyro...'

She's been drifting. This time, she didn't dream; this time, she was walking through the forest, falling through the snowflakes, and now she's here. Drifting.

Millimetre by millimetre, she lifts her groggy eyelids. The voice is real; there's no invisible, shouting entity, and nor is some distant part of her brain tricking the rest awake. Tight-faced with worry, it's Callum.

She blinks. He's leaning over her. She fights her slurring brain to stay awake, and blinks again.

'Oh, sweet Jesus.' Callum tips back his head. 'I didn't want to have to sing. No—' Wild-eyed, loose with relief, he scrapes a hand over his hair and back. 'Whatever. I would have done whatever.' He releases a gale of a sigh. 'This is a daft question, but—are you okay?'

Is she? The ice-fire-ice burns strong. It shakes her body like a candle flame, but she's no longer out in the snow. They're somewhere shadowed, white walls diffusing a pure, faint lightness. The ground is cool but firm. 'I'm cold.'

A whispering croak. She barely feels the words, but Callum must have heard. Raising her torso up from his legs, he tucks his coat around her and hugs her to his chest. It doesn't just feel like come-and-get-warm; it feels like Christ-you-scared-me, and also, I-don't-want-to-crush-you.

'I was half-convinced you were dead,' he murmurs. His breath tickles warm on her hair. 'I thought I saw something going past the branches, so I followed. Not the wisest idea I've ever had, but I'd seen nothing since I left the village. Nothing, and no one, and this was...'

He shakes his head against hers. The friction hurts her tender scalp. 'I don't know what it was. A shadow, I think.'

He pauses, but Kira can't rouse a response. Buried in the cold, it takes several moments for his words to be more than noise. Smarting, drilling, migraine noise.

'Ahh.' Callum shakes his head again. 'It really was a bad idea. I kept seeing this shadow up ahead, and I was starting to think I should probably stop following, but then I found you.' A tiny huff escapes his lips. 'All splayed out under a tree. You weren't moving, and it was so much like finding Romy that...' He tightens his arms around her. A pause, a sigh. 'What happened?'

That is a very good question. The thought comes thick and slow, like sludge. Before she woke up in the forest, where was she? What *did* happen? How did she get from here to home, from home to here? The women were closing in, and then...

'They thought I wouldn't wake up.' Kira lifts her hefty head, washing cold with the truth. Colliding with Callum's cheek, she winces. She's oh-so-sunburn-sore. 'Sorry.' She works her anaesthetised mouth. 'I mean, the women put me in a dream and didn't expect me to wake up from it. The cold was meant to kill me, and I was meant to join them.'

Leering faces, the burning pool. The blood-freezing screams.

'The women?' Callum repeats in a frown. 'The people who chased you from the village? They caught you?'

Shivering, Kira leans into his chest. 'No. Different women. They were...' *The defiled. The denied. The forever.* Her breath hitches, and she swallows. 'They're the last thing I remember from here.'

Callum pulls his coat tighter around them. 'Okay, but I'll need a tad more than that. The village chased you, and you ran, and these different women took you and put you in a dream so you could join them?'

'I guess.' Twisting her defrosting lips, Kira shakes her head. 'But why would they want me to? And why didn't they just kill me themselves? Maybe they couldn't, because they're dead.' The words drop to a murmur. 'But they could *touch* me. They could touch me, and they could hurt me, so they could have killed me.' Her head thunks back to Callum's shoulder. 'God, this *place*. It must have been a game.'

The jumbled thoughts hang before her eyes, impossible but not. 'They could have killed me, but they didn't. They preferred to stick me out in the cold and make me think I was home.' Darkly satisfied, Kira huffs. 'I guess I'm bad at dying.'

She'd sleep, and then she'd die. It's a fair enough assumption. Why would she want to wake up? No outsider would rather be here than home, and would never think home is the lie.

Callum inhales, ready to speak, but Kira cuts him off. 'You were there.' She twists around to look at him, wide-eyed with memory. The dream's end is coming back: the reason she woke up alive. 'I didn't know it at the time, but it was you. Definitely you. You told me the dream wasn't real, that it was the same as the other dreams, even though I don't remember any other dreams.'

Callum's stare is a work of art. Confusion to bemusement to something close to humour, he works his eyebrows. 'What?'

Kira sighs. 'Yes, I know. I hear myself. But hear me out in turn. Maybe there were other dreams, and maybe there weren't. I don't know. But you forced me to listen to you and forced me to stop dreaming. I heard your voice, even though you weren't there when I woke up. When I woke up the first time,' she adds at a bonus raised eyebrow. 'I woke up before and tried to find some kind of shelter, but I fainted. Or I guess that's what happened, because now I'm here. Were you calling, or something? Did I actually hear you?'

Callum raises the other eyebrow. 'Not at that point.' He inches one shoulder up, a careful shrug. 'When I left the village I was, but when I found you, I was following the shadow.' He shrugs again. 'I don't understand what you're talking about, but I definitely wasn't involved.' His lips inch toward their familiar teasing territory. Looking away, he covers them. 'Sorry to disappoint.'

Slowly, Kira nods. 'No, it's…yeah. Of course it wasn't you. It must have been some clever part of my brain, telling me I couldn't stay asleep. Like in any dream, I guess, when you're realising it's not as real as you thought. But the *voice.*'

She taps her lip. 'That was real. It was yours in the dream, but outside… wait.' She frowns at Callum, finger paused in the air. 'You followed a shadow?'

Callum stares. 'And you only pick up on this now?'

Kira stares straight back. 'I was busy.'

She lifts the ends of her hair: frozen. Sweeps a hand along her jeans: damp. 'Coming back from the dead takes time.'

Callum rolls his eyes. 'You weren't dead, but point taken. Yes, I followed a shadow.' His voice snags on the words, an actor struggling to believe his lines. 'Maybe whatever it was woke you up and led me to you; stranger things have happened. Like whatever the hell you're talking about.'

He scratches the back of his head. *Flummoxed. Flabbergasted.* When all of this was just beginning, she was thinking in words like that.

'Can you rewind a bit?' Callum stretches, scraping the ceiling with his gloves. Dust motes of snow drift down to their heads. 'Start again from about three chapters back? Someone tried to kill you? No.' He lifts his palms. 'Someone put you in a *dream* and tried to kill you? What happened to the angry mob?'

Disgruntlement grumbles in Kira's throat. 'When you put it like that, it sounds ridiculous.'

So does the rest, but she tells it anyway.

When she finishes, he's quiet. The wind moans through the silence. Powder patters past the snow-cut den. The Kyo were truthful there, at least: the door of branches, the low, carved space, crudely hacked from the snow. She'd been so concerned about Callum, watching for her through the cracks.

He shifts against the packed wall. 'Well, you really are bad at dying.'

Small and rueful, she laughs. 'I did tell you.' A shrug, between resignation and longing. 'I've had ample opportunity.' She twists her fingers into her sleeves, stained with dusty white. 'It's strange. I never thought I'd miss Devon. It's staid, and it's predictable, but right now, I'd kill for an old grouch to tell me I should dress more like a girl.'

Callum snorts. 'So.' He holds his hands a foot apart. 'On a scale of one to a cave of banshees?'

'I'd take church-based activities, measly public transport, and a lack of supermarkets any day. No.' Kira smiles properly. '*Every* day.'

Callum smirks against her hair. 'And I'd take long-nosed neighbours, endless winters, measly public transport, and all those bloody cats. Speaking of banshees and scales,' he adds, as she huffs another small laugh, 'on a scale of one to dead, exactly how dead is dead?'

'Not zombie dead, if that's what you mean.' Kira pokes the corner of his mouth, turning down. 'Which, by the way, is a good thing. They were more like horror film ghosts. You know, the ones that haunt asylums and run at you in the dark.'

Her skin prickles at the memory. She shakes it off. 'Whatever. They said they were dead, and I believe it. I'm certainly not going back to find out.' She rubs her arms. The prickles have bobbled to goose bumps. 'The longer they think me dealt with, the better.'

And when they realise she's not?

She stills. The bottom of her stomach drops out. 'They'll know.'

She pulls away from Callum, winded. 'Oh, God. They'll know I'm still alive.' She crawls across the tiny floor to peer outside. A blizzard roars around the forest, obscuring all but the night. 'These women watch everything.'

Slowly, she sits back. Beyond the branches, there's nothing but snow. What did she expect to see? The ghost from before she fell? Here, at least, they're huddled, sheltered. Nothing can creep up from behind, take them by horrific surprise.

'They can't watch everything all at once.' Callum traces invisible water, the pool. 'Not in something so small. There's no space. Besides which, they're mad.'

'Maybe not.' Kira drags her knees to her chest. 'But they showed me you, and my parents, and Romy. Even Lena, because of course she's following us.' She lifts a listless hand and drops it. 'Sooner or later, they'll see I'm still alive and come find me. Maybe they can just take me the way they did before. I need to, I don't know.' She rubs a spot on her boots. Snow-stained and scuffed, they're as weary as she is. 'Leave. If they see us both here, they might take you, too.'

Callum laughs, a derisive 'ha.'

'Not a chance.' He nods at the snow. Fat flakes float through the gaps in the web, whipping about in the storm. 'Quite apart from the fact that we're staying together, do you get what'll happen if you leave? You'll either wind up lost and die from exposure, which is what the crazy, dead women want, or you'll wind up at the mercy of the forest's creatures of death. Either way, the banshees are happy. We'—he emphasises the word—'are not leaving here until morning. If the snow hasn't stopped, maybe not even then.'

Her boots are too far gone for salvation. Kira rubs at them regardless. 'What happens when they come for me?' She fixes on the wrinkled leather, pressing hard on the stains. 'They're mad, Callum. They'd kill us both, and you're not'—she juts out her chin, rubbing—'dying because of me.'

'Kira.' Callum borders on exasperation. 'Remember your own words: these women watch everything. If they watch everything, they'll already have seen you. And if they've already seen you, and they want to kill you, why aren't you already dead?'

Panic flares and settles. Kira looks up. He's right; she's alive, but *still*.

Callum spreads his hands. 'You can't be that important to them if they've let you sit here and fret. And there's no point running off into a blizzard because you think they want you to die. Listen.'

He manoeuvres himself to sit next to her. She's never seen him so sincere, so urgent…except, perhaps, in her dream. 'If they want you,' he says, 'they'll find you, and if they don't, then they won't. I know that's not encouraging, but it's more than likely true. Leaving won't make a difference.'

'It will if I go alone.'

'No.'

'No one's dying on my account, Callum.'

'No one's going to die at all.'

Kira lets her head droop. There must be straws; there must be something to clutch at.

Romy.

'Romy's still in the forest.' Straw acquired, Kira looks up. She sounds eager, desperate, but so what if it works? She won't put Callum in danger. 'If I left now, I could catch her up. She was moving far slower than I would, and considering she's half the reason we're here, it makes sense to use any advantage.'

'Kira.' Frustration flares in Callum's voice, like someone revving an engine. 'Stop. I get that you're scared, but you're being stupid. You can't catch your own left foot in this.'

Kira glances from him to the branches, the storm. 'I could try.'

'You could, and you'd die.' Callum's voice is terse. 'Romy'll be holed up like us. You won't find her, and going alone won't change that.'

'Callum.' Kira rubs her forehead. It sounds like a plea. 'Just listen. If I go alone, you stay alive. You've only known me a few days. It's never been your fight, but you've gone through all of this, and it's selfish to drag you through more.'

'Fucking *no*.' Callum clenches his fists on the snow. Kira starts. 'How many times?' he snaps. 'Neither of us are leaving until the storm is over. I don't care what you say, or any reasonable excuse you think you're going to find; going out there would be suicide.'

Callum's face is as set as his resolve. Good. Missing the point and refusing to leave makes it easier for her.

'The whole idea is me going alone.' Kira rocks onto her knees. 'I told you: you're not dying because of me. If I leave, you can go home.' She makes for the branches, steeling herself for the cold. 'You said it's what you want.'

'*No*.' Grabbing her arm, Callum yanks her back. 'You're twisting everything, and it's ludicrous. Did the women turn you mad as well as stupid? *We are not splitting up.*'

'We are.' Stubbornly, Kira wrenches against him. 'Let me go. I'm not a lit-tle girl, and if I want to leave, you can't stop me. Ah!'

Callum lets her go, and she topples. Before she can struggle back up, he pushes her down, pins her arms, and traps her legs between his own. Aggrava-tion blasts through her. Yet again, she's wedged fast.

'Why do people do this?' She growls. Apart from her feet, head, and hands, none of her limbs will budge. 'In the Kyo, they used magic. The dream you used force. He held me to a wall until I listened.' Glowering, she tugs on her wrists. 'The real you has done that, too, if you recall. Hey.' She ramps up her wrenching as Callum starts to smirk. 'It's not funny. I was saving your life.'

'No, you weren't. You were being a martyr.' Although his trap doesn't loos-en, his anger melts away. 'And it really is quite funny.' He bows his head, puff-ing out a laugh. 'Amazing. That's what it is. You're so impossible that live people, dead people, and dream characters come to the same conclusion: if you need to listen, you have to be restrained. I'm sorry, but that's funny. Oi.'

He jams her legs tighter as she tries to lift her knees. 'Is accepting defeat too much to ask? This position is neither flattering, comfortable, nor making me feel like a gentleman. Ow.'

His face flickers with pain. Kira tracks his glance. His fingers are red and leathery, his knuckles yellow from ageing bruises and bubbled with un-popped blisters.

'Oh, God.' Fresh guilt flashes through her. 'What happened to you? Why didn't you say? Get up, Callum. Let me see.'

Suspiciously, Callum sits back against the wall. 'Why didn't I say?' he re-peats dryly. His tone is spiced with teasing. 'Oh, I don't know. Something to do with a bid for freedom? I didn't think I'd be on a winner with "please don't struggle, my hands hurt."'

'Shush.' Scraping a handful of snow from the entrance, Kira presses it to the blisters.

'Ow.' Callum winces. 'I did that already, but thanks. I think. And as for what happened'—he flashes his eyebrows—'crazy women, two-point-oh. When you ran out of the hobbit-hole, Iris kicked her husband, threw her el-bows everywhere, and got away. I tried to grab her, but she picked up a stool and knocked me over. I didn't see it coming.'

He gestures widely: *what can you do?* 'I landed with my hand in the fire. It could have been worse, though. The stool was only small, and I didn't burn that badly. Oh, so now you're smiling.'

He lifts his gaze heavenwards, his arm still swept. Scouring another handful of snow, Kira bites back her amusement. With his arm still out, he's a scruffy-haired Jesus.

Jesus in a ski coat, but Jesus nonetheless. 'Very sorry.' She inclines her solemn head. Praise our Lord and Saviour. 'But now the tables have turned, perhaps you'll be more sympathetic.'

The storm patters snow through the branches. A flurry flutters into Callum's face. He grimaces. 'Puh. Women are cruel.'

'You were beaten up by a crazy lady who said I had a tail.' Slyly, Kira looks up from his hand. 'To quote you, it really is quite funny.'

Deadpan, Callum holds her gaze. 'What she actually said was that your mother had a tail.'

It's too much. His insulted manner, the implications of his words. The whole situation, unreal and getting worse. They argued about leaving a snow hole, in the middle of the night, in a storm. Letting him go, Kira ducks her head.

'That makes no difference.' She starts to laugh. It's the queen of lies, and that makes her laugh more. 'Jesus.' She sinks backwards to the floor. Her chest shudders, hilarity gasping, and she shakes her head at herself. 'What's wrong with me? She—she said my mum had a *tail*.'

Carefully, Callum eases down beside her. 'She did. Or at least, she implied it. And I have no idea what's wrong with you.' He smirks. 'I've stopped trying to figure it out.'

'Hey.' Kira bats half-heartedly at him, placing a hand on her heaving chest. 'I could—wait.' She lifts a finger, breathes in deep, and swallows the last of the laughter. 'I'm done. What I was going to say'—she regards him pointedly—'was that I could be a whole lot worse. I could be beating you up with a stool or breaking my own fingers. All things considered, I'm doing okay.'

She rolls onto her side. The blizzard shows no signs of letting up, and snow has crept into her boots. She nods down her legs at the makeshift door. 'Can some of that wood be spared?'

'No need.' Callum points vaguely into the shelter's dark depths. 'There's loads back there. I was planning on lighting a fire if you hadn't woken up when you did. I'd have waved your hands in front of it, or something. With all your adventures and escaping, I forgot.' He grins. 'I don't know who built this place and filled it with sticks, but I'd love to kiss their feet and tell them they're stunning. Without them, I'd be cursing my life up a tree.' His grin falters to a frown. 'Oh, no.'

Kira averts her eyes, but too late. 'That face.' He taps her cheek. 'I recognise that face. What is it?'

Nothing. Everything. 'Just...' She pulls off her gloves, finger by finger. They're clammy and unpleasant from scraping the snow. 'I know I was laughing about it, but what if the woman was right? The hobbit-hole woman. Iris.'

She flinches at another shriek of the wind. It's too much like the Kyo, like Enny's scream as she broke her neck. Framing it as a wriggle for comfort, she shifts closer to Callum. 'It makes me wonder why all this happened.' She toys with the wool on her cuff. 'How it happened, really. Mum knew where to go to help Romy, so...' She trails off. The thoughts, never mind the words, are so hard to get out. *Huldra.* 'What if she is who they say she is?'

Callum taps her lips. 'Stop worrying.' It's more of an order than a consolation. 'It's possibly even less productive than your middle-earth-martyr idea, throwing caution to the wind to get to Mordor. You can't change what they say.'

'But what if they're telling the truth?' Kira curls her toes in her boots. 'I'd be half a huldra. Half a monster. Everything I thought I knew would be a lie.'

'And you'd deal with it.' Callum squeezes her arm. Her chest shivers. Her belly thrills. 'Rationalise. Use your weird Kira-logic. Your mum is who she is. Whoever that turns out to be, though, it doesn't change anything. It doesn't make you someone else, and certainly not a monster.'

He shifts. It brings him closer, his rough hand warm through her coat. The night seems to be narrowing, focusing around them. Kira is suddenly aware of her pulse. 'We'd all be someone else,' she murmurs. Callum's expression is shadowed, but she looks away regardless. 'Me, and Mum, and Romy. It'd be in us to be capable of...'

Seduction. Murder.

They're monsters.

'The same things everyone's capable of,' Callum finishes deliberately. 'Listen.' He moves his resolute hand to her shoulder. 'Your mum may have been someone else in the past, but at the end of the day, she's your mum. Her past is gone, and it'll never be yours.' He leans into her, his voice firm, hand firmer. 'Don't let it make you hate yourself.'

He's moved so close. Kira shuts her eyes. Thank God for the dark; her face is heating, her chest squeezing tight about her lungs, her heart. She can feel his warmth, his breath, the moment coming where you know, you *know*. This is the least appropriate time. 'But,' she tries lamely, 'what if…'

Sliding his hand behind her head, Callum kisses her. Not like the first time, but certain, less whimsical, more than Whiteland playing games with their minds. The forest pines are in his hair, on his skin. A hint of cologne still lingers. She moves her hand to his face, along the scratch of his jaw, and pulling him close, closer still, everything starts to drift.

Until, abruptly, he pulls away. 'How old are you?' His voice is low, his breathing less than steady.

Kira blinks. So is hers. 'What?' The question swirls. 'How old—does it matter?'

Callum shuts his eyes, puts a hand on her arm, removes it, puts it back. 'I just realised I have no idea.' Heavily, he exhales. 'You could be fifteen and look older. I don't want to be a creep.'

The penny spins, slows, and drops. 'Out of all the things we could be worrying about, that's the one you choose?' A smile touches her lips, almost coy. 'How very noble.' She hesitates. Normally, it would amuse her to freak him out a bit. Normally…but not now. 'I'm eighteen.' She cocks her head. 'You've redeemed your past ungentlemanly actions. That really was quite noble.'

Callum huffs a low laugh. 'Thank you. Good.' He nods, and again. 'Thank God.'

'One thing.'

He tenses. The urge to tease is so very strong, but Kira simply smiles. 'Am I the creep? Are *you* fifteen?'

He blinks, blinks, and slowly lifts his well-practiced eyebrows. 'I sincerely hope not. I'll have you know, I'll be twenty-one in—'

This time, he is silenced. With a breath, Kira pulls him in, and in the cold of the shelter and the echo of the wind, in the dark of the storm, they're warm.

33

Lone walks and night talks

Missing a leg and wobbling mournfully, the wooden stool tips.
Erik closes his eyes. The noise leaps and bounds, and cursing his foot, he
braces for the cataclysm.

Nobody moves. The stool rolls across the floor, taps the rocky fireplace,
and settles. Curled up together, his family stays asleep.

It's where he should be, too. Erik exhales softly, slowly. He would like
to join them, love to join them, but now the wind has stilled and the snow is
but a trickle, he must go. If they've survived this long, the outsiders have been
lucky; any longer without help, however, and Atikur, this forest, this place only
equalled by the Tomi desert, might swallow them whole.

The cave echoes back to silent dark. Slinging his satchel over his shoulder,
Erik treads quietly to the door. A last look thrown behind him as he tugs on
his boots. With a heavy, shoulder-slumping sigh, he scoops up his snowshoes,
pushes through the curtains, and stomps out into the dark.

It shouldn't take long, he assures himself, testy but resigned. He won't be
looking to the ends of the earth. If they've left Atikur and reached the Zaino
river, he has no need to follow. Neither weather nor beasts should bother them,
and Sofia will take it from there.

At the snow bank, he bends and straps the snowshoes to his feet. A brutal shiver makes his back click, and he straightens up with a frown; the weather
may have calmed, but a deadly cold has settled. At the very least, the outsiders
will be chilled to the bone, if not completely chilled to death. He glances behind him. Should he turn around, fetch something warm? A few extra minutes
to the cave and back, for the sake of their survival?

No. If necessary, he can give them something of his; going back risks waking Iris. It was pure, precious luck that he slipped out in the first place. Her anger at his journey would be monstrous.

Retrieving a match-bag, a wind protector, and a candle stub, Erik lights the wick, slips it into the glass, and starts to climb. Whoever Kira is, she did not deserve a manhunt. There may be something in the link to Anneliese, but his discernment is his pride, and it isn't overly convinced. The girl knew little about Whiteland and nothing whatsoever of the Huldra.

At the top of the slope, Erik pauses for breath, for his tired bones to rest. Huldra can be incredibly, convincingly deceptive; is it possible that everything she said was a lie? He holds his cold hand above the candle, thinking. It's not out of the question at all for Iris to have been right. On one point, she certainly *was* right: Callum was helplessly, hopelessly attached. He knows as well as anyone that the Huldra rely on their lure.

Men trailing them like baby animals, following after the mother. Men clueless until it's too late.

Stop. Banishing his doubt, Erik grinds his muscles into a snowshoed-march. Kira was chased in this direction, stumbling, staggering, screaming for her life; whatever her parentage, she's an outsider. They both are, and they'll need his help. He shakes his head grimly. Ørenna, she was chased away with fire; he *has* to help her, in order to make amends for the wrongs of Haavö. He can't let a blatant horror fester unredeemed.

Numbing in the bitter air, Erik secures his hat over his ears. It *was* a horror; the actions of the villagers, *his* villagers, turn his mouth sour and his thoughts dour, and he glowers deeper than deep. They're well aware of Iris—to the skies, a few have wished to cast her out—and yet, at the barest hint of threat, they hang on her pronouncements and scurry off to battle. Were it the first time, it would almost be acceptable—there's more than enough to fear in the forest, and the witch Iris alerted them to would have proved a grisly danger. But the harmless travellers, or the peaceful, daring fossegrim? What community is he a part of that can repeatedly act this way?

Erik sighs so heavily the candle stutters. Not one he can ever foresee himself agreeing with, even if, for his survival, he remains in their midst. Burying his face in beard and coat, his thoughts turn even dourer. Here he is, the stubborn dissenter, trudging through the snow with a solitary candle. Trying to help two outsiders who may be trouble, may be on a questionable quest, and may have already perished. He sighs again, a low rumble. There's no burden quite like righteousness.

He's wallowing in this, pushing through a cluster of elegant thorns veiled by frost and snow, when a darkness snares his eye. In the shadows of a tree on the other side, almost buried, is a shape.

A dark, unmoving shape. At once, his grumbling shames him. Erik bows his head. Righteousness should not be a burden; not if it prevents this. Beneath the tree lies a woman.

Cautiously, he trudges toward her. After each crunch of snow, he listens. No wolves around, drawn by her death. No roaming moroaica. No indication that the Kyo lurk to tow her spirit down.

No sign of Freya. Although, if the huldra was here, he wouldn't know until he died.

Which is something he shouldn't dwell on. Reaching the woman, Erik crouches with the candle. She's another outsider: her legs are drawn into her chest, her fingers locked dreadfully around them. A long black coat has iced to her body, her short hair glittered with icicles, and as the flame flickers over her, there's no doubt; with her eyes squeezed shut, her chapped mouth twisted, and her skin blue with frost, she's frozen.

She's dead.

'Ørenna,' Erik murmurs. The prayer is incomplete, and its full form makes him shudder, but *Ørenna* is enough. *Be safe. Pass on.* All of its meanings sift through his head as he creaks to his feet. The woman's crooked fingertips are black. The blizzard must have caught her.

As wretched as it is, though, there's nothing he can do. The flame of his candle is halfway gone, and whether or not he finds Kira and Callum, soon he must head back. With a last, sombre look at the woman, he moves on.

At least Whiteland, especially at night, is not as vicious as it used to be. The thought is half a distraction. Anneliese's reign was dangerous. She never reigned in any real sense, but she was unscrupulous, ruthless, and reckless, and she encouraged others, whether Huldra, witch, mountain troll, or marsh-dwelling kelpie, to do the same. They may worry about Freya, but she's fear; she's not a nightmare. Anneliese took fifteen men instead of ten. Anneliese was the terror in the dark.

My, my. Erik grimaces. Between Iris's maniacal adamance about Anneliese, and his will not to picture the woman in the snow, he can't help but morosely remember. When the creature got out, it was a shudder, a ripple, a shock-wave known but twice before, and in the backs of their minds, the people felt the Whispers. They were swarming, buzzing like angry bees, and nothing—not the beasts, not the inhumane spirits—were exempt from the rushing of their rage. They're always there, omniscient murmurs like the pressure of a storm, but that night…Erik shakes his head. That night, they were an armada.

Seeping from the northern ice in a misty, insipid mass, set to pour through Atikur in pursuit of Anneliese. Nothing showed its face in the end, but the in-credulous horror was a taste in the air. They were tangible, all-encompassing. All the world could do was hide.

He may be unaccustomed to scathing cynicism, but Erik's mouth curls up. Basking above the ice plains, the Whispers threaten, wheedle, and pompously rule, relying on the loyalty of those who hate the outside to keep their domin-ion. He thinks this sourly, trudging through the snow, through the silhouetted bracken and the close-knit trees. What are they really? Puppet kings? They're not puppets, but in others lies the power. The muscle, the movement. The Whispers have knowledge, they slip to the edges of the outside, but they're not physical. There's only so much you can do with the minds of men and beasts.

Although maybe that's it. He's thought this tens, if not hundreds of times, but he always hopes to reach a different end. The Whispers creep into whoever they need; they listen to homes, villages, mountain walks, and they slither from this world like leeches to take the thoughts of outsiders and bend them. Only the Kyo have similar talents—when they manage to slip beneath the Whispers' watch—and no one, physical presence or no, can leave.

Erik's mouth thins. The only way to leave is through gross sacrifice, and the only way to enter…he hadn't liked to say, but if Kira isn't Huldra, either she or Callum must be *some*thing. If they weren't a part of Whiteland, Whiteland wouldn't have let them in.

And if it's Kira, and Iris is right?

Erik shivers. Ancestry does not beget evil.

He sets this in the front of his mind and moves on. The lingering wind knocks about his boots. The iced air burns his throat. Even though the moon is elsewhere, there are stars; faraway pinpricks, but stars nonetheless. They'll be brighter over the Zaino and bigger above the ice plains; perhaps, over the grass-lands, they shine with the moon. One day, he'll travel beyond the river people's hub. One day, he'll take his girls, and one day, they'll see it.

Away with the luminaries, he almost misses the light. Warily, Erik stops, angling his head. Deep in a snow bank and crisscrossed by branches, flames lick quiet and faint. A fire?

Pushing guardedly through the bushes, Erik studies the bank. Above his head, the spirits click, the ones that watch in the night. The protectors. Which means…

…The outsiders. As he watches, hopeful and statuesque, the branches move aside. 'Who's there?' a low voice calls. 'If you don't come out, I'm going back to bed.'

Erik huffs a gruff laugh. 'Fine way to scare off intruders.'

He steps forward, lifting the sputtering candle. Crouched in the opening, Callum jerks back.

'Calm down.' Erik raises his other hand, too. 'You know me. I saved you and your girl from the mist. You were chased from my village. Remember?' He brings the candle closer to his face. Callum nods, and he blows it out.

Callum watches the wick fizzle and still.

'It has to last the way back,' Erik says. 'I didn't want to wake anyone by rummaging to find more.'

With another slow nod, Callum moves toward him, away from the glowing hollow. As long as she's not been dropped in a dream, Kira might as well stay asleep. She needs it.

'How will you get back?' he asks, pulling his hoodie sleeves down. The hollow was cosy and toasted, like a world within the world. Stepping outside is a stark reminder that the world they're in is cold. 'We can't seem to go anywhere without being taken in circles and separated. Kira couldn't get away from your village no matter how much she ran straight, and when I tried searching for her, I kept coming back to the same patch of snow. This patch, specifically.' He stamps the ground. He came to hate its guts. 'How do you get where you're trying to go?'

Erik strokes the needles of a low-hanging branch. 'You're outsiders,' he says. 'You don't know how to live here. There are ways in which we manipulate the land.' He lets the tree go. 'If I touch this trunk and go left'—he nudges its roots with a hide-wrapped boot laced to a splintered snowshoe—'I'll be on my way to the Atikur fossegrim's island. If I do the same and go right, I may find myself near to Haavö, my village, or somewhere close to the desert. This is why I believe you're being helped.' Erik's craggy face turns to the hollow. 'You and Kira found each other, when you could have ended up with the Huldra, and she in a myrling's path.'

Words. So many unknown words, too many to tackle at once. Callum settles for what he can ten-percent fathom. 'There was a shadow,' he hedges. Erik may not have joined the mob, but he could still lead them here. 'Or something I saw the shadow of. And a...' He digs his hands in his kangaroo pouch. *Hansel-and-Gretel-witch-in-a-cloak?* 'Woman.' His mouth quirks. 'Although I don't know if you'd call saying *child* and vanishing "help."'

'You would, believe me.' Erik laughs softly. 'I imagine she was a spirit, the same as your shadow.' His rugged expression turns thoughtful. 'Was that all she said?'

Callum opens his mouth to say *yes* before the scene replays in his mind. The woman appearing in the space of a blink. Kira scraping her chair back and crashing to the floor. Then, there were two words spoken. *Child* and...

'Actually, no.' Callum thins his eyes at the snow. This never helps anyone remember things, but hey, they can but try. 'She said...' He scours his mind. One second. Two. Five. 'I don't know.' He shakes his head and gives up. 'Something like *Odin*, which would have been cool, but it 100 percent was not.'

Erik's face is still thoughtful. Slowly, his gaze travels to the hollow and back to Callum. 'Ørenna?'

Callum sifts through the scene in his mind. 'Maybe? Honestly, I don't know. We were too'—the word *scared* almost comes out, but there's no way he's admitting to that—'surprised.'

Erik bows his head. 'Of course.' He considers the forest floor in a way that says he's considering his words, too. 'That's good, though. Very good.'

A branch drops snow to the ground with a *whumpf.* Callum starts. 'Good?' He looks back to Erik, more rattled than he'd like. It's snow. It's just snow. 'On the outside, spirits are the opposite of good, and they're really not meant to talk.'

Not that he ever thought they existed. Maybe, out there, they don't.

'I'm sure.' Erik bows his head. 'But whoever your spirit was, she's protecting you. If she wasn't, she wouldn't have said Ørenna, and if she is, you can't be a threat.'

Presumably this makes sense to someone.

'If you were,' Erik continues, 'the mist would not attack you. In quiet ways, with signs we miss, there are those who help the humans they were. You've been recognised as more akin to us than anything else.'

He glances at the hollow. Callum can almost hear his mind, his wife doubting Kira: *Huldra.* 'We're not akin to humans,' he says. A breeze drifts around him. It brings powder, the scent of snow, their fire's syrupy smoulder. He jigs on the balls of his feet with a shiver. 'We *are* humans.'

Huldra.

Stop.

Erik inclines his chin. 'Indeed. Which reminds me.' The corners of his lips pinch. 'Did you know there was another outsider here?'

Callum's intestines twist. Lena. They considered tracking her down before deciding it wouldn't end well; if she followed them here, and puts people to sleep, she may well knock them out and drag them home by their toes.

'A woman?' he asks. 'Short black hair?' Erik's face is sombre, gruffly concerned. Callum's intestines twist out of place. 'Really thin? Probably a long black coat?'

Erik is nodding. His face winces. Callum narrows his eyes. 'What about her?'

Five, ten heartbeats. 'What?' Callum presses. Looking off through the night, through the dusted starlight, Erik's throat is working. 'You've seen her, so what is it?'

Fifteen heartbeats, twenty. Somewhere distant, the breeze rustles, branches creak and sigh. 'I'm sorry,' Erik says grudgingly. His small grey eyes meet Callum's. 'I am. I found her frozen. Dead.'

The rest is white noise, condensing to a ring. Callum stares through him. Lena, frozen. Lena, dead.

Lena, here because of him. Silence settles on the air. Callum tips back his head. The star-dotted sky is ghostly, and he stares through it as well. He never liked Lena—she was a sharp-tongued, acerbic gossip who snapped more often than she smiled—but she shouldn't have died. She should definitely not have died *here.*

She wouldn't have, if not for him.

For the first time, he understands Kira. Drowned with guilt for him being here, for enduring all they have. He's her Lena.

And there, their differences are bared. If Kira had her way, he'd be packed off tonight with a promise to keep in touch. Even having kissed him, she'd want him to leave. They've known each other less than a week, and she's dragged him into hell. She feels it all so sharply.

Good thing they're both that bloody stubborn. Shit, he feels things sharply, too, but while she lets it cut her, he turns the blade. What's the point of this, all of this, if it ends with him going back, alone? He'd feel like a kid sloping back to his house after threatening to run away. It has to mean something. It all has to matter.

What's the point of Lena dying if none of it *matters*?

Shit. Shit. Fuck. Lena *died*.

'Why are you here?' Callum looks back to Erik. A fetid taste lines his mouth, coating his teeth and tongue. 'If it's to make us feel bad about Lena, you can leave. You succeeded.'

Erik regards him shrewdly. He looks away. 'I wanted to make sure you were still alive.' He slips his rough, grey coat from his shoulders. 'And to apologise for how your girl was treated. Is she all right?'

Teeth gritted, Callum nods. He's set to sink through the ground, to the centre of the earth and beyond. Does the centre of the earth work the same in this place? Slowly, he exhales. Jesus. They're so damn far from home.

Maybe he should listen to Kira. Run now, stop when he's out, when he's back in Motalles with its icy ground, its smell of raclette, its ever-present skiers and sledgers and dogs. Better yet, stop when he's back in Madrid, where this'll be nothing more than a nightmare Kira got from the Kyo.

Kira. All images of running erode, leaving him stark and cold. In their place is the sense of losing a balloon and watching it take to the sky. Sure, she's right. He barely knows her. He knows her family less, and doesn't need to help them. But for one, he's turning that blade for Lena, and for another, what kind of man would he be if he left a girl alone in a forest—any forest, magically fucked or not—so he could run home to his mum?

'Good.' As if he heard the mental skirmish, Erik holds out his coat. Callum takes it, arms dipping at the weight of the wool. He has to stay, but God, he can't stand to be awake. He can't. He can't. He—

'If you still intend to carry on'—the skier removes his poncho, shades of brown and thickly spun—'follow the trees with the lowest branches. The ones that scrape the ground.'

Callum doesn't have it in him to scoff. 'Why?'

'It's the way to manipulate the land so it takes you to the Zaino. A river,' Erik amends, securing his hat back on his head. 'You need to cross it to get to the ice plains. Nowhere else has answers to something on the outside. There's no guarantee the Whispers will, or that they'll want to help. If you're following someone, though, that's where they'll be going.'

It takes a moment to process that not all of this makes sense. 'The what?' he repeats. His voice sounds awful and feels even worse. 'The Whispers?'

'Mm.' Erik sounds like a cautionary tale. 'If you don't find who you're following, they might know what to do. Alternatively—' He stops. 'Here.'

Left with a thick, long-sleeved jersey, he hands Callum the poncho. Down, down, down, like an anchor, men drowned. Callum's arms dip farther. He's lost the strength to brace. How does Erik walk at all?

'I'm sorry about my village.' Erik's voice turns sour. 'The treatment you received is shameful. Abhorrent. And'—he puts a gloved hand on Callum's arm— 'I'm sorry about the woman. More than sorry. Is it Lain?'

Dully, Callum swallows. 'Lena.'

Silence. It weighs too much. Eventually, Erik sighs. 'Look at me.'

Callum does nothing. He's spiralling up, outside his head. Lena, frozen. Lena, dead.

'Look at me.' Erik grips his arm so tight that reflexively, Callum does. 'You can't let this bury you. Any of it. If you do, you'll die.'

He searches Callum's face. A memory fades in, stonewashed with age: Clemence, back when they lived in Shetland, grabbing his arms in the rain. *Don't be a bloody diddy*, he barked. Carting him away from the jetty, the old man shook him. His head rattled back and forth. He was only a kid. *I know you don't like it here, but hell, rowing out there would be suicide.* His weathered, walnut face leant right into Callum's. The wind whooped by. *Do you not see the storm?*

Callum blinks the memory away. He'd rather be back in Shetland than here. He could take Kira with him. They could sit and drink tea, have a beer in the other hand, and misquote poets. That night is now the pinnacle of want.

'If I could, I'd help you more.' Erik sighs and steps back. The lines on his face look sad. 'But I need to get home. I may be hardy'—he smiles, a grave, grumbling first—'but I feel the cold. As do you and your girl.' He glances at the hollow. It's silent, flickering. 'Get back inside. Keep yourselves warm. The Whispers aren't easy to reach.'

Wordless, Callum watches as he snowshoes away. The candle sparks, disappearing in the dark as Erik fades into shadow. Callum's gritted teeth ache.

'Thank you,' he calls. It's a hush through the trees, through the quieting crunch of snow. Callum doesn't move. If Erik didn't hear, hopefully he'll understand. There's no burden like righteousness.

34

Following the trees

The morning is muted: no wind, no sound. Not even the crackling fire behind them, which Kira had worried would pop in the night and burn their clothes to ash.

On the climb back to wakefulness, she wrinkles her nose. Maybe it would have been best. Through fleeing and fear and too many days, her sweaty clothes have clung to her for far too long. They could do with exile, or excommunication. Preferably both, and then death.

So could her clammy, tacky body. She can *feel* the grease on her forehead and the grime building up on her skin. They both must smell atrocious.

At least they'll cancel each other out. Is that good? Kira screws up her face, smooths it out, and rolls over.

Her eyes flick open. She's come face to chin with an itch, a grey, woolly one. Eyebrows raised, she lifts it between finger and thumb. It's not theirs, but neither is it murderous, or chasing her with fire.

What it is is unbearably hot. Shrugging it onto Callum, she smiles, a small, melancholy twitch. Considering their bed of coats and snow, his sleeping face is content.

The thought slithers in like a bad habit, undetected until it's too late. She should leave.

If Iris was right, he might be here against his will. Because of some unwitting pull. Because of some inherited pull. Because of some destructive pull, leading them both to…what?

It might be the reason he kissed her, too. Something inside her shrinks and quiets. It didn't occur to her last night—if she'd been dwelling on monsters while kissing, well, the kissing was pretty much doomed—but it would make sense. It would make sense of a *lot*. After knowing her for two days, Callum followed her to somewhere unknown, somewhere dangerous, and won't stop trying to help.

Kira sighs, soft and light to let him sleep. He should have run for his life. Having saved the delirious, frozen Romy and seen the corrupted hotel scene, he should have literally run for the hills. He should have, but he didn't. He stuck to her from the minute they met.

And Romy? This applies to her, too. The lure of them both must have pulled so hard that Callum had no choice.

And Peter?

Kira squashes this like a bug. God, no. Peter was a species unto himself.

And this is getting too much. Kira breathes deep and sighs deeper. The air is warm, pine and woodsmoke and animal fur. The hollow should be comforting, a cosy claustrophobia, but it isn't; she can dance away from the ghost of Anna, but that's the thing about ghosts. They haunt.

Unhappily, Kira stares through the ceiling. Pockmarked snow, matte in the morning in the hollow's shadowed light. Anna. Anneliese. And her mother is a ghost.

She's an only child of only children. She has no family at all. No great-aunt Amanda, as on Mathew's side, who puts socks over shoes and lives on egg. No trying nephews or nieces, who like to draw on walls. Her parents died when she was twenty. After that, she said, the thought of her childhood became too much to bear.

Kira's eyes sink shut as the truth starts to bite. Anna always said that one day, she'd be strong enough, and they'd look through her childhood things together. They were in storage, out of the house. She loved her parents so deeply, she said, that any reminder just *hurt*.

Kira never thought that it might have been a lie. Did Romy? Did Mathew? Has he spent nearly twenty years under some kind of—

'I take it your head's a fun place right now.'

Kira opens her eyes and is met by Callum's. His words are so dry, so pre-prepared, that her face must have been more bleak than *The Scream*. Guilt twinges in Kira's chest. 'You look like someone ate your goldfish. And you also'—he throws the woollen something aside, along with a bulky something else Kira hadn't realised was there—'look like you want to get going. So come on.' He taps her leg, a knowing in his eyes. 'Let's go, while the iron's hot.'

Kira stares. He's tugging his coat from beneath their thighs, but in disbelief, she lingers. He worked out her plan before she'd made it. Not only that, but removing the branches and climbing outside, he's ensuring it's fully thwarted. How did he know it was back on her mind?

'I know how to leave the forest,' Callum calls back into the hollow. 'Erik found us during the night. He knows how to work the land to find your way.' He stretches his night-stiff limbs to the sky. 'Ahh. We're meant to follow branches that touch the ground, which I'm hoping will be obvious. He also gave us those.'

He nods at the blankets. Kira tows them out after her, squinting at the whiteness as she clambers into the day. 'What are they?'

'A coat and a poncho. Throw me one?' Callum zips up his coat, bouncing on the balls of his feet. 'It's freezing.'

Kira half-drags, half-tosses him the poncho. 'You trust him?'

She bundles the heavy coat in her arms. Wool on the outside, fur on the inside; it'll scratch like anything, but oh, it looks warm.

'We don't have much of a choice.' Callum pulls on the poncho. 'Even if he did say, "Follow the branches."'

Kira pouts. 'It sounds like a fairy tale.'

'It does.' Callum pauses. 'Do you need to pee?' He lifts a finger. 'I need to pee.'

'I need,' Kira says as he trudges off, 'to know what else Erik said.'

Silence. She sighs for this world, the afterlife, and hell. 'Callum. Is that all he said?'

Silence. Then, 'Peeing,' he calls. 'Bear with. It's been a while.'

There's something he's not telling her. It gnaws at Kira's mind as she, too, realises her bladder aches and finds a hefty, hiding tree. It gnaws at her mind as they leave, and Callum sets off out in front. Either that, or he regrets what happened last night. Which, while it would mean she hasn't unwittingly seduced him, would also be extremely awkward.

'Hey.' She jogs to catch him up. 'What's wrong?'

Callum cocks his head at a snow-sweeping branch. 'Nothing, bar the knowledge that we're running out of snacks. Why?'

Kira's frown snakes through her skin to her nerves. 'Well, because you're being strange.' She stumbles as he veers toward the branch, close to treading on her toes. 'Like that, really.' She resists the temptation to dig him in the ribs. 'What is it?'

Callum sighs through his nose. One beat, two. 'My arches hurt.' He casts his testy eyes around the forest. 'I don't have my soles in these boots. Your turn. What were you brooding over when I woke up?'

'No, no.' Kira indicates another branch, bowed to the ground in a moss-covered claw. 'We're not doing that. You know you already guessed what was bothering me, so it's still your turn. Your arches hurt yesterday, but you weren't like this.'

'Like what?'

'Moody and evasive.'

He says nothing. Footsteps crunching on the hard-crust snow, Kira aims her full-force scepticism at the impassive side of his head. 'Did someone else come along, as well as Erik?' she tries as they tramp toward a distant branch. Here, the trees are so tall, and so lonely, that it's easy to see what sweeps the snow. At last, something is simple. 'Did he have an ulterior motive? Intelligence gathering for the village? Emissary from the devil?'

'He wanted to apologise and make sure we were alive.'

If her arms weren't full, she'd throw them up. 'That was a joke!' she exclaims. 'If I can make jokes, with my love for worrying, there's definitely something wrong with you. I'm not stupid.'

A moment passes. Another, and then, to her relief, his impassive mouth perks up. 'Let's not say things we don't mean.'

This time, she elbows him. Smirking, he returns to silence.

Better than nothing. If it's not Erik, or her, she can wait. At least until her mind slips, boredom nips, or curiosity gnaws her raw.

Branch after branch, tree after tree. On a scale of one to things she's never liked, walking is pretty high up. The cold is one peg down, just above peanut butter and rum; despite her bundled-up torso, she's numb. It's so much deeper than yesterday. Frost is forming on the ends of her hair, starching her collar and the rims of her boots. Even her eyelashes are iced.

A violent shudder ripples through her. She'd been saving Erik's coat for the last frozen moment, and clumsily, she wrestles it on. It hangs heavy to her knees, and she smiles. She feels like a child in her father's clothing, flapping around with the sleeves.

Burrowing her head low, she pulls her hair over her ears and pushes out her lips. Twists them to one side, then the other. She can do nothing for her feet, those stumpy, blocky things, but she can damn well make sure nothing else falls off.

Rubbing her hands briskly, she shoves them into her pockets.

With a shock through her chest, she pulls them straight back out. Deep down in both pockets, two somethings lurk.

Her first thought is something alive. Her second is something dead. Her third is that she's being silly, and she pushes her hands back in.

A stiff, round container, fashioned from hide. A soft bundle, wrapped in a leathery, more yielding material, almost too large to grasp. Did Erik forget to get rid of them? Kira wrinkles her nose. She wouldn't be surprised; far more pungent than the clothes, they stink of the wild to the moon and back.

Glancing up to make sure Callum hasn't vanished, Kira gently shakes the container. It sloshes. Rum? Vodka? She shakes it again. A killer concoction unknown to the outside? What would be most likely, here in the—

Oh. Her stupidity is staggering. Water.

'Callum!' she cries, jogging to his side. A ruffled-looking ruffian in the poncho, he turns. 'I think we have more water.' She waggles the container. How did vodka come before water? 'And food. No more *crisps.*'

Handing him the water, she unwraps the bundle. Two small animals, cold but cooked, golden and smelling like Christmas came early. If she wasn't so famished, she could cry.

'Not so disgusted this time, are we?' Callum comments once the two little beasts have been scoffed. *Stuffing your face* has never been more apt.

'My stomach realised it was emptier than heaven.' Kira drops the delicate bones to the ground. Bins don't seem to be a thing. 'Right now, I'd eat anything. What?'

Silently laughing, Callum shakes his head. 'Nothing.'

Kira spreads her hands. '*What*, Callum?'

He regards her like she's given him the best joke gift of all. 'It's just…'— he swallows his laughter and rubs his smirking mouth—'we've been together far too long. I'm worrying, and you're politically incorrect.'

Kira blinks at him.

'Never mind.' With a wink, he hands her the water. 'Focus on the fact that one person's been kind.'

Kira narrows her eyes. 'Thanks.' She drinks. 'I'd find Erik and hug him, but the rest would probably jump for joy and grab the nearest stick.'

Callum snorts. 'I reckon they'd stand in a row and take turns to tell me I'm a victim. You know the age-old story: boy meets girl, girl bewitches boy, girl turns out to have a tail. It's a classic.'

Kira's mouth pops open. 'Excuse me?' She bats at him with an oversized sleeve. 'I think you'll find it's *not*.'

'Hey!' Callum rubs his arm, grinningly affronted. 'Don't shoot the jester. Someone has to make light of our murderous new friends.'

Kira rolls her eyes. 'I'm so glad it's this that cheered you up.' She pauses, toeing a tiny branch that squirms across the snow. He may be making light, but it struck her well-played chord. 'Does it really not bother you?'

Callum snaps up his hood. 'What, our murderous friends?'

Kira keeps her eyes on the snow, dotted with drips from the trees. 'More their reason for murder.'

Callum snorts. 'What, that I'm here because you seduced me? That sooner or later you'll decide you're fed up and usher in my untimely death?' He waves a hand. 'You're three feet tall. I can handle you.'

Kira bats at him again. He dodges.

'Besides, I don't kiss succubae.' With a grin, he pivots, walking backwards. 'They've never been my type.'

Kira tries for a beady, headmistress stare, but her cheeks are heating up. Thank God for the cold; with any luck, they were already a fetching red. 'You're not worried, then.'

Or thinking twice. A frisson flitters through her chest, down to her belly and beyond. If only this was more the time.

Callum regards her sardonically. 'Are you worried I'm the male equivalent?'

'No, but—'

'Then case closed, and let's speed up.' He rotates again. 'I'm getting sick of the sight of trees. As soon as we get out of here, I'm moving to Dubai.'

Kira huffs wryly. God, he's stubborn; but then, so is she. At least he's talking. 'Why Dubai?'

Callum nods at a tree, thinner than its fellows and dripping low boughs. 'Not sure.' He nudges a pine cone along with his boot. 'I guess I've never pictured it with trees.'

'I'm pretty sure everywhere has trees.' Kira nudges his woollen side. 'You might want to rethink your criteria.'

'"Oh, you might want to rethink your criteria."' Callum's hands make a mockery in the air. 'Look at me, I like words. I have the best words. Maybe you should be the one rethinking—Antarctica!' His arm shoots out to point at her. 'Antarctica can't have trees. I'll move there.'

Kira tilts her head. 'I suppose that makes sense.' She reins back a smirk. 'It'll be cold, and barren, and unpopulated...oh.' She lets the smirk unfurl. 'What do you know? It sounds like here. You may.' She nudges him again, and again. Begrudgingly laughing, he jerks away up the steepening slope. 'Have to rethink your criteria. Oh.'

She stops. The trunk of a tree has caught her eye, a metre off their path. 'Callum.'

Etched into the bark is a tiny carving. A sketchy tree trunk, four thin branches, and a short line for the ground. Uneasily, it wallows in her mind. It never brings anything good.

She scoots up the slope after Callum. 'That symbol's back,' she calls. 'The one we should have asked Erik about. It's on a—'

'Bloody hell.'

At the top of the rise, Callum pulls up short. Kira slams into his shoulder. Deflating with an *oof*, she pinches his coat for balance. 'Some warning would have been—*oh*.'

Her eyes widen. Her fingers tense. The trees slant down, petering to pebbles. Where the land breaks off, there's blue.

35

The woman from the shallows

'That's a bloody big river.'

Stretched to all directions as far as they can see, there's no land on the horizon, and no horizon at all. It's a deep blue endlessness blending with the sky, painful after days of sombre green and white. Kira shades her eyes. The sun still hides, but everything is light enough, bright enough, for its coyness not to matter. The cloudy mass above the forest ends with the trees, and the blue that carries on is blinding.

I bet you thought it was an ocean, didn't you?

Romy's mockery slips in. Kira brushes it away and scans the water's edge. Now's not the time to feel like a fool, to doubt herself and lose focus; they have a high fantasy quest to complete, and to do that...

'We need a boat.'

She turns to Callum. Staring at the river like a man in love, he doesn't respond. She taps his arm. 'Callum? We need a boat.'

Unmoving, unblinking, watching the blue. Kira frowns.

I bet you thought it was an ocean, didn't you?

It's the water they saw from the cliff-top. The water that Romy knew they'd seen, burning her eyes, transfixing her thoughts, fuelling her rage to a furnace. Of course. Sighing through her nose, Kira tips her head back. After a whole twelve hours without mind games, one was more than due.

'Callum.' Bashing her frustration six feet under, she tugs him around to face her. 'Hey. Callum. Stop it.'

Nothing. His body might have moved, but his eyes have not; they refuse to be shifted from the shining water, glowing, glittering, consuming. If it feels like it did for her, it wants him to look at it, *needs* him look at it, begs him to dedicate himself to it, whole.

Too bad. With a staccato sigh, she stamps on his foot.

The shock snaps his head around. Kira takes his cheeks in her hands. 'Stop it,' she orders. 'You're letting it get to you, the same as it got to me.' She gives his head a short shake. 'Look at me. Focus on me. All right?'

At another shake, Callum pulls away. 'All right,' he grumbles. Wriggling his foot, he rubs the river-facing cheek. 'That wasn't included in the memo.'

Kira eyes the water warily. It's pulling her, too, prickling her scalp and knocking on her thoughts, but it's lost its virgin cunning. 'Maybe everyone else is used to it.' She looks away. 'And yes, it's big, but it must be the river Erik meant. If it was the sea, there'd be waves.' She waves in its direction. 'But there aren't, and the water's flowing. I'd say see for yourself, but don't.'

Callum lifts his forehead, brief and sarcastic. 'Great.' The strain in his face is evident. 'Now I'm a victim to large bodies of water, as well as girls with tails. This is turning into a top-notch trip.'

'At least you're not the girl with the tail. Come on.' Kira takes his hand, suddenly decisive. 'Erik said we have to get across, and standing around being sarcastic won't be how we work it out. If you haven't already realised'—she nods down at the beach—'we're boatless.'

For what feels like the first time in years, her boots don't sink into snow. It's as destabilising as a raft, or a tightrope; thick summer grasses layer the ground, rising, swishing softly to brush against their thighs. Kira runs her fingers through the tips. If this top-notch trip is teaching her anything, it's not to take things for granted.

Including wildlife. Bugs. A bee drones past. A small, squirrelly creature skitters in front of her away from a dusty molehill. A second molehill pools, volcanic, beside a sprinkle of overlarge poppies and a ring of forget-me-nots. By the time she steps from the grass to the pebbles, something unrolls that feels a lot like hope.

Hope: conspicuous by how it was lacking. She hadn't realised how tightly she was wound.

With the forest at her back, she can finally unwind. The beach of sorts is alley-like, hemmed in on one side by lanky bushes and on the other by a jungle of breeze-blown reeds. It's not the most welcoming beach she's seen; it's not *her* beach by a long chalk, but it's a wonderful change of scene.

And it's hot.

Oh, *God*, it's hot. All at once, it's stiflingly, agonisingly warm, like she's walked into last week's hammam. In a fumble, Kira shrugs big coat, little coat, gloves, scarf, and baggy purple jumper off onto the pebbles. At least the hammam smelt of eucalyptus and needed nothing but a bathing suit. If Callum wasn't here, she'd strip to her knickers.

'Whooof.' Callum arrives beside her. Her vest and jeans will have to do. 'Talk about extremes.'

'I know.' Consigning her beaten-up boots to the pile, Kira straightens to fan her face. Her skin is flushing red. 'This is madness.'

Callum's reply is lost, a mumble that may have been, 'We're all mad here.' Pulling off his hoodie, he scrubs his heathen hair. 'I just want…'

He turns back to the slope, scrabbling up the steep grass to the forest. Kira holds her hair above her head and fans her neck, her chest. She should paddle in the river; absolute bliss. With any luck, she'll cool down.

'Aha!'

Kira turns. At the top of the slope, Callum laughs. 'Thought so.' Extending his arms, he angles one hand into the forest and one toward the river. 'You wanted madness, Kira.' He shakes his head, caught between amusement, despair, and disbelief. 'Come and feel it.'

Kira squints up the riverbank. She'd rather not scrabble in such dry heat, and especially not when it ends in snow. 'Feel what?'

'This.' He sifts the air with his hands, intrigue puffing in *hmm*s. Kira gives in. It's not like there's a boat just screaming to be sailed.

'Feel.' He grabs her the second she crests the bank, making her his mirror image. 'See?'

His expectant expression is endearing, but the climb made her sweat rivulets, and she'd really rather paddle, even if she has to shut her eyes. He's waiting, though. His face is brimming, and her mouth is half open, ready to say *yes, that's nice, but I feel like Big Bird*, when she does.

She sees.

She feels. Her right arm, pointing to the river, is hot. Her left, shadowed by the forest, is cold, wrapped in a frost so deep that it's already a wonder they survived. Her face breaks into a startled smile. She can almost see the difference: bleached curls of white and blue, and rippling, sunlit gold.

'I told you.' Callum grins. 'Incredible.'

'Impossible.' Kira starts to laugh, slowly turning in a circle. The temperatures never change, split by the top of the riverbank in a strict slice through her spine. 'Out of all the things we've experienced, it feels really, *really* strange'—she faces him—'but I think it's my favourite.'

Callum's face crinkles into mischief. 'You're sure?' Touching her cheeks, he kisses her. She squeaks. 'Maybe not.'

Wickedly, he grins. Kira brushes her tingling lips. They're just like his: half-hot and half-cold. 'Nope.' She holds up her hands in surrender. 'Nope, nope, nope. Before, it was a curiosity. Now, it's downright weird. Knockturn Alley weird. Back to the beach we go.' She takes Callum's frozen hand and pulls him away, down the wistful grass to the pebbles. 'Try that again when my body's all the—God.'

She jerks to a halt on the edge of the beach. Standing with her back to the reeds is Romy.

Chapping lips, hollow cheeks. Her straggling hair falls in matted knots. The black clothes she lives in hang loose, butchered and dirty on wasting limbs. Kira clenches her fists by her sides. It's not really Romy. It's not. If it was, she'd run up, hug her, and cry with relief and love and shock. The ghost inside her is ripping her to shreds.

'Romy?' she calls, her voice uneven. Her sister is haunting. Kira's insides chill. She's haunting…and alone. 'Where's Dad?'

Romy tilts her head and contemplates. 'I am not Romy.'

Kira falters. It's a stilted version of her sister's voice, as undefined as if she's trying it on. Different to the hotel, and different to the hospital; both times, she sounded raw, a harsher version of herself. This voice is thick and ill-fitting. Kira steps forward, more bewildered than afraid.

'Kira,' Callum warns.

'I know it's not Romy speaking.' She nudges his warning hand from her shoulder. 'But she's there. It's her body, even if you took it over.'

She pauses. Did the figure just flicker? Blur along the edges, lose a little focus? 'I…' She falters again, less sure. Was that another flicker? 'What have…'

The figure shakes her head. 'I am not Romy,' she repeats. The flicker comes a third time, as if Romy's an image, a mirage, unreal. 'But neither am I what possesses Romy.' A droll smile curls her mouth. 'I am not anyone.'

'Okay.' Callum grips her shoulder. 'We should definitely leave.' He drops his voice to a hiss. 'If that's not your sister, in any of her forms, then I'd wager that talking is a terrible plan. We have a history with crazy women.'

Again, Kira shrugs him off. 'Who are you, if you're not Romy?' she asks. Callum may be right, but leaving means the forest, and the crazy women have been the ones to give them answers. 'Why do you look like her?'

The figure thinks. It's an obvious process, muscles working, as ill-fitting in her face as the voice. 'It is difficult to explain,' she says, lifting a lock of hair to appraise. Her mouth wrinkles. She lets the tangle return to her ribs. 'I am a helper; when someone needs my help, I appear in the guise of the one I saw last. The rest of the time, I am nothing.'

She smiles again, a contented curve. 'I join with the air and lie in the shallows. Sometimes I bask on the stones, or swim underwater to watch the fish.' She regards them inquisitively. 'Normally, I am rarely needed, but in two days, there have been five. Do you know why?' Her smile widens. It softens Romy's wilted face. 'And although I am nobody, I am also Sofia.'

'This is definitely a terrible plan,' Callum urges beneath his breath.

Kira steps away from him. 'Who were the others?'

Callum sighs loudly. She shoots him a look that could wither an ox. Sofia hasn't shown them so much as suspicion, and she won't look a gift apparition in the mouth. 'When did you see them?' she continues. The words are a hiccup, a stumble. 'The others? You said there've been five in two days.'

Sofia tilts her head at the water. 'Yesterday,' she replies. 'The man and the girl after the storm, and the woman—'

'The man and the girl?' Kira's fists contract. 'My dad? Is he okay?'

'And the woman'—Sofia eyes her—'in the morning.'

Kira tries not to feel chastened. 'Sorry.'

'I had never thought to meet that particular soul.' Surprise blinks airy in Sofia's eyes. 'She didn't think I recognised her, but I knew.'

Callum's voice is suspicion. 'Knew what?'

Sofia turns her gaze on him. 'Anneliese has a presence that is hard to forget.'

Callum's eyes widen. Kira stops breathing. The name leaves her winded, struck in the stomach and the head and the mind. It's the nail in a coffin she didn't want to close. 'Anneliese?' she whispers, barely there. 'That was the woman? Anneliese?'

Black with the spirit of Romy-not-Romy, Sofia's eyes spark. 'Yes.' Her curiosity looks Kira up and down. 'She didn't say, but she's going to the northern ice.'

'How do you know?' Kira finds her mouth asking. Her lips don't feel like hers. 'If she didn't say.'

Sofia cocks her head, smiling. 'I take payment in a glimmer of a thought. I admit, when Romy arrived, the resemblance surprised me, but she looked too dreadful to be sure. Now you're here, however'—her eyes shimmer in amusement, mischievously benign—'would I be wrong to presume you're all related?'

Behind her own eyes, Kira is spinning.

'Do you care?' Callum steps forward, resting his hand on the small of her back.

Unperturbed, Sofia shrugs. 'No,' she says lightly. 'I am a helper; who I help does not matter. I would advise you to be more discerning about what you reveal to strangers, but'—she turns her attention to Kira—'even if you weren't so similar, your presence is almost identical. Oh!'

She claps her hands. Kira starts. 'I apologise. You asked about your father. He was being unceremoniously dragged, but he was very much alive. Speaking of which'—she squints at the sky—'if you want to catch any of them, you should be going.' She fixes her happy-child eyes on Kira. 'May I take a thought?'

She lifts a hand.

'Whoa, whoa, whoa.' Callum holds up his own. 'What are you—'

'It's already done.' A broad smile breaks across Sofia's face. She presses Romy's bony hands together. They smudge around the edges. 'I have never seen inside the Kyo, and Callum, that brother of yours is unique.' She flicks her fingers at the river. The tips blur and merge. 'Thank you. Your air-drawn carriage awaits.'

'What?' Callum exclaims. 'My brother—*what?*'

Sofia nods behind them. Distant, reeling, Kira turns. A small, reeded rowboat bobs in the shallows.

'There are no oars.' Callum's exasperation bursts. He lifts the words from her mind. 'How can we sail it if there are no oars? And even if there were oars'— he cuts the sifting water a glare—'how would we row against the current? Do we look that stupid?'

'No,' Sofia says, in a tone that suggests *a bit.* 'But you do not need oars. You do not need anything; it will protect you from the river's allure and take you straight across. You need only watch out for the bishop-fish.'

Kira stares. Callum stares.

'Oh!' Sofia laughs. Coming from Romy's face, it's odd, the brightness of wind chimes, or panpipes. 'I love springing that on people. They very rarely know of him, and why would they? He's mad.'

Callum looks at Kira. Kira looks at him. Her temples are throbbing. *She's having us on,* Callum's look says. Kira twists her mouth: *she's all we have.*

Sofia eyes them pointedly. 'I really wouldn't mock. The bishop-fish is ridiculous, and extraordinarily transparent, but still, he draws people in.' Dreamily, she sighs. 'A shame. He sits on an island in the middle of the river and tries to persuade my travellers to stop and hear him speak. Don't.' Her black eyes sober up with warning. 'I am not entirely sure what will happen if you do, but I advise not finding out. And you.'

She directs this straight to Callum. The warning in her eyes grows deeper, steeper. 'You need to watch for the Havsrå. You know of the Huldra?'

Callum sounds incredibly sceptical. 'Yes?'

'They are the Huldra of the river.' Sofia's gaze flits over Kira. 'Should you see or hear any sign of them, close your eyes and shut your ears. The boat will pass on without issue.' She weaves her fingers together, drifting back to lightness. 'At this point, you must go.'

She nods again, to the river and the merry, bobbing boat. Callum hesitates.

Kira does not. Gingerly stepping from the pebbles to the boat, she sits at one end and tries to have faith. It's hard to see how an oar-less boat on an endless river will help them, but they don't have much of a choice. Two vague mentions of an ice plain does not a direction give.

And this shadow of Romy hurts. It hurts, and it's unnerving, and it's making it hard to breathe. There's so much they don't know.

'Remember,' Sofia says, once Callum and their extraneous clothes have clambered into the boat. 'You are dealing with the Kyo. If you catch up to Anneliese, you'll be dealing with the ghosts of the ice plains, too. If you wish to stay alive'—she steps back from the shore—'stay paranoid. Now go.'

She places her hand beneath her chin. A thin breath of air gusts from her lips, scented with metal and salt. The boat begins to move.

'One more thing,' she calls as they gaily float away. 'If you see any normal fish, eat them. Take them straight from the water.' She beams. 'They're delicious.'

Kira opens her mouth to say thank you, but when she looks back at the beach, the ragged Romy has vanished. In its place is a mirror image of Callum, and as the words shrivel up, it's gone.

36

The Whispers and Anneliese

'Where are they?' Carol asks. Downstairs, the twins chatter, playing a game that may end in tears. Jay is next door, fighting robots or trekking through mystical kingdoms. Life is normal.

Except it isn't. *On the river.* The voice sighs. Carol shuts her eyes. *Alive.*

The anchor in her chest is raised, just a little. She's felt too heavy to move, too heavy to speak since Lena left. 'And you can't just…' she flounders, thinning her mouth. Her leg jigs, up and down, as annoying as Callum's tapping. Right now, she couldn't stop if she tried. 'Force them out?'

The voice is a rustle around her throat. *Can your God force you?*

Carol flinches and tenses. 'You're not gods,' she says tightly. 'Even you don't believe you are.'

A laugh slithers softly down her spine. *Precisely.* Flitting across her shoulders, it lifts the hair at the base of her neck. *There are no gods, and no such control. All we have, we fought for.*

Omnipotence, another murmurs, *does not exist.*

If it did… the first voice is a writhing smile. Dread drips through Carol like oil. *We might have saved her.*

The oil oozes, tarring her lungs. The anchor pulls down, down, down. 'Saved who?'

Sighing together, the Whispers lift. *Goodbye, Carol.* The chalet creaks. *Anneliese is getting close.*

37

And so they float

I f his watch is honest, after ten minutes, the beach has merged with the forest. After twenty, the horizon-spanning forest is a horizon-spanning blur. After thirty, there's only blue.

He's never been so glad to see the back of anything. Sofia may have said to be paranoid, but as his lazy, blistered fingers trail, cooling in the ripples from the boat, he can't help but relax. The heat is a haze, the water clear and cold, the air as salty as the sea. It's a summer holiday.

Reclining against the reeds, Callum closes his eyes. A holiday with sirens and religious fish, but a holiday nonetheless.

Sirens and religious fish. His stomach growls like a dungeon door. If they'll give him food, let them come; a puny squirrel a day is not enough. He'd murder for raclette. Raclette, and some caramelised vin cuit, and beer. Hell, if it's summer, why not a barbecue? Chicken wings, pork chops, the burgers they show on *Food Network* at three o'clock in the morning.

His stomach gears up from a growl to a howl. At his feet, Kira laughs. 'I take it you're hungry.'

Callum rubs a hand over his face. His nose clicks. 'Like you're not.' He yawns and stretches wide. His stomach feels like a cavern, filled with flittering bats. 'If you could eat anything right now, what would it be? Anything.'

Kira rests her cheek on her hand, curled against the side of the boat. 'Hmm.' She smiles at him sleepily, but something about it is staged. No wonder; Sofia dropped the mother of bombs. 'Sticky toffee pudding.'

Callum groans. 'Oh, British food.' He slaps his stomach and groans some more. '*Oh.* Toad-in-the-hole. Haggis.'

'I wouldn't go that far.'

'Cullen skink.'

'Now you're just making up words.'

'I'm not!' Callum grins. If he's not mistaken, she looks a tad happier. 'It's some kind of Scottish soup. Maybe fish.'

Kira wrinkles her nose. Still smushed against her hand, her face is adorable, turning pink in the sun. 'I think I'll pass. What about bread and butter pudding?'

Callum's stomach crashes like thunder. 'Okay.' He pats it tenderly. 'Okay. This guy's headed for certain death if we keep going on about food. There must be something else to do.' He squints at the blinding sky. 'We're floating on a river, in a driverless boat, in the middle of an adult Narnia. It's not *possible* there's nothing to do.'

There's plenty. Callum drags his eyes away from Kira, awkwardly shifting his jeans. Sadly, they'd end in a capsized ship.

Pulling away from her mother-shaped monkey, Kira shuffles around to face him. 'What do people usually do when they're stuck in tiny boats?'

Yawning, Callum shifts again. 'Think? Philosophise?'

Kira huffs. 'Since when?' Her gaze lands on his T-shirt, and her lips slide to the side. Dark blue, white emblazoned: *Am I Alive?*

Catching her scrutiny, Callum plucks at the words. 'I know. The irony. And I get the impression'—slotting his hands behind his head, he neatly crosses his ankles—'that that's what people do. From films? Books? Old books? They philosophise all the time in old books. Tea and biscuits? Philosophy. Death of a rabbit? Philosophy. Or maybe'—he wags a finger—'we should be bonding. Maybe that's the reason for the extended boat-trip. Maybe this is the moment for us, as this epic tale's protagonists, to work out our differences, stare in realisation, and figure out we get on.'

Kira narrows her eyes through the silent sky. 'Didn't we already do that? You shouted at me in a car park, I ran away, you shouted at me again. We were huffy for a while, then we kissed and made up. Not literally.' She looks at him slyly, with a jolt of confidence. 'The literal part came later.'

Callum's eyes linger on her, briefly intense. 'Aye, lassie.' He stretches out his arms. 'So if we can't work out our differences, I guess we're stuck philosophising.' He claps the reeds on either side, two underwhelming thuds. 'Fabulous. Where do we start? Questioning how we know that this strange world is real? Questioning how we know that *either* world is real? Maybe I'm a figment of your imagination; maybe you're a figment of mine. Or maybe'—he leans forward, placing a solemn hand on her knee—'we're a figment of someone else's. Take your pick. We can work through them in order, or at random.' He sits back. 'We appear to have all the time in the world.'

Kira picks at her vest. It sticks to her side. 'I'd rather not pick any.' Perish the thought. 'Philosophy was the one thing I ran from at A Level. Well.' She frowns. 'And maths. And biology. And geography. Whatever.' She wriggles around, aligning her arms on the rim of the boat. 'Point being, philosophy can die.'

Resting her chin on her hands, she peers down at her reflection. Rippled though it is, she can tell it's undesirable, undercut by a pure, roiling abyss. She looks away again. There could be far worse things down there than two unwashed, ripe-smelling youths.

'What if we *were* made up by someone else?' Callum slides his hands back behind his head. 'How would we know? How would we even *start* to know? Have you ever had a dream you were convinced was real?'

Kira draws out a stage-groan, topped off with a slump. 'Yes,' she replies. An uneasy stab of longing pierces her chest. The beach. Sun. Home. 'Everyone has. But sooner or later, we realise they're dreams. There's always something not quite real.'

Silence. She feels it coming in the pressure on the heat-hazed air. Quietly, Callum asks, 'What about yesterday?'

I do not want to talk about yesterday. The words are almost out when Kira traps them in their cage. If it's that or working into an existential crisis...

'I did realise that some of it wasn't real.' She settles against the boat with a sigh. It feels like a game from a Shreddies box, sliding plastic pieces around to try and make a picture. 'But when I woke up, I only remembered the last part. Since then, I've had these sprinkled scenes, and I think there were three. Three dreams. Either a dream in a dream in a dream'—she walks her fingers along the reeds—'or a dream conveyor belt.'

Callum scratches the back of his neck. 'And what happened?'

And now you're going to see. An image swims up of her as an ostrich, burying her head in the sand.

'I'm still not sure,' she says. 'It's in bits.' She touches her fingertips together, a photo. There's sadly no sand to speak of. 'Waking up in the forest, seeing Mum with a tail, hearing the Kyo whisper that I had to watch. I think there was a cabin, too.' She wrinkles her forehead. 'That was the first dream. In the second, I woke up in the forest and saw my dad. He was leaving Whiteland with a woman, I think?'

She shakes her head and shrugs. 'I don't know. It made even less sense than the first, but I'd guess they were both there to convince me that the last part, when I was home, was real. Sleep, wake, sleep, wake, relief.'

She watches her fingers trot back along the reeds. What she doesn't want to think—and can't stand to say—is that they felt like a snapshot of truth. Both her mum and dad involved in Whiteland, in different ways and times. Lies, seduction, magic, murder. Someone escaping, ecstatic to be out.

'We can go back to being fictional,' Callum says. Kira looks up. He's also watching her fingers, their ever more fractious march. 'Seeing as I brought up something you're unhappy about, we might now have some differences.'

His tone is only half-joking. When Kira huffs a tiny laugh, she's only half-amused. 'Ah.' She shakes her head wryly. 'Disagreeing, making up again, and philosophising, all while forced into each other's company. Aren't we the perfect story.'

A thought strikes, and she leaps upon it. Oh, how distracting. Oh, how wondrous.

'Actually, we are.' Awkwardly, she twists around. Sure, this may be a magic boat, but magic boats capsize. Right?

Of all the things to worry about.

'If we were a story'—Kira boots this from her mind—'I think we'd be a fairy tale.' She lengthens the words, a façade of reflection, testing them for taste. 'Therefore, we don't need to disagree and then make up. We can just disagree. We're both foregone conclusions.'

Digging in Erik's coat, Callum stops. 'That'—he looks up at her—'is depressing.'

'No, no.' Kira lifts a finger. 'It's literary analysis.'

'Oh.' With a huff, Callum carries on digging. 'Because that's so much better.'

'It is.'

Surfacing with the water, Callum drinks and passes it over. 'Really.'

'Yes.' Gratefully, she gulps. 'Thanks.' She passes it back. 'I wouldn't question me on this, Callum. I would not.'

It's a challenge. She knows it. He knows it, too, because he pauses in his swig, raising his eyebrows as slowly as any eyebrows have ever moved. 'Oh, come on.' He wipes his mouth. 'You know I won't just let that go. You *know* I won't.'

'I do.' The half-amusement creeps into a three-quarter smile. Kira clings to it, as ardent as someone half asleep avoiding errant thoughts. 'If you let me carry on, though, I'm in danger of becoming one of your, what's the word? Fogies.'

He doesn't rise to it. He doesn't call her dramatic, either, which is great because she is. Of course she is. Look at *where* she is. In a magic land, in a magic river, sailing along in a magic boat with nothing but a hologram's wisdom.

After this, she's buying him beer. For life.

'I,' Callum says, almost lazily, 'would very much find that fun.'

She looks at him. He looks at her. Kira smiles.

'You, male lead, are on.' Crossing her legs, she sits forward. The boat creaks. She ignores it. 'So, my reasoning.' She frames it like a photo. 'Fairy tales don't do character development.'

She waits. Most obliging, Callum looks inquisitive.

'Okay.' She wriggles, getting comfortable, as much as she can in a vessel made of reeds. 'Think about it: the wolf wants Little Red Riding Hood, and then, the wolf gets her. The version of the story you read doesn't matter. You never—'

'But,' Callum says, interrupting her suddenly, straightening up from his slump. 'Sorry.' He shuts his mouth. 'Carry on.'

'No.' Kira's three-quarter smile becomes nearly full. He's en*gaging* with this? Really? 'You go.'

He smirks, but as though it's more at himself. 'Well, I just thought the wolf got butchered.' He mimes an axe, or Maxwell's hammer. 'Does that not count?'

'Oh.' Kira laces her fingers together, so fast it almost hurts. 'I'm sorry, but that was such a trapdoor. Sure, the wolf is sometimes butchered, but you never, ever see him think oops, guess I'm a bad person.'

She keeps her fingers laced, tapping on her knuckles. Callum is watching her, almost oddly, but odd in a way that's…good? As if he can't compute her or doesn't think she's real.

If she thinks about that, she'll lose her thread, and this thread is keeping her sane.

'Okay.' She frames the scene again, stamping out fifty emotions gunning to shoot her down. 'Figure two: Sleeping Beauty. A princess goes to sleep for a hundred years. Yes?'

With the same pleased bemusement, Callum nods.

'Yes.' Kira swats at a fly. 'And Maleficent, who *put* her to sleep, never regrets what she's done. Sure, she dies, but she dies like a villain.'

Callum mimes a dagger throw.

'See, you know what I'm talking about.' Kira spreads her hands. 'Also, neither Aurora nor the prince come out of it with any sort of arc. He wanders in all'—she deepens her voice and furrows her forehead—'"Hey, I'm amazing, give me a princess."'

Callum snorts. 'Like that.'

'Like that.' Kira nods. 'And then, he doesn't change. Well.' She turns her mouth down. 'I guess he goes all, "Hey, I'm amazing, I stabbed some trees and was rewarded with a princess."'

Callum grins. 'Not the worst way to be. Also, I have a question.' He wipes a trail of sweat from his temple. 'Don't fairy tales have morals?'

Oh, no. Despite the need for distraction, she didn't really *want* philosophy. Kira eyes him with suspicion. 'Yes…?'

Callum looks at her like he's just solved the mystery of who put Bella in the wych elm. 'Then,' he says, 'wouldn't they count as character development?'

Oh, no. She *really* didn't want philosophy.

'The wolf gets butchered.' Callum mimes his axe. 'And Maleficent is thwarted. I can't remember how, but I like thwarted.' He links his middle finger and thumb. 'Thwarted.' He nods to himself. 'Yeah. Either way, the theme is that evil folk lose.'

Shifting her face toward the breeze, Kira lifts her hair. 'True.' She smiles, unable to stop it. Hopefully, it comes across as cooling down. Out on the water, the heat is more bearable, but still her skin is speckled with sweat. 'But morals aren't character development. Getting killed or outwitted—'

'Thwarted.'

'Thwarted.' Kira flicks water at him. 'That word's going to turn into banister. By which,' she adds before he can comment, 'I mean you'll say it so many times it loses all its meaning.'

He holds up his hands in mock surrender.

'My point is,' she says, making sure he's listening, 'getting thwarted doesn't change the characters.'

'Beyond death.'

Kira resists mime-killing him. Again, look at where they are. Anything could happen.

Stop.

'Beyond death.' She rubs her heat-chapped lips. Just—don't. 'They don't express remorse, and if they survive, they don't try to better themselves. They just'—she twirls her hand, slowly, gracefully, thoughtfully—'lose.'

Callum lifts his shoulders and drops them. 'Good?'

Kira opens her mouth and shuts it. 'Don't'—she taps the side of the boat—'play devil's, um, advocate.'

His eyes flick left again. 'Who says I am?'

Good point. Not, however, acknowledged. Kira decides against declaring it. On under-nourishing sleep, under-nourishing food, and new hormonal boob pains, she could see anything as a good point, or equally, a bad one.

'I guess I'll play both roles.' Kira resists the urge to poke her boob to see if it still is tender. 'You know, good guys still win. On the whole, they don't learn anything. You're meant to find their inherent goodness, cheer their victory, and go home.'

Callum nods, again, again, in the way guys do when they see a girl they like. 'What about a sequel?'

Kira stalls. Her brain just stops. 'What?'

'Or a prequel?' He folds his arms. 'A back story?'

Slowly, Kira frowns. 'You're...' In a blink, all she sees is Disney. *Frozen*. 'Oh. Oh, no.'

'Some of that would be covered then, I'm sure. They can't just leave us hanging.'

'No.' Lifting her hands, she shuts her eyes. 'No. Please. I am not doing Disney. Okay? Please don't tell me you're—'

'What's wrong with *Frozen 2*?'

Eyes closed, Kira clenches her fists. 'Nothing,' she manages. Everything, really, bar the sisters. 'But…but fairy tales are what they are. Fairy tales *should* be what they are.'

'I haven't read the Grimm tales, but I gather they're gruesome.'

'Exactly.' Kira opens her eyes. 'So—'

'It's fine.' Callum winks at her with something more than a wink. 'But if this malarkey's a fairy tale, is philosophy a go?'

Kira ducks her head. 'Um.' Damn him. Damn him. Damn him. Damn him. 'No. Not a chance.'

'Fair enough.' Callum hands her the water. Gratefully, she drinks. 'From now on, we'll be a philosophy-less, simpleton-worthy tale. Although'—he fans his T-shirt over his stomach—'it does mean there'll be some changes around here. What would you say if I renamed myself Richard Parker, transformed into a tiger, and ate you because I thought you were a monkey?'

'Much better.' Kira lifts her hair, angling toward the breeze. Out on the water, the heat is more bearable, but her skin is still dewy with sweat. 'But you're dating yourself with that reference.' She taps the side of her head. 'Got to keep it modern. Get down with the cool—'

The boat bumps into something solid. Knocked forward into their clothes, Kira yelps.

Callum ricochets off his knees. 'Christ!' Groaning, he rubs his forehead. 'What the *hell* was that?'

Face-first in fur, Kira struggles upright. She's never been one for yoga poses, and that one damn well hurt. 'God knows.'

'Just once.' Callum shakes his head. A red, knee-shaped mark mars his skin. 'Just once, I'd like a warning. You know, one of those voices that have been telling you to wake up.'

Kira twists in the boat and gasps. 'Callum.'

'All it has to say is CLIFF, or COLLISION.'

'Callum!'

She's star-struck, snow-blind, stunned. He has to look, has to marvel: half in the water and half on the sand, they've bumped up onto an island.

It's toy-sized, smaller than Erik's cave with golden, grass-patched sand. Pebbles form a scattered boundary. A tired shrub cradles scarlet berries, smelling of a musky spice. In the centre laps the most inviting pool she's ever seen.

Oh. *Oh.* The size of a gnarled old dinner table, the vivid water glitters, as cloudlessly blue as the river. It doesn't pull. It doesn't lure. It's there for one thing. 'Bathtime!'

The boat rocks and shudders as Kira scrambles out.

'Huh?' A thump behind her. 'Ow. Thanks, Kira,' Callum calls. 'More injuries. Just what I need.'

'You're welcome.' Hopping across the scorching sand, Kira plunks into the water.

It's glorious. What's even more glorious is removing her *clothes*. It's a weight lifted, a purification, a sacred religious rite: no one has ever valued nudity quite as much as this. The balls of her feet scrape mossy stones as she wriggles out of her knickers. Glorious. *Glorious.* Spending days in filthy clothes is bad enough, but days-old knickers are disgusting.

No more. Wringing and rinsing as fast as she can, she flings her sopping clothes to the sand and plunges underwater.

Shivery. Glassy. Bubbling. Hushed. Clean, cool, bluish, greenish, and Kira comes up beaming. 'It's amazing.' She turns, up to her neck, the softness billowing about her limbs. It's silky, soaking into her skin. The water seeps through to her bones, and like its own kind of dirt, the clammy, cloying feeling of the forest melts away. Even her mind is clearing: like a painkiller easing an ache to a throb, her worries don't seem so bad.

'Are you sure you've not jumped into a death trap?' Callum pads across the murmuring sand. 'There could be anything in there. Piranhas. Jellyfish. Jesus, it's hot.' He inhales through his teeth, his toes scraping audibly in on themselves. 'Maybe that's where the sirens hang out.'

Kira peers down through the ripples. 'If it is, they're the worst seductresses ever. They'd have to be the size of a seahorse.' She smiles to herself. 'If you're going to be seduced by a fish-sized siren, you deserve whatever you get.'

'Very funny.' Callum's padding stops. 'Sofia just said to be paranoid. Ouch.' He inhales again. 'Did it occur to you that it could be unsafe?'

'No.'

'You wanted a bath, so you took one.'

'Yes.'

'Do you remember what else Sofia said?'

Kira cranes her neck up at him. 'No?'

'Of course.' Crouching beside the pool, Callum eyes her. 'We are on an is-land. Who lives on an island? Who specifically must we avoid?'

He takes a beat to wait, raising his eyebrows in a way that says *come on.* Come on. Come on. Come on.

Oh.

Several things ripple right through Kira. Fear, cold. Idiocy, hot. Pride, hot-ter, and the need to save face, the hottest of them all.

'Well, yes. I thought about that.' She didn't. 'But look. This place is tiny.' She cuts her eyes away from him, the better to mask the lie. 'If he's hiding some-where, he's not even a seahorse. He's a, I don't know'—she waves a hand—'like, a mollusc.'

Callum snorts. 'And if we're deceived by a mollusc, we deserve whatever we get?'

'Damn straight.'

He shakes his head, tracing the water, and shakes it again, and again. 'I'm not going to mention the fact that you didn't think this through, because you're right, there's no daft, alluring fish.' He nods at the pool. 'What about in there?'

Kira peers down through the ripples again. 'I'm pretty sure it's fine.' She hopes. The bottom of the pool is blurry, but solid: pebbles, rocks, and slick brown algae. Pushing down a curl of unease, she makes herself paddle around. No smell beyond salt and the spicy berries. No hand around her ankles, no chasm, no bite; only a sense of cocooned serenity, difficult to distrust, already washing clean her doubts. 'I can't see anything.' She tips her head back so her hair floats out. 'When else will we feel this clean?'

Every inch of her is thoroughly scrubbed before Callum is convinced. 'Ah-hhh.' He sighs a gusty sigh, casts the pool a longing look, and yanks his T-shirt over his head. 'Fine. Fine. Your cleanliness convinced me. But if we die in a ghastly way…'

'Yes, yes.' Kira tries not to look at him, and tries not to heat. 'It's on me. I'll take the—hey!'

She jerks up a hand in a stop sign, even as her belly does a flip. Un-ashamed, he's shed his jeans and is poised to bathe in his boxers. 'No, you don't. You have to wash those.' She dips a sharp finger at his underwear. 'Please. For the love of God.'

For a second, she thinks he might listen.

For a second, she's a fool.

'As you wish, my lady.' With a smug smile, Callum jogs backwards and merrily starts to run.

'Callum!' Kira yelps, but too late. Churning the pool with a colossal splash, he bombs in front of her face.

'You called?' All innocence, he surfaces in the midst of the roiling waves. 'I was just making sure my underwear got clean. You know, for the love of God. Oh, and funny thing.' He settles against the rocky sides of the pool, tapping the stone with his fingers. 'I can't see you up here, but the underwater view is spectacular.'

Her body thinks first, and she splashes him. Her mind catches up, and she splashes him again, rushing with heat and curling her toes and pinching her thighs together. The *cheek*.

He's seen her cheeks. All of them.

Kira's head has never felt so hot. She splashes him again.

'Oi!' Callum shields his face with his arms. 'Beast! You're the one who chose nudity over dignity, or whatever. I'm only a simple man.'

'Even simple men have balls to kick.' Kira lifts her chin and meets his eyes. He can embarrass her to the ends of the earth, but nothing will force her from the pool. Nothing is stealing this halo of calm.

As long as he stays on the surface.

Tipping her head back, she lets the water muffle his chuckles. The ripples cover her ears. His paddling recedes to a pulse. She stretches her legs, flexes her toes, and gazes up at the sky. She could almost be back at the thermal baths. Ringed by peaks, the air was sharp, but the water steamed and the sky was deep and—

The pool around her churns. Taken by surprise, Kira loses her balance, plunging underwater. With a shout, Callum scrambles onto the sand.

At the second shout, Kira splutters back up, water in her nose and honeyed in her throat the way no water should be. At the third, she scrapes her hair from her face, a sodden, slapping curtain. 'What's wrong with you?' she croaks. 'I was starting to relax.'

Wiping her filmy eyes, she sees. Callum is tromping back toward her, grinning in a slightly shellshocked way with a glistening fish in each hand.

'Fish!' he crows.

Kira blinks. 'I can see that.'

Animatedly, he points to the river. 'Look!'

Perplexed, she looks; and as she looks, she inhales. In the river around the island, in a delicate, splashing storm, leap a fanciful, fantastical, bizarre array of fish.

Sparkling rainbows and wings of scales. Silver bodies and mermaid tails. Dipping in and out of the water, the fish arc toward them. Kira's lips curve to a speechless smile. In a rush, a swarm, splashing and tinkling like a rock-pool waterfall, the fish encircle the island. It seems a shame, a betrayal, something sad and stolen, to break their brightened flight, but as Callum hastens back to the water, Kira lets him. If they don't eat, they won't get much farther; and if they don't get to the ice plains, all this will have been for nothing.

When it's over, though, she'll be veggie for life.

'Amazing.' Callum extends his arms, laughing in the wet, sludgy sand beside the boat. Another fish slaps into his chest, and Kira's stomach growls. She'd be foolish to spurn convenient food.

A second fish, almost a third, and Callum scoops them up. 'The job's a good-un.' He heads back toward her. 'Man provide for woman.'

Kira smirks but says nothing. He looks comical enough as it is with his boxers sodden, sand in his leg hair, and his prizes held like babies. He doesn't need her teasing, too…and he *is* catching them food.

Resting her chin on her hands, Kira sighs. The fish are surging away again, dipping toward the blue horizon in a blur of glittering light. Smiling, she follows their dreamy path. Between them and the wing-lit birds, she'll never have painter's block again.

'Dinner,' Callum proclaims loudly. The last of the rush glints away.

Kira shakes the brightness from her eyes. 'How do you propose we cook them?' she asks, allowing a hint of a tease. 'Does man make fire, as well as provide? We're a little low on supplies.'

'Have faith.' Callum lifts a finger for silence, squats beside his bounty, and raises a newly dead fish to his mouth.

Revulsion writhes up from Kira's stomach, stronger than the squirrels in spades. 'Callum!' She covers her mouth with her hands. 'What are—that could *kill* you.'

Callum waggles the lifted finger. 'Mmm.' His forehead creases, and with it his face. Kira's words grind to a halt. '*Mmm.*' Pulling a tiny white bone from his mouth, he motions for Kira to eat. 'Dig in.'

A half-grimace twisting her face, Kira stares. 'Really?' she says dubiously as he bites, and bites again. With his lidded eyes, and the peace between his brows, he could be caught in rapture. 'Because that does not seem like a good idea. In fact, it's extremely gross.'

Cheeks bulging, Callum shrugs. 'Sofia said we could eat them out of the water, so I did. It could have gone terribly, but'—he swallows, whole-heartedly smug—'it didn't. Trust me.' He nods at the sandy pile. 'Sofia was right; they're delicious. And unless that bishop-fish *does* turn up...'

He trails off with a drawn-out shrug.

'I'd really rather it didn't.' Reaching over the side of the pool, Kira lifts a fish between finger and thumb. As much as her belly bawls *foodfoodfood*, it also threatens to heave. They could do without food poisoning. They could do without any kind of poisoning. 'Getting close enough to eat it doesn't sound wise if we're not meant to hear it talk.'

Laying his skeleton bare on the ground, Callum leans in for another. 'It can't if it's in my stomach.'

Grinning, he returns to stuffing his face. Kira regards her own helping. Food. Poison. Poison. Food. She sighs, a resigned, solitary huff. How many dinners are literally going to fly into their arms?

'We should go,' she says a short while later, when the fish have been demolished. Dropping their translucent bones, she arranges them neatly on the sand by the rim of the sighing pool: a tree trunk, four branches, the ground. A flag that, once they're home, no one will understand. 'We've probably already stayed too long.'

Her reluctance mirrors in Callum's face. 'I know.' His eyes fall to her bone design. 'Oh.' He tilts his head to the side. 'I saw that in the hobbit-hole.'

Taken aback, Kira frowns. 'Really?'

'Yes.' Callum traces it lightly, thoughtfully, before reaching for his clothes. 'It was scratched into the wall. If we ever see another living soul, I'll ask them what it means. Hey!' His expression brightens. 'Bone-dry!'

Kira groans. One hand holds a sock. The other holds a bone. 'Terrible.' She fills her face with contempt. 'You're terrible. I'm going to get dressed. Turn around.'

To her surprise, he does. For a moment, Kira studies him, girlishly enthralled. Broad back, muscled arms. His jeans hug his hips when he stands. She smiles. That's what you get for being a ski instructor, or chopping endless wood. If he was a summer lifeguard, all the girls would drool.

'Done?' he asks over his shoulder. Kira shakes her head, staccato. Now, more than ever, is so not the time.

The second they're settled, the boat sails away. Kira lolls against the reeds. Raking back his hair, Callum does the same. The heat has already reclaimed him. Sweat films every inch of skin; the pool made it bearable, but now it's back, arid, vengeful, and, well, bone-dry. Tracing infinity signs on Kira's leg, he smirks. She can say what she likes. He's funny.

He's also a desert, baked and cracking. They filled up the water pouch from the pool, but it's one pouch versus the world. He's a parched, dry-lipped, gasping fish.

He's also a cartoon. Callum dips his other hand in the river. He should have been more careful on the island; either the burn, the bruises, or both are throbbing, and his hand is as heavy as sin. An oversized thumb, scarlet from a hammer. A pulsing hand, trapped in a door and ballooning to the size of his head.

A soft snore flutters from his feet. Callum smiles, but it's jaded. Call him paranoid, and it may be true; but Kira was snared in a dream and left in the snow to die. Who's to say it won't happen again? If the dreams returned, they could be stronger, tethered with chains, not ropes. He could wind up watching her smiling in sleep, growing frail in her fictional life. She could die, and he'd be left knowing that he just had to keep her awake.

Callum rubs his eyes. She was fine last night; he watched her "Every Breath You Take"-style, but by morning, she was alive and kicking, dandy, righter than rain. The screwball Kyo, with about a hundred bats in the goddamn belfry, have either lost interest, think she's dead, or are concocting another wonderful plan that doesn't involve her dreams.

Callum yawns. Half an hour. She can have half an hour, or until something weird appears. Pinching his arm, he scratches his head, sleepily stretching his legs. Whether or not they need oars, in this sunless heat, in this ruthless world, he can't help feeling that they're literally up the creek without a paddle.

38

Turning tides

She's singing. Standing in a dark room, watched by faces, upturned, tilted, charmed. She's singing, and…afloat?

She looks up. A stone ceiling rocks bare inches from her head, and she frowns. How peculiar.

The song is peculiar, too. Changing on its own whims, it lilts beyond control. It's a sea shanty, an aria, an Arabian dance; she can see deserts, merchants, travellers, snakes forming in the dust from the air. She's motionless, bodiless, made up of images. Her lips don't move. Is she singing at all?

Her eyesight stripes with light, and she drifts. Of course she's singing. It's her lullaby, her siren's call. Spreading her arms, she floats to the floor. Landing, alighting, flighty, spritely, with a kingfisher's grace—a blackbird, a lark—she fills her airy lungs and—

Chokes. The song scratches her throat. She coughs, her windpipe pinched like a straw. Her stomach heaves, trying to breathe. Her vision splinters. The faces sneer. Her lungs close up, but the song grows stronger. The arid dust becomes arid air.

The dark room parts like butterflies, and the heat swallows her whole.

※

The song is all around her as she drags herself from sleep. Kira opens her gungy eyes, squinting blearily at the sky. So bright. She angles her head away, protesting in her throat. Why is someone *singing*?

She's still on the boat. Rocking unsteadily, it threatens her sea legs, inviting a meeting with her stomach. If anyone would be singing, it'd be Callum, but the voice is too female, too tuneful, and sounds nothing like Biffy Clyro.

Like a slap, her mind sharpens.

'Callum!' The word is a croak in her sleep-stuffed mouth. Sofia's warning shrieks in her head, and she struggles upright.

Her chest grows cold. Horribly, perilously low, Callum is leaning out of the boat.

Kira gasps. His T-shirt has ridden up. He's on his knees, back arched, hair falling over his face, and as she scrabbles toward him, grasping for anything, he tips gracefully into the water.

'No!' Kira screams, scrambling for the reeds. He drops like a bomb but sinks in silence, two arms swirling him round. Her head is a roar. *No.* 'Call— let him go!'

Callum's head lolls. The arms tighten. As she plunges hers in after him, he slips out of reach.

'Callum!' Kira yells, but he doesn't respond. The black-eyed woman holds him close, her body bare and her short hair streaming. Smiling, she pulls him into darkness. 'No!'

Kira plunges both arms deeper. Far below the surface, the havsrå laughs. A remnant of the lilting song bubbles to the surface, and as the boat bobs on, unfailing, unaware, she and Callum are gone.

'No!' Kira beats wildly at the reeds. It's impossible; he can't be gone. Not so fast, not so— 'Stop! Turn around. We have to go back!'

If the boat has a mind, it ignores her. The wrinkled water falls behind, the singing drifts to nothing, and Callum doesn't reappear. Kira's head screams. Her blood beats fast like a panic attack. She digs her nails into her arms, her neck, her cheeks. Maybe she never woke up; maybe she's thrashing around, lost in another nightmare. Maybe the world will start swirling, breaking down and fraying, and someone will call her name.

She keeps pinching until her skin stings. 'Callum!' she shouts when nothing happens, no one calls. Flinging herself against the side of the boat, she stares through the water with tense, strained eyes. Empty bar her manic reflection, wavering above the black. No havsrå. No Callum.

A glance back across the river. Another whipped forward, just in case. Another around as her heart dances wild, beating like a caged bird trying to escape.

She grits her teeth to creaking, grinding. She screwed up. Oh, God, she screwed up. Shit. Shit, shit, *shit*.

How did this *happen*? Flopping back with a thump and a jolt, she boots the reeds, jarring her leg, driving splinters into her toes. The Havsrå. Sirens. She let herself relax, surrender to sleep, and Callum was left unprotected.

She could have stopped this. She *should* have stopped this. At the first sight or sound of the shrivelled, black-eyed beast, she could have ordered him to close his eyes. She could have slapped her hands over his ears. She could have saved him, but instead, she fell asleep.

A cry starts deep in her belly. Surging through her lungs, it barrels up her throat, getting caught in her mouth, and she chokes. Callum's gone. He's bewitched, or drowning, or both, or worse, being tortured in the bowels of the river. If the Havsrå are anything like the Huldra, seducing their men before gutting them...

The cry rips out of her, so harsh it tears her throat. Callum's gone because of her. She's alone because of her. Callum's gone, and he's not coming back.

How does she find him?

What happens if she can't?

A hundred questions, a hundred more. Chasing each other's tails as she lies, head pounding and eyes raw, coiled in the belly of the boat. Her ears ring from screaming and shock. Talons scratch her throat. She hasn't moved for hours.

The boat has sailed on. Never slowing, never stopping, oblivious to her endlessly willing it back. Back to the point where Callum disappeared, so she can dive until she finds him. That's what she should have done in the first place; she should have reacted more quickly, jumped in after him, wrestled the bug-eyed thorax away. She didn't think. She never does.

But she has to carry on. The thought cuts through her quietly, and with Callum's closed, sinking eyes branded on her brain, she slowly starts to uncoil. She has to find her family. They're the reason she's here, and to give up now would be close to tragedy.

But *Callum*.

Kira clenches her fists. It hurts like hell—the pain, the guilt, the terror of being alone—but she has to shut it off. Push it back into the wings like the thought of her mother. If she doesn't, she could languish for the rest of her days, hiding in the bottom of a rowboat and pretending to the world that the world's gone home. *That* would be a tragedy. That would be failing.

Dim and detached, Kira stiffly sits up. It feels disrespectful, selfish even, to carry on after what she's done. Or rather, what she didn't do. It feels wrong to do more than lie and grieve, praying for Callum's escape, and dream up fantastical rescue attempts. After all he's done for her—

Stop. Kira closes her eyes, just for a second. Languishing. Tragedy. Failure.

Move. Dragging her eyes open, she stretches her unhappy limbs. The day is as bright as when they first found the beach. Does the river ever get dark? Dully, she roots for the water container, rubbing her peeling lips. It doesn't matter. She's never sleeping again.

'He that is…'

Kira stiffens. The last of the water trickles down her throat. There was a voice. Was there a voice?

'…Shall not enter into the congregation of the Lord.'

There was definitely a voice. As it drifts toward her, Kira looks around. Turns around, her dullness splintering. Scan the river. There.

A short way ahead is a small, strange island, and on that island sits a large, strange fish. Her dullness cracks. He's toddler-sized, chunky and squat, propped on his rear like a begging dog. With a bishop's mitre sat on his head, she can't doubt it. Oh, good God. She can't, though it shouldn't be possible: Callum's long-awaited, hunger-provoking, sermon-spouting bishop-fish.

God. The boat sails closer, swift on the blue. Kira shakes her head. Flabbergasted. Flummoxed. All of those and more. Whatever she'd expected from the bishop-fish, it wasn't this. Is this really not a dream?

No. Backed against a scraggy, solitary bush, the fish is utterly bizarre. Round, fleshy eyes bulge fiercely as he speaks in a husky human voice. Fins the translucence of frogspawn, his body a marshy green. He looks like a giant toad crossed with a snake.

And he doesn't yet know she's there.

'He that is,' the fish repeats proudly, the words deep and ringing, 'wounded in the stones, or hath his privy member cut off, shall not enter into the congregation of the Lord.'

He tries to persuade my travellers to stop and hear him speak.

Sofia's words, and Romy's face. They pang deep inside her. *I am not entirely sure what will happen if you do, but I advise not finding out.*

Slowly, Kira holds her breath, shrinking down into the reeds. The boat sails closer, closer still. She couldn't avoid the sirens, but she'll avoid him, sure as hell. Spouting his sermons to the world at large, he hasn't seen her, hasn't seen her, hasn't—

'Young woman!' the fish cries. 'Hello!'

Dammit. Kira tenses, uncomfortable and largely prone. Apparently, his sight is as good as his voice. 'Hello.'

The word slips out before she can stop it. She claps a hand to her treacherous mouth. *Damm*it. What the hell was that?

Nothing. It's okay. It wasn't listening to him speak; it was a greeting. She's been raised to be polite. Taking a breath, Kira stares straight ahead, blocking out all but the gentle blues. If the boat just passes on by…

Slowing to a crawl, the boat scrapes the island.

'Why do you look so forlorn?' the fish cries. Kira's hope sputters out, but she drops her eyes, fixing on her fraying jeans. This is not ending because of a fish. 'Is there any way I can assist?'

No chance.

'Sirens took my friend,' Kira says. The words march out of their own accord, as slippery as fish themselves. 'I don't know how to get him back. I don't even know if he can come back. He sank into the river with a havsrå.'

What the hell? What the hell? What the hell? She covers her mouth again—it worked *so* well—but its explanation is over.

'Ah.' The fish sighs. The corners of his puffed lips droop with melancholy. 'I see. Canst thou fill his skin with barbed irons? or his head with fish spears?'

Kira lowers her fingers and blinks at him. 'No?'

What the hell? What the hell? Her mind hollers on, but another part, a stronger part, rallies to curiosity. 'Even if I could, I don't think it would help.'

'Ah.' The fish shakes what passes for its head. They're parallel now. The boat sails by in microscopic increments; if she wanted to, she could stop it. 'I see. But *I* can help, even if it can't!'

He gestures widely. The mitre slips. With one slimy fin, he rights it.

'Stop here, young woman,' he continues. Kira leans toward the speckled sand. Her chest flutters, and it feels like hope. 'Listen to the wisdom of my speech! I'—he dips the mitre toward her—'will tell you how to find your friend.'

He tries to persuade my travellers to stop and hear him speak.

Kira's intrigue pops like airplane ears. If that's not what he's doing, she'll eat her own foot. She shakes her head fervently, diverting her eyes. Back to the jeans, the sandy reeds. He knows nothing about Callum; he can't. And death by talking fish is *not* the way she's going to go.

She fought the forest from her head. She can fight him as well.

And besides, the boat is speeding up. The fluttering hope billows into relief. Soon, his voice will be lost.

'Young woman!' the fish cries. 'Foreign woman! I can help!'

'I don't need your help,' she calls back, laconic. It's as much of a trick as the havsrå's song. Because of her, Callum is gone.

Stop. Kira bodily shoves this away. Sandy reeds. Manky-looking socks. She can feel the fish bristling, affronted by her rudeness, but he's already drifting out of earshot. Stuck on his sad, lifeless little island, he can do nothing to exact his revenge.

'When the king's decree, which he shall make…' he cries in a last-ditch attempt to win her back. Across the water, the words lose grip, and Kira slides down onto her back. The sooner they're lost, the better; he's a talking fish. '…All the wives shall give to their husbands honour…'

Humourless, Kira snorts. A talking, chauvinistic fish; brilliant. She's Alice in Wonderland, again. She twists her mouth bitterly, kicking one foot up to rest on her knee. Pink from heat, chipping purple nail varnish. Her life is now defined by a drug-induced book.

She's toying with the toe of one of Callum's hefty boots when a bellow echoes out from the island.

'Callum!' the fish bawls. 'Callum Reeve!'

Kira's breath catches, stutters, and balls up in her mouth. Callum Reeve? It knows his name when she didn't.

'What?' She scrambles up, clutches at the reeds, and yells as loud as she can. The talons scrape her throat. 'What about Callum?' Callum Reeve. 'What do you know about him?'

'Callum!' the fish hollers. He's far, far away now, dwindling by the second. 'I know h—'

Violent and unseen, the boat crashes into land.

39

Faded boats

The pain is appalling. Lying on a beach of stones, dazed and barely there, Kira's skull throbs like she beat it with a mace. The water swims through slitted eyes.

The water's all there is. The fish has gone; the island has gone. Even the boat has gone. It kicked her out and buggered off.

Taking with it all hope of finding Callum. Although it was probably nothing, a trick, Kira can't help but hope that it wasn't. The fish knew Callum's *name*.

Did it? It could have said anything, and she'd be none the wiser. Callum Tartt. Callum King. Callum Schwab. Callum Reeve is as believable as any.

But it's so human. So human and so plausible for who he is and where he's from. What's more, when the alternative is to be alone, living with the knowledge that she caused his disappearance, if not his ultimate demise—

No. With a colourful grimace and a series of groans, Kira pushes herself upright. She's been through this already, a hundred thousand times. She has to keep moving.

Dizzily, she touches her temple.

Mistake. The contact ignites such a shock of pain, a firework display of colourful rain, that she almost faints back away. Kira blinks. Breathes. Her eyes are flecked with black, swarming at the edges of her vision. That blossoming lump will become a beauty.

Blink. Breathe. Bit by bit, the black recedes.

A heavy hand lands on her shoulder. Kira jerks away with a strangled shout, scrabbling round to face him. Stones bite her palms. The world sways like stormy seas.

'Sorry,' the man says quickly. Raising both hands, he takes a step back. 'Didn't mean to frighten you. Are you okay?'

His voice is throaty, twisting around the words as if his tongue wants to reject them. Each syllable is carefully formed. Kira doesn't speak. It's all she can do to shake her head, unwieldy and woollen and thick. Her sharp retreat brought the swarming back. Her vision is sick, and her stomach is tipping. The flecks are dancing to black.

Severe and sharp-cheeked, the man kneels beside her. He's dark, browned further by the hiding sun, and knotted with sweat at the neck, his hair rough, curling, chestnut. Too hot, Kira thinks faintly; his bare chest gleams with heat, a pair of loose, dusty trousers tied with twine at his waist. She could do with something like that. Jeans too much, bra digging in. Too hot, too—

'Girl.' The man tips up her chin, forcing her giddy eyes to his. The words are quiet but cogent. 'You don't want to be here when night comes, and night'— he moves her face to the side, to the horizon—'is coming.'

Oh, oh, dizzy. The tug on her chin was too much.

'If you don't leave,' the man continues, 'many things you don't want to see will—oh.'

He catches her torso as she slumps. The giddiness thumps in her belly, but as the black takes over, she smiles. The sun. Setting gold across the land, she's found the sun.

'You can't stay here,' the man urges, but she's going. Alongside the pain, and the churning nausea, the swarm is just too strong. The blackness swirls and connects. Going, going.

Going, gone.

Oh, to the sky. Klaus bows his head. The girl has gone limp in his arms; a sleeping, half-dressed, injured girl, who looks to be an outsider. If he takes her home, the talk will fly.

If he leaves her here, she'll die. The sun is setting, and the land looks friendly, warm, and lulling, but it's not. If she was to get caught by the Night Hunter, she'd be lost. If a myrling was to find her, she'd be terrified for life and never shift it from her back. What can he do?

He can save a life. Lifting the girl to his chest, he stands, steadies, and starts up the beach to Maja, snuffing and scuffing her hooves. To the sky with village talk, too. If they wanted a ruthless patroller, they shouldn't use him.

He won't reach Rana for some time, at least. Manoeuvring them both onto Maja's back, it's some small form of comfort: he has a while to steel himself. In all likelihood, he'll need it.

The pebbles of the beach give way to a sand dune, littered with purple-rimmed shells. From there stretches a rolling vastness of flat, gentle plains. The grass waves tall in the lethargic breeze. The evening sun bleaches everything yellow. It's a wonder compared to what he's heard of Atikur; assuming the forest is where the girl has come from, were she awake, she would have marvelled. The trees grow sparsely, scattered, leafy patches of oasis, and although the ground is hot, rivulets of water trickle freely to the river. It's life over nothingness, colour over white. Positioning her more comfortably in front of him, he takes the reins, casts his eye over the violent sunset, and nudges Maja into the wilds.

The end comes into sight when the colour is almost bled. Huddled around three low, sprawling trees, some way beneath Monte Yuno, appears a pinprick of civilisation: his isolated, close-knit pinprick, ringed by pastures, scrawny but enough. Glancing at the raging sun, Klaus nudges Maja faster. If he's not in Rana when the mountain takes it, the wards will go up and he'll be stranded. Prey for the Night Hunter. Prey for the world.

He digs his heels into Maja's sides. The reddened disc is barely a sliver, peeping over the summit; it won't be long.

Just as it dips, he's there. 'Dad!'

A tiny voice springs from the outskirts of the village. Dusty and brown, Marcus bounds out, bouncing about Klaus's legs as he slides from the horse. 'It's nearly—' He breaks off to goggle at the girl. 'Who's that?'

Before Klaus can answer, he bounds away. 'Mam!' he calls. 'Mam!'

Klaus frowns at his back. And so it begins.

'Marcus says you've found a girl,' a new voice calls, preceding her out of the trees. Marya, in a thin, wraparound dress, ducks under a branch to meet them.

The ideal first inquisitor. 'She was on the beach,' Klaus explains, lifting the girl in his arms. Her head lolls backwards. Her bruises stand stark. He flicks a fly from her cheek.

Marya ducks back into the shade. 'Bring her in.' She beckons for him to follow, and dotting between gratitude and defensive apprehension, he weaves his way into the village.

Two dozen people are waiting, as he expected them to be. Half of the villagers are always here, lying against trunks, wrapped in idle tasks, or talking by their tipi flaps. As he steps into their midst, they look up.

'You cut it fine,' Ingar calls, grain trickling absently through his old, stubby fingers. The horses at his side protest, but he nods at the girl and ignores them. 'Who's she?'

'I've never seen the like,' little Heike comments. Her head pokes out of a slouching tent, and her girls poke out their own.

'Me neither,' they say from her armpits. Amusement rumbles through the congregation, but Klaus brushes it off. He needs to get the girl inside, and when his wife slips beneath a heavy, bowing branch, he follows without a word.

Still inclined to goggle, Marcus waits inside the tipi. 'Who is she?' he asks eagerly, shuffling to the edge of a low-slung bed. Lowering the girl on top, Klaus says nothing. 'Do you know what happened? Why is she sleeping? Why is she *here*?'

Their larger bed rests by the first, surrounded by a parted scarlet screen. Motioning for Marcus to run and play, Klaus sinks down heavily onto it.

'I found her on the beach,' he repeats when, with much scowling, his son leaves them alone. Stretching his strained arms, he winces. Even before the beach, it had been a long day. 'I don't know who she is or where she came from. There was a boat disappearing as I got there, so I assume she was sent by the shapeshifter. All I got before she collapsed was that she wasn't okay.'

Marya kneels beside her. 'For a start, she's from the outside.'

Deft fingers check her pulse, feel for her temperature, brush back her hair to reveal the lump on her skull. 'And she's taken a beating from something. If I were to guess'—she skims her hands over bruises on the girl's arms, her chest, the skin where her skimpy clothes have ridden above her hips—'I'd say she's linked to the travellers.'

Climbing to her feet, Marya moves to the large chest beside the beds and pulls out her medicine pouch. 'Which travellers?' he asks, between suspicion and intrigue. 'No one mentioned them to me.'

'Last night.' Marya retrieves a cream, speckled with herbs, and returns to the girl's side. Carefully, she parts her hair around the inimical lump. 'I saw them in the distance. Clara did, too, but we didn't think it important enough to report. They showed no interest in the village.' She pauses, the poultice almost complete. 'We thought at that point they might be linked to the woman; the one the children said they saw earlier in the day. You knew about that?' She glances at her husband.

Forehead wrinkling, Klaus nods. 'A woman'—he runs his eyes over the girl's pale skin, her dark clothes, her long, white-blonde hair—'who looked like this one.'

Marya tilts her head. 'I suppose. I couldn't see the others clearly enough, but Clara said there was a limping man.' She eyes the girl shrewdly. 'And a pale, long-haired woman.'

Klaus meets her eyes. 'An Atikur woman?'

'Perhaps. We'd be fools to think they're not connected. Although'—Marya checks the poultice with her fingers—'I doubt this one's a threat.' She shakes her head. 'She's injured, and she's not wearing shoes. No weapons, no provisions.' She sighs. It matches her expression, the look she gives Marcus when he sneaks off to seek out snakes. 'Who knows what she's doing here. Who knows what any of them are doing here.'

Disapproval merges with a sweet exasperation. Klaus almost smiles; even with outsiders, she can't resist mothering. 'If you call Marcus back to watch her,' she continues, 'I'll find her some food. She can spend the night and go through the Yunavida in the morning.'

With this, she leaves. Klaus's almost-smile slides away. Rather than a blessing, that sounds like a curse.

40

Holding lies

Kira comes to in the falling dusk. A pinkish-red stains the canopy above her, and as she watches, not truly awake, it melts through magenta to a purpling blue.

Sunset. The thought is a coalescent dream. Her mind is slow to drift back to itself. Where is she?

Not relaxed, not alarmed, she angles her eyes to the side. She's lying on a foot-high bed, her feet close to the walls of a tent. Rough material, smelling of the wild. The ceiling's gentle apex is propped by wooden stakes. A long slit opens to her left, fluttering in the mild scents of evening, fires, and nearby water and warmth. Kira tilts her head. On the tent's far side sits a large wooden chest, a tumult of canvas bags, and a pile of toys and implements, leading to a screen and a—

Somewhere, there's food.

She knows it as keenly as if she were Callum. A stronger smell than evening wafts through the air, and with her ever-stiff limbs complaining, she rolls over.

Next to the bed is a bowl of soup, neatly coupled with a spoon. Kira stares at it, unashamedly hopeful. It must be meant for her; she's the only one here. There are people outside, talking and laughing, but why would it sit a foot from her face, with such a strong aroma, if it was for them?

With only a flicker of guilt and warning, she reaches to scoop up the bowl.

Is it a bad idea? Maybe. Does she care? No. At this point, it's more important to eat something that doesn't still have a face. After all of this is over, she thinks, around something herby like basil, a piquant tomato, or lemon, or lime, she'll definitely be veggie for life. She's said it before, and it's gospel truth.

On her third glorious, faceless mouthful, a woman ducks into the tent. Kira starts, swallows quickly, and drops the spoon back into the bowl, splattering her fingers with soup.

'Feel free to carry on.' The woman smiles, wry and tickling. At her rich, thick voice, Kira remembers: she was found on the beach by a man. A dark-skinned man, chestnut-haired; the woman is a shorter, curvier version, her braided hair looped behind her head. He must have brought her here once she'd passed out again. He did say she couldn't stay where she was.

Self-conscious but starving, Kira delicately licks her fingers and returns to the soup. The woman has set to work on the larger bed, moving the screen aside to beat rough-stitched pillows, rearrange blankets, and create as much space as she can. She's a matronly, rustic presence of solidity, but surely they should speak? She's a stranger, saved from the night; if she, or someone she knew, had saved a stranger, she'd want to know all about them. She certainly wouldn't go about her business, leaving them in bed eating soup.

Unless she was fattening them up for sacrifice. Kira's mind leaps with fan-tastical fear, her chest leaping in actual fear as the tent slit opens. Oh, God. Her fingers tighten around the bowl. They're coming for her with knives; they're coming for her with fire. They're coming for her full stop, having realised who she is. They've called the Kyo, they've called the mist—

A young boy enters, mouth downturned. Kira's face heats with shame. Paranoia is one thing, but how distrustful has she grown? 'Sorry, Mam,' the boy mumbles. 'I only left for a bit.'

'Or a lot, apparently.' The woman turns, dry but stern. 'If your dad asks you to do something, you do it. Yes?' She beckons him over, splashing water on his face from a jug by the chest.

'Yes,' he says glumly, tipping back his head so she can briskly wash his neck.

The woman flicks water from her hands. 'Good.' She indicates the rear-ranged nest of blankets. 'Now bed. You're with us tonight.'

The boy nods again, as sorry for himself as a dog in the rain. 'Sorry, Mam,' he mumbles again. 'I am.'

'Sleep, Marcus.' The woman rolls her eyes, pulling the screen in front of the bed. The dusk-light glints off the shimmering fabric. 'I have other things to do. How are you, other things?'

Kira jumps, setting the empty bowl on the floor. 'Um.'

'How's your head? No, don't touch it.' She crosses the tent in a second, slapping Kira's hand away. Kira jumps again. Sacrifice. 'I dressed it not long ago. What did you do to get a lump that big? Actually, never mind.'

She kneels beside the bed. Kira's nerves clatter, but all the woman does is tilt her head. Her touch is light, familiar, like the nurse back in October when she sprained her ankle in the art shop. Tripping over an easel; even her boss had laughed.

The woman sits back on her heels. 'It's looking better.' She nods her approval. 'Another success for the magic poultice.'

She smiles, and there's something of Callum in it. Smugness and teasing, satisfaction and fun. 'Thank you,' Kira says quietly. Callum, lurching along with Romy the first time she saw him. Tipping limp into the river, the last. 'Can I...' She bites on her cheek, forcing back tears. Is it grief when he might be alive? 'Can I ask where I am?'

'You can.' The woman moves to the chest, returning with a pot and a pouch. 'You're in Rana. We're nomadic. My husband found you on the beach. Although'—she tilts Kira's head again—'shouldn't it be me asking about you?'

Kira's nerves clatter into shame. She drops her eyes. 'Sorry. I—'

'But I'll indulge you,' the woman finishes, meaningfully, purposefully: *listen before you speak*. Face heating, Kira's insides squirm. Oh, to faint again. 'I'm Marya, my husband is Klaus, and that'—she inclines her head toward the screen—'is Marcus. We live in the grasslands. Your turn.'

Surprised, Kira's eyes flick back up. She hadn't even known there *were* grasslands. 'I'm—ow.' She winces as Marya dabs at her head. Up close, the woman smells mysterious, open, unfamiliar wilderness and summer smoke. 'I'm Kira.'

'Nice to meet you, Kira.' Marya eyes her briefly, scooping cream from the pot and continuing to dab. 'Your head is doing well. It was swollen to the skies when I first saw it, but by the morning you should just have a bruise. An ugly bruise'—more cream, and the pot is set down—'but a bruise. And call me presumptuous'—she eyes her again, inviting, searching—'but you appear to be an outsider.'

Kira hesitates. *I would advise you to be more discerning about what you reveal to strangers.* 'Yes,' she says carefully. Sofia's advice has proved unhappily sound; she should probably listen to it now. Strike three. 'I'm here because of my sister.'

Marya arches a dark eyebrow. 'Oh?'

Careful. 'I followed her,' Kira explains, as naturally as she can. Her fingers twist in the covers on the bed, an airy, cotton-like mauve. 'I don't really know what she's doing here. I got the feeling it wasn't good, so I followed.'

Both eyebrows arch now. Kira struggles for an innocent face, to fight her fingers still. The lie in her voice is painful.

'I see.' Sitting back on her heels, Marya studies her. Thoughtfully, amicably. 'Who told you to lie?'

Kira's eyes fly wide. 'I'm not lying.'

'You are.' Marya rises to her feet. Her face falls into shadow, and Kira sickens with despair. Has she grossly offended her? Ruined her chances of any more help? 'You sound like a child putting on a performance. But that's okay.' She smiles, dry and teasing. 'We live by actions rather than words; say you're a witch or say you're clueless, it's nothing. As long as you're not a threat, you can be whoever you want.'

Replacing the pot and the pouch in the chest, she rummages, careful and quiet. Watching her flitting silhouette, Kira sighs. 'The last time I told the truth, I was chased.' She shivers. *Huldra.* 'They wanted me dead.'

Marya withdraws a spindly candle, narrowing her eyes as the wick bursts to life. Kira sighs again. 'After that, I was warned to watch what I said. I'm sorry.' She shakes her head. Everything slumping, everything drained. All of a sudden, she's so, so tired. 'I don't mean to seem ungrateful. Everyone I meet just wants something different, or has their own opinions about how I should act. It's getting hard to follow.'

Marya huffs. 'I can imagine.' Placing the candleholder on the floor, she lowers herself to the bed. The darkness sits with her, shadows flitting up the soft-lit walls. After a moment, Kira looks away. The looming shapes that pattern the hide remind her of her frailty. In such a virulent land, it's a reminder she doesn't need.

'Are there...' she begins. The words seem to tumble back down her throat. Does she really want to know?

Yes. If she's travelling alone, she *needs* to. A third, heftier sigh whooshes from her throat, and she forces herself to meet Marya's eyes. Inviting, searching. She needs to trust someone. 'Are there things I need to be careful of here? Like the havsrå in the river, or the mist in the forest? Well.' Her forehead puckers. 'It was the world and his dog in the forest. Your husband—Klaus'—she amends with a bob of her head—'said I shouldn't be out after dark.'

'The forest?' Marya clears her throat, hitched on surprise. The dryness has dropped, and she's watchful, serious. 'Klaus thought you looked—did you come through Atikur?'

Slowly, warily, Kira lifts her shoulders. 'I…don't know. I never heard a name. I'm assuming there's more than one.'

Marya smooths the scratchy blanket. 'Correct.' She holds the fabric taut with both hands. 'This is Everla, the Everland.' She scrapes her hands together, the blanket trapped between them. 'And this is Atikur.'

The crude distinction creeps like bugs beneath the skin. She scratches her arm. 'Then Atikur.' She scratches the other. Goddamn bugs. 'You and Klaus were right.'

Marya regards her. This time, it's impossible to read. 'To look at you, you'd never think you'd get out alive.' She shakes her head, eyebrows rising. 'Anyway. During the day, you'll meet nothing here. Animals tend to stay away.' She glances over her shoulder. 'There are things that come out at night—on the beach, in the grasslands, and through the Monte Yuno tunnel—but they're not for a certain someone to hear.'

A fake snore grumbles from behind the screen.

Kira's lips rebel and become a smile. 'The village is safe, though?' she asks. Outside, the light is deepening, more raven-coloured than blue. 'At night?'

Returning to wryness, Marya nods. 'We have wards. Weavers put them up in the evenings. Stay here until morning, take the tunnel while the sun's still up, and you'll be fine. The ice plains are on the other side.' She stands. 'Whether you really are following your sister, if you've come this far, I'm sure that's where you're going. Unless it's Skarrig?'

Kira opens her mouth and shuts it. 'No?'

'Skarrig is a lake.'

'Then no.'

'Good. Skarrig is'—Marya glances at the screen—'unsavoury. Anyway, now you and Marcus must sleep.'

Halfway through the tent slit, she turns. 'And when you're done in Whiteland, don't go back to Atikur. There are entrances everywhere.'

Kira stares after her. Through the slit, fires pop and spark, leaves whispering on low-hung branches—was it only this morning that they followed the trees? It must be, but it seems impossible. Impossible and cruel.

With a final, lung-emptying sigh, she falls back to the bed. So, so tired. Adults chatter outside, children laugh at their passing bedtimes, but inside the tent, with Marcus's snores growing real, it's not long before she sinks toward sleep.

Maybe she should be more cautious; maybe she should stay awake and keep watch, just to ensure she's safe. Maybe she should do many things, yet none of it—the stuffy heat, her worries, *wards, weavers,* the bishop-fish shouting *Callum, Callum Reeve*—seems to matter. She's away with the night and doesn't wake.

41

Fleeing from the things that bite

'You'll need a horse.'

Klaus appears beside her, unannounced. Kira startles. Marya coughs. Clearly, the foliage is not as private as they thought.

'Well, you will.' He shrugs. Apparently, her surprise came across as a protest. 'Marya told me what you're trying to do. If you've any hope of achieving it, you'll need a horse.' He pats the animal's flank as it ambles up to join them, a bay mare with a bright white nose. 'Maja's good. She'll take you to the northern ice. Farther, if necessary, as you'll have these.' He indicates the furs tied to Maja's back. 'Blankets for her body. And these'—he holds up four pouches—'for her hooves. I see Marya found some for you.'

Kira joins him in regarding her feet. It's an effort to adjust to the moccasins, laced from her ankles to halfway up her calves, but her gratitude is exponential. Everything she had must have stayed in the boat, never to be seen again. Alongside a hollow ache—for Callum and Erik, rather than the things—Kira can't resist a twinge of amusement. Whoever receives two iPhones and a *Breaking Bad* hoodie will be confused for the rest of their lives.

'Thank you.' She looks up at Klaus. Tucking the pouches into a hide-hewn coat, he positions it carefully on top of the furs. 'Both of you.' She smiles between him and Marya, hands folded beside them. 'For everything. Bringing me here. The food, the bed, the water. Whatever you did to heal me. I no longer hurt, which is insane.'

'I told you.' Marya's eyes spark. 'I'm the one with the magic poultice.'

Kira smiles properly. It almost feels real. 'Well, I'm grateful to the three of you. Are you sure about the horse?' She glances at Maja. It's the bed and the floor in the cabin again. Absently, she bats at a bug. 'I don't know if I'll be able to get her back to you. I've not been too lucky with choosing my own direction.'

'We're sure.' Marya inclines her head. The humour is light and alive in her eyes. 'I hadn't thought of giving you a horse, but it'll help you catch up to your sister.'

She doesn't need to add the rest. Kira sees it in her face, curious but quiet: *if that's what you're really doing.* If she had more time, maybe, eventually, she'd tell the whole truth. Rana fed her, kept her, and fed her again, intrigued but accepting. They're open in a way that Erik's village wasn't, that Callum's wasn't, that her own small town tends not to be. People for people: actions over words.

'And Maja will find her way home,' Klaus adds. A hint of a smile curls his full mouth. 'Do you know how to ride?'

Kira barely has time to think *kind of, but* before he lifts her up, plants her square on the horse, and steps back. She sways, unready, unsteady. *Yes, but I haven't in—*

Too late. With a smack on Maja's rump, Klaus sends them on their way.

'Ørenna,' Marya calls. From around the village come echoes. Too fast to look back, to speak, to wave, they fly from the trees, past startled chickens, through a garden of sorts, and out into the grasslands.

Pressing her legs tight to Maja's flanks, Kira clutches the reins in a panic. He didn't wait for an answer! Did he assume she'd refuse if she couldn't ride? There wasn't *time* to think, and a pre-smack warning would have been nice. Kiddie riding lessons take time to remember.

Especially mid-gallop. Daring a glance down, Kira quickly slides her right foot into a loop in the blankets, burying her left in their bundled midst. He didn't even wait for that; what if she'd fallen? What if she still does? What if she rides Maja into a *tree*?

For that, there would have to be trees. Come on. Kira breathes, embracing the air flying into her lungs and skimming over her skin. The horse isn't going *that* fast, and she's already adjusting to the rhythm of the run. It's a steady line, at a steady pace. They're going to be fine.

After a while, she starts to believe it. The morning is scorching, hotter than the previous day, and it would even be nice to go faster. Their speed-blown wind is a godsend, keeping her alert as it beats at her face, refreshing as it whips through her hair; it's coldly delicious all round, and she slowly starts to settle. No predators will bother her, and she knows the way. Ride to Monte Yuno, ride through the tunnel, ride out and look for her family. Done.

Probably not done. Marya said this, too, sheltered beneath the dappled leaves: nothing is ever that simple, and if it has been, it's something else's design. All that has to happen is for Whiteland to tire of her, to decide she's worth toying with, and she could end up anywhere. The Yunavida mountains move at the whims of many, as does the ice and snow. Even if that doesn't happen, while the grasslands aren't dangerous, danger will come.

She just doesn't want to think about that. Not yet. As endless time elapses, and the vast mountain range creeps closer, she focuses on one thought: *I will find my family.* She nudges Maja faster. She'll find them today, and all of this—whatever it is—will be done.

Not for Callum.

Kira steers away from this, nudging Maja faster still. It's reared its ugly heads a hundred times, but they all boil down to one thing: she can't help him now. Maybe when she gets to the ice plains—maybe if she talks to what Sofia called the Whispers—but she can't do that unless she rides.

She leans determinedly into Maja's neck. Faster. She has to reach the tunnel while the sun's still up.

It's barely risen to the middle of the sky when the Yunavida range is upon her. Rumbling unbroken for as far as she can see, they're a looming stretch of rock, a blockade, a legion. Kira slows Maja to a trot. What was Callum muttering in the forest? *We can't go over it, and we can't go under it. I guess we'll have to go through it.*

She pushes out her lips. Her insides are turning coffee-jittery, like when she studies until 3:00 a.m. How far along does the dusty mass go? How far *back*? It could last for acres, kilometres, *leagues*, until the end of the earth is closer than home. She could be stuck in the blackness forever with the monsters that sleep until dark.

Unless you make noise and disturb their peace.

Kira shakes this off with a vague sense of bravado. Her repeated dramatics are annoying; she'll be fine. Marya told her what to do: traverse the tunnel quietly, as most of Rana, for hunting, trade, whatever, has done, and if Maja is as obedient as Klaus said, they shouldn't meet trouble. She's survived mist phantoms, a squalling fish, multiple injuries, crazy dead women, and crazy *real* women; she can deal with being quiet. *It's all,* Kira thinks stoically, *going to be fine.*

Her bravado lasts until her eyes find the tunnel. A short way to the left, marked by a dead, spindly tree, it's unmistakeable; Marya was right to say she couldn't miss it. It's a dark slash in the sandy rock, and as they trot closer, Maja whinnies.

'Shh,' Kira murmurs. Stroking Maja's sweat-sodden neck, it's as much for herself as the horse. 'Shh. It's still morning. Nothing's going to hurt you.'

Still, the tunnel couldn't look less welcoming. Despite the angle of the sun, its crooked entrance escapes the light, barely wider than the bishop-fish's island, which is not very wide at all. Apprehension grows feelers and crawls inside her, joining the jittery coffee. It could be a B-list horror film, where darkness shrouds evil places and animals won't go in. All they need now is a lightning bolt or maybe a scattering of bones.

It's got the symbol.

That godforsaken thing. Kira swells with distaste. Scratched into the rock by the tunnel's entrance, it mirrors the white-bleached tree beside it. She glares at them both. Stupid thing. Stupid, nonsensical thing. Is that the tree it's based on, or a tree based on it? The way to the Whispers, the so-called lawmakers? Surely it must be option two; option one would be the least impressive kingdom marker ever.

The last time she came across it, Callum was with her.

For God's sake, *stop*. She closes her eyes briefly. She can't blame the symbol, or its corresponding tree, for his disappearance, no more than she can for never asking about it. It always just slipped away.

So, stop.

Casting a delaying look back, she sighs. The grasslands are so light, so bright; it's not right to have spent so long in the dim, grim forest and so little time somewhere like this, where nobody wants to kill her, and the sun tends to exist. If it's designed, it's particularly cruel.

Building up her resolve, brick by dreading brick, Kira turns back to the tunnel. She has to go on, and she has to be logical. The tunnel is sinister, a primal maw leeching light from the land, but Marya told her how to take it. No candle; no sound; no quick movements. It may be cut from a B-list horror film, but that doesn't make her the heroine. Not a B-list one, at least.

Romy. Mum. Dad.

Settling herself straight and firm, alert and as present as can be, Kira nudges the horse toward the tunnel. Maja had been slowing, so subtly she'd hardly noticed, but before she can change her mind, she urges her back into a trot. A deep breath, another grumbling whinny, and they head bravado-first into the mountain.

The first thing, before the daylight has faded, is that the tunnel is oppressively hot. She'd expected the chill of ghosts, but the air is musty, stale, and muffled, as if it's been trapped in here for eras. Knowing Whiteland, it probably has.

She's sheened with sweat within minutes. Her breath is airless. Her eyes are dusty. Her palms rest slippy on the reins. Good God. She shakes the hair from her neck, wiping her face with her knuckles. Her jeans are damp around the waistband. Her vest—she can practically feel it darkening, from midnight blue to black—clings over-zealously to her armpits. If the grasslands were hot, this is an inferno.

An inferno that Marya neglected to mention. She'd have remembered a warning about hellish, cloying heat; she'd have been mentally preparing all the way from Rana. As it is, however, she feels set to faint, to let the fusty air constrict her throat and siphon off her strength.

Which is what the mountain wants. Kira shakes her head to clear it. No. It is not an inferno; it's an illusion. She can breathe. She can think. She can remember Marya's advice. After all of Whiteland's mind games, her thoughts are growing strong.

Follow the path. Tightening her hands on the reins, she firmly sets her sights. Follow the path, ignore the hellfire illusion, and she'll be fine. The tunnel only has one major change, and she's meant to know it instantly, from the drop on either side and the water underneath. Other than that, it's all the same. She just has to stay quiet.

Which is going weirdly well. Maja hasn't made a sound since the entrance. Perhaps she's too afraid; perhaps she's done this enough to know how to act, even if she'd rather stay away. Perhaps—and this is the rock-and-the-hard-place option—she can feel whatever waits in sleep and knows to stay quieter than death.

For there *is* something here. The tunnel seems to breathe. No one in Rana could or would tell her what, but a heavy presence wraps around her, pulsing in the air. There's something here, and it's something that normal life fears.

That's the other thing. Kira's eyes adjust to the dark and see: normal life does not exist. Step by step in front of her, Monte Yuno's underbelly materialises, but it's barren. No lizards, no spiders, no bats. Nothing scuttling, nothing lurking. Nothing growing in the walls. Tiny crystals glint above her head, Kyo-like, nesting in the low ceiling. Other than that, the rock is bare.

A sharp bend looms in the narrow path. With mindful quietness, Maja steers herself around it. Kira's heart bounces up and down and back again, swooning. She's got to pay better attention. The harder she concentrates, the harder it is, but she has to stay focused. It's her *life*. Her family's lives. Maybe—hopefully, please—Callum's life.

After an unknowable amount of silent time, she's disoriented and immersed. How far are they into the mountain? No one told her how long it would take.

No one told her a lot of things. Gripping the reins tight through her sweat, Kira tenses her legs at another spiked bend. Both her pulse and Maja's beat ten to fifty dozen. If this part of Whiteland is as crafty as the rest, how will she know if it's slinking into night? If the dead are set to—

Behind them, something plinks and skitters. The echo of a stone, loosed from the wall or kicked by the horse's hooves.

Oh, God.

A shiver snakes through Kira's skin. She forces herself to gently halt Maja, her heart skipping over the surface of a drum. Oh, God, oh, God, oh, God. Straining every limb to listen, she waits, rooted in horrified silence. She was being so careful, too; she thought they were doing so well! Flicking her eyes from left to right, the drum beats faster, faster, faster, ready to ramp up and burst into terror. What happens now?

She can see nothing but darkness and rock, hear nothing but the lingering echo. How long should she wait? Is it wise to wait at all?

Seconds. Minutes. More minutes. Nothing. With her pulse still thrumming, beating hard and sickly against her belly, Kira presses her heels cautiously into the horse's flank. The sooner they get out of here, the better.

Minutes, and minutes, and minutes. Dejected, Maja walks with her head bent low. Her hooves barely click the hot stone. Kira watches her closely, and when the horse dips lower, she flattens herself against the heaving, sweaty neck. They're one pulse, pounding.

In a breath, the ceiling drops. Kira's heart beats ten to fifty dozen, gripping the horse so tight it hurts. Maja knew. She's walked this tunnel, knows its ins and outs…and still, she's so afraid. Pray to the gods, to the Whispers, whatever, that they never find out what of.

It can't be this passage, at least. The crystal shines gold, jutting in swathes from the ceiling and the walls. Pressed to Maja's mane, Kira turns to watch it go. It's iridescent, jagged and gleaming; if she ever gets home, she'll paint it. Not just the tunnel, lit in the dusty gloom by sparkling stones, but everything: the bleak forest, the glittering river, the hummingbird and cliff face from when it all began—

The tunnel curves. With a jolting of her thoughts and chest, the inspiration becomes a sun-facing flower, a peacock butterfly. A stalactite dips down in the corner, a translucent, bloody scarlet. She stares at it in awe as they gently click past. It's surrounded by golden, clinging crystal, mirrored at the tip by its stalagmite twin, and together—a glowing hourglass, two straining lovers—they're perfect.

They're also falling behind. Kira lifts her head for one last look.

The ceiling scrapes over her skull.

'Agh!'

Pain slices in a bright, hot line. Kira claps her hands to her mouth, but too late. Beneath her, Maja whinnies, skidding to a startled stop, and out of the rocks, somewhere behind them, drifts a faint, echoing howl.

The hairs on Kira's arms stand up. Her sticky, throbbing skull thuds. Oh, no. Oh, no, oh, God, oh, no. Louder, longer, and closer, a second howl reverberates. Her breath stutters. The passage tunnels, narrow and pulsing with fear. What has she done?

What can she do? The sounds ricochet around them, slipping out of crevices and battering the bends. If she and Maja stay perfectly still, the creatures might go back to sleep. Maja has turned to stone, wide-eyed and terrified. If Kira does the same, maybe the mountain will think them gone.

Not a chance. Not a hope in hell, not a crow in heaven. A harsh voice tears the air apart, and Kira's insides quail. It's unfamiliar, a tongue that drills into her bones, pooling and spreading in her marrow. She whips her head around, bending low. Rock, darkness, crystal, nothing.

Fear whumps down like a smothering pillow, clamped to her nose and mouth. Faint and pale, there's something else. A glow, a glimmer, a gleam, gliding onto the path behind them, and beyond…Kira swallows a whimper. She needs to vomit. She needs to scream. Beyond it is another, and another, and another, drifting toward her from the depths of the dark.

Oh, God, oh, hell. The glimmers solidify, becoming crooked figures. Her mind starts to bellow, battering its walls, horror gushing up, up, up. Their heads snap to the side. Their long, disjointed bodies bend, clicking and cracking and hollow. The smell of metal fills her nose. Something sour. Something acrid. Something dead.

A chitter sounds behind her. Kira spins, unbalanced. A small creature skitters toward her, low to the ground and inhuman. Its arms are too long, its spine bent back, and approaching the horse with a clattering of claws, it blasts her every atom into raw hysteria. It has no eyes.

Caution be damned.

'Go!' Kira screams. Breathing in a gust of foul, musty air, she chokes, yanks the reins, and drives the horse with her hips, her weight, her slippery legs. 'Go, Maja!'

Maja won't. She rears up as the creature crawls closer, skidding in reverse along the twisting path. Kira flings a wild look back. The passage is full of hazy figures, contorted bodies, shimmering lights and stretching arms and the darkness splicing her guts.

'Maja!' Kira yells, whipping the reins. Hooves scrape rock as Maja tosses her head: *no, no, no, no, no.* '*Maja!*' Kira kicks her sides. 'Maja, come on! *Move!*'

Maja takes off screaming. The rush tips her backwards, giddy. The path starts to fly. Kira propels herself forward into Maja's neck, jarring and hanging on for life. This is it. A low moan leeches from the ceiling, and she flinches. After all the times she thought it was the end, it's here. She'll die alone, in a haunted mountain, because she got distracted by a stalactite. If anyone was here to tell her tale, they'd revel in the irony.

A screech echoes in her ear. An empty-eyed, blood-streaked shape grins, wagging its face into hers. Kira screams, with mind and voice and more. Skulking up the wall, a shadow crooks a broken hand. A bodiless beast bays beside her. Its breath blasts like sewage. Kira sobs, pinching her eyes shut. Fireworks spark red behind them, but that's worse, not seeing, only jolting along, every bone rattling, her chin rebounding, and she urges Maja faster, faster. Skidding round bends, scraping past walls, vaulting over rocks that make vertigo whine—

Maja stops and clatters back. Kira holds on with a fresh rush of terror, clawing back her balance with a sick, swooping moan. Water. Rippling below a wooden bridge. They almost barrelled into a pool.

That can't be all there is. It looks like death, no more and no less. The sturdy bridge is railless. The pool pulls with a cold, grey gravity, and stamping and shrieking, Maja still backs away.

Oh, God. Wildly, Kira looks back.

Oh, God. A whimper bubbles up and out of her throat. They can't retreat. They can't fight. They can't run. The figures have been following her, drifting, scuttling, bounding. A rich shadow rolls out a keen, dead howl. The others squall. They yowl. They hunt. Kira's mind chills to nothing. If they go back, they'll die.

A resonating groan shakes the ground. With her eyes spotting black, she whips around. The rippling water gurgles to a boil. A grumbling darkness blooms beneath the bubbles, spilling a sweet, fleshy burning. A second groan throws up waves, and as the howls and the screeches, the moans and the laughter, crescendo and roar, lights flare at the water's edge and something breaks the surface.

Kira doesn't wait to see what. A hot, dry hand clasps her arm, and with a guttural scream, she implodes. Her mind bottoms out. Everything releases. She kicks Maja as hard as she can.

Bellowing, Maja takes off. They hit the bridge and fly into a gallop, the wood booming and the hand torn away. A horn sounds. They're hunting her. Kira flattens herself against Maja's neck. No thoughts, no words, just an aching horror swamping her mind with red. She's brittle, made of matches. They could tear her apart.

Once you realise this, the world realigns.

The wood stops booming. The bridge falls behind. The crystals glow violet as they tear through the tunnel, but the caterwauling dead keep up. Nails slash her skin as they try to hold her back. Maja's hooves echo, and it sounds like there are more, a snorting, roaring army, the *mist*.

A wailing sob breaks from her throat. She can't win. Let it end. Let it be a dream, if that's what Whiteland wants. Let her wake up to sirens again, to murderous cold again. She shuts her eyes. It's a scalding, bloody nightmare. She'll jerk awake once she can't breathe, once the rot and stench of fiery death has finally stifled her lungs. She screws her eyes up tight. Behind them, golden-red fireworks fly. Either that, or she'll die.

Cold erupts around her.

Light.

Light that sears, light that blinds. Kira's eyes fly wide, the clamour dying with the dark. With a scream of disbelief, she bursts into tears.

Pushing back the mountain, pushing back the dead, the ice plains have arrived.

42

Ice and fear and wolves and light

Maja keeps running until she drops. Tired beyond her wits, the tunnel is a crack in the distance when she stops, huffs, and shrugs her burden to the ground.

Kira lands in the snow with a thump. Her elbow rebounds off the underlying ice. She jerks her head up to avoid it cracking and finds she doesn't care if it does. Falling back into powder, she breathes. They're out.

She lets out a single, hysterical laugh. Silence, bar a distant whooshing of wind sweeping over the ice. Crisp, frosted air. No smell but the cold, and the tacky tang of sweat, and something stale from her jeans. Kira ignores it. They're *out*.

Flanks glistening, Maja shudders and sits, huffing a snorting breath. Kira lies and breathes, in her vest and jeans. The ebbing terror drains as it fades, leaving a viscous, thumping heart and a tired, throbbing mind. Before long, the cold begins to bite.

The heat from Monte Yuno fell away with the tunnel, and the heat from the gallop fell away with the drop. Shivering, Kira rubs her arms and sits. Snow trickles from her hair and body, and gingerly, she taps her skull. Raised and painful, but dry. The blood has dried on her arms as well, from a dozen cuts and scrapes. A ring of bruising nail marks, and that's all. She was lucky.

It doesn't mean she has to look at the damage. The claws, the hands, the mountain…they tighten her chest and stir her stomach. Now she truly knows the meaning of fear.

Maja neighs softly. Kira looks up. Rising on weary legs, the horse shakes free of slivers and snow and gives her a plaintive look.

With the slightest vibration of an inward smile, Kira stands. If Maja could speak, she'd be right: it isn't just cold here, but forest-cold. Shrugging on the lightweight, fur-lined coat, she sets to work on the blankets.

Thank God. Meticulously cut to shape and size, they take no time at all. One for the neck, two for the middle, and one for the rear; even done inexpertly, in minutes Maja's covered. With the hoof-pouches on, she nuzzles Kira in thanks.

'You're welcome.' Kira slumps against her. Fatigue is starting in tremors. It leaves the world spark-bright and unreal, but also fades the horror. She'd rather it fade to a dream than a lucid, haunting nightmare, but it's better than not fading at all. She looks around with a sigh. 'But what, Maja, do we do?'

Maja snorts, harrumphs, and turns to clop away, her hoofbeats dull on the ice.

'Right.' Kira dips her chin until it meets her chest and sighs again. 'Okay. Just me.'

Snow and ice, ice and snow. What, indeed, *do* they do? Fishbone clouds scud across the blue sky. Kira shades her eyes and squints; despite the lack of a blazing sun, the day is bright and far from night. The plains themselves are just as blinding. Sloping to a ridge far to the right, below it is much of a muchness: unbroken, stretching white, and scattered, lurching peaks. Craggy dips and water holes, a group of dark specks.

Kira drops her hand. No people. Nerves pluck her strings and sing. She's still too far behind.

Fastening the coat ties, she scans the ice for Maja. The horse meandered away, and now, burying her mouth in a hole, she's drinking for her life.

Averting her eyes from the innocent mountains, Kira carefully treads toward her. Damn mountains. How white they are now, how august, how pure, like the view of the Alps from the plane. Kira turns her back. 'Maja,' she says, to focus herself. The horse is gulping from a water hole.

Kira's thirst is suddenly ferocious. Sandpaper? No, it's a desert, starving, as though the baked tunnel air has made her its home. Kira's eyes snag on a second hole a few metres away. It's tiny. It's blue.

She shouldn't trust it.

Maja does.

Kira's moccasins slip on the powder-brushed ice. If it's good enough for wonder-horse, it's good enough for her, and crouching by the chipped hole, she braces.

The water is the coldest thing her hands have ever touched. She dips her cupped fingers, quick enough for her skin not to burn. Again, and again, and again. She drinks until her lips are numb before pulling up her hood, pushing her purpling fingers in her pockets, and, shattered but determined, pushing to her feet. Time to go.

In theory. Maja looks up as Kira approaches, chewing on her cheek. The blankets formed both stirrups and saddle. She's going to have to jump.

For once, it's a godsend to be so alone. Planting her hands on Maja's back, Kira bends her legs to spring.

One, two, three, and up. Landing hard on her stomach, winded and gasping, she squirms around before she slips off. One leg on either side. Hands lodged behind shoulder blades. There. Pushing herself upright, Kira wriggles her hips for balance. Done. And unless it's a dire emergency, she's never doing it again.

What a jinx. As Kira retrieves the dangling reins, Maja pricks her ears.

'Hmm?' Kira wriggles back a bit more. Maja whinnies, fretfully shifting her feet. As comfortable as she can be, Kira looks up. 'Oh.'

The dark specks she saw before have left the far distance. Narrowing her eyes, her strained heart jolts. They're loping toward her and, with their fur greyblack and their long tails flat, they're unmistakeable. Wolves.

'Oh, shit.' Kira fumbles with the reins, digging Maja with her heels. The horse kicks into a trot, a canter, veering away across the empty plains. The wolves curve toward them. 'Oh, *shit*.'

From a canter to a gallop. Kira's hood whips back. Snow flies up to spray her feet, her legs, her frozen fingers, her freezing face. She slits her eyes against the wind, but it stings. Maja neighs in panic, slipping off balance, wildly careering over patches of ice. The plains slope up. Maja's legs quake. A wall of ice looms tall against the sky.

Still, the wolves curve closer.

Oh, God. Tongues lolling, paws pounding. Everything's a rush of white and grey and blue and spray. Kira can hardly breathe. The terror's back like it never left. She can barely see, whirling, blurring, but suddenly, they're here.

Tongues lolling, paws pounding. Darting in front, the wolves cut her off.

With a cry, Kira jerks Maja to a halt. Three in number. Gargantuan in size. Panting, they trot to stand together. Maja skitters back, back, back.

Nothing moves. Maja stops. Kira's breath is loud and shallow. The wolves are only watching, gold irises thin. Their focus is anthropomorphic. Kira can't think. It's disconcerting: the wolves stare straight into her face, each pair of eyes unblinking on her own. They lull her into a state of hypnosis, lull her into a state of trust.

One by one, they break away and turn tail to trot.

Kira blinks, hard. Heading toward the ice wall, the wolves don't look back. A whirl of unreality, she watches them go. Was that all they wanted? A chase? God, if she could *think*. Bewilderment, exasperation, fright, relief. Do wolves attack people unprovoked? Can she go?

The foremost wolf stops dead. Its patchwork face turns back toward her, and poised like a dog whose owner is dawdling, it seems to be waiting, expectant.

Bewilderment overcomes everything else. Kira stares. It can't be waiting for her to follow. No chance. The birds did when they took them to the cabin, but this is different. These are wolves. Huge, folkloric, winter-wild *wolves*.

Knowing her luck, that's exactly what it wants. The wolf doesn't move as the others pass by. Its eyes latch onto hers again, and tensing each muscle, dredging every ounce of will, Kira prepares to squeeze Maja's sides.

Maja moves before she can. Kira's eyes widen. 'What?'

Maja grumbles a whinny but walks on. The wolf turns away, trotting off in satisfaction. Kira shuts her eyes. Wonderful. They *are* meant to follow—the horse understood that and took it upon herself. Kira swallows, lifts her chin, and breathes, gritting her teeth to a grind. Wonderful. At this point, life can't get better.

At least they have a direction. The wolves break into a sprint, and Maja speeds to a gallop, making a beeline for a gap in the ice wall. Kira shakes her head, rueful, wry. If Maja's not afraid, they must be safe. Everything here is so much more intelligent, so much more alive, that she shouldn't be surprised anymore; even when it's hunting her, it's alive. Even when it's trying to kill her, it's alive. The land, a thing in itself, is alive. The animals are intuitive in a way that humans miss, and even though Whiteland is dangerous, merciless, it has something the outside has lost.

Kira lifts her eyebrows. She's referring to her home as the outside; after a few days, Whiteland has taken her over. Who knows how she'll ever readjust.

A flash of textured white catches her eye. Meandering close to the edge of a ridge, off to her left, is a bear.

A polar bear. In a way she's only read about, Kira's mouth drops. She's seen bears in zoos—brown bears, pandas—but never a polar bear. Vast and proud, it gazes over the plains and, as she watches, shifts to reveal a smaller, rounder companion.

Kira's breathes hitches. Awestruck, dumbstruck, thunderstruck. Two? Two polar bears? How *will* she readjust? Lips apart, she twists around to watch them fall behind. Peace, in the midst of chaos. Something else she'll never forget.

A cold shadow falls over her. With a wistful sigh, she turns back to the ice. The gap in the wall is upon them.

It's not a tunnel. She breathes her shuddering relief. One is enough for a lifetime and a half, and thankfully, this is more an open-air pass. Two opposing swathes of white stretch high into the sky. A stone's throw apart, as if they can't stand to touch, the path in-between creates a valley. Snaking to the right, it could last forever. Unflagging, the wolves plunge in.

Kira's nerves are plucked like a harp, but she doesn't have a choice. Maja follows.

Blinding whiteness on three sides, scudded blue on the fourth. Time passes, and passes, and although it curls, and coils, and curves, the valley doesn't change. Flurries of snow trickle down the walls. A small grey creature shoots across the floor, but the journey is as constant, as smooth and unthreatened, as the windswept grasslands gallop. The wolves never tire. The horse never falters. Kira's nerves steady to a constant thrum. Battered by air, buoyed by speed, they run, and run, and run.

Romy, Mum, and Dad. Kira's spine stiffens, and her legs start to numb, but through everything—exhaustion and mayhem and terror and grief—there's hope. By now, unless she's been lured off course, they must be close. Everything must be ending. She can finally—*finally*—get out. Away.

Romy, Mum, and Dad.

Away.

43

Everything she hides

Anna knows she's arrived when the Whispers start to sigh. They're soft at first, lilting breaths, before growing louder, more urgent, some close, some far.

The first of them brushes her legs. Anna stops. Approaching from all sides, in blurs of rustling, physical sound, they stroke her face, lift her hair, drift around her gloves. If she wasn't sure before, she knows now.

She's arrived.

It's just as she was told when Whiteland was still her home. Bleak and barren, there's nothing for miles; nothing but the Yunavida range, but once you're through the ice wall, they're so faint they hardly exist. All she has is white.

The ice plains dwarf her. Their endless nothingness shrinks her inside, their uninviting arms opening wide to meet the sky. She fights the urge to shiver, to push her hands in her pockets. She can't seem weak. Is it almost finished?

She's deflated since the tunnel. Every creature knew her, and most of them stopped her, hissing that she'd soon be one of their own. It wore her out. What she used to be is scalding, peeling back her skin, as raw and sore and oozing as though it's not been twenty years.

What infects the wound more is her family. They were never meant to know this, see this, touch this. They were never meant to have the slightest thought that it exists. Anna tenses her face and grits her teeth. However she'll be punished, let it come soon. Maybe, if she surrenders herself, the Whispers will be pleased. Maybe they'll make them all forget.

Anne…

Anna slides from her thoughts. The Whispers are coming. It doesn't hurt to be alert.

Another thing that scalds: how easy it is to remember. She's forgotten so little of Whiteland, a fact that's ached and grown and ached since she stepped into Atikur. She's forgotten so little, but still…she keeps her teeth gritted and her face composed. She lacks so much. The Whispers are an authority, living in the ice plains and watching the worlds. She should never underestimate them, and as keen on justice as they are, they'll have had something to do with Romy.

But that's *it*. That's all she has. She's bringing a knife to a gunfight, if it counts as a knife at all.

Annel…

The Whisper flutters through the air to her ear. Anna focuses at once. It's not quite real, not quite in her head; and as it softly repeats, it's whole. *Anneliese.*

She stares ahead at the ice and the sky. A snow-hare bounds in the distance. *Yes.*

You are different.

If her life wasn't in the Whispers' hands, she'd laugh. *I've been gone for twenty years,* she says. *Of course I am.* She lifts her chin. *I'm not a huldra, which is all I wanted.*

That's not true. You killed for fun.

Another Whisper caresses her neck. *You made a mistake, Anneliese. You shouldn't have let curiosity win.* It sighs, trailing breaths along the top of her spine. *We've been watching for a very long time.*

Close to a chuckle, it's sinister, soft. *Did you not realise we would be waiting?*

Inside and out, Anna shivers. It's cold, colder than anywhere else. Cold enough that her mind spins, her skin burning blue. The air is almost physical. *Maybe,* she says. *But I had to go back. Just once. Just to see.*

She blinks, hard. Her eyelashes frost, her eyes growing heavy, but she can't start to weaken. Not here. Not now. *When my husband suggested Switzerland, I couldn't…*

Just once. To see. I couldn't.

The Whispers don't repeat it but she hears it again, again and again and again. How feeble will it sound for Romy, Kira, Mathew? She endangered them because she was curious and took Mathew's suggestion as a sign. She hid her past because she used to be a monster and couldn't bear for them to find out. Burrowing her neck deep into her collar, she blows out against the Gore-Tex. It warms her lips but not her mind, freezing to ice. Did she really not think they'd be waiting?

She could lie. They'd hear, though, and call her out, and it might make everything worse. *I tried not to think about what might happen.* Anna shakes her head. Denial; it all comes down to denial. *I felt it pulling, and I had to go back. I did think you'd be watching, but I didn't let myself think you'd be waiting, too.*

Humourlessly, she huffs. *I figured out who you were using as soon as I got to Lally. Your female helpers aren't exactly subtle, but I accepted them. After a couple of days, I ignored them. I didn't expect an unremarkable return, but I never*—she thins her bitter lips—*thought you'd involve my daughter.*

A hiss of a laugh. Air trills on her cheek. *One was involved*, a new voice says, a damp, misted breath. *The other made a choice.*

One second. Two seconds. Three, four, five. Slowly, Anna's stomach drops, along with the penny. *The other made a choice?*

Yes.

Her head rotates to follow the voice, tittering across her skin. She stamps down her wash of alarm. *What do you mean, the other made a choice? Are you talking about Kira?*

Another laugh. The Whisper wisps around her ankles, chilling the rims of her boots. She flinches. *Maybe.*

The word is thoughtful, teasing. *She came with the boy that found her sister, even after we sent the mist. She is close.*

They both are.

Another murmur chuckles, flitting up to her ear. Anna's breath slips back into her lungs and stays there. *No*, she says faintly. *They're not. You're—*

Lying? She can almost imagine the Whisper shrugging, matter-of-fact and amused. *Because of you they are linked to Whiteland, so Whiteland let them in. You cannot blame us for that.*

Kira. Romy. Anna shuts her eyes. Kira in Atikur, Romy on the Zaino. Both of them caught near Al-Sanit and packed off to Skarrig as playthings. The images run wild. They were never meant to know about any of this. They were certainly never meant to come here.

At least if they're close, they're alive.

I know what you want, Anna manages over the drowning horror in her head. *You want to punish me for killing and punish me for leaving. I'm not stupid.*

Yet still you went back.

I don't need reminding. Clenching her fists in her pockets, Anna makes herself breathe. *Whatever it is you've chosen, do it. Before Kira and Romy get here. If it'll give them and Mathew back their—wait.*

She breaks off. A question has struck her, so obvious, so catalytic, that she can't believe she hasn't asked. Before they take her from herself, she has to know. *What did you do to—*

She is hosting a woman of the Kyo.

A new voice, snaking inside her collar before her question has formed. *When the entrance in Atikur opened up around her, the Kyo were ready to take. You know how we despise them, but they served us well.*

The Whisper is smug, almost gleeful. Anna's skin crawls. *Why Romy?*

It could have been either of your girls. It smiles. *We simply waited until one of them felt the pull and ventured out alone. Whiteland would have opened its doors for them both and closed them just the same. We had to enable the girl to be found.*

The Kyo. The crawling intensifies. The women are a thing of dread, and to know they were lying in wait for her girls…Anna swallows a pincushion of tears. Oh, Romy.

The Kyo. If they took over Romy, is that where she'll go? A wave of pure-bred panic grasps her, and she has to grit her teeth, clench her jaw, ball her hands into fists to break its fingers and shove it away. She'd rather be nothing than become one of them. She'd rather be trapped in a cave of trolls, slowly withering away, or eternally wandering the forests with a leshy. Anything but the Kyo.

You will not join the Kyo. The Whisper swirls around her neck, its eager breath brushing up and away. *It will be the desert; drifting and alone, lost among the souls above the sands. It is what you need for the men you killed.*

The men. The men. It swells to an echo.

Again, Anna has to push herself to breathe. *I know,* she says shortly. The words gnaw at her insides, and she tries to block them out; there's no way she'll let herself remember. She's worked to the bone to forget. *I know exactly what I did. I know that I revelled in it more than I should, but I had to get away. Whiteland was too oppressive. Too much.*

You were weak, the first Whisper buzzes. Anna jumps; angry in her ear, it's a sting. *You were born here, and you should have found the strength to stay. You know it's forbidden to leave, so now*—it hisses closer, almost spitting—*you make amends.*

Before she can stop herself, Anna snorts. *So it's not about the men?* Her caution slips away. *I should have known. You don't care about morality; that only matters to the people. You just hate that I got out.* She pauses. *I'm right, aren't I?*

Nothing jumps to stop her. Nothing says she's wrong. Anna shakes her head, incredulous. *All of this for envy? I'm not here because I killed.* Her mouth contorts. *I'm here because of your fancy that nobody can leave. That nobody* should *leave, even when there's a way.*

We can't mix, the second Whisper says. Less angry than the first, it flicks across her cheeks. *It's less about leaving and more about collision.* Down the hair curling pale from her hat, it rests cool on her lips. *The colliding of the worlds. You know that; everyone knows that, as much as they might disregard it. Whiteland is not a place for outsiders.*

It lifts up again at an echo of assent. *They are not wanted, and they are not needed. There are too many dangers. If they knew—if they were brought here by one of our own who'd escaped, and they saw, and angered, and died—it would cause an uproar on the outside.*

Another echo, a crackling agreement. A summer storm, power lines. *More would try and come. If they succeeded, they'd interfere.*

It works the other way, of course.

A new voice murmurs in, faint and far away. Anna strains to hear. Static rustles in her ears. A draught drifts about her boots. Atop the ice, the Whispers are gathering.

She suppresses a shiver. *What other way?*

If others leave as you did, the distant voice murmurs. *Ones who can't pass as human. Where would we end up? There would be more interference, more chaos, more death. Outsiders would die; we would die. Everything we all have now would die.*

But if both are separate and the outside is ignorant—another sighs—*then both are safe. Surely, Anneliese, you can see?*

Anna can. She can also understand, perfectly well, but the Huldra are reviled. Rejected if accidentally born to humans, they're exiled, left to cluster in the forest's heart. They could be killers. They could be innocent. Either way, if they're spotted, they're threatened with death. There's no mercy or a sniff of a chance of a life. It wasn't enough.

She believed it then, filled with rage, and she believes it now: it wasn't enough. It's not enough for her and shouldn't be for anyone. Out of Whiteland, she could live. She could be what she invented.

I was careful, she says. It may be futile, but the nails are in the coffin. There's no harm in one last try. *I wanted a life where I wouldn't be hated, so when I got out, I left Whiteland for good. I never even said the name to myself, let alone anyone else.* She huffs. The irony is awful. *You've endangered us all more than I ever did. By releasing women of the Kyo, using inept women as spyglasses, and messing with my daughter, the worlds well and truly collided.*

And yet. The Whispers rustle closer, swirling around her in a windy cocoon. Whatever they're building up to, it's close. *Quite apart from justifying why you're hated, you set an example that anyone can leave. You posed no threat once you were out, but others who try to follow might not be so careful. If we're all to stay safe...* They pause, and with a surge of bitterness, Anna knows what's coming. *You must be an example.*

Hook, line, and hypocrisy; out comes the truth.

It's not like I'm the first to have left! Anna flings out her arms in anger, despair. *We grow up hearing the stories. Things have schemed, and waited, and escaped. Even outsiders have stories; the Havsrå, the Huldra. That stupid bishop-fish. Why should I have to be an example? If you're that concerned, make it harder to leave.* She drops her hands. *Or are you not as omnipotent as you make out?*

A breeze tears across the ice. It pierces her cheeks, and she winces. *You for your daughter,* the Whispers hiss. Together, they're a rumble, menacing, provoked. Moving on from reasons, spinning the cocoon. *A trade, as you said.*

Anna's head swoons, out and back. She knew this would happen from the minute the boy appeared with Romy, but now it's here. *I...*she tries. Winded, hollowed-out, resigned. Her fight drains as quickly as it came. *I know. But please. When it's done, let her go.*

She releases a shuddering, ice-flecked breath. *Her, Kira, and that poor damn boy. Wherever the nearest entrance is, send them there. I don't care if it lets them out in Peru; just get them away from here.*

Another breath, and another, fighting to stay even. The cocoon is closing around her ankles, ready to spin, to rustle, to whirl its way up her body until there's nothing left. Despite her sacrificial bravery, she's afraid. They're slowing her heart. They're taking her life. She's so, so afraid.

Don't hold me against them, she continues. Even in her mind, the words are frail. *You can help them get out.* Spin, rustle, whirl, breathe. *Please.*

A shriek slices the end of her words. Anna looks round sharply.

No. Anna's breath catches and stays caught. Emerging from the ice wall is someone, something, too distant to make out, but there—a hundred metres away—is Romy.

Romy and Matt.

Oh, God.

'Stop!' Romy shrieks again. Rigid, Anna stares at her husband. How is he here? *Why* is he here? Head drooping, feet dragging, he appears to be unconscious.

Fearful longing constricts her throat. Romy's desperation is furious, hauling Mathew across the ice. The sight is wretched, impossible; what happened after she left? What brought them all here? *How?* The questions start to race. Anna's hands start to shake. What does the woman want? Is Matt okay? Is *Romy* okay, hidden in herself? Even from here, she looks so thin. She's corners and bones.

Anna nearly chokes. She screwed up. Oh, God, she screwed up. She's a carousel, spinning and spinning, gravitating toward inevitability. She thought she could do this, be strong enough for this, but they're here, now, here, and oh, God, oh, God—

She likes her freedom, the Whispers breathe when Romy wails again. It's racked and hoarse and hurts. It *hurts. The woman. She always knew she couldn't keep it, but she wants to. She intends to bargain.*

Anna's head swoons again, but she pushes it down. *What?*

The Whispers ignore her. *Interesting, to choose Mathew.* They're mild, musing, amused. *She must have sensed the vulnerability of his mind.*

Stop the horses. Calm the carousel. Anna's lungs are paper. *What do you mean?* she asks. *How would she—no.* Her mind drops to frozen, paralysing dread. *Please say you didn't. Not Matt, too.*

You said yourself that he suggested your holiday. A voice slithers by her elbow. If it had a face, it'd be smirking, unpleasantly pleased. *Do you recall the business trip to London? It was fortuitous. Stepping into someone's mind near an entrance, especially when the mind is unguarded.* The voice laughs softly. *He had no idea we were there, and obeyed. It's a shame the woman chose him.* Smug, sly, dreadful. *He was such a good boy.*

Anna closes her eyes. They got to Matt. She curls her fingers, her toes, her lips. They got to Romy. As a result of both, they got to Kira. For what?

No. She didn't come here—she didn't leave her home, scar her family, and abandon the life she carved from nothing—to be beaten by a leech from the Kyo.

Whoever the woman is, she says fiercely, ramming down the pain, *she can't keep her freedom. You said there'd be a trade.*

There will be, they say. The cocoon swells up to her knees, tying her in place and beginning to roar. As much as its climax scares her, its stolidity is a relief. *We don't want her free. It defeats the purpose of making you an example. Rosemarie will be released, and they will all return to the outside. The other two were never supposed to be involved.*

'No!' Romy screeches. Grimacing, straining, she speeds up. Anna chokes on a sob. Her daughter and her husband, one dragging the other like a disobedient dog. Mathew thumps against the ice. His kneecaps thud. One elbow cracks, scraped along the ground. Anna swallows.

That's not her daughter. Her daughter's not the one shrieking, dragging. She's not the one with the haunted face, the hateful fury, the air of a ghost. Romy will be okay. The Whispers are brutal, but they don't lie. And Matt...

Anna shuts her eyes. She can't look at him. It's a gruelling enough fight as it is, simply knowing he's there. Everything inside her aches to run, to check he's alive, to hold his hands and kiss him awake. To apologise for his role, for the catalyst he became. If it wouldn't stop the trade, she'd already be gone.

But the trade has to happen. It aches, it breaks, every possible anguish, but it's the way she has to save them. She can't stop it, can't risk the woman wreaking havoc. She can't risk it not starting again. She can't do anything but stand, submit, and hope the Whispers keep their word.

'Anneliese!' Romy shrieks. It's ragged, raw, animalistic, but even with the raging woman inside it, it belongs to her daughter. Her sixteen-year-old daughter.

As the Whispers swirl up her thighs, Anna opens her eyes.

At once, she wishes she hadn't. Pushing Matt to his knees, half-awake and swaying, Romy plants her hands on either side of his head. 'Anneliese,' she says. Jerking his chin so sharply that he gasps, she fixes Anna with a dead-eyed threat. 'Stop.'

44

No

The valley of ice took forever. Kira's relief is unrivalled when it ends: never slowing, never stopping, they pelted around so many bends that she lost all sense of direction. Her eyes stung from real, sparkling snow-blindness, her mind growing giddy with unsteady speed. It was nauseating, and as she gallops after the wolves onto the glittering, endless ice, she doesn't look back.

She's found them.

In the distance, three figures bob into view. Kira's heart surges up to her mouth. They're toy-town tiny, and rattling on Maja's back, she can't make them out, but it doesn't matter. Romy, Mum, and Dad.

She nudges Maja faster, but the horse is faltering. Her mane is sweat-matted, her legs out of time. She slows, judders, and comes to a halt, far from the toy-town shadows. Kira's heart sinks down, down, down. No.

The wolves lope on. 'No,' Kira pleads, digging in her heels, tugging on the reins. Not when she's so close. 'You have to move, Maja. Please.'

She's close enough to hear Romy shouting in desperate, inhuman shrieks. Close enough to see her hauling Mathew over the ice to their motionless mother. Jabbing her heels into Maja's flanks, Kira thrusts her hips forward. The wolves have stopped, now, looking back and pacing. Their impatience growls. *We have to go.*

Kira throws them a helpless glance. Maja is trembling, hanging her head, going nowhere. What can she do?

She can run. Stiff-legged, she slips from Maja's back, stumbling toward the wolves. Her apprehension has ground to dust; compared to the scene ahead of her, they're nothing but puppies, or petals. Mulled wine, chestnuts, cinnamon, candles. Wintry, unthreatening things. She staggers into a run.

Useless legs. Stupid stilts. Romy is yelling, Anna doing nothing, and as the largest wolf dips its muzzle toward her, her sister stops, drops Mathew to his knees, and places her hands on his head.

'Romy, don't.'

Anna's mind quakes, but her voice is calm. It has to be. If she loses her calm, she loses everything.

Not everything. If she stepped away from the Whispers, she could stop this; they're swirling up her stomach, a corset of air replacing the cocoon, but she's not powerless. Not yet. She could drag Matt away, disable the woman, and start over.

'Move.' Romy jerks her father's head again. A painful whine keens from his lips. Anna's very being judders. She could hurt Matt fatally in a second; she's fighting for her freedom, she's unnaturally strong, and as a result, she's ruthless.

'Romy—'

'*Move.*'

Anna flinches at a third jerk, this time to the side. What can she do? If she stops the trade, she loses Romy; if she continues, she could lose Matt.

Oh, God.

With her chest shot with shock, Kira gasps. She expected something like this, but seeing it here, so close to coming true, with her dad's life in her sister's hands—

The bending wolf yips. Horror vaulting, soaring, roaring, Kira turns to it, wide-eyed. It's bowed its front half, haunches high. Waiting.

Waiting for her to get on. Time staggers. In a long, looping moment, Kira sees what the wolf wants, sees the danger, and sees that she no longer cares. The wolves were strange from the start.

It's her dad's life in her sister's hands. She has to get to Romy.

The wolf's bent snout is as tall as her waist. Kira doesn't think as she heaves herself up, gripping its coarse grey-black fur. Its broad body is hot. It neither helps nor hinders. Her mind whirls and shouts, chaos, hell. Has she made a mistake?

No. In one fluid movement, the wolf straightens, yips at the others, and runs.

'Step away from them,' Romy hisses. Her human façade is slipping. Her eyes shine large and black. Anna glances around, panicked. The dark shapes are getting closer, but whatever they are, they're too far away. Contact lenses aren't something that exist here, so she didn't think twice about leaving them behind.

There's still some of Whiteland in her.

'Romy.' Avoiding this thought, Anna cuts her eyes back to her daughter. Her not-daughter. Her husband, God, the man who loved her without knowing any of her secrets, slumping on his knees. Choosing between them is no choice at all. 'Romy, don't.'

'I said, step away,' Romy snaps. Her nails are sharp on her father's skin. His eyelids droop and flutter. 'I'm sure you can see what'll happen if you don't.' A smile tears the slipping face apart. Impossibly, gapingly stretched, it leers. 'Can't you, Anneliese?'

Anna chokes. Tears blur in rainbows and spill. She throws her eyes around again. The dark shapes have grown to wolves. A girl rides the largest, her long hair streaming, flying across the ice. Anna can't stop the tears. She needs to scream. She needs to die. They're close, so close, and it's Kira, her Kira, the girl who reads and paints and studies, who took to snow like a fish in the heat. It's Kira, hurtling on with the wolves. If she can just buy a little more *time*.

The Whispers need to take her. She needs to stall, help the process, before the thing in Romy does something the real Romy can't forgive. At the very least, she needs to stall until Kira gets here.

Despair sweeps through her like suicide. God help her. God help them all. She's relying on one of her daughters to stop the other from murder.

'All right.' Somehow speaking, somehow lucid, Anna looks back to Romy. The Cheshire grin is fixed, the head slightly tilted, and it makes her want to run. That is *not* her daughter.

This is all her fault.

'All right.' Breathing, riding out the despair, she steps an inch to the left. The Whispers cloak her shoulders now, creeping up her neck. 'There.'

Romy moves a hand, an inch from Mathew's head. 'More,' she says, sing-song-sweet. 'All the way away. Move.'

Steadying her breath, Anna takes another step. It's a struggle to mask the discomfort bleeding through her as the Whispers slide up. Beyond her chin, up to her mouth. Although they won't smother her, it's a thin thing to breathe, like a butterfly trapped in a net. She's nearly gone.

Another tiny step. Can Romy tell she's lying? Does the woman have enough of a mind to see, from her tautening face, her rigid limbs, that while her body looks alive, it's nearly dead?

Maybe. Maybe not. She's light, tingling, grainy, adrift. Narrowing her eyes, Romy's hand retreats. Anna moulds her face straight. Come on. Come on.

The wolves are almost here.

Romy's hand moves away from Mathew's head. The wolf pushes harder toward them. Kira's blood roars like an ocean: they'll make it. They will. There'll be enough time. Run her down, scare her, whatever. As long as she doesn't hurt Mathew.

But why isn't Anna stopping her? Kira squints through the rushing air. Romy must be a waif, a wraith, fragile and dwindled after coming this far; Anna could overpower her. She must be missing something. Their mum looks nothing but terrified.

Romy's hand retreats farther. Kira releases a precarious breath. Anna's talking to her. Convincing her not to do it. Reasoning, threatening, something. Anything.

The wolves are so, so close.

'More.' Romy nods twitchily. Anna's heart stops. She can't move, even if she wanted to; with the Whispers crawling up her face, her body is no longer hers. '*More*,' Romy repeats, her leer warping to anger. 'Can't you hear me? It's not enough!' She slaps her hand back. Her 8-ball eyes are on fire. '*Move*.'

I can't, Anna thinks faintly. *I can't, I can't, I can't.* She's lifting, drifting, sifting away. The Whispers eddy above her head, and as she fades—it's in her dispersing bones, in the nothing of her skin—Romy's face morphs into horror.

'No!' She jerks the man's head back up. 'You won't go.' She squeezes his skull between the heels of her hands. It's not too late. It can't be. It won't be. 'You won't.' Fury. Freedom. Nothing. Another jerk. 'Not before—'

'No!' Kira hears. Fifty metres. Forty.

'You won't go.' Thirty.

'You won't.' Twenty. 'Not before you see.'

The wolves scrape to a frenzied halt. Gripping Matt's slumping head, Romy snaps his neck to the side.

Kira shrieks. Tumbling from the wolf, she crashes to the ice, scrabbling over to her father. His eyes are closed. His breath has gone. Chest bursting, heart a storm, Kira's leaves her body.

'What did you do?' she yells. The words are hoarse. Linking her fingers, she slams them into Mathew's silent chest. Again, again, again, again, trying for a heartbeat, searching for life. 'Romy, what did you *do*?'

Throwing back her head, Romy screams. Her body bends so far back that her hair scrapes the ground. Kira flinches away in horror. Romy's spine creaks with the strain, cracking as her chest pushes up like a puppet, and at a second, agonised scream, Kira scrambles to her feet. Where's Anna? She has to stop this. She has to make it right. That's the reason she's here, the reason any of them are—

Her urgent, searching eyes find Anna. Her hope plummets through the ice. 'Mum?'

She was ready to run to her. She was ready to hug her, beg her, shout at her, but she stops in her stiffening tracks. It's Anna, but it isn't; it is her mum's face, her mum's hair, and her mum's winter clothing, but as familiar as they are, they're not there. Not quite.

'Mum?' Kira repeats. It pitches with confusion, with roiling distress. Step forward. Falter, step back. Anna is still, quiet, bleached, whipped by a translucent wind and fading to the ice. Distress smashes back up to horror. 'Mum?' Dread, hysteria, dismay, a whirl. 'Mum?' she cries. 'What's happening?'

Romy wails again. More bestial than human, it's a ghastly, volucrine screech. Kira throws a wild glance at her. Down to her dad, back to her mum. What does she *do*? Why does she never know what to do? Anna's eyes close, paling. Her expression glints sadly away, and it clicks.

Anna for Romy.

'Mum!' Kira flings herself forward. Her skin tingles as she passes through the wind, rustling against her like cold-fingered leaves, but she ignores it. She has to keep her mother here. Whatever Anna's done, as Anneliese, as a huldra, there must be a way for her to stay.

It's not too late. Anna's witchy perfume drifts, faint and mingled with the smell of her skin. Kira gulps, sobs, grapples. It's not too late. It won't be.

She reaches for her mother's hands, but there's nothing left to touch. Nothing to hold to, nothing to keep. Her fingers wane, her arms become air, and when Kira looks up, Anna's face is gone.

'Mum?' she whispers. The wind leaves her skin. The air settles and stills. 'Mum?' She turns. Wolves. Mathew. Romy, collapsing with a final, breathless cry. Everyone but Anna. 'Where are you?'

Nowhere. Romy's body goes limp. A cold rush of air flies up from her chest, and Kira's legs buckle and give. Romy's unconscious. Mathew's dead. And Anna…

Anna's gone. The ice jars her knees as she lands. Anna for Romy. Tears drown her throat. Her stomach convulses, and trying not to retch, as heavy as the ground, Kira drags herself toward her sister. It's obvious; perhaps it always should have been. Anneliese, wanted for her past, lured back to Whiteland for punishment. Brought down by love for her possessed, wandering daughter. And Mathew?

He was blackmail, then revenge. After all the time spent working it out, in the end, it's simple. Simple and cruel.

Collapsing onto Romy's shoulder, Kira clenches her fists and cries. Heaving, merciless sobs wrench through her, ripping her to strips; she wanted it over, but not like this. She'd rather be away with the dead than left with the pieces, the memories. After all of this, all this hell, all this *shit*, she's alone.

A hot, sniffing nose burrows into her neck. Angling out of its reach, Kira curls into Romy. The wolves are wild; they'll go away.

They don't. A paw bats her arm, as impatient as a cat pining for food. Wrecked and blurry, Kira looks up.

The wolf who carried her across the ice stands close beside her head. Ears pricked, its nose nudges, even as the others lope off. Kira swallows. Her lips are swollen. 'There's nowhere,' she croaks. Coughing, she returns to Romy's shoulder, closing her bee-stung eyes. Please, just leave. 'There's nowhere to take me now. Go home.'

Her dark, deflated peace doesn't last. Yipping, the wolf bats her again, snuffling its nose into her hair. *You will move.*

I will not. The ice crystals cool her cheeks. The painful ground is justified. Romy smells awful, of urine and blood. It's all they both have left.

The wolf whines. Its hot breath billows across her face. Kira drags her hooded eyes open. Its human gaze on hers is golden.

She's wrong, and it's right. The realisation is gradual, reluctant: this isn't all they have left. They have a home. They have a world. They need to move.

Step one. With a whole-body sigh, Kira slowly sits up. Her mind is numbing. Good. Dragging her cold, tired legs upright, she bends down. Even unconscious, Romy's light enough to lift. Dully, Kira manoeuvres her onto the waiting wolf. Okay. Step two. Gripping Romy's spectral arms, she casts a last look back.

Dimly, suffocated and cold, she pangs. Both her dad and Maja have disappeared, traceless in the white. How?

It doesn't matter. Deadened, Kira turns back to the wolf. The thoughtless, wonderless feeling swaddles, and she lets it take her whole. If she starts to think, she'll never get home.

Home. The outside. Go.

Using Romy as a teetering anchor, Kira clambers up behind her. One arm cinching her sister's waist, she buries the other in bristling fur and squeezes with her thighs. Step three.

The wolf takes off across the ice.

The Whispers let them go.

ONE YEAR LATER

Almost skipping, almost running. Her feet barely skim the ground, and she's glad the night is still. A touch of wind, never mind a blizzard, and she wouldn't have left the forest alive. The ground glints with frosted snow. It's the coldest she's ever been.

Her new form is blasphemy. Continuing her floating path down the road, Freya shakes her head. To live in such a body is a crude, cruel joke. It's sluggish, ignorant, weak. Without the Kyo, she wouldn't survive.

As she runs, she feels them. They watch, they spy, they sigh directions. They show her what to do.

Make them scream, and make them run. Make them try in vain to hide. Send them to the hellish veins of nowhere, and then…Freya smiles. Mathew steps out of the trees.

It's time to find the sisters.

ACKNOWLEDGMENTS

Acknowledgments seem simple until you come to write them. Where do you start? How do you choose? Writing is never one solitary person, hammering away in a caffeinated storm...although a lot of the time, that storm is life.

First, a massive thanks to all at BBC Blast, who supported me as an eager teenager bursting with lyrics and still support me now. Particularly gargantuan thanks go to Kimberly, Chantal, Molly, and Lisa. James, someday, *Kathy Carlton* will see the light.

The Fiction Café, you're beauties. You put up with my endless questions about publishing, writing, and everything in between, as well as my sardonic despair about the writing process: Emma N, Kiltie, Wendy, Sue, and everyone who fills these groups with irreverence and banter. Jenny, your support everywhere is amazing. Madeline, I couldn't have done without your advice on publishing. Antonio—you're still learning from the best!

A huge, giant, colossal thanks to Becky Rawnsley for your LWA tutoring—you taught me about deep POV, and finally made it click! All the thanks and more to Margie Lawson, for creating the courses that turned my writing around. Rebecca Rue, what's bigger than gargantuan? Leviathan? Leviathan thanks for being my editor, for clicking with *Whiteland*, for getting the irreverent British humour, for loving Callum as much as I do, and for leaving comments in the margins that make me grin and nearly make my mum cry—which is the gold standard of reactions.

Lana King, Easter-egg finder and discoverer of secrets—thank you!

Vern and Joni Firestone, my publishers at BHC Press, for offering a three-book deal to an awkward unknown author, *thank you.*

I joked about this on Twitter, but I genuinely need to thank my village. Lally, you're cold, snowy, and snug on a mountaintop, and I love you. Your winter mists and eccentric villagers stopped this book from flailing. To everyone else who stopped this book from flailing—thank you. Emily, we were such imaginative kids that I'm sure it sparked my love of magic. The Harry Potter obsession, the caravan in the playground that we dowsed over with cardboards moons, the fox that we thought haunted a star...I reckon they led to this. Mr Hay—you'll always be Mr Hay to me, no matter if I'm ten or twenty-six. Your expectations for me meant a lot, and still do. Anna, I love that we still keep in touch—you amazed *me* at how much amazement you showed at my year six stories about magic.

Last, but in absolutely, positively no way least, my family. You've read my stories since I started writing them, and hopefully seen an improvement since *From Peace Into Peril*, the *Lord of the Rings* meets Busted adventure from my nine-year-old self. Ben, your random comments inevitably end up in my books. Josh, your music does the same, and I'm throwing one out there for "Wintertide." Also, your unflagging enthusiasm for Callum is exceptionally fab. Dad, for reading everything as soon as it was ready-ish, and adding your own paragraphs to every book in this trilogy. Several beautiful scenes, and one major writer's block, have been turned on their heads this way. Mum—for the characters you created (Erik!), the tramps through snowy forests to take atmospheric pictures, the endless discussions about this trilogy, through every single draft... as well as the endless tea and wine, thank you.

Hugo, my old, wonky cat—you have a scene, and it doesn't even make you look grumpy.

ABOUT THE AUTHOR

Rosie Cranie-Higgs is an English writer obsessed with folklore, wine, bullfinches, and the magical worlds inside her head. She pines for mountains and snow, loves true crime, and coffee. She likes to write about darkness and ghosts.

She plans to visit all major cities and try their food. She grew up across Europe, and now lives in Lally, Switzerland, the alpine village where her debut horror novel, *Whiteland*, is set. Other books in the series include *Karliquai*, releasing 2021 and *Memento Mori*, releasing 2022.

CPSIA information can be obtained
at www.ICGtesting.com
Printed in the USA
LVHW041742011020
667692LV00004B/774

9 781948 540735